Penguin Books 16/05/2000

The Fishcastle

Elizabeth Stead was born in Sydney in 1932 and is the niece of writer Christina Stead. She was inspired greatly by her grandfather, David George Stead, naturalist and conservationist, and father of Christina. Elizabeth has published numerous short stories. *The Fishcastle* is her first novel.

The Fishcastle

ELIZABETH STEAD

PENGUIN BOOKS

Penguin Notes for Reading Groups are available for this title

Penguin Books Australia Ltd
487 Maroondah Highway, PO Box 257
Ringwood, Victoria 3134, Australia
Penguin Books Ltd
Harmondsworth, Middlesex, England
Penguin Putnam Inc.
375 Hudson Street, New York, New York 10014, USA
Penguin Books Canada Limited
10 Alcorn Avenue, Toronto, Ontario, Canada M4V 3B2
Penguin Books (NZ) Ltd
Cnr Rosedale and Airborne Roads, Albany, Auckland, New Zealand
Penguin Books (South Africa) (Pty) Ltd
5 Watkins Street, Denver Ext. 4, 2094, South Africa
Penguin Books India (P) Ltd
11, Community Centre, Panchsheel Park, New Delhi 110 017, India

First published by Penguin Books Australia Ltd, 2000

1 3 5 7 9 10 8 6 4 2

Design by Nikki Townsend, Penguin Design Studio
Cover illustration by Anna Walker
Internal illustrations by Michelle Katsouranis
Typeset in Century Old Style by Midland Typesetters, Maryborough, Victoria
Made and printed in Australia by Australian Print Group, Maryborough, Victoria

National Library of Australia
Cataloguing-in-Publication data:

Stead, Elizabeth, 1932– .
The Fishcastle.

ISBN 0 14 029162 8.

I. Title.

A823.3

This project has been assisted by the Commonwealth Government through the
Australia Council, its arts funding and advisory body.

www.penguin.com.au

To my sister, Janet, and to my grandchildren,
Lily, Leah, Naomi, Emma and Zac.

ACKNOWLEDGEMENTS

My gratitude to those who have encouraged, advised and helped me through a challenging and wonderful slice of life. Professor Steven Goldsberry (University of Hawaii); Professor Elizabeth Webby (University of Sydney); John Brooker; Bryce Courtenay; Robert Knox; Dr James Wall; Joy Storie; Stephanie Dowrick; Louise Porebski; Joseph Danieli; Lucia Pelissier; and my valued friends and editors, Clare Forster and Rachel Scully; and to Hector Berlioz, who taught me to leap boundaries.

My thanks also go to Trinity Grammar School, Sydney, for a delightful year as Writer in Residence, and The Society of Women Writers of NSW, for graciously offering me a term as president.

George Atkinson
Purser.

Chapter One

VIEWS FROM THE SANDPATH

Of all the early summer times in Proudie Bay and its village, it is thought November is the sweetest. That is when the air of summer licks across the spit of land that separates the ocean from the harbour like a tongue to kiss the skin naked and demand it be stripped of winter wools.

It is then that the Sandpath, an old ribbon of road that snakes in a design of its own making through its clutch of households, begins to funnel late spring ocean breezes with less chill, less bite, along its twists and turns.

It is time for carpet scrubbing, window polishing and painting, for curtains and covers in rich houses to be sent to the cleaners and washed in tubs by 'old Proudie' poors. And it is the time, regular as clockwork, when developers prowl and real estate agents leave goodwill cards in mailboxes on both sides of the Sandpath – but messages more full of promise if the mailbox is on the harbour-view side.

1

At the old end of Proudie Bay, the Sandpath twists a hap-hazard way in only one direction – to where the sea meets the harbour. It gravels past houses that lead to the grass and rocks, hide and seeking children on Greys Point and the swimmers at Cove Beach.

In the newer and developed part of the Bay the Sandpath levels and trims its way to the Beachwalk – cleans itself up for the proper end of it, the tourist end of it, the council's pet end of it – and leads to Dolan's Cafe, the hotel and McKenzie Park, before it curls into nothing more than a lizard's tail track that winds up to Shack Hill and the high cliffs over the ocean.

On its way to the park, and opposite the cafe, the Sand-path hesitates near the oldest structure in Proudie Bay – a long wooden pier of hardwood logs sawn once and preserved by a hundred years of fish scales and gut and grease, and warmed by a thousand suns.

And as though to keep the traditions alive, small boys still dangle small lines over the side for small fry, old din-ghies tie up at the sea steps, and lovers still wind each other in for sunset kissing, as they've done for a hundred years.

But now on the pier, there's a white metal rail with *Queue Here* in black and white and *No Entry* in red for the ferry stop. There's a man with a glass eye who sells ice-creams wrapped in plastic from a plastic trolley under a plastic umbrella and outside tables and chairs for the fish-and-chippers, and bins and buskers and day coach-trippers, ferries that load and unload regular as breathing, and a place where tourists can have their photographs taken – a place marked with yellow paint, in front of an historic plaque, and where something secret is done to frighten the seagulls.

A journalist, once asked by a newspaper to write about the character of Proudie Bay, wrote that it was *like stepping out of Shit City into a clean bath*. He described the bobbing dinghies and other craft – cruisers, more graceful on the harbour swell, having their decks scrubbed and their brasses polished for the season. He wrote of the smell of salt-sprayed hair and skin; sun oil and insect sprays; meat cooking somewhere on a grill; sticky, sick sweet wrappers half-buried in the sand; fish dead and alive; and kelp beached by the tide.

And he wrote about the sensuous feel of the Bay. Sand, damp and good under his feet, toe curling through spear points of pipis in rock pools and the live fanning of red anemones waving and contracting in tepid water. He described young, white winter breasts bared to the sky at last, laid out in nippled pairs on Cove Beach and on the sand below Dolan's Cafe, and men in tight, wet Speedos lying next to them, backs turned to the sky to hide their new summer excitement. Hot pier planks, cool park grass and water bubblers, ocean winds and harbour breezes – all the senses of the Bay's summer he wrote about, and of all these senses, experienced for as long as old Proudies could remember, and thought by some to have formed part of the beginning of the world – of all these senses, the sight of bare breasts below Dolan's Cafe was the one that made him a headline. Middle section. Just before the letters page.

One of the old Proudies – one of those who'd been at the Bay all their lives and had not 'come in', as they refer to the newcomers, is brown Bindi Hope of number twenty, the Sandpath. Spry and clear-eyed despite arthritis and the bowed bones of age, Bindi welcomes the coming of summer to the Bay as she always has, with the windows and doors wide open to warm and sweep dry air through the heart of the house, the way her family had welcomed summers years before she was born the colour of sweet, milk chocolate on the kitchen floor on Boxing Day, 1921.

As for some of the other old Proudies who still cling to the Sandpath, there are the Hughes who once owned a corner shop and were left stranded when a supermarket opened in the village. They stir themselves in memories of busier, happier times, and potter around their yard sighing, tending plants not in need of it and mending things already fixed. The Perkers look out at the blueing sky as they do every year and cry new summer tears in mourning for their son. Old Hughie Pheiffer, in his ruined, wifeless cottage on the wrong side of the road, strips to a singlet over his tanned hide – a torn, yellowed thing she'd nagged him never to wear in public, and goes off plodding the streets, barefoot and randy, dreaming of pinching young bums with his nips of old fingers. The Carters open their door for their thin and yapping water-eyed dog in number sixteen, who'll lie outside at last in the warming sun with his daymares, even in his yelping sleep, of being chased by gulls.

And in number fourteen, Marlin Hardwick chippers and putties and spruces around the old house known in the Bay as the Fishcastle, and prepares for another summer of sea stories and sea fishing. He checks the wire of the pigeon coop, weeds the carp pond, counts the lizards, strokes the tortoises and opens the python's cage with little hope of it moving a muscle. He cleans his row of salt-water tanks in the back hall for the welcoming of fish gone wrong, collected by locals from nets and hooks and trawlers, deformities of fish, for studying. And last but not the least of it, the king of the Fishcastle spruces himself, it is said, for the landing of women, wrong or right, who flop, hook lined and sinkered onto his bed, and a'trawling for their children, for their company and for their devotion when he casts his spells of madness upon them.

Bindi Hope, in her old house on its bigger than average block on higher land on the harbour side of the road, prepares, as do one or two others similarly situated, for the seasonal raids by developers and agents. But it has seemed to her for over two years now that her house had become their Mecca.

Bindi has lived alone since her husband died in 1979 and though the raiders' visits are short (for she always gives the same answer, and occasionally the answer Steven would have given them if they show rough manners) they bring a change to the day. She strolls around the ground with them, watching greed flood their eyes, feeling their tension as they try to be casual – 'Yes, great view,' she says, teasing – 'Yes, pretty well two blocks you could say – yes, all the way up-harbour to the city, you can see everything when it's clear, and isn't it a good clear day today. Ha ha ha, wouldn't you love it!'

And she's always ready with the life story of every old Proudie on the Sandpath if a raider wants to know – stories sometimes illustrated with her husband's photos spread on an outside table. But she never admits them to the house.

Later, when they slide away sly as money to try their luck somewhere else, she sits at the kitchen table, anchored by memories and place, and determines that the anchor's chain will not be broken.

It is in this kitchen with its square table, its Early Kooka stove in a bricked niche, the dresser with its crooked drawer and wood crumbs and the grubby pressed-tin ceiling that she forges the links that hold her fast to the Bay. Like most of the old Proudies it was the house of her beginning – her afterbirth had been put in the icebox for burying later under a tree, and there it was still, she liked to think, feeding its roots. In this kitchen there'd been generations of dinners and breakfasts and squabbles and lovings and couplings and births. There'd been chickens scratching in the yard and fat harbour rats down by the wet rocks, and cats full of crickets and sheeps' hearts frightening sparrows with their eyes. There were fresh eggs with their birth feathers stuck to them, a rabbitoh, an iceman and a milko – there was even a Chinaman who sold vegetables from a horse and cart, coolie hat and all, and fish! My God, if you wanted fish you just went down to Cove Beach and waited for them to land at your feet, belly up and scaled. No money in the world could buy better than Proudie Bay. That was the gospel according to Bindi Hope. And she'd planned not to leave it at all or leave in a box.

'And it's never the houses they're after is it?' Having her say to passing old Proudies at her front gate.

'No, it never is.'

'We didn't come down in the last bloody shower.'

'No, we never did.'

'They don't fool me. You see what they're up to – bulldozers right through! House, trees, gardens, everything. Good solid old places been here for ever and what do they put up? Cement squares like toilet blocks with cement yards. God help them they should have anything to do! And cement pools right next to a harbour full of water, for God's sake!'

In the late salt air of an afternoon when old Proudie washing was taken off clothes lines and 'new Proudies' unloaded dryers, Bindi shook and folded in the old way and wondered if the raiders had had any luck that day.

She knew Meryl and Victor Hughes wouldn't leave but she could not understand why the Perkers clung to the Bay – losing their blue-eyed boy to Shack Hill as they had, and only fifteen when he jumped off the cliff into the ocean, full of drugs or drink they think, or both. Then of course there were the Hardwicks down in fourteen. Just him and the two children since poor Lissy died. Three generations in that big house and only three of them left in it now. But she knew *he* wouldn't sell, not Marlin Hardwick – the stud of Proudie Bay, so they say. And didn't he have it made now with Jennifer grown up and waiting on him hand and foot after working all day at Dolan's Cafe. Him and his brat of a son. Not that she ever went near them now. Not since poor Lissy died. Poor Lissy Gibson, a sweet pretty thing until he married her and wore her out. Wore out her body first then scraped away at her mind until she was ragged as a dishcloth fit for the bin. *There's no justice in the world*, Bindi thought, when a man marries a woman and her property then chews her up and spits her out and ends up with everything in his lap like Christmas, there's no justice in that.

There are, for Bindi, clear memories of Lissy. The clearest on the Sandpath.

She remembers her eyes – she'll never forget her eyes – big as night pools with the moon gone when Bindi had hurried to the Fishcastle after seeing Jennifer wandering out on the road, half-dressed for school. She had found Lissy crouched and dying in a corner of the laundry with the door closed so the children wouldn't see the cancer eating the last of her, curled up on the floor like a pile of old clothes.

And she remembers the smell – clothes soiled, a rot – death still breathing.

'Where's your mum and dad?' she called to Jennifer down the road, before she knew the truth but had a feeling something was wrong.

'I think they're sleeping in. I can't find Gulliver.'

'Your brother's down on the rocks watching the fishing boats go out. I saw him from my place. You'd better tell him to put some clothes on.' And she'd followed an instinct and gone to the house and found Lissy.

She'd said to the children, 'Sssssh, don't disturb them if they're sleeping, and you know where to find me if you want anything, darlings,' and shaking like a jelly she'd hurried them off to school. And Marlin? He'd slept in, all right, but not in his own bed and not with his own wife. Making himself un-sick, hale and healthy – not like ordinary mortals – sickness being the worst of human weakness to him.

'Ol' Marlin wouldn't let nothing like sick get the better of him,' Hughie Pheiffer once said to her. 'He's a man pulled up high by his own boot straps. Tough as hide. Sharp as sharks. Taught himself everything he knows – you've got to give the man his dues. A man who never set foot in a university till he was asked to give a lecture in one. He's a do-it-yourselfer, ol' Marlin. Doesn't worry me they call him professor round here, he's worked for it.'

And then she remembers a time just after Lissy's funeral when the kids were howling every other minute – just before she was cremated, there was a story going the rounds that that Irish biddy, Angie Frost, was heard to say to him, 'Poor Marlin. Poor you who's lost his wife and the mother of his children, how in God's heaven can I help you?' And how he'd said back to her in that sly way of his, 'In the easiest way of all, Angie girl.' Maybe true, maybe not.

Bindi remembers a photo Steven had once taken of Marlin, all dressed in white, all blond and clean and proper, leaning against a tree and grinning and she'd thought, *He doesn't drink. He doesn't drive because of the pollution. He eats plain. He won't let the kids swear – butter wouldn't melt on him but I never trusted him for a minute. He's like a devil tarted up as a saint to fool you.*

Steven Hope had begun to photograph Proudie Bay from the day he and Bindi returned to the Sandpath from their honeymoon. He'd photographed everything that moved and most things that didn't. Bindi had them all stacked, dated and named. She thought of them as her Steven in two shoe boxes, to be brought down from the top of the wardrobe any time she wanted him. Now she wanted him. She made a pot of tea and put the boxes on the kitchen table.

She sorted through stacks of black and whites and coloureds of Proudies who'd either moved or died. Weddings, anniversaries, harbourscapes and oceanscapes blurred when the wind was too strong. Views from Shack Hill and from the church on the high point opposite it, and then selected a bundle that included the Fishcastle.

One was of a young, slim Lissy, simply dressed, looking with huge, dark eyes at the camera. On her head she wore a patterned scarf. A girl child hung back behind the curtain of her mother's skirt. The child was not smiling. The background of trees and harbour glowed soft like a watercolour, but the mother and child looked as though they were pinned to it, startled and wide-eyed like insects. When Bindi had seen this she knew that Lissy was already ill and that her small daughter somehow knew it.

Another photograph was of Marlin and his firstborn, Gulliver, sitting in their dinghy and grinning up to the camera, handsome, arrogant, and not caring about the two trembling females on shore.

And another of Marlin's sister, Hesta, who came to do what she could for the children during the worst of the motherless times, but a dreamer like her brother, play-acting for the camera and probably anxious to go back to the Blue Mountains, where her new love had bought her a nest.

There was a photo of the boy child, Gulliver, standing under the flame tree, holding a lizard in one hand and a tortoise in the other with a snake coiled at his feet.

And another of Jennifer, not long before Steven died, grown tall, and with brown lank hair and the resigned eyes of a drone. Taken not long before she took the job of waitress at Dolan's Cafe. Not long before she waitressed all day for the Dolans then went home to the Fishcastle and waitressed all over again.

But then, Bindi came to her favourite photograph of Proudie Bay. Her favourite, and Steven's too. It was protected by a cover.

They had gone for an early morning walk around the point and had looked back across the bay. They'd watched a fishing boat cruise past the Fishcastle in a sky mist and a mist of its own, but Marlin's garden could be clearly seen: the flame tree, the fig, the dinghy cave, the jutty, the clothes line with nothing but a pair of panties flapping from it, Marlin's royal standard, so they said. The cock's flag flying when he'd had a woman in his bed. It was a photograph in all the subtle shades and shadows of black and white (Steven's choice for scenes like this). There was a surreal quality to it and if it had not featured the Fishcastle she would have had it enlarged and framed.

She'd always thought he could have won a prize for it. Medals for memories ... *Pity about the subject ... Pity the best go and the worst are left,* she thought.

Chapter Two

DAWN FISHERMEN, NOVEMBER MORNING

When Steven Hope took that misty photograph of the bay in its softest light, it was after the briefest time of mourning that followed Lissy Hardwick's death. She was 'privately cremated'. She had no immediately available relatives, her friends were few and not encouraged to be close, but brown Bindi, though she was not at all surprised to have been ignored, thought she might have been asked to attend. She would like to have spilled at least one tear near Lissy's pine box – said goodbye, one human to another. Jennifer and Gulliver had been too young to be involved and Marlin refused to dwell on death. 'Dead is dead,' he'd said, as comforting as ice, after the plain service. And at the end of it the spirit of the dead passed him by with its eyes closed and stroked its soul only on her children.

And so it was that a hoony few of the dawn fishermen cruised harbour quiet past the high garden and the house near the point of Proudie Bay that morning. Men who grinned up at it with their grimy, yesterday teeth, happy to snap at the baits of local gossip. These were the ones who saluted and called out at the top of their salt-sea voices, loud enough to make the locals toss furious in their beds:

'Here's to Marlin Hardwick, boys! Salute the king fisher and his rod!' And there'd be a bellow of laughter strong enough to roll the boat. 'That house there, that's his Fishcastle,' they'd tell a new boy, unsteady on his land legs hard apart, and shining with spray from his young, fuzzed cheeks to his hand-me-downs. 'And that up there, flying on the clothes line, they say, is his royal standard.'

'All I can see is a pair of panties,' says the new boy, green as weed.

'That's it,' they'd tell him.

And the new boy, with his legs planted firm and rolling with the swell, grins under their back slaps and considers himself cock-wise like the rest of them. And even if there was no motor below drumming them forward through the dawn, there'd be fuel enough from their chiacking and bellows, spiriting around them like a stiff wind of morning breath, to carry them through the salt mists and out through Sydney heads to the ocean and their deep green hunting grounds.

But lately the cocksure have been more careful to keep their boat steady on course because on one occasion, not a month back, one loud cock had shouted to another, 'Those pants look a bit like your Angie's come to think of it.'

'No, they're not his Angie's,' shouted the other, 'because she don't wear any – ha ha ha ha ha!!!'

And that cock had hooted so much he'd slipped and fallen over the stern, caught his hand in the screw and it was cut off, neat as a butcher's chop, just above the wrist. 'Best steady through the dawn now,' they say – 'steady now,' they whisper in their minds since the accident, remembering the hand, fingers up, waving at nobody and lost in blood and churn until a fish took the lot.

The curse of the joke of Angie's pants, they'd said at the time, but it happened that those pants were old ones that had belonged to poor Lissy. Good, strong cottons that Marlin now used to wipe the fish tanks.

The Fishcastle stands proud and high over the Bay as is right for a house with such a name. It is built square, of grey weatherboards stacked like fish scales, scale over scale two storeys high, and near enough to the harbour for its flight of stone steps to tumble down over two tiers of land in order to touch the salt swell, where it slaps against rocks, and breaks against the base of a sandstone sea wall.

It is close enough to hear the slaps of ebb and flow through a cave cut into rock below the wall where the dinghy shelters. And it is near enough to watch the water lick up onto a spit of oyster-shelled rock – a stone 'jutty' covered in old shells, sharp as razors, and with an iron ring set into it for a mooring.

And close enough, when the weather turns and howls, for curls of tide to climb the stone steps, one lap at a time, to get at the yard grass, the carp pond, the pigeon coop, the lizards with their blue flicking tongues and the diamond python's hutch.

But the house stands solid against bad seas as well as good, and the winds that blow from the ocean side of it. Marlin keeps it weatherproofed and sealed and painted fast as a ship – clean and spruce as himself, on the outside. Three upstairs windows, three square glass eyes in a row, that only blink when the sun catches them, keep watch, ready to rattle a warning if the sky swings a mood.

Storm eyes for black ocean moods are never far away from the bay – just beyond the point of it. Just outside the heads. Bad-temper skies and dark water, deep swells of it, sevens of waves of it, ready at any time to turn from pounding the high cliffs that face the ocean and howl through the open gates of the heads and into the harbour to frighten old women and children and dogs and babies in their night dreams.

Jennifer Hardwick is afraid of sea storms, and the temper of their high water crashing against the cliffs and the swell that threatens the harbour. She always has been. For as long back as she can remember; from times of suckling and nestling against her mother when the clouds hung heavy – and her mother just as nervous, hugging her daughter to her like a comfort toy.

It is not so much when the storms hit the house and rage around it. Not so much then, though she is happier locked away in her room at the top of the stairs – away from the worst of it, and away from the wind whistling through the rambling, slopping, fish-tanked house she lives in. It is the feel of the storm's approach that disturbs her, a feeling in the pit of her stomach – a dread that makes her much more nervous than when it breaks. She was never sure why she'd been cursed with 'storm willies', as her father called the feelings, she'd had them for as long as she could remember, but she learned early enough in her life that there were other humans who reacted to seasonal changes, atmospheric disturbances and that sort of thing – thousands – so it was some comfort to know she was not alone. She knew that dogs reacted in their own way. The Carters' dog next door always barks, noisier than usual, if a storm is coming. Like a signal. 'All right, all right,' she calls over the fence if she's at home. 'I hear you. I hear you. I feel it too.'

Of course, there was the story her father told her, when she was very small, of a great tidal wave that swept high as sky over the tops of the ocean cliffs hundreds of years ago. Over the cliffs and across the spit of land to smash into the harbour, leaving enormous sandstone boulders scattered about like bottle tops.

'Could the water come again?' she'd asked him.

'O yes sirreee,' he'd said, grinning. 'That old wave's just waiting round the corner of the world, hanging still, just waiting,' he'd said, and he'd shivered his lips in mock fear while he bounced her, tense and wide-eyed on his knee.

Her storm willies probably started then, she thought, *on her dear father's knee.* But after it all – the bad sky moods – when the sun shines out over the bay and the water peaks and sparkles as though it's covered with tea candles, and the

17

breeze is dry enough not to leave salt on the lines of washing, Jennifer's gut feelings subside considerably – the weather-dread feelings, at any rate.

Jennifer Hardwick had been named simply Jennifer, just one name and in honour of no one in particular. A naming ceremony had been conducted by Marlin under the flame tree in the garden. But it was not a Christly Christening. There was no font or holy water – there is no Christ in the Hardwick house except between the covers of reference books on all the world's gods. He made up his own ceremonial words like the storyteller he was, but they had nothing to do with gods.

Jennifer, however, had always wished there'd been a photograph taken of her 'naming'. She wished brown Bindi and Steven had been asked to attend. She would like to have had some memory scraps of it – and her mother – and to make more clear her misty memories of soft milk breasts and soft smiles and fresh-smelling cotton. She would have liked that, even if the ceremony had been something that probably only lasted five minutes between Marlin's lunch and his horsing around with lizards or the snake for the entertainment of children who were not his own – just the locals and strays – the ones he likes best for what they see in him. But there was no record of those moments under the flame tree – nothing. It was as though it might never have happened. It was as though she hardly existed. 'I name this brown, tumble-down, flame-tree leaf Jennifer, after nobody,' she once imagined him saying.

She had often wondered if she would have been less plain if she had not been a Jennifer. A Jennifer, she'd decided, needs to be either very beautiful or very rich. A Jennifer needs accessories – high strap heels and curled copper hair and gold chains.

She had always been fond of the names Lilian and Victoria and thought that perhaps even Emily Hardwick had something of a tune to it, but when she saw images of herself she knew it was too late, that she had grown into the name she'd been given. Except for the times her father, when his mood was right, called her Blue Wren or Jenny Wren, or something else like it.

Her mother had once been introduced to a new baby in the village. The baby's name was Angela and her mother had said, 'Angela is a beautiful name, it's a name I've always loved,' and she wondered if her mother might have preferred Angela for her daughter but was overruled.

She once asked her father, 'Did Mum ever say she wanted to call me Angela?'

But all he said was: 'Jennifer Angela? Jennifer Angelica? *Jennifuss Angelicuss.*' Twisting it all around like an academic clown. 'A good Latin name for a weed. Yes. Not bad.'

'I wish you'd died instead,' she had said.

Jennifer had grown with a disability – a difference so small that only she is aware of it. Her disability is not visible to the eyes of others – only she can sense it. Only she can tell that her brain has a slight limp – something that trips her thinking from time to time and allows uninvited thoughts and tensions to invade, unchecked. A slight limp of the brain, she might say, as though one lobe was shorter than the other, with nothing to protect either of them.

'I feel bad,' she used to say to her mother before her mother died. 'The inside of my head feels white. It stings.'

'It's just the strain of it all. You're a worrier, like me.' Her mother would tell her softly, white-faced with her breath smelling of death, 'You're just too young for Mummy to be so sick, darling.'

And when she told her father about the 'white feeling' he dismissed her as being a 'poor weedy worrybelly', making as much fun of it as he could for her sake, and for his. But Jennifer knew she was different. She'd always known. And even now she can look into a mirror and count the rings of it under her eyes, as fine as they are, just as she might count the rings of a troubled tree.

Because of her height, she believes, and her strong bones, she is sometimes described, if she is described at all, as being 'handsome' – a word she hates. She is slim and tall, with a fine-cut face whose features long to be softer than they are, long legs, muscled like a dancer's, and hands that work like a man's – ugly hands, she's always thought, worker's hands that no man would ever kiss. She moves her body in a tight, fidgety way – a nervous way, with her head and shoulders slightly bowed in the way of tall women, so that her straight dark hair falls forward against her cheeks. 'Shoving along, head on into the wind, even if there isn't one,' someone at Dolan's Cafe once said of her, but Jennifer has known no other way for most of her twenty-five years.

Solemn and contained and tense as a screw-top jar full of frights is Jennifer Hardwick.

She has the pale sea eyes of her father. She'd always wished for her mother's dark satiny eyes but her brother had inherited those, and what a waste that was, as things turned out, she thought. She did, however, have her mother's smooth cream-tea skin that easily browned but she often thought that against all the rich, seaside brown of her, her father's pale water eyes faded to nothing and made her look as though she had none at all. Or eyes made of glass. The kind of eyes in which other people can watch their reflections and not notice her at all.

Jennifer is not a lover of the sea as her father is. She's a dry-lander, a sky-flyer – a cloud-traveller, even if only in her day and night dreams. She does not love the sea with the passion of her father, or her brother, or other men who live on it or in it.

When she and Gulliver were barely more than babies, Marlin had slipped them into the harbour from the rocks below the sea wall when the tide was up to teach them to swim. It was his way. Lissy was horrified.

'Your little nips will come up with their fins flapping and their gills puffing, girl, so shush, you'll see!' he told her. 'It's the natural way of things – breathing!'

And Gulliver did come head up out of the harbour sputting and coughing and splashing his legs and laughing for more, but Jennifer choked and swallowed enough salt water to fill one of his fish tanks and had to be scooped up like a screaming carp.

'Worrybelly damn near drowned that time,' he roared, laughing, as he handed the slippery child to its mother. 'Better tomorrow!'

At which she screamed more loudly and clung, terrified, to Lissy's blouse.

After that she was always afraid of the sea – afraid of its alien life with its slithering shapes and sharp scales and staring eyes. She still has nightmares of white-horsed, tossing, powerful tops of oceans that only just hold down a fright of creatures that live on the floor of their world. She never minded much going to Cove Beach where the harbour water gently lapped at her paddling toes, or quiet rock pools where she watched minute shellfish and poked them gently with a finger, but she had always hated climbing with her father up the path that led to the high cliffs, and looking way down into the furious ocean. And she *never* walks along the dark, back hallway of her house – the cold-floored linoleum corridor where the fish tanks are lined up, full of wrong fish staring out of their slimy glass, despite Marlin's complaints that the floor needed a scrub.

'You can clean that part of the house yourself,' she said to him, 'or get Gull to do it. I'm not going anywhere near those terrible things.'

And once he said to her in the teasing voice he knows she can't stand, and with the sly grin he thinks is funny – or sexy: 'But what about the floppy with two heads, Jen? He needs dusting before his dinner.'

But she'd closed her eyes at him and turned away. She'd

willed the two-headed fish to die when Gull told her about it, but it seemed to live forever.

'I've seen him feeding it,' her brother told her, grinning at her revulsion. 'He feeds it one mouth at a time,' he told her, 'and you should see the other head going for it!'

'You both make me sick!' she'd cried, angry and repulsed.

Something else to dream about, she'd worried, in the quiet of her mind. Something else to make her curl more tightly in her bed.

'Some day some person with a hammer will smash every one of those tanks and that will be the end of it.'

'But it won't be you, will it, Jen?' Gull said, still grinning.

'Don't you be so sure about that!' she'd said. But the thought of all those creatures loose and slithering on the floor – the two-headed fish, the octopus dragging one tentacle after another across the lino – the eyes, the eyes, and the stench of sick sea water almost made her gag with fright.

The wonder of it was, she worked in a fish cafe, but the cafe fish somehow looked different, as though they had all been grown in a different sea garden where the colours were brighter and the sun shone through the surface.

Her work at Dolan's cafe was the only part of her day, she'd considered, the *only* hours worth living. It was like going from a madhouse to a laughing. From somewhere twisted to where it was all Sunday best ironed, and French perfumes and popping corks. And nicest of all, a place where she was *thanked* for hard work. Even by old Mother Dolan on her good days. Dolan's was Jennifer's sanctuary. Her dreaming. Her shoulder-rub with sanity. And as much as she hated fish she would stay there even if she had to stuff cotton up her nose.

Gulliver Hardwick is two years older than Jennifer.

Gulliver had been named under the flame tree too, but had been given a second name. He became Gulliver Darwin, in honour of the great naturalist, and Marlin had congratulated Lissy for giving him a male child. And for a few short years Marlin was content enough for them to have one child each. Like the lyrics of the old song, 'A boy for him and a girl for her', except there was probably never 'tea for two' and Jennifer could not 'picture Lissy upon his knee' – and as far as she knew there was nothing in the old song about a cancer gnawing away at the insides of the sweetest of the pair.

'A poor motherless Gull and a poor motherless Wren, both with their wings clipped,' Marlin said, in a perfectly straight voice after Lissy's death, as though their child lives had suffered nothing more serious than stubbed toes – both children faced with living their lives like ferals, in a serious, exploratory way within the boundaries of the Fishcastle, learning survival with all the rest of Marlin's creatures. Learning cunning from the lizards, patience from the carp, strength from the python and resignation from the death-row pigeons.

Gull crawled naked amongst them all and learned everything. Jennifer tried but in the end her limping brain chose only resignation.

It was a pity, Jennifer thought, *that when their mother died she could never have known what a beautiful man child she had made, despite the sire.* Despite the clean on the outside, strutting, seed spiller she was sure her father must always have been.

Gulliver's body was formed in her mother's image – olive skinned and smooth and sweet as lick. Kept safe and warm in her mother's womb, Jennifer imagined, while she painted him perfect for the world. There was not a touch of the pale sea colours of his father, and after their mother died Jennifer had taken her dark-eyed brother under her wing as easily as a child would have taken a doll, with willingness and love and not a second thought. And with the occasional, haphazard help of their aunt Hesta, and under the eye of brown Bindi, in the first few bitter months she had mothered him herself. Her father praised her when the occasion suited him and sometimes called her 'little mother', which thrilled her at the time, but as she grew older she realised that his praise had been no more than an expression of relief that there was still a female to service his household. She learned to cook and clean, and even when she couldn't reach, climbed on a chair in order to wash up in the sink. Marlin rewarded her by giving her the upstairs room that was her mother's 'quiet room' and left her alone in the evening to watch television, listen to music or pretend in her 'dress-ups' away from the kitchen and his watching eyes.

She felt safe in the 'mother' room. Protected. Safe, with the door closed and wrapped in the warmth of her mother's nursing chair that still held a faint, good smell of her.

But it was a great disappointment to Jennifer, as Gulliver grew older, that she might have mothered the boy too well. Spoiled him too well. Done too much for him – spoke too much for him – encouraged him to become lazy and to lie too easily. She was afraid that her love of his beauty had made him love himself too much – and that others did not had escaped her notice. She tried not to blame herself for the wickedness that developed in her brother's eyes. *That could not have come from her, and it could not have come from her mother.* It had to be, she knew in her heart, the part of him seeded by his father. And as the years passed she was sure of it.

Locked away in her mother room on still nights she sometimes worried that she had failed Lissy Hardwick. Once, she'd confided this to brown Bindi but Bindi had only laughed.

'You think any of us gets a book of instructions with kids?' she'd asked. 'Especially in your case when the kid's older than its "mother" and ought to know better! You're doing your best, darling. You do more than your best. You deserve a medal!' And Bindi had taken the opportunity to wrap her brown arms around Jennifer and hold her close. 'If you want to know what I think,' Bindi had said, 'I think it's a pity Gull's little mum isn't strong enough to give him a good pad on the backside when he needs it. I'll lend you my wooden spoon if you like.' And Jennifer had laughed and was reassured for a while.

Gulliver Darwin loved the sea. He swam in it, rowed on it, fed from it and floated about so that his skin shone forever wet and slippery as one of its fish. It seemed to Jennifer that as Gull grew older the mother parts of him she loved so much withered and died before her eyes. It seemed to her that he had betrayed his mother by living the ways of his father.

Gulliver grew as close to the sea as he could, away from his dry-land sister. He stuck to the lives of fishermen – all the closer in their drinking hours, and the rougher the better. He shared their sea language and chased their women. And as he aged it was clear that Marlin's affections for his son cooled as his appearance reminded him more and more of his wife, and his ego more and more of himself. Two nagging thoughts, sharp as shards, he would rather have kept locked away in the strong boxes he housed in the shadowed back of his mind – with all the other disturbances that had road-blocked the path to his own glory.

Gulliver Hardwick lives off the Bay like a limpet, content to cling to its rocks and suck into itself whatever passes its way. His home rocks are placed in the half moon of the Bay between the Fishcastle, the pub, the dole office, his dinghy and his room full of motorbike parts, closet magazines and secret bottles.

Gull is not tall – not six feet, but a straight spine gives the illusion of height that he displays with the conceited skill of a runway model. A movie dream, a Mel Gibson with brown eyes, he was once told to his delight (and a likeness he could now clearly see in his mirror). His eyes and hair are the colour of night kelp, and his head is held high and light as the air inside it. But to any lip-licking passer-by sniffing the air for sex, Gull is a body primed and cocked. To watch Gulliver Hardwick work the Bay strips, when he feels like it, is to see a certain theatre of the streets at its best. A skin-flick character from one end of the waterline to the other.

If Jennifer sees him as she clears tables at the end of her work day, she burns with shame.

Marlin Hardwick once watched the theatre of his son, silently, from a distance. He watched him strut along the beach below the cafe in the late afternoon, bare to the waist, jeans rolled up and flexing for the staring, wetting, tipsy women after their late lunches. And when Gulliver had come home at eight, Marlin's rage was so great that Jennifer took the stairs two at a time and locked herself in her room, leaving their food to grow cold on the kitchen table.

'You damned loader!' he swore at his son. 'You damned horny goat! You disgrace me! You disgrace this house! There's no honour in you! You're nothing but a parasitic walking cock!'

And Gulliver, buoyed by beers chased by whisky, had replied, 'And who would I have caught all that from, old Dad?' and winked.

For the father, the pride in his son had soured. There was a confusion, a self doubt and a helplessness that was alien to him and they were feelings that pricked his nerve ends. His work with the natural world and its special laws, its straightforward laws, and all his knowledge of creatures of the sea and the land and the air had not prepared him for a rutting son.

In all of his studies and all of his teachings he had not

learned how a human sire of a young male should act –
especially when the young male openly challenges the sire
in his own territory – without fear. A lion, he knew, would
have killed him.

Marlin's body had not surrendered in any way to its fifty-six
years. The sharp, hard and clear features of his face were
lined, but only by the best of the elements – the sun, the salt
sea air, the moon and night squalls: a strong face. There was
only a certain looseness to his lower lip, spit wet at times,
that betrayed a strangeness – weaknesses in hiding.

His hair, the colour of sand, showed no signs of greying
and his eyes were still the sea deep, deep grey eyes of his
young life. He was taller than his son, and moved with the
easy grace of all the wild things he knew better than humans,
and in his mind he imagined he could still move every
woman within hip-swinging distance of the Fishcastle. Even
their wintering eyes wandered slyly when he padded along
the Sandpath on his bare feet, his hide covered with little
more than shirt and shorts in the cold air and sometimes
only sarongs wrapped and tied. But no matter his reputation;
no matter how he'd treated his poor wife and the mother of
his children, they licked their lips and hid secret thoughts
behind their eyes.

'Look at you!' Jennifer once admonished him on a cold,
southerly day, irritated to the point of screaming. 'For God's
sake put on a sweater – it's freezing! Who do you think
you're fooling, poncing around like that? I can see the goose
bumps!'

'Cold toughens the skin, Jen Wren. You should try it.'

'You do it to show off!' she'd snapped. 'You can't think people love you for it?'

'But they do, Jen. And I love dem people right back,' he'd said in his smart-arse voice.

'You don't know what love is! They're not fools. You only love animals and sex!'

'Is that what they say? Still, sex is people, Jen,' he'd said, grinning at her.

'Sex is sex!' she'd said, before hurrying away from him and slamming the nearest door. She hated being so close to him when he talked like that – slack-lipped, his eyes grinning and wetting behind their lashes. Her belly churned when he talked like that and thoughts like a tangle of worms filled her mind. And slid together. And touched. Warm and breathing. Jennifer kept a box in the back of her own mind for worm thoughts. That's where they lived and that's where they'd stay – locked away until she died.

It never occurred to her that there were other boxes of worms locked away in the backs of minds in the Fishcastle.

There was, apart from women, a clutch of human adoration that Marlin could always rely on. And that was the powerful admiration bestowed upon him by the 'after-school children'.

The children of Proudie Bay loved him without reservation and without judgement. They loved his wild, outrageous ways. They loved the Fishcastle made eerie by the stories he told them, and its scaly, feathery, twisting menagerie.

The 'after-schoolies' came to the house in packs, as

many as six or seven and sometimes ten, on the days when Marlin was not lecturing at the university or working at the museum, rushing up the driveway, shrieking like invaders, crunching white gravel under their boots or bare feet, calling his name to draw him out, shrieking all over the yard, frightening the pigeons awake in their house, scuttling lizards, tripping tortoises and play-acting a terror circle around the python's hutch.

The after-schoolies bellowed into the yard about an hour before Jen arrived home from the cafe, and even though she longed to kick off her sandals and get as far away from serving as she could, she would automatically go to the kitchen, take butter from the fridge and reach for plastic cups and paper plates and bread – and wait for Marlin's orders.

Jennifer would have loved the children to come to her. She often wished for it. She imagined them all sitting at her own feet, gazing up at her, listening with all their ears to her own stories, just as they did for him. She had tried. She'd invited them to her warm, dry part of the house where it was safe. She'd asked them to choose a book to be read, or listen to music or to dress up and eat cakes or chips, never mind the crumbs, but as soon as Marlin called they'd race downstairs to him and squat on the grass, glued to the spot, eyes wide, mouths open, waiting for the best or the worst to happen, and she would be no more than the invisible kitchen appliance again, with a spreading knife, a pot of honey, a jar of jam – and no hope.

It was on such an afternoon, a typical afternoon, that she watched the show from the house for the hundredth time. Marlin's audience had arranged themselves as usual in a semi-circle, cross-legged on the grass of the harbour front yard, and Marlin made his entrance from a side door, wearing nothing but one of the sarongs he'd brought back from a study tour of Malaysia, and a wide, wicked grin. Jennifer watched it all from the kitchen window. The way the man swung along on the bare pads of his feet, his head high and his expression giving them permission to cheer when all he was doing was walking towards them. It infuriated her. She'd watched this entrance so many times and it still infuriated her, but she couldn't take her eyes off it.

She resented it all so much – her father, the idol of children who were not his own. *The storyteller, the spellweaver, the liar.* The enchanter of other women's children, with his own forced to stay backstage and work the ropes, pouring lolly water and counting bread slices.

But she still watched him and listened to him, as she had done for years. She couldn't help it.

The storyteller slid to the grass and, like the children, sat easy-limbed and cross-legged, but centre stage. 'Now!' he began in his clear, strong stage voice, 'This here is a story about —'

'Start at "once upon a time"! Start properly! Start at "once upon a time"!' the children shouted, and Marlin laughed on cue, working into his routine. 'Once upon a time!' they chanted in unison.

'All right – all right! "Once upon a time" it is, then!' the man shouted, and in the smooth air of the yawning sun that made the green grass greener, he began an old story as though it were a new story – as though they had never heard it before. 'Once upon a time there were three sons of a father . . .'

Same old thing! she thought angrily, glued to the spot. *Why aren't they sick of it! Why on earth don't they tell him to shutup!* But still watching and listening from behind the kitchen window, watching, in a fury of envy.

'Yes!!' they cried. 'That one!'

'Once upon a time there were three sons of a father, the North Son, the South Son and the Middle Son, as handsome as you like!'

'You!!'

'The North Son grew snakes for belts and pigeons for the pot.'

The after-schoolies recited with him:

'The South Son grew cows for shoes and spiders for eggs . . .' They giggled now – nudged and clapped their hands.

'And the Middle Son! The Middle Son grew a Marlin to swim in a sea when he's wet and tell stories when he's dry.'

'You! You!!'

They shrieked the words with him, and Jennifer, at last entirely exasperated, marched outside and across the grass. She tried to look as though she was doing nothing more than getting some fresh air. She kicked off her sandals and one landed near the low, wire hutch beside the hydrangeas.

Marlin ignored her. 'To tell stories to all the little ones – all the little fun ones who loves him.'

'Oh my God!' Jennifer called, over their heads. 'Why on earth do you go on talking that nonsense to them, Dad? It's so stupid! It's insane! It's a wonder to me they're allowed to come here at all!' She retrieved her sandals and glared at him.

'My, my, look you all! The Wren's flown out!' he shouted in his play-acting voice. 'Who let the Jen out of its nest?' A yard full of small faces were turned and laughing at her.

'Their parents couldn't possibly imagine the sort of rubbish you tell them if they thought for a hundred years!' She knew she was flushed red.

'Their mummies and daddies,' Marlin said to her in a low, even tone, 'are happy their little funs aren't on the road under a bus, or staring at telly or shouting their houses to the ground. Now, how about you make us all a nice snack.' And he smiled at her with a certain look in his eyes – a snare of a smile, a noose of a smile, and as usual her insides turned to jelly. 'Sugar tea and bikkies for the funs and a coffee for your dear ol' dad, eh?' It was his low hiss of a voice that she hated. The sound of it brought back the worms soft weaving their way from her ears way down to the floor of her belly – under the navel – to the parts of her that twitched hot with love and hate. She knew she was flushed again. And she knew he saw it, as usual, and watched it, above the noise of the children, with his moist, sea eyes.

'Don't you know the snake's still out of its hutch!' she snapped angrily, to cut the tension she felt all through her. Three of the children screamed happily and ran around in circles. 'I told you it was loose before I went to work.'

'Get brother Gulliver to put him back, then.'

'You know very well Gull's out!'

'So! Two snakes out of their hutches hey, hey? Is that what we've got here?' Marlin crept around, bent over, peering slit-eyed with his hands up shading them, whispering, 'Two snakes in the grass, kids. Let's root 'em out,' to the delight of the children, who copied his every move. Jennifer folded her arms tight across her chest.

'It'll get in the pigeon house one of these days, then you won't think it's so funny!' She wanted to sound angry, but she was tired. Her period was near and she'd been forcing smiles all day. The end-of-the-day stuffing was out of her. 'You wouldn't be laughing if the damn thing ate your pigeon roasts! Think of Sundays!' was all she managed.

'In that case,' said Marlin, 'you'd better make it some party tea as well, Jen Wren. Nice sugared tea for ol' diamond snake and some sugared mice to go with it – but make sure they're alive and wriggling!'

There were squeals of frightened pleasure from the children.

'You'll have them dreaming terrors all night!' she admonished.

'There'd be no point to it if they didn't, Jennifer,' he said, still smiling that smile. 'Now, go make one of your nice teas for us.' Then turning to the children, 'Who wants to hear the terrible, horrible, fearful story about the rats that ate through the bellringer's rope?' And paid his daughter no further notice.

'Me!' shouted the children.

'Very well then . . .'

'Once upon a time!' they reminded him.

'Once upon a time . . .' he began in his secretive, for-their-ears-only voice. 'Once upon a most terrible, nightmare time there were two bellringers in a church tower – and the tower was built one thousand metres above the ocean . . .'

You could hear a pin drop! Jennifer thought, as she stalked off to the kitchen, invisible, wild and frustrated. Before she reached the door she saw the python coiled tight and still under a shrub. 'Probably trying to block its ears,' she muttered. 'Trying to bury itself as far away from him as it can get! Why doesn't it kill the pigeons, the lazy great lump! Why doesn't it kill something!' And she slammed the door behind her as hard as she could.

At the kitchen bench under the window she forced herself to breathe easy while she stirred her father's mug of coffee – milk, two sugars. Breathe and out . . . breathe and out . . . She buttered the bread slices with deliberate, slow strokes and made herself pour drinks into plastic cups without dripping. There was a familiar hard tension in her neck – a stiffening that became an ache at the top of her clamped jaws and behind her ears, and her ears feeling as though they were filled to bursting with a dam of water. Fire water and brimstone.

She spread jam on the bread slices, carefully to the crust line – not outside the lines. She cut the bread into quarter points and pressed every stray crumb onto the tip of her index finger and put the strays into a saucer – into the middle of the saucer, where the indentation for a cup was formed.

She arranged the children's tea on a tray, the cups in a neat row, the bread placed point to point to point ... attention to detail – everything in its place, in line, in order, meditative things she forced herself to do when tension threatened to explode her brain – when she felt it limp – a care for detail she was praised for on those occasions at the cafe but admonished at the same time for the length of time it took.

Jennifer was unsteady as she put the stacked tray on the grass, but with an effort tossed her hair in what she hoped was a casual way and smiled at them all. But she smiled only with her teeth – her eyes were pale flints.

Marlin had reached the part of the story where the jealous bellringer had his pet rat gnawing through the pig fat on the skin tied in bows around his victim's rope. The children were perfectly still – absolutely quiet, listening to every breath he took, watching every twitch of his body, every movement of his hands with wide eyes, waiting to be frightened out of their wits by the story's end.

Marlin ignored her. He saw the tray but he did not see her. The tray could have floated out by itself, held by the hand of a breeze. The only reaction to her presence was a shifting of small bodies whose view of Marlin the tray blocked for a moment.

On her way back to the house she saw the python still coiled, hidden under the shrub. She blew it a savage kiss. 'Eat something,' she whispered to it. 'Strangle something, you fat lump! Strangle him, but slowly!' She had no intention of telling any of them where the snake was. They can look for it themselves, she thought angrily, and they can all damn well clean up after themselves – she didn't care. She just didn't care.

As Jennifer climbed the stairs to her room she felt the tension move to her legs. The stairway seemed almost insurmountable, as steep as a ship's ladder, and she climbed slowly, her hands pulling, one after the other, along the banister.

In the safety of her room, with the door closed and locked against another world, she lit a candle under a burner of calming ylang ylang oil. She switched on the TV but the early evening programs did nothing to relax her. She switched through the candy-floss conflicts of 'The Bold and the Beautiful', violent early newscast previews, cocky screeching commercials, and finally turned it off and slipped a CD into her player. She took two pain-killers, curled herself in her 'mother' chair and forced her eyes closed to the nocturnes of Chopin.

For a few precious moments she would drift onto her own floating place, where she and her room floated in a space of its own, too high for anyone to reach and held to earth by a cord so fine that only she could see it. A world where there was for a time no limp to her brain, where everything could be as good as it wanted to be. As sweet as the burning oil.

From a table beside the chair she took her journal out of the green lacquer box her mother had used for letters and pressed flowers, and began to write:

*It's after half-past four and the strays are still here listening
to you-know-who! He's telling them the story about the rats.
I hate that story. It makes me want to scream. Did you hate
it too? Did he tell that one when you were alive? I can't
remember. Today I thought again about leaving this place
and leaving the two of them to do for themselves. I think
about it all the time but I'm like a pin stuck to a magnet.
I feel like a moth stabbed to a board – do you know what
I mean? Of course you must know what I mean. You were
pinned down like one of his specimens too, weren't you.
I wish the thought of leaving didn't scare me so much. Today
at work a man told me he liked my eyes. He wasn't rude.
He was about Dad's age and looked very nice. He was alone
and he ate crab and salad and he was reading a book of
poetry and I wished I could have had him but I was too
embarrassed to even squeak. The council rates are due and
there's no money as usual. I won't get a chance to save anything this month, either. I'm curled up in your chair,
Mummy. I wish you could wrap its arms around me. I miss
you so much – A.*

The 'A' was for Angela. A secret.

Jennifer put the journal into its box and locked it. She
lay on her bed with her eyes firmly closed and pictured as
clear as she could the man who ate crab and salad and read
a book of poetry. Only with her eyes shut tight could she
bring him closer until she could feel his hands stroking, his
fingers probing, and the wetting smell of him. The air over
her mouth became his mouth and the pillow against her neck

became hot skin and breath and the sea wind through leaves outside her window became the soft, mewing sounds of sexing. She saw him clearly through the blood red of her eyelids. 'Make it last – make it last,' she whispered, until she was breathing wide-mouthed and shuddering, her own fingers moist and warm between her legs. She stared at the ceiling and tried to trace a picture of the man and keep him there, and his body that she had so carefully re-created, keep him there on the ceiling forever in a frame, but the face of her father kept getting in the way, leering with his pale eyes and grinning his loose lips.

She even imagined Marlin saying to her, 'Been swimming, Jen Wren? You're all wet.' She imagined too that he'd yanked hard on the cord to her world and brought her crashing back to earth. And disgusted and ashamed, she rolled off the bed and hurried to her bathroom.

After her brief glide of intimate fancy in her room – a precious hour – Jennifer washed, patted her hair with wet hands and reluctantly went downstairs. She could hear the sound of her father's bare feet padding around the kitchen. From the doorway she saw there was a doll lying on the long, pine table. Its arm and a leg lay beside it.

'Whose is that?' she asked, setting out a chopping board and knife.

'Poor lil' dolly bwoken,' he said, with his eyes wide like a child's. She ignored his ham-acting. 'I can't find the super-glue, Jen.'

'Well, I haven't touched it,' she said. 'Whose doll is it?'

'Little Beattie's. She had it all wrapped up in a towel bleeding, then she says to me, "Marwin make dolly better."' He smiled smugly. He was scraping old glue from the doll's joints. Beside him were pins and elastic.

'Can't you do that on newspaper, Dad? It's going all over the place.'

'Stop your fussin', woman!'

'Anyway, I think Beattie's too young to come here and listen to your murderous stories. I think she's too young to come here at all. I can't think why her parents let her – she's only four.'

'The wisest age of all,' he said. 'Every house should have a four-year-old to be wise – and who else would she ask to mend her dolly?'

'Her own father?'

'Bob Hart couldn't stick a paper bag together. Little Beattie thinks I'm God.'

'*You* think you're God!' she said. 'Is Gull home?'

'If he is he hasn't said so. I can't smell no fish boy, can you?'

'I wish you'd talk in a normal voice for a while. I'm tired.'

Marlin ignored her and busied himself noisily glue hunting. He slid out drawers and banged them shut again, opened cupboard doors and flipped them shut again. She tried to ignore him but he upset the whole room with his hunt and bang.

'It's probably in the tool room,' she said, and began to strip potatoes and de-skin pumpkin for one of their good, plain dinners that died of boredom as soon it was served on their

41

plates. Old potatoes still with dirt in their eyes, tough skin pumpkin that needed a special knife, carrots with green tops and snake beans long enough to tie bows. Cheap produce he picked up at the markets when he was in the city. She would love to have used some of the cooking ideas she'd picked up at the cafe but Marlin would not even discuss cafe food, and in particular, the fare at Dolan's cafe. Food was food for staying alive; for keeping the motors running. Just good, wholesome fuel. Good staple peasant stuffing. Honest worker's staples. Stinking cabbage and the stinking fish he cooked himself – vegetables or rice and not even a drop of wine to wash the tastes away. The only blood-dark meat he ate was pigeon from his own yard – the slaughter of animals was sickening to him but he didn't mind murdering his pigeons, screwing their necks until their eyes popped. Jennifer kept her own supply of meat. She made sure that while she prepared *his* vegetables, *her* meat was displayed in the centre of the table where he couldn't possibly miss it, better still if it swam in a pool of its own defrosted blood.

'Got it!' he declared suddenly, waving the glue tube over his head. 'In the drawer with the egg slice and the cleaver – glue in wrong drawer!'

'Well I didn't put it there!'

Marlin slid her a look that could have meant anything she wanted to make of it but she didn't react.

She put a bowl of vegetables next to a saucer with a lamb chop in it, wiped her hands and set places for three at one end of the table. Marlin said, ''Taters baked in the oven would be nice, Jen Wren.'

'I'm too tired,' she said, even though it wouldn't have been any more trouble than boiling. 'You want baked potatoes, Dad, you do it.'

'Can't. I'm breakfast,' he said, and that was the end of it.

What she would really like to have done was cook clean, scrubbed, gold-fleshed potatoes the way the cafe prepared them – quartered and parboiled and roasted crisp in olive oil and served with rock salt. She would happily have done that if she didn't have to dish up to two preoccupied, food-ignorant munchers, one considering the dimensions of a hammerhead shark brought into the bay that morning and the other dreaming of himself.

Jennifer wondered how her mother had coped as she scraped away at plain dirt food at feeding time. Brief scenes of the past flashed in and out of her mind at times like these, like fragments of an old picture book, the pages turned too quickly to dwell upon, but just long enough to recognise.

There were fragments of the smell of Sunday roasts, flowers in vases, waxed floors, her mother's clean morning smell in the kitchen, the light, starchy feel of cotton. After these the memories were stronger. Different smells – fever and sick and a clinical clinging and a different touching, dry and hot and sometimes oily moist, and boiled soup and cabbage instead of roasts when Marlin cooked and cotton was rarely washed at all. Hushed whispers. Empty vases. Aunt Hesta suddenly arriving and making too much fuss of them. And the beginning of anxiety and black fear in the pit of her belly when she knew her mother was going to leave them alone. And knowing even then that she must be the one to take her place and not really knowing how.

In memory of Lissy she placed a single red geranium in a jar of water on the table. She was not aware that her father watched her gesture, moved in his way by some memory of his own.

Gull came home at ten minutes to seven. His hair was messed and damp and the grin on his face had been pushed to one side by drink. There was a tell-tale heaviness to the lid over his right eye and his breath was all rum and chasers.

Without a word he tore the paper off a bundle he held under his arm and threw a huge schnapper across the table.

'There's a fish for you!' His loose words ran into each other like running dyes. 'What d'you think of that!'

The fish's tail lay on top of her lamb and its head sent the flower jar flying. Jennifer stood by the stove, horrified, her hand over her mouth.

'You know I hate fish near my food!' she shouted at him, while he clumsily dragged the dead, wet thing away.

'Tabby gave it to me,' he said, loose-lipped, and stabbed a finger at her chop. 'Better than that scrawny thing!'

'Well, it's no good now! I couldn't touch it now!'

Marlin moved towards Gull, his eyes wide with anger. Jennifer let her end-of-the-day nerves explode:

'Everything in this house stinks of dead fish. Everything! You both smell of it – it's always there on your clothes. Even the air around me,' Jennifer howled. 'Even the vegetables smell as though they've been caught in a net! You can finish dinner yourselves. I couldn't eat anything now.' Tears flowed to the corners of her mouth. She began to storm out of the room but turned and retrieved the jar and the flower. They shook in her hand. 'If cancer hadn't killed Mum, you two would have found some way of doing it,' she said to them as she left the room, shaking with misery. As she left she saw Marlin take the swaying Gull by the hair, hard enough to yank it from his scalp. She was, thankfully, only barely aware of what followed in the kitchen.

'You never, never come into my house in this state again!' Marlin was hissing fury at his son, only inches from his face. 'You come to this house with a pub slopping in your belly, you go straight to the dinghy cave, push a finger down your throat and drown it off! You hear me?!' Gull whimpered. 'And what's that other smell on you, you bloody tom cat? Is that woman?'

'You should know, ol' Dad,' Gull mumbled with a drunk's courage.

Marlin tossed his son aside and in his fury swept everything off the table. Not a plate was left. The fish lay in a slick of its own death on the floor.

'Now, clean it up.' Marlin's voice was low and even and there was space enough between his words for menace. Gulliver was shocked into a silence. 'And when you've done that, finish cooking what's fit to eat.'

Gull stumbled suddenly to the sink and vomited noisily while the tap ran hard.

Jennifer ran up the stairs and locked herself in her room, and despite the warmth of the evening she felt cold to her bones. She felt no hunger at all. She set the flower in its jar beside the chair, took two pain-killers, turned the radio volume high enough to cover the sounds of her misery and sobbed from below the very base of her soul.

Time passed. It could have been an hour or two, she couldn't be sure, but she heard the pad of her father's feet on the stairs. She remained perfectly still when he tapped on her door.

'Jenny,' he called softly, in a voice that was almost normal, as though he wasn't sure which of his voices he should use. 'There's some tea here and hot buttered toast – just the way you like it.'

'Go away!'

'Not so much as a sprat's fin's been near it.'

'I'm not hungry. Go away.'

'I'll just leave the tray, then.'

'Leave it! I don't care what you do.'

She heard the rattle of china and the tap of something against her door, then she listened until his barefoot pad back down the stairs was out of hearing. She did not open the door. She switched off the radio and fell into an exhausted, nervous sleep with a pillow hard against her, and slept until the first light, the first bird call, the first throb of fishing boats rounding the point woke her.

On the way to her bathroom she saw that the tray had been removed. She would say nothing about it. She would say nothing about the night at all.

Early morning in Proudie Bay was as always, exactly a new day born. No matter how dramatic the day before or how exhausting the night, early morning was a new leaf turned – fresh and crisp and sharp. It was difficult to find darkness in any of its shades – especially in summer.

Jennifer kicked off her sandals at the kitchen door and walked through the morning grass, down to the harbour wall, pressing her toes into damp, green tufts. She had passed Marlin when she'd walked through the kitchen and they'd exchanged glances. He'd nodded her way and continued to measure meal into a pot. Outside, she caught sight of Gull, on his way to the dinghy cave. There was no unpleasantness – nothing was said – and she was hungry.

Marlin is breakfast, and his breakfasts are as ritualised as a Japanese tea ceremony or a play entitled *Breaking the Fast* in three acts.

Breakfast is oatmeal and the recipe and method has not changed since he'd inherited 'breakfast' from his own father. Act one is the preparation. Act two concerns the eating of it and act three, the finale, is the celebration of seagulls.

The preparation for breakfast is as follows:

1: Beat the sides of an old, black iron pot to signal that the curtain is up.

2: Stir, boil and simmer enough oatmeal for exactly twenty minutes for three people and a harbour full of birds.

3: Set the table with porridge plates big enough to piss in and spoons as big as paddles.

4: Give one loud call, 'PODG ... !' when it's ready and serve with milk, sultanas and black sugar with toast and marmalade and coffee on the side.

The cast will sit at the long kitchen table and eat, with

47

the window open to fresh air and flies. There may be a rustle of newspaper or notepaper or the rake of knife across toast or spoon stirring, but during this act there may well be no dialogue at all.

The finale comes after the cast has eaten. Marlin takes a good portion of meal left in the pot down to the harbour wall. He bangs upon it three times again with his ladle and feeds the flocks of gulls who have been waiting, chattering and feather-fluffed on every vantage point within sight of the Fishcastle. Some he calls by name and some he feeds by hand. The scrapings from the pot bottom are then put along the wall for a last noisy scrabbling of beaks. The spectacle often causes people, afloat or ashore, to pause a while and watch, and Marlin acknowledges them with a slow wave before he turns towards his house and the curtain comes down for another day.

Breakfast, Jennifer thinks, might well be the longest-running play in memory, certainly in Proudie Bay: probably as long, Gull once said in a moment of rare wit, 'As 'M*A*S*H' repeats, back to back. You know what's coming but you still watch.'

Jennifer had her own morning rituals, of course, but they were very much 'backstage'. While Marlin fed his gulls she hung stiff jeans and towels on the clothes line and tossed Gulliver an old, dry one for his first swim of the day. The early sun warmed her back and the breeze that came with it dried her showered hair. She was comforted in a way by the sounds of their mornings: sea birds and boats and cooing pigeons. She put the wash basket away and strolled through the yard, shaking her damp hair with her fingers. The second act of *Breakfast* that morning had been ordinary – silent, but ordinary and reasonably serene, in view of the night before it. They had all, it seemed to her, decided in their own ways to let the night lie dead and buried.

Under the shrub where Jennifer had last seen the snake there was nothing but a flattened circle of grass. Its hutch was empty. 'Did one of you put the snake to bed last night?' she asked, with little hope.

'Well, I didn't,' Gull said.

'That ol' snake man – he be sunning himself, I reckon,' Marlin said, pretending to search through a jungle of shrubs. 'Gully, check the pigeons have all their feathers and heads so Jen won't worry.'

'They're all feathers and heads, Dad.' Gull was grinning near the coop. 'Yep! Not a beak out of place.'

Jennifer knew they were trying to amuse her and it was difficult not to smile but she refused to give them the satisfaction.

Marlin found the python, eyes staring wide asleep in the sun, its black and yellow coils big as tyres, and he scooped it up in his arms and rocked it gentle as a baby.

'Jen say the snake man has to go home.' He cooed, 'She's very cross with her ol' dad.' He glanced at Jennifer. There was still no smile but he saw that she'd had to cross her arms tight across her chest. 'Gully,' he said, 'get a nice fat mouse for snake man.'

'There's only white ones left,' Gull said, easily falling into the part.

'Perfect!' said Marlin.

She wanted to tell them how mad they sounded – like idiots, but on that warm, salt bay morning she couldn't be bothered. Still barefoot, she walked down the stone steps towards the harbour. She had time. Ten-thirty was time enough to leave for work. She stepped out onto the sandstone jutty and tiptoed around its crust of pipi and old oyster shells. And with the breeze running warm through her hair she heard her mother's voice: 'Mind the shells, Jenny – put your shoes on, darling' – a voice soft, out of love. And she sat on the jutty with her toes just touching the surface of the tide and shook her hair in the morning warmth. Her cheeks shone damp and salty but not from sea spray.

She stayed quiet by the water's edge but safe from it until her breathing slowed and the tightness eased from her neck and shoulders. She stayed until the sun formed mirror tips on the waves and the slap of oars and echoes of sea motors faded into somewhere. She stayed until her eyes were closed and made images of their own – and when she finally eased herself up she found she'd been sitting hard on her hands and there was blood on them.

She walked back to the house to change. Gull was squatting by his fishing tackle, surrounded by old tins and rags. He smiled but did not look at her.

'What time do you start work, Jen?'

'Fifteen years ago,' she said quietly and went inside. She closed the wire door gently.

Chapter Three

A PEBBLE IN AWE OF AN EMERALD

Dolan's Cafe sat snug inside the horseshoe of the bay. It was within the sound of the ocean wilding against the cliffs behind it but nearer to the gentler harbour, weed slapping onto the sand below it.

The cafe had grown over three generations from a rowing boat selling traps of yellow tail to barefoot wives with baskets and pennies, to a hole-in-the-wall fish and chip shop, clap-trapped together with splintered wood, next to the boat-shed, to the present bright, scrubbed fishery with tables on the Beachwalk and striped umbrellas and diners from everywhere, all fashion and chic, flocking and chattering and queuing like elegant pelicans. At the new Dolan's, reservations were essential – except for sparrows and the park pigeons who roamed free and pecked under the tables of old people, knowing they were the ones who spilled their food.

Dan Dolan's grey, sharp-voiced mother, tight-lipped in

memory of harder times, wanders amongst the theatre of tables in an ancient flowered apron, nagging the role of fishwife – playing a part she created, 'the village fishwife' – to entertain the tourists and to add a bit of old rough to the classy new, and in secret honour of the old oars and nets and floats of their beginnings that now hang from the walls as decorations – lest they're forgotten. Lest her son forgets the tools that made him.

'You want to order lobster,' she'll shout to a table of businessmen, florid with sun and wine. 'They swam up here just five minutes ago and climbed into the pot themselves.'

'Okay, Mother,' they'll say, enjoying the boisterous image of her.

'You look hungry to me, love,' she'll say to a Chanel-slim woman with black pearls and expensive hair. 'We've got a chowder today that'll knock your socks off!'

'If you say so,' the woman will say, with good humour and smiling designer teeth.

And everyone within earshot will laugh at the fishwife's antics, unaware that behind the facade are eyes as sharp as hooks and brain cells quick as cash keys.

Marlin Hardwick had never entered Dolan's. It was even an irritation for him to walk past the cafe and, if he did, he never acknowledged Jennifer. Contemptuous, nose up, and head turned the other way is how he passed Dolan's. One reason for it was the 'pathetic sight of pamby city idiots with their Panama hats and draped jackets eating oysters swimming around the tops of soups, drowning in muck so they won't taste the stale'. But Jennifer knew the real reason was deep resentment. He resented that a family of ordinary hook and liners – uneducated trappers, as he referred to the Dolans – had produced a son with a brain and a going business. But more than that was his vexation that the Dolans were his daughter's employers and he could not afford to do anything about it. Paying the bills with Dolan money was a humiliation he could barely tolerate – but never once did he dare tell Jennifer, in case she thought she might leave the job for the sake of his feelings and ruin them all.

Quiet, reliable Jennifer Hardwick suited the Dolans very well, and that she was Marlin's daughter suited them all the more. First to start and last to leave, filling in for sickness or injury without a question, willing and able and sober – they all agreed that the 'professor's daughter' could work for the 'fish trappers' for as long as she wanted to.

In contrast to the other waitresses, curved and sexy with brown legs and short, bright skirts, Jen moved through the crowd quick and invisible as one of the sparrows. There were so many times when she wished she could be like the others, but then simply being at the cafe on bright, fine days – near laughter and full bellies and good cheer – under the blue bay sky with clouds flying like birds joined together, was compensation enough.

She had recently bought a batik skirt, similar to one of Marlin's sarongs: a design of black and gold on light brown, so that the sparrow now looked as though it had been airbrushed. With it she wore a white shirt that didn't show too much of her chest. One of the girls told her she looked great;

out of kindness, she imagined. It was an improvement, she'd thought, but she knew she would probably always be a brown bird amongst parrots, working invisible as sea mist instead of strutting about with colours flying. Even the hippies who shuffled across the beach below the cafe late in the afternoons on their way to Shack Hill, draped in hand-me-downs and carrying their babies on their hips like comforters, had more colour in the beads on their dusty arms than Jennifer had from head to toe.

She had once dreamed – one of her dreams of freedom – of becoming one of them – a hippie, an alternative, a 'Bombay Cottonhead' as Marlin calls them, but she'd observed their aimlessness and their need to band together, their depend-encies, for a long time and she knew it would be like escaping from the frypan into a fire. She could think of few things she had in common with them.

But then she had not met Miriam Holt.

The first time Jennifer saw Miriam Holt it was a late after-noon and she was walking back along the Beachwalk, on her way home from work.

Miriam was with a group of Hill people on the beach below the cafe, looking for shells. Miriam and Jennifer might have been about the same age but likeness ended there. The woman on the beach had skin the colour of milk, and Irish red hair, thick enough to hide birds. Jennifer could not see her eyes but guessed they must be blazing green or blue, or turquoise. She was almost as tall as Jennifer but not angular, not all bones and joins; she was soft looking and curved, and pausing to watch her, Jennifer thought, *That's what a Jennifer should look like, there's a Jennifer with all the trimmings!!* And she wanted with all her heart to know her, to touch her, to stroke her glowing hair and stand in the light of her and absorb some of her beauty – as one strokes jade or a pearl, warm in a hand. The attraction was not, in its truth, sexual, but simply a pure admiration of something beautiful – a pebble in awe of an emerald.

There was a small, dark-haired child, a girl, sitting at Miriam's feet, sitting silent in the lap of the wash, staring out across the bay, her elbows on her knees and her chin cupped in her hands. Behind them on the sand a flock of gulls feathered around in their own tight group, wheedling, picking and fussing like old bus-trippers, pecking at the remains of the day. Then, as if by a signal from Jennifer, the woman took the child's hand and walked towards her, towards the path, where it rose higher than the sand and, in a movement that seemed right at the time, Jennifer sat on the edge of the path and hung her legs over the side. She wondered briefly, watching them, how the sun seemed not to have affected the woman's white skin. There was a Celtic look to her, with none of the brown and baked hide of an Australian. She noticed too, that the child had a limp – barely there, but Jennifer saw it. Miriam and the child sat, not far away to her right, and for a while they all silently watched the harbour as if something might happen that was important not to miss. There were quick, sideways glances.

Jennifer wanted to make contact but was unsure how to go about it – she had no talent for spontaneity. Never in the memory of her life had she been able to easily begin a friendship – there had always been a moat of separation and a tense self-consciousness on her part that made others wary and equally tense.

She remembers clearly her school reports – *Jennifer has great difficulty making friends. Jennifer is often alone with her lunch box. She should make an effort to mix* – and so on, and so on. It was even difficult for her to exchange small talk with Dolan's customers – she left that to the bright, serving parrots. And there'd been no use looking for help at the Fishcastle. She had always lived in a house of cold spaces that friends might have filled and warmed but they would remain chilled forever. Adult visitors were not encouraged unless they were for business or sex. She could not remember her mother sitting with friends for tea and gossip and laughter. Not once. How terribly lonely she must have been. She wondered if Gull had similar problems. She had never talked about it – social isolation had been their lives from their beginnings and it had never entered her head to discuss it. She wondered if it was the pub that helped loosen his tongue and shake others' hands. Maybe he thought that vomiting at the end of a night was better than loneliness. They had grown, Jennifer and Gull, with the ability to easily make friends with animals, but the same skills with humans had passed them by. If only Miriam was a bird or some other wild thing, Jennifer could speak to her in a minute.

She thought she might speak to the child – she could speak to children now that she was no longer a child; that would not seem an unusual thing to do. She would speak to the child, that would not be so difficult, but when she turned her head it was Miriam who made the move.

'Hi,' she said, and smiled. And Jennifer, with immense relief, smiled back. She saw that the woman's eyes were not green or blue, but hazel. It didn't matter. It took nothing away from the light of her, the lovely easy manner of her.

'Hello.'

'Don't you love it here this time of day.' Miriam took a deep breath and stretched back her swan of a throat. 'Everything looks so soft, doesn't it?'

'Yes – it's more quiet, too. I sit here sometimes after work – unwind a bit.' Jennifer did no such thing. But that didn't matter, either.

'I think I've seen you down at the cafe,' Miriam said. 'Would that be right? Is that where you work?'

'Yes, that's where I work. I've been there for ages.' The child had not turned or spoken but sat still and gazed out over the water, her wide, dark eyes all but swimming in it. Jennifer called to her. 'There's always something to watch on the harbour, isn't there?'

'Sometimes.' The child's voice was barely audible.

'This is my girl, Rebecca. She's nine. Say hello, Bec,' her mother said to her. 'Everyone calls her Beccy.'

'Hi, Beccy.' Jennifer began to relax. She moved some of the tension out of her shoulders and sent it, stiff as a board, to bury in the sand.

'Hi.' The child's voice was as flat as a wrong note. She did not turn or fidget or move, but continued to look out over the harbour, separated in her own way from her mother and Jennifer and the rest of the world – like something in a snow dome.

'She's a quiet one, Beccy. It's just the way she is,' said her mother, answering an imagined question. 'My name's Miriam Holt, by the way.'

'And I'm Jennifer Hardwick. It's nice to meet you.' And she waited for, 'Oh, so you're a Hardwick. You're one of them, are you?' But there was no reaction. 'You must be new at the Bay. I only saw you for the first time today,' she said. 'Do you live up on the Hill?'

'Yes. But we've only been there a couple of weeks. It's going to be nice, I think.'

'I hate it!' Beccy said with a passion.

'Oh, she'll get used to it.' Miriam patted her daughter's back. 'You know what kids are like in a new place.'

'I'll always hate it!' Beccy said.

'I'm sure you'll like the Hill when you get used to it.' Jennifer was sorry for her. 'You'll make lots of friends, then you'll like it.'

'No I won't! The kids up there broke my doll – and I hate Crystal.'

'We're living in her shack until we can get one to ourselves,' Miriam said. 'Crystal's shack.'

'She takes everything. She never asks, she just takes stuff,' Beccy yipped like a small, angry terrier. In a few years, Jennifer thought, watching her, the world had better mind its manners!

'I'm sorry,' Jennifer said.

'Beccy!' Miriam said sharply. 'She's just taking a while to settle in. The kids really have a good time up there.' Miriam tried to honey over the outburst. 'There's lots for them to do.'

'Like what?' Beccy had her arms clamped tight across her.

'Well, like, what about the kite party last Sunday? And what about Paul's puppies?' She told Jennifer all about the wonderful, fun things there were to do, but she was not smiling. 'That's a friend of ours, Paul. His bitch had pups and the kids gave them a birthday party, made them little presents. It was really cute. You watched them being born, Bec, didn't you.'

'He threw two of them over the cliff into the sea!' the child said angrily.

'They were dead, Beccy. Those two were dead.'

'They weren't! They weren't dead,' Beccy cried. 'One was moving. I saw it move!'

'Oh, God, Beccy, don't. I'm sorry, Jennifer.'

'It's all right. I don't blame her for being upset, really.'

'She'll get over it. She's having a hard time at school as well. Some of them make life pretty tough for the Hill kids. You know what they're like – kids. They can be real little shits.'

'Yes, I know.' Jennifer could see that it was not just Beccy who was finding it hard to settle in. *But there'd be plenty of time to help them*, she hoped. She'd do anything.

For a few uncomfortable moments they didn't speak. Then Jennifer moved and sat next to the child.

'I live just over there.' She pointed across the bay. 'Over there to the right. Can you see? It's that old, grey wooden house with the flame tree in the garden.'

'Is it a real house?'

'I suppose it is – in a way.'

'Does the roof leak?'

'No.'

'Do you have real beds?'

'Yes.'

'Can I go there one day?' Beccy suddenly asked.

'Bec!' Miriam said to her.

'It's okay, really. I'd love it.'

Jennifer could not have been more pleased. She sensed for a moment that a light had been switched on inside her and her shadow parts were lit up. There was an energy in Miriam that reached across to Jennifer like a line of sparklers, and there was something about the solemn child she recognised and had sympathy for, and loved her for. There was the memory of another child life, a tension, a wariness that she knew so well. She had, even then, a strong desire to put her arms around Beccy and hug her tight and tell her everything would be all right. She longed to know her – and her mother, the glory woman she thought a Jennifer should look like, the lush, copper-top who Jennifer Hardwick wished she looked like. She gave silent thanks to whatever allowed them to meet that afternoon. She would be their friend, their shelter, their protection. It all flashed through her mind in pastel frames of mothering. *She would watch over them and be their friend forever.*

'Of course you can come and visit!' Jennifer touched the child's arm, 'I'd love it. There'd be nothing better! I'll pick a day when we can have the whole house to ourselves, Beccy, and you can both come home with me after work and I'll make the best, fancy tea you've ever had, and you can play with my dress-up box or dolls or watch TV or look at books – whatever you want. How about that?'

'Okay,' Beccy said, still watching out to sea, but outside the snow dome for the moment.

'Thanks,' said Miriam. 'That'd be great. We'd love it, too. I guess we'll catch up with you soon then? Thanks,' she said, briefly taking Jennifer's hand. 'It'd be so good for Beccy.'

'How about Wednesday then – about this time?' Jennifer asked with remarkable placidity, casually – all an act for she was afraid to let them go without commitment.

'Okay, Wednesday's fine. We'll wait on the beach for you – and Jenny, thanks again.'

'Jenny! Oh yes!, the joys of Jenny, the joy of it all,' Jennifer whispered to herself, after they'd gone their separate ways, but then, thinking of her father and her brother, *If they spoil this for me I'll kill them!*

As she turned into the Sandpath she was still in the state of pleasure the events of the afternoon had given her. Two pleasures in fact, she'd been given, giftwrapped in milk white and tied with thick red hair. It was as though someone kind, someone she'd not thought existed, had said, 'Jennifer, it's time you had a friend – well, here's two. A bonus.' There was a lightness to her step that was rarely there when she slow walked to the Fishcastle at the end of the day – 'dead girl walking', she often said, but not that day. She looked down for a moment to swing her bag to the other hand and almost collided with old Hughie Pheiffer.

'Hey there!' Hughie said, hopping from one leg to the other to block her way.

'Sorry.' But Jennifer, in her new, good mood, regretted her apology. 'Didn't you see me, either?'

'I seen you, Jen Hardwick, but you didn't see me.'

'Oh, for God's sake, Hughie,' Jennifer said.

'But I forgive you this time,' Old Hugh said, winking and folding his bones of arms, old as driftwood, across his chest and across his ancient singlet, now almost rusty with age and grime. Like some of the old men of the Bay, his teeth needed fixing, he had a hide, tanned and creased and dry as something dug up, and bare soles on his feet thick enough to walk on splinters. As a child, Jennifer would cross the street if she saw him coming. The local 'bogey man'. He never seemed to change – always the old, gap-toothed, bandy grinner spying on Proudie Bay – peeping like a Tom. *He must be a hundred!*

'You off to the shops, Hughie?' she asked him, forcing herself to be civil.

'Been to the shops, girlie, but forgot the newspaper.'

'Oh.' It was obvious from the look in his little eyes that Hughie was digging in for a gossip.

'But the first time I go to the shops, I seen you talking to that hippie.'

'Oh?'

'Yes, young Jen, I did. I seen you messin' round with hippies on the beach.'

'And?'

'And I reckon old Marlin wouldn't like you hangin' round with that lot.'

'It'd be none of his business!'

'Well, I won't tell him, girlie. It won't come from me. I can keep me mouth shut.' Jennifer and the sky winked to each other. 'But they're a lot of dirty bludgers, they are. Kids runnin' nude.' He made it sound obscene, the way he spat the word out through his broken teeth – *nyuude*. 'But like I said, it won't come from me. I won't give the game away.'

'I don't care if you do!' Jennifer snapped.

'Oh?'

'Look, Hughie, I've got to get home. I've got things to do.'

'What's in y' bag then? Somethin' nice for his tea?'

'No! It's something nice for *my* tea.'

'What?'

'Veal, if you must know. Do you know what veal is?'

'I do, girlie – and he won't like you eatin' little cows either, hardly out of their mummys' backsides,' Hughie said, grinning, with his bandy leg sticks planted apart and his tongue picking and clicking around his mouth like a cockatoo's.

'Oh, for heaven's sake! I'll see you later, Hughie. I've got to go.'

'And one more thing I'm tellin'. You want to tell those girlies you work with at the cafe to wear proper skirts. I can see their pants – you know what I mean? Every time those girlies bend over to pick somethin' up, I can see their pants and some of them pants don't give much cover – you know what I mean?'

'Then don't look at them, Hughie. Don't go round there and spy on them.'

'You can't help not seeing bottoms, girlie!'

She turned quickly and walked away. 'Goodbye, Hughie.'

Head down and frowning, she walked briskly. She heard him dragging his feet away, across the surface of the Sand-path like a soft-shoe shuffler, a brothel creeper. The thought of old Hughie maybe bumping into Miriam and looking her up and down in his leery way and calling her a 'dirty bludger' appalled her. And she couldn't bare the thought of him touching Beccy. She never considered the Hill crowd as bludging any more than her own brother, if the truth were known. It was just a matter of geography. There were, of course, some Hill people, the Ferals, who were a pretty grubby lot and would probably die by choice if they didn't get their Government handouts, but Miriam was not one of *them*. In fact, when Jennifer looked once more at the bright image Miriam had painted in her mind, it seemed to her that she was an unusual addition to the Hill tribe. In their struggle to be different, they had all become exactly like each other – a sort of uniform light brown – skin, hair and eyes – with beads, hemp and babies as accessories. The sixties' ghosts. Miriam stood out in the tribe like a flame on marble.

When she was close to home Jennifer swung her bag from her right hand to the left in order to open the gate and clear the letterbox.

'Something nice for his tea,' she said to the gate latch. 'As if I'd ever bother.'

There was nothing in the letterbox of interest – junk mail, offers from real-estaters for free valuations and two newsletters for Marlin. There was nothing for Jennifer. That was not unusual. She had hoped there might be a card from Hesta. She knew her aunt had not been at home for some weeks but they had no idea where she'd gone to this time. But Jennifer knew that if Hesta had become nomadic again it would be her niece she'd write to, and she looked forward to getting her off-beat postcards. 'The cracked biddy will tell us where she is, soon enough,' Marlin had told her when she'd asked him if he'd heard.

As she walked up the driveway she could see that the pebbles had not been disturbed. The pussy willow tree, just inside the gate, sat rooted with all its furry buds intact. From the side door she could see no circle of warm, pressed grass where after-school children sat at the feet of their 'master'. The snake lay coiled, quiet in its hutch. Lizards slept under warm stones, thankful for the peace and quiet, and pigeons dozed uneasily on their roosts, one fearful eye half-cocked for their keeper's Sunday lunch. There was even a lull in the screaming of seagulls. The Fishcastle, it seemed, was at rest for the moment, taking deep, sea salt breaths through the breaches and cracks that had escaped Marlin's putty.

All around her was at sacred rest.

Jennifer cherished the few precious hours allowed to her in the house alone. She felt she could breathe easy, move around the house with less tension – there was an air about it that seemed lighter. It was a fitting end to a good day – a *good* day! She put her veal in the fridge, switched on the jug for coffee and read the note propped against a glass on the kitchen table.

'Your ol' dad's away talkin' and readin' and teachin'. Don't wait up, Jen. No dinner on the stove, I'm eatin' with the high an' mighty.'

'Good,' she said. She had no idea where Gull was but she imagined he was pub-drinking or tom-catting around the town and she didn't care if he came home late as a top moon, drunk or sober. She took her coffee up to her room and closed the door.

Before she changed from her work clothes, Jennifer looked in the mirror.

'God Almighty!' she said to her image. 'You could hang me out to frighten birds!'

In honour of Miriam, she threw her clothes on the floor, including her chastity stitched, hard cotton bra, strong enough to stop spears, and put a thin blouse over her that clearly showed her nipples. She kicked off her sandals, brushed her hair until her scalp stung and smoothed colour on her lips. She even took off her pants and pulled on a skirt that easily let the light shine through – and imagined what dirty Hughie would think of that!

'Sorry, Mother,' she said, drinking the last of her coffee. 'I'll tell you about it all later.' And she ran downstairs, through the quiet, breathing kitchen and out into the yard, feeling air brushing soft and cool around the whole of her, and with it, a sense of freedom and daring.

The python was too heavy to move but on an impulse she put two lizards in the pigeon house – and left its door open. She turned back a corner of the wire over the carp pond to give scavenging birds a better chance at fishing. She put a tortoise in the letterbox and one on top of the sleeping snake. In the grass where the after-school children sat, she drew corn circles with a rake and a face in the pebble drive. Then she walked inside, feeling foolish but pleased as Punch. She prepared her meal and planned for Special Wednesday, the day following the day to come.

In her journal she wrote about a day that made the page crackle with change. She wrote about events that had rolled smooth as syrup – not the usual at all. She described Miriam: *Today I think I made a friend.* She told her about Hughie Pheiffer, knowing she would laugh, and she told her about Beccy, thinking she might also recognise her as a child she used to love. She wrote about the pigeon-house door and the carp-pond wire and the others and she ended with *You-know-who is out for the night, and so is Gull – but you mustn't worry about your boy; I'll look after him . . .*

She watched television until eleven and at that time, as far as she knew, Gulliver had not come home. She hadn't heard the creak or slam of doors or the yawn of his jaws loud and clear down the toilet bowl. An hour or so later, after she'd fallen asleep, she was only just aware of the sound of the gate and of feet on gravel, two of which she recognised as her father's – two she didn't, but they giggled like a female. She turned over and ignored it all. She was only grateful that his bed was so far away from hers, she wouldn't hear them grunting.

Very early the next morning, reluctant, but with the sanity

that came with a new day, Jennifer crept downstairs to the yard and put right all the wonderful wrongs she had committed the night before. The tortoise she had put on the python was sleeping in on its coiled bed, undisturbed; the lizards had escaped the pigeon house, but the pigeons, loyal to their last, choking breaths, had stayed put, frightened of the open door; the tortoise in the letterbox rested under its shell and waited patient as a stone for release, and the carp in their unprotected pond swam safe and lazy while gulls waited like fools on the harbour wall for porridge.

'What a menagerie of idiots!' Jennifer said to it all. She did, however, leave the face in the pebble drive, if only for the short time it would last, but the 'corn circles' she had raked into the grass had been crisped back to plain green by the dew.

She was still in the yard when Marlin came out, stretching and wearing a sarong and a grin. There was a female by his side.

'And fancy the Jen up already,' he said, with his hands up, play-acting surprise. 'What brings the Jenny Wren out so early?'

'Well, you know what they say about early birds,' Jennifer said lightly.

'Is it worms you're hunting, then?'

'Oh, just checking around.' She didn't call him 'Dad'; it didn't seem appropriate. 'Letting the snake out for a bite, feeding the spiders – that sort of thing.'

He passed her a certain look. 'This is Deirdre Morris,'

he said. 'She's a marine biologist, Jen – knows all about dem fishes, like your poor ol' dad.'

And one or two other things as well, Jennifer thought. The woman had red hair from a bottle, cropped short. Nothing like Miriam's. My God, she looks younger than me! How could someone like that possibly stand him! Thank goodness the days of pennant panties on the clothes line seemed to have passed into legend.

'Hello,' she said.

'Hello,' said Deirdre Morris, uncomfortably.

'Are you staying for breakfast?' Jennifer asked her, as though Deirdre Morrises were a daily occurrence.

The woman looked at Marlin. 'No, I don't think I can. I'm working early today. Thanks anyway.'

'Jennifer,' Marlin said quickly. 'Why don't you go and wake up the Gulliver and get him going for the day?'

'Oh, Gulliver didn't come home last night – that's my brother,' she said to Deirdre, and still addressing her said, 'You know what men are like? It's hard to keep track, isn't it?'

But she thought it best to go inside, anyway. There was a definite storm brewing in Marlin's eyes. And a certain curiosity, she was pleased to see.

After a later than usual breakfast was consumed – just the two of them, and in silence, Jennifer asked: 'Are you lecturing as usual tomorrow, Dad?'

'Yes.'

'All day?'

'Yes, all day.'

'And night?'

'I hope so!' Giving her a side glance, sharp as a probe.

And while Jennifer smiled in the privacy of her mind, Marlin left the table and carried the porridge pot down to the impatient, empty gulls.

Wednesday was Wednesday all over the Bay. There were Proudies who knew it was Wednesday and couldn't be bothered one way or the other, and perhaps even some who didn't know what day it was at all. But to Jennifer this Wednesday was a day to be cared for from the moment it rose with the sun until it went to bed with the moon.

Towards the end of her day at Dolan's, Jennifer hurried through the closing and fastening of table umbrellas, wiping spills, gathering lost spectacles and dropped handkerchiefs and shaking crumbs onto the Beachwalk for the cleaning birds to dispose of – and all the time keeping an eye on the sand below for Miriam and Beccy. When she saw them she held up five fingers. Miriam nodded.

Jennifer found mother Dolan counting a forest of blue water bottles used for the tables. They were popular as souvenirs, despite their size, and the old fishwife, sharp as a pin, counted them at closing time every day, with the cash and the cheques and the cool-room food.

'You off now, Jennifer?' she said, with her back turned.

'Everything's done. The umbrella over table eleven has a broken spoke. It'll last tomorrow but we'll have to fix it. Any bottles missing?'

'Not today. There'll be a different answer come the weekend, but you know that, don't you?' She did not have to

A Pebble in Awe of an Emerald

turn from her counting: she used the eyes in the back of her head to sense that Jennifer had something else to say. 'What is it you want, dear?'

'Would you mind if I took some leftover cake with me? And maybe some cookies? Of course I'll pay. I have a little girl coming to visit this afternoon.'

'Take it – take it. Orange, carrot, chocolate – whatever you want. But not the cookies. Danny's taking them home for *his* kids.' All this with her back turned and counting bottles. She missed nothing!

'Thanks, Mrs Dolan.'

'Who is this child?' she said to the bottles.

'Just a friend. Beccy and her mother are waiting for me down on the sand.'

'Oh, them.' Making notes now, and adding figures at the same time. Still not looking. 'You want to be careful with that lot, Jennifer. They've got more problems than you can shake a stick at. You don't want to get saddled with them, you've got enough of your own.'

Jennifer wanted to tell her to shutup! And tell her to keep her hundred and one eyes out of her bloody business! But she said, 'I'll be careful,' and hurried away to the cake stand.

They walked along the cooled water's edge of the beach, the three of them; toe curling through wavelets and their offerings of sea grass and shell grit. In the air was a drum roll of early summer cicadas from park trees and late gulls wheeled in slow motion over cruisers moored in the bay, looking for a luxury roost for the night. Here and there, Beccy would stoop to pick up an object sacred only to

71

children, turn over jellyfish drowned in the air or pop dead bluebottles with a stick.

'I can't think why you don't burn to a crisp, Miriam. Don't you ever wear a hat?' Miriam looked scrubbed fresh for the afternoon in clean cottons and, looking at her, Jennifer felt as dull as yesterday's bread.

'I don't go out in the sun much. Early mornings or late afternoons, that's all,' she said. 'And I can't find a hat to fit me – all this hair – I've got a head the size of a pumpkin, it's a worry.'

There's problems for you – hats! Jennifer thought, wistfully.

Jennifer handed over the box of cake to Beccy as they walked back up to the path. 'Can you carry this for me, darling? It's cake for our tea.' She so much wanted to make the day special for the child – for them both.

'Okay.'

'I like your school uniform. It's smart. It suits you.' The child wore small pink checks with a round white collar.

'It's second hand!'

'Well, so was mine when I was your age. Everybody buys at the clothing pool.'

'Melissa doesn't,' Beccy said with disgust. 'She gets new.'

'Beccy! I'm warning you!' Miriam glanced at Jennifer, and shrugged and raised her hands in a gesture of copelessness.

Jennifer wondered briefly if any of the Hill tribe's brown, beaded mothers of the infants they wore as love tokens ever considered their milky bundles would soon grow to be bothering children with tempers and questions of their own.

'And I'm getting new shoes too,' Beccy said, with one

eye on her mother. 'Shiny black with bows.'

'Not!' said her mother.

'Am!' said Beccy – and if she had known, would have added, 'check and mate!' But instead, she simply stamped her foot.

Away from the sand, the pathway was hard and dry under their feet, but cool enough at that time for them to walk upon it bare-soled. Beccy trotted behind them, carrying the cake box out in front as if it held something alive. As they turned the corner onto the Sandpath, the child asked, 'Are we nearly there?'

'You just count the numbers till we're at fourteen,' Jennifer said. 'And then we'll be there.'

At the gate, Jennifer felt the familiar tension around her as if she wore a belt too tight, a notch tighter every time, even though she knew they would be safely alone for hours. It was a feeling she imagined would never leave her as long as she stood at the gate of number fourteen. She swung her bag from her right hand to her left (another 'ritual of the gate') and lifted the latch. Beccy was the first inside and on the pebble drive, all eyes and jumping around like a pink-checked bag of beans.

'Cool!' she said.

'It's huge,' Miriam said. 'How many live here?'

'Just my father and my brother – and me. But it's sort of divided up so we all have our own space – I'm upstairs. We have it to ourselves this afternoon. Dad's out lecturing and I never know where Gull is.'

'My God! Who looks after it all?'

'Guess,' said Jennifer.

Beccy had disappeared. She'd run on ahead, up the pebble drive, but not boisterous like the army of after-school children. She was calling from the harbour front.

'Mum! Quick, come here! Come and look at the birds.' She was standing at the pigeon house with her fingers hooked through the wire. 'There's two white ones with tails.'

'They're called fantails, Beccy,' Jennifer said, and added without thinking, 'he doesn't eat those.' Miriam looked at her with her brows raised. 'The pigeons,' Jennifer said quickly. 'My father grows the pigeons to eat, you see – but I was just saying, not the white ones. Sorry, I forget that any normal person would think that's insane.'

'I guess it's no worse than farming chickens. I'm mostly vegetarian, myself.' Miriam looked for Beccy but she had already flown to the carp pond, chased two lizards through the grass and nursed a tortoise.

This was not what Jennifer had planned. The picture she'd had of their first visit was of them all walking up the drive, turning into the side door to the kitchen where she would slice cake and make whatever drinks they wanted – talk at the table for a while then go upstairs to her room for bonding, friendship and to entertain Beccy in her own way, with her own normal, good child things. 'Please tell me a story.' She wanted the child to say. 'Something out of a book – with a happy ending.'

'Beccy,' Jennifer called to her. 'We'd better have our tea before it gets too late. You'll need to wash your hands after those dirty things.' *For God's sake get off my father's land – get off it and come to mine!* she wanted to scream.

'I don't want any cake or anything,' the child said, lying on her back on the grass with the tortoise sitting on her belly. 'This is so cool! Can't I stay out here, Mum?' Beccy was already up again and stroking the back of a blue-tongue lizard. 'Please!'

'We'd better do what Jenny wants, Bec.'

'Come on, darling.' Jennifer went to the door and held it open for them. 'I have something really nice for you upstairs. There's a beautiful doll, and books and a whole box of dress-up clothes – or you can just watch TV if you want.' But it was too late – she'd already seen the snake.

The python was outside its hutch and, for possibly the second time in its life, it moved. It was coiled around itself like a skein of rubber, its variegated scales squeezed tight, one layer after another, contracting in a sluggish show of belly over grass. A blank-eyed head came up slow from the coils and listed to one side as though the effort of lifting it was too much, and the head's tongue licked the air and tasted it, and of all the flavours the air offered, it fell in love with the taste of Beccy Holt.

'Oh look, Mum! Just look at him.' Falling head over heels in love herself, with the python and the whole zoo. 'Can I pat him, Jenny?'

'DON'T TOUCH IT, BECCY!!' Miriam screamed. 'My God, Jenny. What is all this? I hate snakes!'

'Don't worry, Miriam. It's okay.' Fright was clearly in Miriam's eyes but Jennifer was pleased she was afraid; she was pleased even to have fear to help keep this child away from the influences of the yard. 'It's a dirty, great lump of a thing, but brain dead like everything else in this place.' But she called to Beccy, 'Your mum's right. Better not touch it, Bec. Come upstairs. Come quickly and we'll do something else.'

'I want to stay out here!'

'Come – NOW!'

And there was no answer to Miriam's order. Jennifer held the door open for them and smiled, grateful for the miracle of intervention.

Jennifer's room, the mother room, had been arranged early that morning as an elegant chamber of treasures. She had placed books, floor cushions and a flower posy on tidy, dust-less surfaces. The dress-up box, with scraps of net and ribbon trying to escape the lid, was within easy reach and the doll sat on the corner of the dresser, facing the door where Beccy would see it before anything else. She'd put magazines that might interest Miriam by the mother chair, thrown casually down, and she had sweetened the air with drops of lavender oil in a dish by the bed. Miriam admired it all with charm.

'It's really nice, Jenny – beautiful. You've made a won-derful world here. It reminds me of that movie *Flowers in the Attic* where the kids make their room like a magic place. You didn't go to any trouble for us I hope?'

'I didn't do a thing,' Jennifer lied. 'Nothing's different. Can you get that movie on video? I'd like to see it.'

'I guess so.'

They'd had tea by the window and Beccy threw crumbs to the sparrows. Now she leaned her small arms on the sill and watched out over rooftops towards the heads that led to the ocean.

'When I was about your age, Beccy, I used to call this window my "lookout". My mum used to sit in that chair and I'd tell her what was happening outside.' And as if it were a signal, the superstructure of a freighter sailed past with a blast from its horn loud enough to shatter ears.

'It looks as though it's sailing over the tops of the houses,' said the child.

'Maybe it is.' Jennifer stood behind her and lightly hugged her shoulders. 'Tell us if you see anything else unusual. We don't want to miss anything.'

The two women talked around their lives, circling them wide enough for the moment, and only brushing the hems of things that touched their souls.

Miriam told Jennifer of an early relationship with Paul of the Hill and then about Queensland with another man called Gates, who fathered Beccy.

'But it didn't work out,' she said. 'He got himself a head full of shit. I didn't want Bec around a scene as bad as that. Paul said to come down here and, well, here we are. He used to live with Crystal but he doesn't any more, and that's who we're sharing with now.' She took a deep breath. 'I guess that must all sound pretty messed up.'

'A bit.' Then Jennifer thought of her own situation and added, 'I've heard worse. But what about your family, your parents?'

'Maybe another time. Tell me about yours,' she hedged.

'I don't want to intrude, Miriam. It's just well, you don't exactly look like the rest of the Hill people. I thought you might be Irish or something. Something like that.'

'Well, I'm not, but it's not the first time I've been asked. I'm just an ordinary Aussie, except I'm Jewish.' She laughed. 'No one knows where my colouring came from. Some blast from the past.'

'Was it hard, in the beginning, to leave home?'

'Harder for them.' Miriam's hands twisted in her lap. 'Family dinners on Fridays, two sets of china, two kitchen sinks. The whole "chicken soup". You can imagine. They called in the rabbi when I left. He was there for a while, I'm told.'

'So, I shouldn't ask you why you left.'

'No,' Miriam said. 'Well it was no big deal. I just felt too stitched up I guess. I couldn't wait to break out. Some people asked me to go to Cairns with them and I dropped out of school and went ... not the sort of thing a sixteen-year-old from a nice, straight Jewish family does, hey, but who knows why kids do anything. I don't hate my parents, we keep in touch. They know Beccy. They love her. I've seen Mum and Dad a few times. It was just something I needed to do. I hated the fences they'd built around me. Do you know what I mean?'

'I think so,' Jennifer said, with just a pinch of envy.

'Once or twice I've wondered what I'm doing here but I am here and that's that,' said Miriam. 'Now, what about you?'

Beccy stood quiet as a watchman by the window. It had

been one of the attractions in the room – the 'lookout' window and the camphor chest full of dress-up clothes that Jennifer's mother had added to from the moment she could walk. The doll that had been so carefully displayed had been admired but not touched 'in case it gets broken'. Beccy stood quiet by the window but Jennifer knew she was listening to every word.

'Well, my father is a naturalist . . . '

'That figures,' Miriam laughed. 'Sorry, go on.'

'But he really specialises in marine life and the sea and that sort of thing. He's – well, he's an unusual sort of man. Strange. He doesn't work all the time but he usually goes to the university or the museum on Wednesdays, that's why things are quiet today. My brother doesn't do anything much. He messes around with old motorbikes and pubs and women. You should stay away from the two of them! I wish Gull could get himself together but it's a faint hope. He drinks too much. It makes him sick. My mum died when I was about Beccy's age. This was her room – and that's her chair. It's all I've got left of her. Well, that's about all there is, really.'

'A truck ran over me when I was a baby,' Beccy said, without leaving her post.

'No!' Jennifer was genuinely shocked. 'What happened?'

'We don't want to talk about this, Beccy!' Miriam almost shouted.

'What happened?' Jennifer asked. It was Beccy who answered.

'It'd been raining a lot and the mud was soft and the truck

79

ran over me and I was pushed down into the mud and I got a broken hip and at the hospital they said it was a miracle that the mud was so deep and Mum told me they told her off, and Gates, too!'

'Thanks a lot, Bec,' Miriam said nothing more for a minute. 'It happened in Queensland. We were living with her father. Beccy was two years old. It *was* a miracle. It could have happened to anyone, anywhere, but, well, it happened to us and they knew we all smoked pretty much a lot of the time then and they accused us of being too stoned to look after kids. That wasn't true. It was an accident – I didn't even see her go under.'

'You must have been scared out of your wits, Miriam.' It explained the limp, but Jennifer would say no more about the accident in Beccy's presence.

'It was, as they say, a life-changing experience.' Miriam brushed the memory away for the moment with a sweep of her busy hands.

'The wind's changing and the sparrows are flying backwards,' a low voice of authority suddenly announced from the lookout as though all they had been discussing was the weather.

'Thank you, watcher!' Jennifer saluted. Some clouds were grouping together in clusters of grey and the light in the room was dimming.

'I guess we'd better start up the hill before it gets dark.' Miriam looked across to the window. 'Come on, Bec. Jenny must have lots to do. Say thank you, and get your things together.'

'Not just yet,' said the watchman. 'Something might happen.'

'I'm sure Jenny won't mind if we come another day – but upstairs,' she added, with a shivery smile.

'Mind?' Jennifer said. 'I would never mind. We're going to be friends forever, aren't we, Beccy?'

'Yes, okay.'

Miriam gathered her own things and motioned for her daughter to do the same. She looked around the room and sighed.

'It's been a great afternoon, Jenny. It's been great for Beccy. It's made all the difference to her. I'm truly grateful for that.'

As they went downstairs with a reluctant and surly Beccy, Miriam asked, 'Is Gulliver your brother?'

'Yes. Gulliver Darwin of all things, but he's mostly called Gull.'

'It's an unusual name, Gulliver, but the Gull fits in around here. What's your dad's name?'

'Marlin.'

Beccy swung around on the edge of the stair so quickly she nearly toppled over. 'Is this the Fishcastle!?' she asked loudly.

'Yes. Well, I suppose it is.' Jennifer's spirits fell to the floor. She felt absolutely defeated – absolutely powerless. The man was everywhere. He was on the stairs. He was in the house and outside in the yard even when he was miles away from it. He would be in the house if someone had the guts to murder him. He'd still be here. If the place burned to the ground with him in it, he'd rise from the ashes! 'You've heard of it, have you, Bec?'

'They talk about it at school. They say Hill kids aren't allowed to hear Marlin's stories. They say he hates Hill kids.' Enormous, bright eyes saw everything around her all over again. It all had a new meaning. 'But I'm here. I'm here! I'll show them. I can come any time I want now, can't I, Jenny? He won't hate me, will he?'

'Of course he won't hate you.' Jennifer spoke to the stairs in a futureless tone. 'How could anyone hate you.'

'Beccy! How about that!' Miriam was curious about Jennifer's change of mood but she was delighted to see her child so animated, and laughing at the world for a while.

'Can I, Jenny? Can I come to the Fishcastle any time I want?'

'I expect so,' Jennifer said in a voice from somewhere below her. And as she escorted them safely down the drive to the Sandpath, she thought, *Beccy was right. The wind had changed and the sparrows were flying backwards*. It was storm time again. She wondered why the Carters' dog wasn't barking.

Chapter Four

ICE FISHING, ALASKA

There was, at last, a postcard in the letterbox from Hesta Mainwaring – aunt Hesta, sister Hesta – and it had lain like a favour between the power bill, a bank statement and a quarterly from the university. It was addressed to only one of the Fishcastled dwellers. It had been delivered by the god of mail on Friday following the first visit by Miriam and Rebecca Holt, to make Jennifer happy.

The postcard had been recycled in the way of Hesta's postcards. On it was a photograph entitled *Ice Fishing, Alaska* – a tiny boy cosied in fur with expectant eyes, a line on a stick, a half barrel to sit on and a hole in the ice. That the postcard had been posted from a place near Iquitos on the Amazon River in melting-pot heat was of no concern to its writer or its recipient. Hesta recycled cards by pasting labels over used words and whiting out addresses long forgotten. She gave no thought to matching pictures with content. The most memorable in Jennifer's opinion was 'Magic Mountain Disney World', sent in 1986 from the holy site of the Reclining Buddha in Sri Lanka.

In recycling writing paper Hesta was convinced she helped to save her planet's forests; but that in order to write upon the paper she might sit at a tabletop cut from one tree and on the chair of another in a house made of wood, never occurred to her.

Hesta had stayed at the Fishcastle many times – between flights, between ships, between lovers – but the most memorable visit was immediately after the death of Lissy Hardwick. She had come to the Fishcastle for the sake of the grieving children. She had fussed and feathered around them like a disorganised Mary Poppins, her hair cobwebbed around her head, moist brandy-nip eyes, quick feet picking their way around loose threads of her ankle-length skirts. Another storyteller, another play-actor – but stories better at their ends. Happier than her brother's. She had cloaked the lost children with the love stored in a woman who'd never had the bother of children of her own. Jennifer and Gulliver had worshipped her for the relief it gave them.

And for their sake her brother kept mixed feelings about his sister to himself.

On that occasion she'd walked, with determined geniality, up the Sandpath, dragging her luggage behind her in a trolley. It had excited every dog on the strip, except the Carters', who'd had the feeling he'd heard it somewhere before and had curled back to his snoring sleep.

'Did you know it's snowing heavy on the bus stop at the

junction?' she'd said in her way. 'A blizzard it is up there!'

'But it never snows on Proudie Bay,' young Gulliver had said at the gate where they'd waited.

'Well?' she'd said. 'Who's to say it couldn't, young man?'

'It can snow if it wants to,' Jennifer had tucked herself into Hesta's skirt, wrapping herself in the soft, protective parcel of it.

'Tell them the truth, sister – this is no time for play-acting,' Marlin said. 'Tell them it's a truck lost its load of shredded paper. We already know.'

'Think it's paper if you want,' she said. 'I say it's snow!'

'And so do I!' shouted the children.

'Then snow it is! They're ankle-deep up there.'

'You're insane,' Marlin had said, in his sorrow and confusion.

But it was their aunt's insanity (if that's what it was) that saved the children's reason.

Hesta's home is now in the Blue Mountains, a good three-and-a-half hours from Proudie Bay – a *good* three-and-a-half hours from her brother, depending of course, on whether the crow flies straight or stops to admire the views. On a slow day, it could be four hours or more – better still.

Her home is a warm nest of a cottage, at the end of a fire trail off Wellings Road, and thanks be, too difficult for a brother without a car, and much too far west from the sea for a brother to survive more than half a day. It is a fine house in a fine timbered heartbeat of the world, and given

85

to her by one of the dearest of her gentlemen, Mr Mainwaring – God rest his soul.

It was from trees and the earth that Hesta drew her strength, and the only swimming she did was through the blue eucalypt mists that rose from the valleys and curled around the houses like sweet incense. There was a cleansing in the mountain air that had nothing to do with salt spray and cutting shards of sand on the high-wind days of Proudie Bay. She had grown away from her iron-headed brother and his coastal ground and planted herself in this wooded place like a hybrid, and the hybrid had thrived so well she wished she'd transplanted herself much earlier in her life.

Hesta was once described by the president of a local charity, in a vote of thanks for a contribution she had made, as being a woman of regal carriage, given to wearing mauve but with a tendency to sudden flight – a remark, she later .confided to Jennifer, that made her sound like a capricious horse in mourning. But at sixty-two, her posture is still good, her face unlined and her hands slender, and she still has the eyes of an artist, strong and interesting, forever curious of the colours of the world, though she has never painted a picture or thrown a pot or written a verse in her life.

Hesta had written the postcard to Jennifer while sitting on the top step of the stamp-sized porch of her cabin in an animal orphanage for creatures found abandoned in the surrounding Amazon jungle. Her cabin lay on a clearing of the mud bank of a tributary of the great river, about ten kilometres from Iquitos. The orphanage, operated by a Belgian veterinary surgeon named simply Phillipe, boosts its running costs by offering 'Amazon Adventures' to tourists who have wearied of Tuscany and Tahiti and room service, bar service, clean towels, and suites where the quilts and the bathrooms remind them of their own. The orphanage offers none of that. Animals howl and grunt through the night. Kings of cockroaches, brown and shining as scarabs, roam their range unchallenged, birds scream and screech, everything in the thick air bites, and spiders as big as plates hang framed in the dining hut, precious as a gallery of Rembrandts.

Hesta was hot as she wrote, and insects in flocks of irritations that drank from small patches of exposed skin bit her if a suggestion of breeze dared to dry her sweat for a moment. Under a rusted canopy of tin, she sat only three low steps away from a gum of river mud, from steaming knotted twists of jungle, from tropic rain that fell heavy and suddenly as if buckets were tipped from the trees, from thick, curling smells of river bubbling like ochre porridge. She wrote to Jennifer:

It is teeming heat, dear. It's coming down in sheets. I am soaked with heat. Everything bites and I'm sealed in clothing, even boots to my knees. There are flying clouds of savages around my head screaming with frustration. There is a woman from California who's allergic to everything. She sprays herself and everything else with lysol and doesn't care if she dies of it! She wants to go home but her husband insists they stay until they have spent the last cent of the cost of their tour package. Mr and Mrs 'Boston', a nice couple, left

yesterday after only two days here with an album of photo-
graphs to visit in the comfort of their den. That has left only
four of us this week. We are all having a most exciting time.

'They come and they go,' Phillipe had told her. 'They like
these adventures for their dinner parties but at the end of
the day some miss their martinis and their five stars.'

One of the four who remained was a German woman
from Bonn. Hesta had so far only spoken to her briefly at
the evening meal table and had thought her loud and coarse
and unmannered but relentlessly cheerful in a boisterous
way. During the day she seemed to spirit away into the wilds
like one of their own, but now, as Hesta wrote, the German
woman walked heavily from the river towards her and sat
dripping beside her on the step.

The dark hair of her head and her arms was swept to
one side like flood grass and decorated with red mud and
sprigs of river weed. Her black swimsuit, struggling to corset
her body, revealed a great deal of hair under her arms and
where the leg joined the groin. There was a distinctly Euro-
pean strength and smoothness to her skin and power in the
grin of her teeth.

'Hallo,' the woman said loudly, even though she was
close enough to be touched.

'*Guten Tag*, Lucretia.' Hesta noticed with some annoy-
ance that the woman's skin displayed not one single insect
bite or any signs that she had been troubled by them at all.
'You have been swimming again, I see.'

'Yes, is *gut* – it is good, the water.'

'And you did not see any of the dear little river fishes again, Lucretia?'

'*Nein* – no!' She laughed loud enough to disturb the flying cloud above Hesta's head for a moment. 'The piranha fish do not eat German women. They do not have the courage.' She laughed again and spread her legs and more dark hair escaped in moving knots to breathe.

'But you must be careful not to swim if you are bleeding, Lucretia – that will give the piranha fishes courage, German or not.' Hesta capped the pen and slid it over the postcard. 'German or not, my dear Lucretia.'

Hesta had, so far, learned from the woman – had been told by her – that she was forty-two years old and an assistant in the department of zoology at the University of Bonn, and had come to holiday with animals. That is what she had learned. Hesta had observed, however, a rough, rivery woman, deep-throated and thunderous in her ways, always hungry and thirsty, who cast herself for bait in the river by day and probably, Hesta suspected, through the workers' cabins after dark. From the beginning Hesta had observed her with distaste and had prayed to the god of piranhas every night for four nights without shame at all – or luck.

'You are writing to your husband?' The woman dripped a puddle of river between her legs. She had a vaguely sulphurous smell.

'I do not have a husband, Lucretia. I have had three delightful companions and sadly they are all dead.'

'Ha! You get rid of them? Good!' She drew her finger across her throat. 'That is *good*.' She laughed. 'You know,

89

I have a man only for screw – maybe lunch, maybe dinner – then I get rid of him. That is better I think.'

Hesta felt that her observations of the woman had not been nearly rich enough, and watching her teeth as she laughed, she thought, *Of course the piranhas would not eat one of their own.* 'My companions, Lucretia, went their way peacefully and of their own accord,' she said. 'I did not *get rid of them.* It would never have occurred to me to get rid of them. I am writing to my niece in Australia.'

'You are Australian? I think maybe you come from England. Your voice is very nose-up Windsor Castle.'

'Indeed! Well, I most certainly am not English, Lucretia. I am Australian – and a republican!'

'Okay.' She dismissed the subject with a grin. 'So – is your niece beautiful? You are a beautiful woman.'

'Aaaah.' Hesta looked closely at the woman's face to find the expression of fawning she knew must be there, but there was no guile in her dark eyes, no sly flattery. Her eyes were wide and candid with something of a light that came from deep behind them. In regarding Lucretia more closely Hesta was reminded that indeed it might have been careless to judge this book by its cover. She reminded herself of something she had once been told – that when the gods are bored, they cover beauty with the hide of pigs and wait for wisdom to find it. Somewhere from the far forest a bird called with exquisite throat. Around them the thick canopy of leaves shone like glass slivers in the parts pushed aside by fingers of sun. And despite the dense, clinging air there was, at that moment, a mood of gentle seduction that had either wound its way from the spirit forest to the step they sat on, or had flowed from their step to the river and the trees. 'She is beautiful to me, Lucretia. There are some difficulties in my niece's life, but she is beautiful to me.'

'She is lucky to have you to love her.'

'Thank you,' Hesta said gently. 'I have no children of my own, you see. Loving my niece is not in the least difficult.' She regarded the woman again. 'You are a very, very confusing woman, Lucretia.'

'I know.' In the German's grinning teeth was caught a thread of green weed, like spinach. She picked it away with her thumbnail.

'Tell me about yourself, Lucretia. You have an unusual name, I think. Forgive me for remarking upon it but it is unusual – and your English is very good.'

'But my Spanish is not so good,' she said. 'Here, the men laugh when I talk Spanish. My English is good because my father was from Scotland – he said to me, "You must speak like a Scot" – he never said to me, "Speak English". It was my father who named me Lucretia.'

'I wonder ... I wonder if he meant to name you Lucia – you know, after an opera set in Scotland – and perhaps confused the names. The name Lucretia brings to mind something entirely different, I feel.' It was an observation Hesta immediately regretted making but the woman smiled over it. 'Never mind, dear, of course, I was just thinking of Scotland, and the music of *Lucia di Lammermoor*. Do you know it? The opera? My mind just rambling along ... the heat, I expect. Tell me, are your parents in Scotland or Germany?'

'There is no father now. He ran away from us,' the woman said. 'There is a mother in Germany but there is no father. It is better, *ja*?' And she laughed loud, with a throat wide enough to swallow eels.

Hesta glanced past the woman and saw an infant capybara, a fat-bellied, oversized rodent, tottering on its toddler legs from the river towards them. She recognised it as the same animal that had emptied its bowels on her feet the day before, and she stood and excused herself.

'I'm feeling very hot, dear, and a little tired. I think I'll finish my cards in the cabin.' Hesta turned to go inside and said, 'By the way, that capybara walking towards you loves to be petted but be careful if you do. I think it eats too much.'

'I do not touch that little one! And you should not touch that little one! It's sick and it runs from its arse.' And Lucretia firmly but gently chased it away from the cabin.

Hesta hurried inside and rubbed her yesterday-spoiled boots hard with disinfectant until there was no shine at all.

A light rain that had begun as little more than a veil of moisture now fell on Hesta's cabin like a thousand bead curtains. The sound of it on the roof was almost deafening. She stood just inside the shelter of the door and shook her cards free of damp. Lucretia walked casually through the torrent as though it meant nothing at all. She turned and waved to Hesta and roared at the top of her voice, 'What is your name?'

'Hesta Mainwaring!' Her words drowned through rain.

'What?'

'Later, dear. Later.' She held out her arm and pointed to her watch. Lucretia waved and nodded and strolled through the torrent back to the river with the capybara toddling behind her. Hesta thought it a most unusual sight.

That night – at the meal table which accommodated guests, Phillipe, some of the staff and an ill-tempered pet macaw, Beppi – Hesta answered Lucretia's question when the German sat next to her.

'My name is Hesta Mainwaring.'

'Okay, Hesta Mainwaring. After four days,' Lucretia said to the licking and chewing eaters, 'I talk to this lady and I do not know her name. Hesta Mainwaring, I am pleased to meet you.'

Lucretia had come into the dining hut still wearing her swimsuit but had tied a transparent black wrap around her waist. *Dressed for dinner*, Hesta thought, *but at least she's combed the mud out of her hair and brushed the leeches from between her toes*. The men ate rice and beans, sucked fish bones and chickens that had grown too old to escape, and they watched the woman's cleavage and the tops of her yeast-pudding breasts, rising and falling with every breath. Watching one then the other with bouncing-ball eyes. Hesta imagined a row of penises, under the table, risen to attention and saluting in honour of the sight of her.

George 'California' concentrated on his food, picking through it like a surgeon through gut, looking for things that moved or had died – too occupied to notice anything above or below the level of his plate and 'Mrs C', slapping at mosquitoes and in her constant headache of tension, forked only at rice and wouldn't have cared if Lucretia had been stark naked. Mrs C appeared to Hesta to have lost weight, due probably to the amount of food that fell from the fork in her shaking hand. At a time written long ago on the tourist schedule Phillipe announced coming activities between gollops of beer and fish.

'Tomorrow,' he told them, 'we visit an Indian village. We will take a path through the jungle and we'll see the real giants of the Amazon – the great trees – and we will see plants that will be strange to you, but your guide will be able to identify. And then we come to an Indian village. The people there are shy; try not to frighten the children. We can take photographs but it is best to pay them something. The Indians in this village are very poor. Also, they do not wear clothes – just to warn you.'

'Oh yeah? Naked *and* poor,' said Mr C, his mouth stuffed full of diagnosed food. 'Hear that, Karen? Naked *and* poor. Like poor, like they need new TVs in their real houses in Iquitos? How often do they come out here to pose their butts?'

Some of the staff, Indians themselves, moved uneasily in their chairs and the bird flicked an irritated tail.

'George, shutup!' his wife snapped, close to snapping in two like a twig herself. 'You're the one who wanted to stay on, so just go along with it and shut the hell up!' She was beyond any pretence of domestic harmony – way beyond embarrassment. Mrs C was too far drowned in misery and homesickness to care. In her dreams she had already poisoned his roses, sold his fishing tackle and divorced him.

'Well, I think it sounds interesting,' Hesta said. 'Do they make things in the village we can buy, Phillipe?'

'Are you kiddin' me?' George laughed, and picked at a meatless chicken bone.

'Okay?' Phillipe said, ignoring George – as though he'd heard nothing at all. 'And now I tell you, in this Indian village we are given a special drink. It's very strong this drink – the Indians make it themselves – you must be careful just to taste but it is okay to say no.'

'Their trash soaked in a drum, is it?' asked George.

'No, no,' Lucretia winked at him. 'Better than that, George. Listen. I can tell you about this drink. It is a drink fermented in their spit. The women chew roots until they are soft, George, and then they spit them out and leave it all to cook in their spit! They say this drink gives a man great strength.'

Mrs C pressed her handkerchief over her mouth and sat perfectly still. 'You should enjoy that, George,' she said, smooth as a razor.

'Yeah? You never know. It might taste better than the crap we get here.'

'And then . . .', Phillipe was expressionless. There wasn't a spat he hadn't heard, there wasn't a tension of nerves he hadn't seen strung from one end of the camp to the other – but there was a tight schedule to making what he could from his visitors and he would not be diverted from it. 'And then the Indians will give a demonstration of the blowpipe which they traditionally use to kill their meat. They are very accurate – they can blow a dart through the forehead of dollar bills.'

'Nothing less than a Ulysses S. Grant, I betcha!'

'Shutup, George!'

'It will be best,' Phillipe said, like a recording, 'to wear insect repellent for the jungle walk, a hat and strong shoes.'

'And what about those tarantulas?' asked Mrs C. 'I hate those spiders.' She pointed to the framed giants hanging on the wall. 'If I saw one of those out there I'd pee my pants!'

'There is no defence from the big spiders.' One of the Indian staff who had scraped the last of his fish and string-bean chicken from his plate looked at George with mortuary eyes and a hardly perceptible twist of a smile. 'You better stay close to your woman, sir. Those big spiders can jump twelve feet off the ground, no trouble.'

'Well, he won't have to stay close to me cause I'm not moving from my damned cabin! I'm not moving till the boat comes and takes me out of here and the plane comes and takes me home.' And Mrs C wiped sweat and a moth from the back of her neck. There were tears in her eyes that had nothing to do with the heat. Hesta felt sorry for her.

'Take no notice, dear. I'm afraid of spiders, too,' she said. 'But I'm sure the jumping is a story they tell to frighten people. My brother tells stories like that – just to frighten people.'

Above their heads there was such a density of insects around the light they were almost in darkness. Mosquitoes gathered in organised squadrons under the table and fed on selected blood. Lucretia ate everything on her own plate and then finished what had been left by Mrs C. She grinned and joked and appeared to be having no end of fun. She rapped the table for attention.

'I have another story for you,' she said to everyone, but concentrating on George. 'This story is also true. There is a tribe of Indians in the jungle that hunt tarantulas for food. Is this not true, Phillipe?' He nodded, and grinned. She had exactly the reaction she'd expected from the two Cs and Hesta. 'They cook them on the fire and if they are lucky to find a pregnant female . . .' She ballooned her hands out over her belly. 'They make an omelette from her eggs.' She laughed widely at their expressions. 'And when they have finished eating them they pick their teeth with the fangs – nothing is wasted!'

'Lucretia,' Hesta said. 'Is it really true? Good heavens! I think you and my brother could terrify each other with your stories forever. When you visit Australia I will introduce you to him.'

A wooden platter of local fruits and nuts was put in the centre of the table. There was a clatter of spoons and bowls and fingers as campers hungry for something familiar and safe served themselves. The platter was decorated with the carved head of a monkey with large, astonished eyes – as though it had just heard some very bad news.

'I have not been to Australia,' Lucretia said. 'Tell me why I should go to Australia. What is in that country? I know there are good animals. Is it easy to see the animals?'

'For you, dear, I think the animals would come to see you. They would suit you very well – in all their forms.'

'But I hear there is nothing to do. At night there is nothing. What would I do at night?'

'In the desert you would lie down and watch stars close enough to touch – and you would breathe clean, sharp air.' There was a defensive edge to Hesta's words, and nostalgia. 'In the cities you would go to the theatre or the opera and coffee houses or eat good food by the side of harbours or rivers. You could even visit the Blue Mountains, where I live – I cannot imagine that you would not like the mountains. Or, my dear, you could wear your swimsuit by the sea all day and I am sure you would meet someone who would find something for you to do all night.' She tried to smooth over the edge to her words. 'But tell me, Lucretia – where in Germany is your home? Your mother's home?'

'It is in Koblenz. Do you know it? When I am not at the university I am living in Koblenz. My mother has a small hotel on the river.'

'Aaaah, Koblenz.' Hesta was unable to resist a smile. 'If your home is in Koblenz, my dear, then to visit a country where there is nothing to do would not disturb you in the least.'

'Okay,' the German grinned, as though she'd been kissed on the cheek. 'I understand what you say.' She shovelled papaya into her mouth and reduced it to a river of juice with one bite. 'Tell me about your Blue Mountains. Are the rocks blue? Is the snow blue?'

Hesta passed her cup across the table to Phillipe, who poured strong tea and palm sugar. 'Are your mountains cool?' he asked.

'Yes,' she said. 'For most of the year it is cool – cool and sweet.' She told them that the blue of the mountains had something to do with the oil of the eucalypt trees forming a haze in the atmosphere. She told them of the glorious wind-fallen world of autumn and special winters when snow came to surprise the children, and of places, not far from her home, where she could stand alone and see mountains and valleys and canyons stretch as far as the edge of the world, where the air is clear and fresh and perfumed and filled with birdsong. And as she told them, she could almost feel the cool air against the skin of her mind, taste the scent of leaves on her fingers and feel the crush of bush tracks under her feet, and when she closed her eyes she could clearly see mountain falls of water fine as virgins' veils, and just for that moment the hot stew of air around them dried and cooled her face. 'It truly is a beautiful place,' Hesta said, and blinked herself back to the dining hut and saw that Mrs C had been listening, her chin cupped in her hand.

'I don't hear these kind of things about Australia,' she said. 'George went there once, to Sydney, on business – didn't you, George!'

'What?' his head lolled back and dozing.

'You went to Sydney once.'

'Yeah. Great oysters!'

'See, that's all I get,' she said, 'when he comes back from a place. The food.'

'Well, Hesta Mainwaring. I would like to visit your Blue Mountains,' Lucretia said.

'And you will be most welcome, dear.'

The Fishcastle

Hesta Mainwaring, nee Hardwick, nee Peace, nee Knight, if she'd bothered to take the names of her two young life lovers, has nested on and off in her Blue Mountains home since the last of her companions, Colin Mainwaring, died.

Of the three, Colin Mainwaring was the only one she had more or less married in a more or less ceremony conducted by an astrologer in their house. Her first love, Eric Peace, a telephone linesman and amateur magician, left her on her nineteenth birthday to join his uncle's mission in the Admiralty Islands with a view to teaching the vulnerable and innocent God's own tricks, and had posted only one letter to her and a Bible for Christmas before cutting her off entirely. Her second love, Edward Knight, who literally swept her off her feet, for cycling was his passion, fell head over heels in love, after two years with Hesta, with her friend Robert Kenny who collected stamps and paperweights. The last she saw of them was when Edward cycled like a demon away from their two rooms with sink, with Bob Kenny doubling and clinging to Edward's waist, his milk-white legs splayed out like wind fins. She had wept to her brother in her loneliness but Marlin had no patience for tears. She had begged to stay with her brother but the room and the bed had been as cold as his welcome. And so it was, within the vastness of the Blue Mountains, as far away from the city as she could afford to travel, that Hesta found warmth, a job, new friends and a house to rent.

The wooden cottage stands in the grounds of what was once the garden of a grand guesthouse, long since fallen to a ruin of scattered pillars and broken columns, lost under a tangle of vines. And the original garden, marked in places of former glory by the tops of conifers, maples and elms, lies also beneath a wilding of bramble and bracken and vine, looking for all the world like a stage set for a gothic drama. What was once a tree-lined drive from the main road to the property had become a fire trail that can be negotiated safely only by work vehicles or by foot. When she is at home, Hesta depends a great deal on the generosity of her neighbours and the Volunteer Bushfire Brigade, who call from time to time to clear the worst of the scrub hazards away from the property.

Hesta's house is a shelter for strangeries – a journal of her life and loves expressed in objects and oddities. It is a sanctuary for chipped treasures, orphaned still lifes and ruined exotica, rescued during her travels in fits of passion and sympathy for them. Curious visitors who have the patience to sift through her shelves find little more than potters' rejects, disabled dolls, driftwood, stones carved by a thousand years and flowers loved and preserved. And if the visitor looks up from the shelves and studies the walls and ceilings he will see landscapes and seascapes, portraits of children no one knows, baskets of shells and pods, shadow puppets from Malaya, masks from India, penis covers from New Guinea, next to strings of garlic and garlands of chillies too hot to touch – menus, programmes and stall tickets, photographs and stacked CDs. It is a crammed theatre of a house where delights can be found wherever the eyes rest – entirely suitable for the curious, for children and the moonstruck.

Some of Hesta's visitors found it so enchanting it was difficult for them to leave at the end of the day, and one of those had been her third and longest partner, Colin Mainwaring, whose name she had taken because he'd been kind enough to buy the house for her and provide sufficient funds for her nomadic instincts even though he had no taste for travel. Colin Mainwaring was a vegetarian but had become wealthy from the proceeds of a chain of butcher shops strung like sausages along the east coast of New South Wales. A plain man with the plainest of minds, he'd lived his life through the spirit of Hesta for nearly twenty years – loyal and in awe of her until the very moment he choked on a curry puff in Bellen's Health Cafe on the Heath Falls Road and died, leaving the proceeds from butchered animals to Hesta, and a vacancy at the golf club. She thanked his photograph in its silver frame frequently.

'I really would like to go to my cabin now,' Hesta said. 'Could someone please escort me? I'm a little nervous in the dark.'

'I will,' Phillipe said. Hesta glanced at Lucretia but she was busy teaching some of the locals to play pick-up-sticks with a box of matches. Someone played a guitar. Insects slept on the swaying globe, drunk with light. George dozed again, at peace, with his paw around a beer. Mrs C scratched her arms with her eyes closed and dreamed of Marina del Rey. It was clearly the end of a day.

The next morning presented itself to the campers as a hotbox of steam – a simmering stew of red mud and water.

The rain had stopped in the early hours but the pools

that had formed in the leaves of trees rained upon the ground as heavy as any cloud shower. Mud-dwelling creatures sucked and plopped just below the surface of their world, forming strange shapes and keeping their identities a secret. And river fish flapped lazily in and out of the warm, thick water with their mouths open and their dull eyes looking up and dreaming of seas. And above it all, everywhere in the sulphurous air, was a wail of insects in their billions, searching for suck, and in the forest was a quiet whispering of sound – a muffling of grunts and coughs and small, faint cries from birds too tired to open their beaks.

More than half an hour had passed since Hesta had heard the breakfast gong but she was reluctant to leave the mosquito netting around her bed. She had slept badly and felt on edge. All around her, on the floor, she listened to the scrabbling giants of cockroaches as they clawed against the cans of water in which the legs of her bed stood. She'd forced herself to become accustomed to roaches but as she lay against her pillow, she watched, through the netting, a large spider slowly picking its way across the ceiling, carefully lifting one thin leg after the other until all eight had crept a spider's length forward. She was afraid – she had never overcome her horror of spiders, no matter how hard she'd tried. And there would have been others above her, she knew that – they crept softly from everywhere in the camp – but she watched the progress of this one with nervous fascination.

She knew she must dress soon and face the day but all she was able to do was cower under her sheet and watch the slow and slide and sidle of the thing across the ceiling – and she watched until even through the heat she shivered.

'Hesta! Hesta Mainwaring!' An unmistakable shout of the German. 'Come to eat.' Lucretia gave such a violent rap to the cabin door that Hesta watched with horror as the spider lost its footing and fell onto her net. She covered herself completely with the sheet.

'Lucretia!' she called as loudly as she could.

'*Ja*? Are you sick?'

'No. Come in – come in. The spider has fallen.'

'What happens?'

'The spider has fallen – quickly! Please come in – come in. You must catch it for me – quickly!'

The woman stormed into the cabin and in very nearly one movement knocked the creature down from the net to the floor with a slap of her hand and stamped on it with her bare foot until it was no more than brown paste. Hesta struggled to regain her composure.

'These spiders have no poison,' said Lucretia. 'You should not be afraid of such things.'

'I am sorry, dear. I slept badly. It was like a bad dream – the spider. I am sorry, Lucretia.'

'Are you all right? Do you have a fever?'

'I am perfectly all right, dear.' Hesta put one foot gingerly onto the floor. The cockroaches had scuttled away to their day lairs when Lucretia had come. 'Have you been swimming already, Lucretia?' The woman wore her swimsuit but it seemed to be dry. 'Or perhaps you're about to swim?'

'I do not swim this morning. The river is thick like soup.'

'Then perhaps you won't wear your swimsuit to breakfast. I think you would look very nice in a skirt.' Hesta patted her face with a handkerchief and struggled to make small talk.

'I wear this because it is cool,' she said. 'You should dress cool, Hesta Mainwaring, but you dress hot like a white hunter in an American movie.'

'I dress to ward off the insects, dear.' Hesta shook her clothes and boots. 'I will wash and dress and be ready for breakfast shortly. Will you wait for me?'

'Yes, I'll wait.' Lucretia sat on the step of the cabin. 'The Indians brought Phillipe a young puma this morning.'

'Not for breakfast, I hope.'

'It is very young and very hungry – and very beautiful.' Lucretia paused for a moment, and added, 'Oh, and the little animal died.'

'What little animal?'

'The little rat you like so much.'

'You mean the capybara?'

'*Ja* – the little capybara died last night.'

'But why? How did it die?' Despite the unreliable functions of its bowels, Hesta had become attached to it. 'I tethered it safely near the river yesterday afternoon. Out of harm's way!'

'It is drowned,' Lucretia said with little emotion. 'That is why I do not swim early. Something ate its face.'

Hesta held her hands across her mouth; she was mortified. She had tethered the animal to a stake before she'd gone to dinner. She had tethered it by a stream that ran through the camp, for its safety, she'd thought – for its safety and to prevent it wandering into her cabin to leave its foul turds on the floor. She had used a length of twine long enough for the animal to have the freedom of dry land or wet.

'It was caught with string around its back legs,' the German was saying. 'Head in the water and legs in the air – a bad death, I think.'

'But it was me!' Hesta sank back onto the bed. Her head throbbed. 'I have killed it – it was me! I thought I might be of some help by coming here, Lucretia, but look what I have done.'

Lucretia gentled herself at the sound of Hesta's distress. She sat next to her on the bed. 'It was very sick, the little animal. It had a bad sickness. Phillipe said it would die soon no matter how much he cared for it.' She held Hesta's hand for a moment. 'Don't worry. Come! Come to eat. Put on your hunting trousers – I will help with the boots.' She swept the remains of the spider out the door with her foot. 'Ha! I think this one die of fright.' She shook the net and inspected the corners of the room. 'There are no more. Come – quickly now – I will wait. I will show you the puma. It has teeth like a devil's child!' And she drew her own lips apart and snarled. 'This one will not die – it will live forever.'

There was an explosive energy about the woman – Hesta had felt it through her hand as strong as a current – but there was a warmth with it, a comforting strength. She was, Hesta thought, a warrior of comfort, an Amazon of protectors only lacking a shield and spear, and on that particular morning she would have been disappointed to find the layers of weakness, no matter how fine, that stilled below the surface of every human soul. Hesta was glad to have the woman's strength to lean upon that morning.

In order to reach the camp's dining hut, it was necessary to negotiate a long, raised and uneven wooden walkway. It was also necessary to run the gauntlet past Phillipe's pet macaw, Beppi.

Beppi was a very large and alcoholic bird that had long since lost the will to fly but still had enormous strength in his beak and claws. He tolerated the males of the camp but attacked women on sight – without a second thought. It was not unusual to see female visitors, screaming with bleeding ankles, running for their lives with an old, faded tart of feathers in hot pursuit. Mrs C had tried to spray him with lysol but he had torn the strap from her sandals. He had been one of the main reasons for the early departure of Mr and Mrs 'Boston'. There was usually a tension in the air during the walk to breakfast that had nothing to do with the climate, for the early hours were when the bird's mood was at its very worst.

At the sound of the breakfast gong, Beppi found hiding places along the walkway where he crouched in wait, as quietly as his age allowed, and attacked without warning. Hesta had five beak nicks in her boots and was very glad she'd had boots to wear. Lucretia, on the other hand, bore no scars at all on her bare feet and legs.

'I wonder where the bird hides this morning,' Hesta said.

She walked a few paces behind Lucretia.

'I don't know. But he will be waiting.'

'I have also wondered, Lucretia, why you don't show the scars of battle?' She watched over the woman's shoulder for signs of movement.

'The bird does not bite German women!' Lucretia laughed.

'Great heavens, Lucretia. Fish don't eat German women, birds don't bite German women? You must not imagine these things will never happen.' Hesta, watching ahead, thought she saw a movement of colour, but it was a fallen leaf. 'You *are* a woman, German or not!'

'It is the way I am,' she said. 'I am not a frightened woman.'

Aaah, thought Hesta – then her shield must be round and stout and there must be a cape for her shoulders and a helmet with horns. *There must be rings on her fingers and bells on her toes and the music of Wagner wherever she goes ...*

'Well, be careful dear, for afraid or not, I see Beppi just ahead of us.'

The bird had pulled itself up onto the walkway from a hide somewhere under the planks and stood facing them, his feathers bristling with hate and his beak open, ready. It was a fiercesome sight and if Hesta had been alone, as she usually was, it was the protection of her boots that prevented her heart from beating fast enough to run out of steam.

'This is a very stupid bird! Do you see this stupid bird?' Lucretia stood firm in front of him and spoke harshly to him in German, and to Hesta's astonishment Beppi lowered his body to the floor and crawled to her with his head on one side and one parrot eye looking steadily into her own.

When the bird reached her, Lucretia slipped a hand into the copious nest of her bosom and slid out of it a small bottle. She unscrewed the top and, squatting in front of Beppi, poured whisky into his open beak. She turned to Hesta and laughed loudly at her expression.

'You think I don't know the tricks? You think maybe I have some magic power to make birds lie down?' Still laughing, she took Hesta's hand and pulled her forward. 'It's drink that makes him mad. He is like a baby, that Beppi – he wants his bottle. He wants his bottle and I want my breakfast. Come quickly now or it will be gone forever!'

'And the piranha, Lucretia? Do you bribe them with something sweet?'

'Maybe when I am in the river the fish don't taste fear; it is a taste that excites, I think.'

'Lucretia,' said Hesta, 'from whatever storms you've battled through in your life I think you have emerged victorious. Am I right? Is it possible that you're one of the strongest people I've known? Are you as strong as you seem to be?'

'No one is strong all the time.'

'No – of course. I know that. Some of us wear our strength for show, don't we? I'm sure I do. With me it is a thin shell and easily cracked. You know now, after the spider, that I'm not so brave. I'm glad I've had the chance to know you better, Lucretia – and you, me. I hope we'll always be friends.'

The focus of the remains of the early morning was directed upon the young puma. Its injured paw had become infected and the animal snarled with the pain of it. It was very thin and very savage but Lucretia put her face close to the wire of its cage. 'But look at the teeth.' She purred to it. 'We see how beautiful you are.' Hesta stood well back. 'You will be hunting soon, little man, and all the animals in the forest will be frightened of you.' The animal snarled and snapped as close to her face as the wire allowed but Lucretia blew it a kiss as though it had just licked her cheek. 'My friend will help me look after you.' She turned to Hesta and took her hand as though she were introducing one to the other – woman to animal.

'Yes – yes. Of course I'll help.' Hesta had nothing more to say. There were times when it was unnecessary to reveal inner thoughts – when it was better to let them lie still for the sheer pleasure of their being. This was such a time, but as Lucretia covered her hand with the warmth of her own it was as though she had already read her mind. 'We will be sorry, I think, when you go home to your mountains and I go back to Bonn, yes?'

'Yes, I'm sure of it.'

'But now we should be ready for the great adventure to the village, I think. I will guard you against blowpipes and spit.'

The German woman constantly surprised her.

Almost two weeks had passed for Hesta in the camp, and for the last four days of that time Lucretia came to Hesta's cabin an hour before their evening meal to talk and enjoy a drink. The 'happy hour' was something they both looked forward to. They had found a common link in their love for the ways of worlds beyond their own and Hesta enjoyed the spice of sexual encounters that Lucretia sprinkled hot as chillies over her travelling tales. On one occasion she told Hesta about the year she traced her runaway father's family to a small fishing town north of Edinburgh and of the affair she had with the proprietor of the guesthouse in which she stayed while his wife visited her sister in Glasgow.

'He liked me, I think.' Laughing and flexing her muscles. 'He said his wife was all weak tea and milk. He liked a bit of muscle, he said. I did not pay him.'

'Lucretia! Really!' Hesta cried, shocked and enjoying every word.

'I can stay with you if I come to Australia?'

'Of course you can, my dear. I'd love it.'

'And your beautiful niece? Is she near your mountains?'

'Oh no. She lives with her father – my brother – and my nephew in a place called Proudie Bay. It's really a very beautiful bay by Sydney Harbour, at a point where the harbour is almost swallowed by the ocean. I have lived there on occasions – the longest time was after the death of my sister-in-law. It was a difficult time then.'

Lucretia saw that Hesta struggled with the memory and interrupted her. 'What is this beautiful niece's name?'

'Jennifer. Just Jennifer. I write to her, but not often enough, not as frequently as I should. She has a hard life, I think. She stays with me sometimes but of course she works and can't spare much time. I should see to her more often, Lucretia, shouldn't I? I will give more attention to her in the future.'

'Does she have a man, a woman, a lover?'

'At the moment I don't think so. But I think she dreams. I know she dreams – I will pay more attention, Lucretia, and *listen*. I will *listen* to her.'

They were quiet for a while, the two women, each one, it seemed, reflecting on loves shared or needed or lost or wasted in the solitary bravado of their hearts and souls, until Lucretia broke the spell.

'And tonight I will write to my mother.'

In the hours of early evening a hushed agitation surrounded the camp. It came from the jungle, the river, the canopy of the trees, the line of mud bank and the wetting air. From Hesta's cabin near the river it was possible to watch light shards probe through a lacework of green, to see birds swoop and catch foolish fish and water in their beaks, and small day beings with nervous eyes, edge slow, slow, close to the river to drink, and end-of-the-day insects swarming to their nests to wake night flyers, peevish with hunger – and above them, far beyond their sight in the canopy of darkening green they could hear the howls and cries of things never seen, worshipping the setting sun, and below it all, below where the sky is hidden, river water, mud red and splashed with fading light, running fast and shivering in a boil of fish.

The Amazon in the hours of early evening was for Hesta a spectacle of forest – a celebration of mystery as rich as a mural in a gallery of oil greens and darks and lights – and when the sight of it and the sounds and smells of it flooded her senses, her own mountain eucalypt and the salt spray of southern oceans vanished from her mind.

'It's all very seductive, Lucretia,' she said. 'I wish I'd come here when I was young.'

'There is no need to be young for it.'

'I think so. There are passions here that belong to young women and hunters and lovers. I can only taste and dream.'

'I feel them, Hesta. I feel every day and I am not so young.'

'I know that, dear, but you're so involved and active and young in your head. I think I've been jealous of you because of it. From the beginning.'

'You don't hate me now?' Lucretia said, in her disarming way.

'Oh no, dear. I've grown to like you very much indeed. I'm ashamed of my thoughts. I'll miss you terribly.'

The walk to the evening meal was less hazardous than in the morning. The great macaw had had the day to drink himself to a limp, loose-beaked shadow of his breed. As they passed, Beppi lay still, on his side, wings and tail feathers oddly fallen under the light of oil lamps along the walkway, looking for all the world as if he had been caught and dumped by a gale of wind. Lucretia crouched and poked his belly while he snored like a sot.

'It's a bad sight, Hesta,' she said, still by Beppi's side. 'It amuses us to kill him slowly with whisky. We laugh when he's mad for it and we laugh when he's mad with it. We are

113

very cruel to show innocents like Beppi the way to their death.'

'We show innocents the way to their death,' Hesta said. 'In my country we've killed thousands of our native Australian people in this way, with alcohol, just like Beppi. And we all profit from the liquor that poisons them – the sellers of it, the government – all of us profit from their misery. The financial gain from alcohol is immense!'

'What happens in your country happens in many countries – how is it in English – *culling*? And not with wine and beer, my dear Hesta. In my mother's country they used guns and gas chambers and filled great holes in the fields with bodies, some still alive. In the Middle East they poison lungs and cut the throats of babies, and so many bad things in so many other places – and all over the world, like this Amazon that we call primitive, are the agents of the gods of murderers, men of one cloth or another with one ball between their legs to share and half a brain, making pure minds rot – killing with disease and lies. In Australia you use wine? I wonder if that is the worst way to die?' Lucretia angrily pulled herself to her feet. She glanced at the surprised expression on Hesta's face and knew that Hesta must now know what lay behind *her* shell, at least one of the hidden layers of her: a Jew who believed in none of the gods for all the trouble gods caused. A woman who took animals as friends and harnessed humans for amusement. She looked down at the bird, her hands on her hips, breathed deeply and exhaled with force, peppering the air with emotion. 'Poor Beppi – poor bird,' she said gently. 'He dies with his whisky and he dies without it, and tomorrow morning he'll be waiting for me and I will open my bottle and kill him a little bit more, so he will perform for the tourists.'

But Lucretia was not to know that Hesta's reaction to her outburst brought memories of a young and passionate brother who had raved similar words in the same way to her for years before they grew apart – the same anger, hair-triggered by injustices and hypocrisies and lies.

'It's difficult for you to understand us. We must seem so shallow. We've never had the experience of booted strangers kicking our doors down in the middle of the night and dragging off our families: we can only imagine the terror of it and bombs destroying whole cities or landmines blowing off children's legs – or the real starvation of hopelessness and loss. We haven't suffered any of these things – not even the extremes of climate that you know so well. The only Australians who know about these things are the poor innocents who went away to fight other people's wars.'

'Then your country is very lucky.'

'As a matter of fact,' said Hesta, 'I think we're a bit too comfortable. Lazy, really. We don't know what it is to fight for freedom because we've had nothing else. There's no glory in the capture of a beachhead in Australia – we do it every weekend for fun.'

'I do understand. You live an island life. I have been to many islands in the Pacific. But I'm glad you don't have to live a hard life, Hesta. I would like to know you will be always happy in your mountains and have no enemies to destroy it.'

Lucretia paused and smiled briefly. 'It is hard to explain the passion of hate. It is passed down through families like a sickness. My mother lost four of her family in the death camps: my grandmother, her uncle, a cousin who was only fourteen and my grandmother's sister who was a dancer. She was good looking, the dancer. She was shot. She was told to strip her clothes and she was ordered to dance on the ground outside the Nazi barracks and then she was shot. The others were gassed. I'm glad you don't have that hate in your blood, Hesta. Every day my hate dreams of killing those *bastards* – every day. In this place I laugh a lot, but every day I want to kill these men, blow their balls off, shoot out their eyes, do to them the worst I can imagine – but almost all are already dead, it is so long ago. I feel cheated, we all feel cheated. Those killers should not be allowed to die of old age comfortable in their beds, it isn't right. There should have been another way.'

'An eye for an eye, Lucretia?'

'Yes!' she said. 'Eyes for eyes! There are many of these beasts here in South America. I see old white men with their heads held a certain way – arrogant – in La Paz, in Santa Cruz, comfortable in their hotels and clubs and banks and I think, if you are Nazis why is it you're still alive? You are so easy to kill. I wonder what kind of deity protects monsters.'

'I know I would feel the same way if my family had experienced your loss – but I wonder, Lucretia, if you could kill someone now, away from the heat of the moment? I think it would be difficult for you – your heart's too big.'

'We will see. I am told I should forgive a little for my

health; forget a little, but it's impossible for me. My mother has cancer now. She was told it has grown out of anger: that she is sick because she could not stop the hate. How can any of us forgive? You see how they are still killing us?'

Beppi hadn't moved. He lay and snored on the board-walk with lank feathers slipping between the gaps like old silk. Hesta used the bird to break the intensity of Lucretia's emotions.

'I simply can't imagine why a man like Phillipe allowed this to happen to the bird.' Hesta had put her arm around Lucretia's shoulder and hugged her. It was a gesture that needed no words.

'He told me the bird was drunk when it was left at the camp. There was nothing he could do – or so he said.' Lucretia took Hesta's hand and together they stepped over the rag of feathers. 'Come along – enough sadness for now. If I don't eat soon, Hesta, the noise in my belly will start all the jungle growling.'

And as if it were a signal, from the cages came a sharp coughing snarl of the young puma.

'Listen. That puma is nearly better.' Lucretia grinned and winked. 'When he is ready to be put back into the jungle and to hunt I will tell him to hunt the ghosts of Nazis and eat their guts!'

The two women held hands for comfort and friendship as far as the dining hut – Lucretia, calmed with the relief of spilled words, and Hesta with a strong sense of belonging and knowing. Beppi heaved himself onto unsteady claws and followed them on an undecided line of path.

When it was time for them to leave the camp and say good-byes, there were holiday pledges and the usual exchange of addresses from George, Mrs C and Phillipe – all never to be seen again – but Hesta had tears in her eyes when she held Lucretia tight to her. Here was a difference. They had become linked in friendship by a thread of a substance unknown to humans. It had not been necessary to speak. In pouring rain Lucretia boarded the first of the boats that would take them to Iquitos. She wore a cotton dress over her swimsuit.

'You look very nice!' Hesta called to her.

'When I come to your mountains I will wear only a dress!' she shouted, and she laughed back to the shore and waved her arms crisscross above her head as the boat chugged through the thick river towards the first bend that would take it out of sight.

Chapter Five

TWELVE BELLS FOR BUTTERFLIES

There is, of course, a church in Proudie Bay. It is small and quaint and Anglican and very old. It stands like a miniature bought from a gift shop, in its Sunday-best churchyard on a point close to the high cliffs overlooking Shack Hill. It stands on the northern point of the bay and not far from an even higher point and the lighthouse.

The Proudie Bay church is at the mercy of all of its God's elements but it shoulders them bravely like the Christian soldier it is, with sandstone and leadlight and strong, hardwood beams and hushed evening prayers. Its defiant finger of a steeple has for its nail not a cross but a star. St P's 'thou shalt not' finger is visible to every sinning, guilty soul in Proudie Bay, landbound or watered.

But it's thought by many at the Bay that St P's has lost its way, its true calling, and is now little more than a gathering place for strays from Shack Hill, a 'something old' and

photogenic for fancy weddings, a rustic set for tourists'
cameras and Sunday gossips and shelf-bosomed do-gooders
with their spaniel-eyed husbands at heel, who fuss with
flowers and urns and look forward to funerals.

Marlin Hardwick, however, is not one of these. He has
not once set foot in St P's and when asked one Sunday by a
rare visitor to the Fishcastle if the high sound he heard
ringing across the harbour was a church bell, had replied:
'Of course it's a damned church bell! What other menace
would disturb the weekend peace of a working man but a
church?'

Dr David Poll, who had driven to the Fishcastle to
discuss a paper on the parasites of harbour fish, thought of
his Catholic wife and his Baptist mother and his Sunday-
schooled son and his convented daughter who changed her
mind – and shaved her head to pot-smoke and kneel at the
churchroots of sentenced trees – and himself, trotting along
with it all for the sake of peace and quiet.

'Well, you know, Marlin, I have to say, I don't think it's
all that bad, the sound of bells. I like the sound of bells, any
bell you know, it doesn't have to be in a church. I can't say
this one disturbs me a great deal.' As diplomatically as he
could, he said that. To a degree David enjoyed Marlin's
explosive nature – perhaps because his own was as plain as
bread and milk – but he'd learned over the years not to be
afraid to speak at all. Flashed lightning in the old dun halls
of the museum, he'd thought, when he'd first encountered
Marlin striding along a corridor dressed in white pants and
shirt with head high and a cockish expression as though he

were an admiral performing a surprise inspection on one of his ships – and the man only three hours into his new job. God Almighty! he'd thought at the time. 'Well, if that bell is from the church on the hill then it's the one I passed on the way here. I think it's quaint,' David said.

'It's a mosquito of a church.'

'But nevertheless quite attractive, I think – architecturally speaking, of course. It must be very old to have been made so small.'

'Don't underestimate the wretched pile!' Marlin said. 'A church's size is of no consequence. The bite of a speck of a grass tick can lay a man low.'

'Then I gather you don't regularly take the flesh and the blood on Sundays, Marlin?' It was meant to be a joke but David Poll had never been good with jokes. It was impossible for him to meet Marlin's passions: his blood moved too slow through his veins; he was too soft and timid. And living, as he did, in an inner-city terrace house with his books and his wife's cats and where the only view outside was of Glory Watson's washing hanging on a line on the verandah across the road, and that view only changing in colour if she drip-dried her red skirt, it was difficult to be passionately disturbed by a church bell. A bay sun warmed his back and he smelled grass when he moved his foot and he heard the lap of waves against the sea wall and the sound of gulls and pigeon cooos and the new cicadas of summer. He was, in fact, unable to suppress a yawn of pure serenity. 'You shouldn't let the sound of a bell irritate you, Marlin.'

'And of course it's all but opposite the school . . . Ha! But of course you'd know that!' Marlin continued, as though David was a mute shadow. 'There's usually a church near a school, or worse still, a church *in* a school ... All those inno-cent bleaters jumping in their playground – and a pen with a cross on it ready to round them up! Kidnapping them before they can think for themselves, suffering them to come unto it with bribes of fancy lies and pictures of clean white Christs, all teeth and the wrong-coloured eyes, and little black books, eh, David? What the hell gives them the right to stuff the brains of babies with their fire and brimstone garbage! What the hell gives them the right?'

A vehement spit of a word landed on David Poll's cheek and in his mind he remembered his mother's old adage: 'To acknowledge hell is to believe in heaven', but he didn't repeat it to Marlin. 'I really don't think they imagine they're doing any harm, Marlin, and kids make up their own minds eventually.'

'Not enough of 'em. They set superstitions and fear into them like cement. Those wet geezers with white bands round their Adam's apples and their wandering hands. "Come into my parlour" ... like the spider to the fly, they say to the bleaters,' Marlin said. 'Remember that old rhyme, David? It could have been written for church and children. "Come into my parlour said the spider to the fly ..." but I've taught my little ones the rest of it: "Not today thanks, Master Longshanks, I have other fish to fry!".'

'*Your* little ones, Marlin?'

'My little ones. My maties. The after-schoolies who come here to play real life and listen to stories with guts.'

'Then I take it you'd rather they were "suffered to come unto you" instead?'

'Ha! David, are you telling me I sound like a geezer?' But Marlin grinned and spread his arms. 'Though now you've offered me the role I know I'm a damned sight better value for those youngsters. At least I let them be *them*, and they know they won't burn in hell at the end of the day.'

David Poll looked at Marlin. Here was a man of ordinary height standing taller than it, blue eyes clear with confidence and looking down on the world, and sun filtering through leaves onto his hair, and he was reminded for that moment of a certain statue that towers over Rio de Janeiro. *God Almighty!* he thought.

'Then I take it you're agnostic?'

'Atheist, David! I'm an atheist – an agnostic simply takes a bet each way. I'm not so wishy-washy. Atheist!'

'Absolutely sure?'

'Of course! And as a scientist, surely you are too! How can a disciple of Darwin be anything else?'

'Oh well, you know, I do go to the odd wedding – maybe a christening here and there. Can't say I entirely agree with it all – but it doesn't bother me a great deal, Marlin. Family commitments – that sort of thing. But once, Marlin, I have to tell you, you know, it was a long time ago, I remember I cheated at a game of cards – poker – and I asked a Catholic friend of mine to light a couple of candles at mass, just in case.' David smiled and shrugged at the memory of, what was then, an amusing incident. 'Better sure than sorry, I thought at the time.' He grinned and turned his eyes to the harbour and the boat sails bobbing through it like clean washing, then looked again at Marlin and saw his expression of distaste. The bell had stopped chiming. 'But for the most part, Marlin, I just go along with it on occasions. I don't make a meal of it, you understand.' And he quickly changed the subject as the first of the afternoon clouds cottoned the sky and laid shadows across Marlin Hardwick's rustling, winding, scuttling and bird-calling yard. The Carters' dog yapped half-heartedly at a currawong on a branch above it.

'And that's the other noise I'd like to murder,' Marlin said to the common fence.

But not all of the Reverend Robert Brae's flock were Marlins. There were, still scattered through Proudie Bay, those who were dutiful and pious. There were fishermen and their fish-wives who still prayed for hauls, as generations had prayed before them, and who kept St P's alive with whispered confessions, their quick, bulging marriages, and its font splashing with babies. There were the out-of-town Saturday brides with shy eyes and heads bowed, pretending under their veils never to have seen their man naked. And communions of small girls in true virgin white for the first and only time in their lives. Then outside in the windy churchyard with its gravel path and stones and milkweeds and bushes with leaves combed to one side by gales, artists worked at easels, small children played and picked wild-flowers among the gravestones, and photographers snapped like lightning at christenings and weddings before the wind blew them all away.

And there were the stray, daydreaming roach smokers from Shack Hill who ocean dreamed on rock perches on the cliff side of the yard.

One of these was Kris Carpenter.

When Robert Brae first saw the man from Shack Hill, Kris was perched still, on a rock, staring out to sea. The breeze flapped through his thin hair and through his raggy hemp shirt and pants so that scraps of it flew around his body like pennants at a fete. The man, Robert thought, could have been a very thin embalmed tribute to the sixties: only the flowers were missing and some sort of musical instrument. Robert viewed him from behind with a guilty mixture of sorrow and distaste and impatience.

There had been other times since his appointment to St P's two years ago when his ambivalence towards the Hill people had troubled him; despite having not yet reached the age of fifty, his manner still stiffened in their presence like a prude's. It was his British country church reserve, his safe picket-fenced background he imagined, that was to blame for it. He had thought long and hard upon it and prayed long and hard upon his difficulty with it and had concluded that in every way it was to be a constant test of his capabilities to communicate with each and every one of his flock, and indeed he was determined to try, with all of his God's powers to support him, to do the job he was paid to do. But on that particular occasion, dear God, it had been a Wednesday.

On Wednesdays there were weddings at St P's – special and well-paid picture weddings for Japanese 'Butterflies', as he called them, and with respect to Christian charity he had to try to clear the Hill people away before two-thirty. The strays did not look good in photographs, he'd been told, and they gave a down-at-heel look to the church grounds. Mrs Kerslake of Blossoms Complete Wedding Service had been quite determined on these points. For Robert, it had become a dilemma of insomniac proportions.

'Hello there,' he said to the man's back, with all the enthusiasm of a man greeting a relative he disliked. There was silence and stillness, and the thin body did not move – it seemed to be in some sort of trance. What he'd call meditation I suppose, Robert whispered in the unholy part of his mind, and drug-enhanced, I shouldn't wonder. It occurred to him that to wake the man too suddenly might cause him to leave his soul behind. 'Hello there.' There was the silence of a drawn breath taken, a swirl of wind and the break of a seventh wave on the rocks far below them ... then, from somewhere in the hemp, the crack of a fart.

'Hi.' The man spoke without turning his head – or indeed anything else – at all. 'You're the minister here, right?'

'Yes – I'm Robert Brae.'

'I'm Kris Carpenter. Can you see the fish porpoising?' He didn't look at Robert but pointed to a splash of sea far away to his right, almost as far as the horizon. 'Isn't that a shit of a sight?'

'A *shit* of a sight?'

'Filthy – great – good! You know? Feelgood!'

'Oh, of course,' Robert said, and felt a fool for saying it. Hill language was a haze to him. He clasped his hands behind his back and walked around Kris in an instinctive attempt to mark his territory. 'I have to tell you that I don't exactly know what you mean by "porpoising".'

'It's when fish jump out of the water – when they dance over it.' Kris glanced briefly at the fool who had spoken to him. 'To "porpoise" is to be like porpoises – to jump, to dance, cut through the air over the sea – like fish dancing!'

'Of course,' Robert said again. He could only imagine what substance the man used to enable him to see so far away. Whatever it was, it formed a barrier between them – probably pot. There was always the smell of it around these people. He could not get through to them. It seemed to him that they shared a secret world and he was never going to be allowed through its gate. He could spend a lifetime trying to cut through their fog of pot-secrets and move under the blanket of them and lie where their souls lay. But in the back of his mind he knew that the reason he could not reach them – the truth of the matter – was that he didn't really want to.

'You haven't got a clue, have you?'

'I'm fairly busy right now,' Robert said. 'I really don't have a great deal of time to watch the flight of fish. I have my first wedding at three-fifteen.' There was an edge to Robert's voice that he wished he could have smoothed, but he was only human after all, please God know that, he prayed. 'The fact is, Kris, I need to clear the grounds for our Wednesday weddings. You know how it is – photos and that sort of thing.' *Lame, lame, lame!*, he thought. 'The brides of course are the problem – and Mrs Kerslake – they like to think it's all theirs, this place ... when the time comes.'

'Of course it could be a shark attack.' Kris waved towards the flurry of ocean with a languid, skinny arm, pinched and veined and almost hairless.

'I beg your pardon?'

'It could be a feeding of sharks,' said Kris. 'What do you know about sharks?'

'Not a great deal, I'm afraid.' Robert was already strung tight with impatience. 'And I really don't have the time.'

'You're a Brit, aren't you?'

'Yes – but –'

'Then maybe you should know about sharks if this is where you're going to stay. Those could be sharks out there because sharks don't usually hang around in shallows the way you see in movies. They don't hang around thrashing about with bloody plastic toys in bloody frenzies like *Jaws* – not unless they're old or sick or maybe a bull. Bull sharks don't mind shallows, but the rest will swim quiet for hundreds of sea miles to a place where the food is. It could be sharks feeding out there. You've got a lot to learn.'

'I have a Japanese wedding at three-fifteen.' Robert pulled his sleeve back from his watch.

'Good on you,' said Kris.

'I have to go,' Robert said. 'But look here, I've quite a few young people who come to church.' He continued, on calmer second thoughts, 'I'll tell them what you've just told me about sharks. It's very interesting. They're all keen surfers.'

'Then you'd better tell them something else.' Kris folded

his skinny knees up under his chin. 'Tell them there's a place off the coast of California where they study sharks, and when they want to film them they tow surfboards around. You know why? Because surfboards look like seals to sharks and sharks like feeding on seals more than most stuff. Tell them that.'

'I'll certainly tell them that, too – thank you for sharing that with me – but right now . . .'

'You could save a shark from swallowing something it hates.'

Robert glanced at his watch again. Further up the road he was sure there must be, coming towards St P's, a plumed horse and carriage carrying the first Wednesday bridal couple, closely followed by the van from Blossoms – a procession that had become a familiar sight midweek at St P's. A straggle of school children and their parents had already gathered outside the gate to watch the show.

'Kris, perhaps you'd like to join the others outside the gate and watch our wedding.'

'Shit no!' said Kris. 'Mock-western weddings for Japanese? It's a bad scene – it's a rat's way of making a buck!'

So is the dole if you don't need it! Robert thought, peeved, as he hurried away.

Robert Brae changed into the vesture designed for Wednesdays by Blossoms – long and noncommittal white linen with purple sash. Mrs Kerslake had told him the robes suited his good height. 'And your bones,' she'd said. 'You've got a good face,' she'd said, 'and a fine nose, almost Hawaiian but the wrong colour, but never mind,' she'd said, whatever that meant. He pushed a brush through hair she'd persuaded him to grow down past his ears. He glanced in the mirror and pushed his lips up into a Blossoms smile with his fingers, and at the sound of horse's hooves he moved to the door, head to one side, smiling and fingers tipped together, and waited while Mrs Kerslake cleared onlookers from camera range and had every move of her bowing doll clients photographed. A liveried coachman held the feisty horse, a cream- and caramel-coloured veteran that snorted in anticipation of a day's end. The bride's gown, used only twice before, flashed a Milky Way of diamantés, while the groom, in pinstripes too long at the ankles, looked to Mrs Kerslake before making a single move. Robert thought the first of his brides, despite her finery, looked pained and thick and awkward with a tussock of hair that defied gravity. Mrs Kerslake was very good at making sow's ears into silk purses but every now and then, he'd discovered, she'd found the sow too much for her – but Mrs Kerslake, sister of the organist, mother of the bride, mother of the groom, maid of honour, witness, congregation, dresser, make-ups and hairdos, fussed around the bridal pair, smiling in her tight celebration of blue polyester with its tricky zip that she'd worn to almost every Wednesday wedding for the past six months, as though the couple were the first and last flowers to bloom in a cherry orchard.

After a mercifully brief ceremony the steeple bell tolled twelve times, rung by the driver of the Blossoms van – not a student of the bellringers' craft, it was understood, but a master of timing: twelve chimes rung quick or normal depending on the time available. The twelve bells for 'Butter-flies' was included in the package, as were photos of Robert shaking hands, pecking the bride on the cheek, handing them up to their carriage and patting the horse on the rump. And upon their departure Mrs Kerslake, for the thousandth time, waved her white lace going-away handkerchief and dabbed her dry eyes.

At the gate the horse clopped through ragged cheers of school children, some of whom narrowed their eyes by stretching the skin beside them with grubby fingers, and Robert, who had half an hour to himself before the next wedding, skulked like a schoolboy behind the church and smoked a cigarette. Out of the corner of his eye, he noticed that Kris Carpenter's rock was vacant.

When that Wednesday had ticked and chimed towards its end, after the last of the school children had been driven or had walked home, and after Blossoms had packed and stacked their van, there was a period of stillness and peace that Robert welcomed every bit as much as the wedding horse welcomed the quiet of its stall. It was a time when the sound of waves below him washed cool through his mind and salt-breathed winds were tasted, clean and sharp. It was the feeling of peace that comes when a day begins to fold itself away to rest and it was when Robert allowed an hour or so to stroll through the church garden and its tiny grave-yard. Armed with secateurs he might trim an edge or cut back fearless portulaca that threatened to engulf a midden of sandstone. He'd nip and prune fine-leafed heath and coast rosemary, and weed around wedding bush and flannel flowers struggling near the graves. He is a gardener of limited knowledge but then the sparse beds in their shallow-earthed yard require little skill – the strong survive and the weak are never seen again. It is, to Robert, a garden created with the beauty of simplicity in mind and his task in it is simple. There is, however, one part of the grounds he leaves undisturbed: the shrub that hides the sign on the gatepost. The shrub is where small birds nest, cosied from the elements and predators, and all that is visible of the church's name are the letters that spell St P – deep inside the shrub a bird's nest covers the *ETER'S* that is the rest of its true name. But to Proudie Bay the church's pet-name remains St P's and will be so, even if the bush is blown to sea, birds' nests and all.

On that late afternoon, Robert Brae pruned his way to the graveyard. It was the smallest graveyard he had known in his twenty-year career. There were just five graves and they occupied the only pockets of deep earth in the yard. All the graves were old: the most recent dated 1911 and the oldest, 1896, and it was this, the earliest of the graves, that Robert tended first. Its stone stood away from the others and was protected by a low iron-rail fence and sheltered by a straggle of banksia, pointing away from the wind, and it said in simple script:

My Sara
first a maiden
one year a bride
one hour a mother
and then she died.

And below that,

> *Sweet Alice*
> *one hour my daughter*
> *in God's hands.*

It was this grave Robert tended first, in memory of his own dead wife and the child they might have had, twenty-one years of a mourned lifetime ago. It was on this grave of Sara and Alice he placed flowers he would otherwise have laid on his own wife's grave in another churchyard in the English countryside near Kent.

But at the end of that Wednesday he saw, next to Sara's grave, a child sitting crosslegged and alone and threading a ribbon of yellow weed flowers. She hummed to herself a barely audible sound and appeared to be so absorbed in her flower chain that she was unaware of his presence. It was a solemn child Robert observed, and he judged by her appearance, even though she wore her school uniform, that she was from Shack Hill. Ordinarily he would have been irritated to have his precious quiet hour disturbed but on that occasion he stood very still and watched her with the feeling that she somehow belonged there, linking flowers by Sara's grave.

'Are you all right there, young lady?' He wished his tone had been softer. He had no way with jokes or children. The child, however, did not look up. 'Shouldn't you be home by now?'

'No.' Still making her weed chain and humming.

'Do you live on the Hill?'

'Yes!' She shot an angry glance at Robert with dark eyes.

'Then you should be home by now. Isn't there someone to collect you?'

'I can go home by myself,' she said. Defiant as a salt-air weed was this child, Robert thought. 'Kris came up to get me but I told him to piss off!'

'Where is your mother?'

'She's got the flu.'

'Why didn't you go home with some of your friends from the Hill?'

'They're not my friends.'

'There must be one who is.'

'I just wanted to sit here and watch for a storm.' She went on with her weaving and did not raise her head to him – only pushed hair from her face where the wind had blown it. She licked her fingers and stuck it down behind her ear.

'Why on earth would you want to sit here and watch for a storm?' Robert prayed she wasn't stoned as well.

'This is going to be *my* 'lookout' – like the one in Jen's room.'

Robert became lost in her words at that point. What a poor stick of a child, he thought, but old and knowing and talking Hill talk. 'Why didn't you go home with Kris?' he asked her.

'He's off his head.'

'And why are you sitting here, next to this grave?'

'Mum said Alice was a little baby.' She looked up at him with her serious eyes. 'I come sometimes so she won't get lonely.'

'What's your name?' Robert asked in a voice more gentle than he was aware. He felt a salty wet in his eyes that did not come from the sea.

'Beccy.'

'Beccy what?'

'Just Beccy,' she said.

'Well, just Beccy. I've got to get you home before dark.'

'Just another minute,' she said. 'I've nearly got this finished.' She lifted the flower chain. 'It's for my mum.'

'It's very nice. It will make her feel a lot better ... but what will happen when Kris gets home without you? Won't she be worried?' Robert suddenly wanted to be close to this child but he dared not touch her. She so easily sat beside Sara and Alice, so much at home among the weeds. She looked, sitting there, absorbed in her work, as though she might have opened the grave and come out for a breath of fresh air. She could, in a moment of imagining, be Alice grown older. He even allowed himself for that moment to imagine she might be like the child he and his wife had lost – that lost baby could very well have grown dark-haired and spirited like Beccy. 'Is Kris your father?' *God forbid*, he thought.

'No way!'

'Well then,' Robert said. 'If you told him to go away maybe you don't like to be with him. Maybe you don't feel safe with Kris?' He felt that the question needed to be asked.

'He's just mad, that's all,' she said. 'They call him the Carpenter at home and he tells everybody on the Hill what to do. He thinks he's God or something but Mum says he can't even roll a roach right. He stuffs them too thick.'

Good grief! Robert clasped his hands behind him and marched around her in his territorial way. 'How old are you, Beccy?'

'Nine.'

Nine going on fifty, Robert thought. 'Can I phone your mum? Do you have a telephone?'

'No. She'll just think I'm at Jen's place.'

'And where does she live?'

'She lives in the Fishcastle – you know, the Fishcastle?' She pointed down towards the bay but his blank nod called for the slower words she used with fools. 'The . . . Fishcastle! Hullooo, anyone home?'

'Aaah, you mean the Hardwick's house! Yes. Now I know what you mean, Beccy.' But poor child, he thought. Poor kid. From the frypan of the Hill to the fire of Marlin Hardwick's mad unholy zoo.

'Jen's nice. I might go and live with her one day.'

'I think your mother would miss you a lot.'

'She could come too.' Beccy suddenly stood and started to walk away. Her uniform was crushed and dirty and part of its hem hung at the back. 'I'm going now.'

Robert would like to have held her hand but she clutched the flower chain high in both of them, out of harm's way. He walked with her as far as the roadside. There was a straight-backed independence about her, a defiance in the manner of a child so young that impressed and saddened him. She was a grub of a thing and smelled of the earth, as though she'd been born from it. He liked to think that his God, out of

kindness, had sent the child from the Hill to help him tolerate the rest of them. 'By the way, Beccy. Do you happen
to know what "porpoising" means?'

'Don't you know anything?' She looked up at him
through the circle of dying weeds. 'It's fish dancing! Everybody knows that.'

He stood and watched her, all the way down, until she
reached McKenzie Park and watched her as she walked
towards the path up to Shack Hill. At the bottom of the road
she had turned and looked back at him and he'd waved, but
she hadn't returned his gesture.

The path from the back of McKenzie Park to the Hill had
in no way been the work of a planning authority: it had, in
fact, not been planned at all. It was a climbing, narrow track
that twisted through salt-toughened scrub and, like all true
tracks, had been stamped bare by armies of padding feet:
first by fishermen and lately by Hill people of all kinds – true
spirits, sick spirits, tribal spirits searching for lost directions,
hazed potheads and sots with bruised arms and no courage
and no hope, and the magic rings of their children who
gathered like apple-cheeked windfalls under bushes, sweet
innocents playing games of comfort.

The track to the Hill was worn in parts right down to the
roots of scrub and old stones and shards of shells. It was
edged with sharp grass tufts that barely covered paper, snack
wrappers, plastic bottles – some half-filled with mysterious
substances – a scatter of used syringes and dried patches of
stained grass still smelling of piss. Here and there were

bushes of heath and coast rosemary, the same plants that grew in the churchyard, but here by the track they seemed abandoned and tired and sad. Beccy touched one with her flower chain, to let it know she was there.

At the top of the track where the wind blows strong from the ocean and where there is a fence at the edge of Gap cliff, Beccy turned her head away so she couldn't see it. She held her head to the left and her eyes down and tried not to be afraid of the crash and pound of the ocean as it tried to smash its way through the rocks below her. The wind blew her hair and whipped her skirt around her legs and she felt a sting of sea on her skin, but she hunched over with her school bag bobbing on her back and walked doggedly on. She did not run. She never tried to run when the ocean was attacking the cliffs because she knew that if she did her legs would move slower and slower, as they did in the bad night-dreams when a great, green wall of water climbed from the bottom of the cliff, higher than clouds, and curled towards her until she was cowering under it and losing her breath and waiting to die. So she did not run but bent her body over so that all she could see was the dirty track – but the track was dry land at least, and when she was frightened it was dry land as sweet in her eyes as the green grass at the Fishcastle.

'Don't you get me, you *sea*! Don't you get me!' was the mantra Beccy Holt chanted to the track on her way home. She would like to have put her hands over her ears, but the flower chain was using them. 'Don't you, don't you, don't you!' she said in time with her steps and in time with the wave's crash in fearful sevens. 'Don't you!' she said, until she saw her shack.

'God, where've you been?' Miriam propped herself on an elbow as best she could, every movement, every strained breath, producing a cough. She lay on top of her bed in the draughty, two-roomed ramshack that she and Beccy shared with the woman called Crystal. There was a rusting caravan outside, leaning against it as if its purpose was to hold the shack upright.

Miriam's skin had a pale and liverish tinge to it, her hair was stringy and damp and her eyes were smudged grey. She pulled a length of toilet roll and dabbed at her roughed, red nose. Her voice sounded swollen. 'Bec, why are you so late?'

'I walked home after I did something.' Beccy slipped her bag from her shoulders and stroked her mother's arm. 'I was all right. I made you this.' The chain of flowers had suffered for their windblown journey home.

'Nice, Bec, thanks. But . . . ' Her coughing was sharp and sudden.

'I made it next to Alice's grave. It took a while,' the child said, and tears dripped down Miriam's face.

'But Kris was supposed to pick you up, I've been really worried. Didn't you see Kris?'

'No,' she lied. 'But I saw a bride.' She pulled back the corners of her eyes to slits as the others had done. 'It was one of those horse-and-cart brides with feathers. Do you want me to make you some soup?'

'Yes, Bec . . . .Yes, sweetie.' She was crying now. 'Make

your mum some soup. Get a can of mushroom and . . .'

'Don't cry, Mum.'

'I'm not. It's just the flu.' Miriam blew her nose and took as deep a breath as her congestion allowed.

'Do you want me to tell Jen you're sick?'

'No.'

'Why?'

'She's a worrier. She'd fuss too much.'

Beccy had never wanted Jennifer Hardwick to see their dump of a shack; it was something deep in her heart she had not wanted, but in the wisdom of her child mind she sensed that help might be needed – more help, she thought, than the oil of wintergreen burning heavy as a shroud in the room, the stained bottle of herbals on the floor next to the tissue box – and Crystal.

'Maybe she could get some real pills or something.'

'No, Bec. Just make me some nice, hot soup and then find Crystal.'

'But she doesn't know anything, Mum!'

'Beccy . . . oh, my God, my head feels like a watermelon.'

'I can look after you myself! Crystal only makes things worse.' Miriam was too weak and her head ached too painfully to argue. She lay back onto her pillow and Beccy picked up the bucket filled with used paper. She filled the water glass from a bottle by the bed and, like a little mother herself, pulled the cover up to her patient's chin, smoothed the damp forehead and whispered, 'I won't be long.'

'Be careful lighting the stove, then. Find something to stand on so you can see what you're doing – and don't put any milk in the soup, just water.' Her voice squeezed its way through a gauze of congestion.

Beccy took a can from the cupboard at the foot of her own bed in the second room and went to the caravan that was the common kitchen and Crystal's space.

The gas-bottled stove top in the caravan was second hand and cranky and did not always behave as it should. Sometimes there was barely enough flame to heat a can of beans and at other times it would flare like a firework and would have to be turned off altogether. Beccy stood on a milk crate and lit the stove, then emptied the soup into a saucepan. That afternoon the stove played a decent game and while the soup heated she buttered and honeyed a piece of bread for herself. She washed a scuttle of small cockroaches down the sink drain, tidied away cups and glasses that Crystal had left like litter around the van, and emptied Crystal's joint butts from a chipped, porcelain tile with its green painted peacock that Beccy had found near the park. The peacock tile had been one of her few precious possessions. She thought for once she'd hidden it where Crystal could never find it. Beccy would never understand the Hill rule that those who had must give to those who had not. Miriam told her it was something that happened in *true communities*. And as part of a *true community*, Beccy should not mind about the tile and she should not have howled like a wild thing when the Warner kid took two of her dolls just because it had smashed its own – Beccy would never understand *true communities* if she lived to be a thousand. She thought it was crap.

But early summer evenings when the light was soft and

the hums and smells of the bay were drawn up and away to sea to make room for new days were good times to look down and over the Hill. While she stirred the soup, Beccy saw through the dirty window of the van smoke from wood stoves ghosting through its poor scrub and it gave the Hill a veil less harsh than during the day. From her perch on the milk crate, she watched late birds flying low, up through the wind to their nests, and the west sun dipping low and red from the last of its reflection in Proudie Bay windows. Beyond the base of the Hill she could see part of the bay, furling and closing down for the drowsing night. And to the right of it there was just a glimpse of the Fishcastle. She wondered if Jen was standing at her 'lookout' and maybe watching her.

In the old days, Shack Hill, protected from developers by the difficulty of its terrain, had evolved as a squat for weekend fishermen: out-of-towners who hammered together basic shacks and fished from the cove, the bay, and even risked a Jacob's ladder down the cliff face to fish from the rocks below. And Proudie Bay councillors, poor-sighted from reading the labels on whisky gifts and pound notes, turned their blind eyes to them and their shelters, big enough for fishing tackle, bed and booze and sea stories and fish tales and the biggest lies in the world, but too small for wives or lovers, unless they were mermaids. And the councillors kept their eyes blind until the two sons of Dr Marcus Hamlyn, one seventeen and one nineteen, drowned off the ocean rocks, one trying to save the other. Marcus had been the first to abandon his shack and then, when the council forced open its eyes again and banned rock fishing and drowning, one by one the shacks stood empty but for crusts of dried gut and scale and nets and knotted lines.

There is no plaque on Shack Hill to tell the story of the sons of Marcus Hamlyn; nor is there a plaque to mark the day that Henri Duchamps leased land and built a yurt on the Cove Beach side two years later, had a powerline strung for a fee and town water run up for another, and was the first to open the Hill as a squat for other out-of-towners whose weekends came every day of the year.

'Is it okay?'

'Yes, Bec.' Miriam felt better, not so much after hot soup but from the relief of having her daughter safe home. She lay back against the pillow and her damp hair strands felt cool, as if she'd been caught in a torrent of sweat. The pillowcase was stained with her fever. 'I don't feel so hot.'

Beccy wiped her mother's cracked lips with tissue paper even though there was nothing to clean away. She stroked the back of Miriam's hand. 'You've broken your nail,' she said. 'Do you want me to file it?'

'No. It's okay. You're a good little kid, Beccy.' Miriam shivered. 'See if you can find my purple wrap. It might be in the van.' And she pulled what covering she had up to her chin.

'Have you still got a headache?'

'Only some – it feels a bit better.' Wind whistled through the scrub outside and the sound of it through cracks in the shack had grown louder.

'Do you want a tablet?'

'No, Bec. It's all right.'

'I can run down the shop.'

'It's too late for you to run to the shop, Bec.' Miriam's eyes had begun to focus away from their feverish stars and dots. 'I just want to get dry and warm,' she said. 'Try and find some dry clothes and something to put over the mattress and the pillow.'

'Why don't we have any proper sheets for the beds, Mum?'

'We will one day.' Miriam coughed loose and full. She spat into paper. 'Just find some dry things, Bec – and my wrap.'

Beccy took the cover from her own bed and her pillow-case. She found a blouse and skirt in the wash basket then went to the van and rummaged through the pile on Crystal's bed. There was no sign of the purple wrap but Beccy knew in her mind who'd taken it. She dragged Crystal's blanket from the bed and cared less that it caused the heap of mess to fall to the floor.

'Couldn't find the wrap, Mum. I bet Crystal's got it.' She helped Miriam change her clothes and smooth her damp bedding. Then she threw the blanket over her and tucked it in.

'Where did you get that, Bec?'

'Off Crystal's bed.' Beccy grinned. 'I dragged it off her bed and all her stuff fell on the floor.'

'Beccy!'

'She won't care. She took my tile and I took her old

blanket! Like you said, you wanted a blanket and she had a blanket so she's giving it, okay?' The child tucked the stained green wool around her mother but her nose wrinkled at the stink of it. It smelt of old smoke and sweat and dead things that would be there until it rotted. She was grateful that her mother's nose was too blocked to be sickened by it. Beccy wished it could have been like the bedcovers in Jen's room, clean and proper and smelling of sun, or like a fleeting memory of things in her grandmother's house in Brisbane, where breezy curtains flapped white at the windows and soft wool floors that had felt so good against her knees and toes. Picture memories that came to her in the flash of an unexpected second.

Miriam slid down into the bed, limp with the exhaustion of a fever passed. She breathed slow and deep into her clearing lungs. She could barely speak above a whisper.

'Go to Leah Morrison, Bec – she'll give you something to eat. Go to the fire dance after that, if you want, Bec – I'm just too tired. I'm sorry. You'll have to look after yourself.'

'It's okay, Mum. You go to sleep.'

'Don't be late home, Beccy.'

'Okay. I'll be all right.'

'Don't take any bullshit.'

'I'll be okay.'

'I love you, Beccy.'

Beccy would rather not have gone to the fire dance – especially this one, organised by Kris to celebrate his own birthday. When Crystal had asked her why she didn't like the fire dances Beccy had told her she thought they were only for dickheads like Crystal and Kris. But on that night she'd gone for three reasons. She was hungry and knew that Leah Morrison would have lentil stew, she wanted her mother to rest quiet and she wanted to see if Crystal was wearing the purple wrap.

Since they'd come to live on the Hill she had been to two fire dances with her mother and she had felt out of place, self-conscious and uncomfortable – and deep inside her afraid, though she never allowed her fear to show.

'I think he's mad,' she'd said to Miriam on the first occasion. 'Why are they all painted up like Indians?'

There'd been coven rings of children running around a bonfire like small flames themselves, naked, their faces and bodies painted with dreaming symbols of foreign design, and ribbons tied to their ankles flew out like May Day reds when they spun around. There'd been men chanting like native Americans with feathers and stripes, and women dressed or undressed any way they liked. Away from the painful sparks of fire, Tim Love and Henri Duchamps played flute and drums like zombies, with their mouths open and tongues working like demented frogs. No one laughed. Not even the children.

'I hate this, Mum,' Beccy had said. 'I wish we could go back to Grandma's.'

On that Wednesday night the fire was well alight when Beccy went to it. She'd eaten with the Morrison kids and now she was looking for Crystal. Red-winged sparks flew around her hot as Hades. Children juggled hot potatoes and snatched bread from a sliced pile on the ground. A few had begun to dance. Babies crawled, left to themselves in their own wet worlds, and communal women – some bare-breasted, sweating oil in the heat – moved from one group to another, gossiping in the way of the women of Proudie Bay and indeed of all the women of the wide world, though the Hill women would not like to have been told that what they did was not extraordinary.

Not far from the edge of the bonfire, Crystal sat in the low fork of a tree flashing colour in the strobe lights of flames. Her bare feet were crossed, she nursed a can of Vodka mix, she grinned down at Beccy like the Cheshire in Wonderland and the purple wrap trailed filthy and spoiled from her shoulders. Beccy could see that it had been torn. Crystal's mouth was curled, dripping in the wake of alcohol, and in her eyes Beccy recognised the dead brown expressionless flakes of dope. She stood under the tree with her hands on her hips.

'You better give back Mum's wrap, Crystal!' she shouted. 'Right now!'

Crystal looked down and focused as best she could with her tired face and its second-hand eyes. 'Get stuffed, Bec,' she slurred. She lifted the can to her mouth but the interruption had put her off balance and she dropped it to the ground. 'Shit!' she said.

'Anyway, I took your blanket for Mum. I pulled it off your bed and everything fell on the floor.'

'You leave my stuff alone, you little bitch.'

'You took Mum's wrap.'

'So?'

'So I took your blanket.'

'Get lost!' Crystal rummaged her hands around her body with the sharp movements of a monkey picking for nits but not finding any. 'Oh Jesus!' she said.

'The blanket stinks, anyway,' Beccy said. 'You're dirty, Crystal.'

Crystal tried to spit down on the child but instead suddenly urinated in a quick, dense stream that splashed foul dustballs onto Beccy's legs. The child stood and looked up with a mixture of disgust and wonder. She didn't see the tree. She'd erased the tree, and saw Crystal suspended above her in the night sky like a wet witch; a stinking witch sitting astride a shaft of air – and if there had been a wall of water behind her she could have been part of a nightmare.

'Go up the van and get us another can, Bec.' Crystal wound her voice down to a whine. 'Go on, Beccy, pleeese.' Her moods never swinging – just ups and dives.

'Get it yourself.' Beccy kicked the dropped can into the scrub.

Somehow, as the child watched her, Crystal, still flickering red and gold, slipped from her shaft of air and jumped onto the dust. Beccy stood her ground. It did not occur to her to run away. She watched Crystal's eyes. She was mesmerised by her eyes. They looked to her like red splinters – the sort you get in bad colour photos. Crystal grabbed Beccy's arm in a crab-claw vice. Her legs were unsteady and she swayed and Beccy swayed with her. Mouthing obscenities she shook the child, picked up her own pee mud and rubbed it into Beccy's face, then in the seconds that remained of that minute, she dragged the child to the fire.

'Here's your fuckin' shawl,' she screamed at her, and threw it into the fire. And Beccy, already crying, ran to the edge of the flames and dragged the smoking, tattered thing out. She stamped on the smoulder until the smoke had gone. She faced Crystal like a small, fisted fury, and cried, 'I hope you die soon,' then, still sobbing, ran up the path to her shack. Crystal yelped behind her like a banshee and pretended to give chase.

'Give it a rest, Crystal!' someone shouted.

Crystal sank to the ground and wept. 'Jesus!' she said. 'Oh, Jesus!'

'Go smash your brains out somewhere else,' shouted another.

Tim Love put his flute down and rubbed his smoky eyes. 'It never used to end up like this in the old days,' he said, knowing no one heard – or cared.

Beccy crept into the shack. She rubbed her eyes with the heel of her hands. She heard soft, congested snoring from her mother's bed then fell, exhausted, onto her own. And despite tears streaking through the filth on her face and the smell of her and her scorched feet and arms, she held the purple wrap close to her and was asleep even as she tried to cover herself with a tie-dyed sarong.

In the light of morning – in the soft, buzzing sea-breezed light of morning when it was impossible to think that such a night had preceded it, Miriam walked, weak-kneed and wispy, to Beccy's bed and looked down on a child she barely recognised. She was scratched and filthy, streaked and smelling of piss and fire, and curled into a ball tight as a possum. The sight of her daughter made her moan. And through emotion and weakness her tears flowed again. Shaking, she stroked the child's hair until she woke. Beccy opened her eyes and smiled.

'You better now, Mum?'

'I'm – I'm all right, Bec.'

'Don't cry any more, Mum.'

'But what happened? What's happened to you?' Beccy uncoiled. 'My God! Your feet are burned, Beccy!' She cradled the child in her arms. 'Oh God.'

'I found Crystal, Mum.' Beccy grinned.

'What?'

'I found Crystal. She had your purple wrap.' She still grinned despite everything. 'I bet myself she'd have it but it got messed up.' Beccy pulled the ruined thing from under her and handed it to Miriam. 'Maybe we can fix it up, okay?'

'I don't care about it, Bec, look at you – I mean – what happened last night? You've got burns!' Miriam was at the cupboard at the foot of Beccy's bed, looking for aloe vera. 'Your feet must be hurting like hell.' A blister was forming under Beccy's right heel.

'Nothing happened.'

'You smell like a toilet. Did anyone hurt you last night?'

'Nobody can hurt me, Mum.'

'You sure, Beccy? You look as though you've been

howling your eyes out.' Miriam began to wipe the filth from her child and replace it with cool green aloe. 'Everything looks burnt.'

'I just got too close to the fire. It was an accident. I didn't cry.'

'Bec?'

'I never cry.' She was not so much ashamed of the lie as she was of showing weakness to Crystal. 'Can we go back to Grandma's, Mum?'

'Oh God, Bec!'

'Well, maybe go to Jen's place, then?'

'I don't think I could walk that far today.'

'Have a good rest and then maybe later.' Beccy sat on the edge of the bed. 'I'll make you some tea and then you'll feel better.'

'You can't walk around on those feet.'

'Yes I can.' Beccy stood gingerly and squeezed her eyelids together. 'See?' She limped towards the van. It was all too much for Miriam. She sat exhausted at the table and covered her face with her hands.

'You're staying home today, Bec, with me.'

'Okay.'

At the bottom of the van steps, Beccy smelled the sick. It was strong enough to make her stomach heave. Inside the van she found Crystal moaning over the electric jug. She was the colour of death's last breath and her eternal blue sarong was creased and stained, back and front. She opened a dead eye just enough to see Beccy.

'You better turn the jug on if you want it to boil.' Beccy

tried to blot out the smells by breathing through her mouth but the foulness was a living thing, strong enough to penetrate skin pores and tongues. 'You burnt me last night.'

'I'm sorry, Bec, okay?' She tried to lift her head. 'I'm sick, Beccy.'

'I don't care.'

'Oh, shit!'

'Shit yourself!' said the child.

Chapter Six

AND HERE IS THE COCK THAT CROWED IN THE MORN

Beside the road to Proudie Bay, between the lighthouse and St P's, sits a huddle of shops and a bus stop. The shops are old (except for a small chain supermarket, circa 1979) and the bus-stop seat has worked its way out of the footpath on one side, giving it a list to port. There is a chemist, a butcher, a greengrocer, a real estate agent and the Spendrite Supermarket. There is, further down, standing alone, a small window with a door to the left of it that displays tie-dyed fabric, pewter dragons, Indian sandals, whale songs and cheap toe rings, but the established shops do not consider this to be a business of any substance and mostly they ignore it.

The shops above Proudie Bay cosy together in a smuggish small-town way – in the way of shops and their keepers in all the world of small towns.

Outside the supermarket stands a gossip of old
Proudies – women of all shapes but with scopes for eyes and
spectacles thick enough to study microbes and sharp enough
to see everything and ears keen enough to hear to the edge
of the earth. They're waiting for the bus to the Bay but they
hope it will not come on time. They stand on their strong
pins with their suds and sun-dried arms plaited across their
chests and their mouths moving tight and disapproving
against the worn hinges of their jaws. They are gathered with
their plastic shopping bags, full of 'specials', arranged around
their feet like litters.

'The trouble is,' says one of them in her bible voice, 'the
trouble is – and you mark my words here – all Gulliver Hardwick has to do is flap those eyelashes up and down and grin
his grin and he gets away with anything he wants.' She juts
her chin to the road and moves one of her litter with the toe
of her shoe. 'Male, female, the half 'n' halfs – doesn't make
a damn difference who he bats his eyes to.'

'What's he done this time?' asks another. 'And let me tell
you every time I hear his name I thank the Lord he's not
mine.

'Same here!'

'What's he done?'

'He ran the red light on the crossing outside Crainbrook
Post Office. Amy Pitts says if the queue hadn't been that long
inside she would have been on it. He got a caution.'

'A caution?'

'That's all.'

'You think I'm surprised?'

'Well, you wouldn't be, would you?'

'I'm not.'

'Now I'm giving you one guess who picked him up . . .'

'Stevie Thomas?'

'Constable Steven Thomas.' They share a look with the underside of the shops' awning. 'Probably got a bloody love note for a ticket.'

'I'm damned if I know why Stevie sucks up to Hardwick; he's not that way. Unless he's changed sides since last time we talked.'

'He wouldn't have time to change, Patty. I mean, he hasn't worked his way through the women yet.'

'He's too wild for my liking.'

'And too pretty for mine.'

'Nothing but trouble from top to bottom.'

'Especially the bottom.'

'Thank the Lord he's not ours,' they say in a Proudie chorus, and unplait their arms as the bus to Proudie Bay comes into view, late enough.

The trouble is – the trouble was – that on that particular day, Gulliver Hardwick had been riding home to the Fish-castle and at about three-ten in the afternoon had driven through a red light at the post-office crossing with not much more on his mind than the vibration of his new, old BSA A65 650 cycle against the inside of his thighs and crotch. He'd given the bike full rein to beat the hour when the slow milk mothers in their 'Mum's taxis' tooled around the school, gathering children. Not much more than that on his mind, except maybe how good he looked in his black-visored helmet, the blue-tint shades across his eyes, and the hand-me-down Stagg Brando leather jacket streaked with battle scars that Max Bank of Western Cycles had given him after they'd restored the vintage British bike together, and that Gull had bought barely a month before for just over four thousand dollars – twenty-five hundred of it being a loan from Jennifer, which he assured her (and she even half-believed) he would pay back.

Having raced through the crossing light – which he would swear to the end of his life was amber all the way – Gull had slowed to a saintly speed and had displayed the very paragon of riding skills as he watched Steve Thomas ahead of him slide out of a patrol car, ready to flag him down. He smiled inside the privacy of his shades. He knew Steve would be blushing. He knew the notebook in his hand would be trembling. And he knew that behind him, up the road, outside the supermarket, would be the old Proudies watching them, like a beached pod with their mouths flapping and their fins folded.

Poor bugger, he thought, as he pulled into the kerb.

'Hi there, constable,' Gull had said as though he'd never seen Steve before. One booted leg on the road, steadying him, and the bike still humming, impatient. He lifted his visor. 'I swear to God that was no run out, constable. I swear to God I made the crease before the red!' He slid off his dark glasses, easing them away from one side, then the other, so he could look Steve full in the eyes – and Steve could look into his own.

'Everybody saw you, Hardwick,' the constable said. Steven

Thomas, as fair as Gull was dark but taller, spoke quietly. He crossed one foot over the other and lowered his eyes away from Gull's, not at all in the way of an arresting officer of the law, but Steve's cheeks still burned in memory of a late night in the McKenzie Park toilet block when Gull had burst, gagging on drink and bile, into a stall already occupied by Constable Thomas, a friend, and their two cocks at play. Gull's jaws were already yawning and he'd thrown up over the two of them, sending them shrinking and wailing to the basins. But there was never a word spoken about it afterwards. Never a word. Steve had known the incident had been filed for future reference – never a word. And Steve had thought, in the humiliation of the day that followed, Just knowing what the shit knows is worse than words. But he said to Gulliver, 'I've got to book you. I've got to do it this time!'

'Then you go right on, Stevie! You throw the bloody book at me. Give me a lecture, Stevie – I'll hang my head in shame, honest to God!' He glanced back up to the shops and saw the thin, grey line staring down at them, arms crossed tight across their breasts, settling back and ignoring the buses. 'Do it right, Stevie. They're all watching. Here, licence, rego – get as tough as you like, Stevie!' Gull had already hung his head in a mockery of shame and slumped his shoulders to the extent that he was staring down below his crotch. He was grinning like an ape.

And when Constable Thomas, almost numb with embarrassment, did as he was told, Gulliver, in a final show, held out his hand, palm down. 'Now you slap my hand good and hard, Constable Thomas – that'll really make me see the error of my ways.'

'Ah, for Christ's sake get the shit out of here!' Stevie hissed at him. 'It won't always be me to pick you up. It won't always be me!'

Gull swung his leg over the saddle.

'But I hope it is always you.' He kissed his lips together. 'I'd be a mess if it wasn't you, Stevie. I'd have bad dreams.'

As he rode away he glanced in the rear mirror and saw that Constable Thomas was scribbling hard in his book, hard and fast, just as though it meant something. But of course it didn't. It meant nothing at all. To the old Proudie women who stood watching until the bike and the patrol car were out of sight, it meant nothing at all. They simply saw one rolling off quietly, tail between his legs, and the other gunning to a roar loud enough to scatter the pigeons window-shopping for scraps.

More of Gulliver's theatre of the streets – disapproved of – played to a packed house.

There is a point on that road, a slight dogleg to the left, where it leaves the high plateau and begins the steep slope down to Proudie Bay. At this point there is a vista so suddenly spectacular that even the oldest of the Bay residents slow and catch their breaths, excited by the knowledge that part of what lies below them is their home. The air changes and is flavoured by the sea, and light paints moving pictures on the sandstone cliffs. To the left, cloud shadows brush gentle across rooftops, ancient Moreton Bay fig trees and harbour boats; and to the right, the ocean carries ships like toys to China or Alaska or Xanadu. It is possible to sense all of this from that point on the road. It is possible even for Gull Hardwick to sense these things, and he regrets having to shield himself against the smells and tastes and the salt wind, for to feel these things in the face of the wind against his own is one of the true, pure pleasures of riding.

As Gull turned into the Sandpath, however, the power of the day began to leave him. He felt the lump of his own home tighten in his belly and there was a familiar dryness in his mouth. The vibrations of his machine slowed to nothing as he pulled the engine back to a purr. The elation he had felt until then, and the aggressive smell of heat and fuel, disappeared into the air with no more potency than a dull fart. It was the end of the day, and the hours between the end of his days at the Fishcastle and the beginning of his nights were hard times. He was in no hurry to reach the gate; he needed to be home for something but it wasn't home sweet home. He cut the engine and walked the bike along the road. From one of the new houses came the sound of Axel Rose's 'Stairway to Heaven', loud enough to reach the sea – so loud it drowned a cat fight and the yapping Carters' dog. Up ahead he could see Bindi Hope talking to Hughie Pheiffer while she hosed the garden, but when she saw Gull she turned the other way. And Hughie, always out, always hunting – the eyes and ears of the Sandpath, bandy-hopped down to Gull, rocking from side to side, grinning and winking and scratching the dry creek beds of his armpits and the brown skin of his chest, dry enough to shed. Hughie came close and Gull

159

caught his smell: stale sweat and randy grease and old salt and something like dead kelp. Hughie with his antennas and eyes all over him and his little ball of a head full of bottoms. He'll never die, Gull thought, or maybe he has died and this is his corpse ... he couldn't stink any worse.

'Hi, Hughie. Doing the rounds?' Gull asked, resigned to it.

'Can't hear m'self think,' he shouted over the music. 'Bloody *hoons*!' He pointed back with his thumb.

'He's only twelve, that kid.'

'I'd give him twelve!'

Suddenly the noise stopped and the cat fight, startled by silence, stopped too. The Carters' dog still yapped at nothing at all.

'Been round the Cove lookin' up bikini bottoms, Hughie?'

'They don't come any better than the Cove,' he said. 'How'd the British ride today? Get anyone strapped to the back seat, boy? Get a couple of lady arms wrapped around your leather?'

'Not today, Hughie.'

'In my day,' he slid his mouth close to Gull's face and breathed foul on it. 'You listen to what I'm tellin' you. In my day we used to cut a slit along the side of the pillion seat, slip in a tennis ball, sew it back up, and when the girlies rode that, boy, they'd be breathing hot in your ear and have their knees up so quick you'd have to stop some place and put 'em out of their misery. You want to try that, boy.' Hughie hitched what was left behind his flies. 'That gets 'em going.'

Gull couldn't help laughing. He could never picture Hughie Pheiffer looking any different, smelling any different, being any other way, and he could not imagine, as hard as he tried, any female in an entire universe of women desperate for a quick roll on the side of a road with him, tennis balls or not. Gull could hardly believe he'd once had a wife. The word is he got her through a dating agency that specialised in women half-blind with no sense of smell.

'Look, I'll see you later, okay?' Gull wheeled away from him.

'You remember what I tell you, boy – about that ball in the seat.'

'Hard to forget that one, Hughie,' as he walked on, up the Sandpath.

The old man scuttled off in the other direction and Gull guessed he was headed for the video store, but at the corner he saw him whispering old dirt in the ear of Vic Perker. Tennis balls in bike seats, Gull had no doubt, for they both looked his way and laughed. Gull grinned and gave them a thumbs up. He walked briskly now. He unlatched the gate of fourteen and rolled the bike quietly around the side towards the garden shed. He wasn't hurrying to be home. He needed a drink.

From the shed he heard a hum of voices. He knew that the after-schoolies would be settled in their half-circle on the harbour front grass listening to his father – wide-eyed disciples of his hot air and bullshit – and Marlin there, spreading them with vanities, buttering them with his tongue.

The dryness in Gulliver's mouth had sunk to his belly and there was a dull, gnawing pain in his right side. He wheeled the bike into the shed and parked it where it did not disturb cracked shelves, ruins of terracotta pots, glass jars and rusted trowels that lay in the place where his mother had propagated cuttings and seed. His plan had been to give one side of the shed to a sort of memorial for her – a memory bench – and the other side to his own rags and oils and tools. Never did one side disturb the other. Only once were the two sides of the shed remarked upon, and his explanation barely scratched the surface of their true meaning. He had arranged the mother side in a particular way from images in distant memories of her, when he had stood in the potting shed by her side, while she worked and hummed, tugging her skirt, handing her little fists of soil, being given a seed to plant in a pot of his own. On the floor, under the corner of a shelf, a small, broken pot lay with dead soil and gravel spilled from it and full of web. He'd let it lie there for he thought he remembered a day when she'd suddenly cried out and let the pot slip from her hand. The rest of the floor, however, he kept clean for the sake of his bike. Jennifer was the one who'd once remarked upon the altered state of the shed. She'd come to see the bike for the first time and she'd shouted, 'How *could* you push Mother's things around like that – push them to one side like that – how *could* you!' And he had just said quietly, 'They were in the way, is how.' But the shed was his, now. The potting shed was now the bike shed and only he had the key to the padlock.

From the inside of an ancient can labelled *Castrol* he took a half of vodka. He briefly toasted the mother side then swallowed until the dry in his belly disappeared into a burn of liquid that made him wince with gut pain. But he knew that in a few minutes he would feel strong enough to walk past his father's grass playhouse, past the audience, and down the steps to the harbour and the dinghy cave. He capped the bottle and slid it back into its hide. He flicked dust from his bike's wheels with cheesecloth, hung his jacket and helmet and boots on their hooks, stepped outside and locked his shed.

Marlin sat with a tortoise in his lap, a lizard in his right hand and seven children at his feet. He was dressed only in shorts even though the wind had turned southerly and a quilt of dark cloud spat a warning.

'Well now, look who's come to visit us schoolies.' Marlin's glance was flinty and his voice had an edge to it and Gull guessed that some part of the day had not suited him. The man called over small heads, 'I do believe it's our brave Gulliver.' One of the boys whistled through a new gap in his teeth. 'And what's our Gull been up to today?' Marlin addressed the children.

'He's been working, that's what he's been up to.' Gulliver stayed where he stood so his eyes would not betray the secret of the bottle.

'And where has he been working?' Marlin looked at him.

'The bike shop.'

'Banksy's cycles and bikes and things that roar in the wind,' Marlin told them.

You bloody clown, Gull thought.

'So! Who wants to hear what our Gulliver does for Mr Banks?' Marlin asked the nodding, big-eyed children. 'At Banksy's our Gulliver puts bikes together from a thousand bits. Clever. Then he polishes the heads of cylinders till those cylinders can see their faces and he shines up the spokes of wheels so bright you can't look at 'em in the sun. Is that right too, Gulliver?'

Gull, sick of it, folded his arms and looked out across the water.

'Are we right?'

'Whatever –'

'How many hours did he give you this time?' Marlin asked. His voice was suddenly normal and the question disconcerting because of it.

'Six.'

'You get paid, Gull?'

'Of course I got paid,' Gull said 'What do you think!' But of course he lied, for every hour he worked for Max came off the cost of his bike.

'Then alleluia! Let's hope our Gulliver gets to shine Mr Banks's bikes forever and ever amen!'

Gull wished he hadn't spat on the grass at that moment. Fourteen small eyes and two old slits of anger watched him spit on the grass and, uneasy about it, he pushed the blob to earth with his bare foot. Small eyes watched Marlin and watched Gulliver, loving it – a dramatic scene played only on occasions, and all the better for it.

'What're you going to do to him, Marlin?' a small voice asked.

'Well, since our Jen's not home yet we'll tell Gull to make Marlin's coffee. How's about that?'

'*Shit, no!*' Gull strode off towards the steps. 'I'm going fishing.'

'And he can take the rest of his drinking spit with him,' shouted Marlin, '. . . and his *bad word* and give 'em to the sea to wash clean!'

Gull started down the steps to the rocks. He didn't look back.

'You think I didn't know that was drinking spit?!' Marlin shouted behind him. 'We could smell it soon as it hit the grass!'

On page 171 in *The Book of Water*, one of the Fishcastle's bibles, the reader is taught that 'the height of harbour waves depends mainly on the strength and duration of the wind, and the fetch or distance the waves have run . . .'

But below the jutty and outside the dinghy cave the waves that splashed against the rocks seemed not to have run very far at all, despite the southerly. The wind had steadied itself to a stiff breeze but the water was still grey and had a heavy look to it. The tide was high enough to soak Gull's jeans to the knees when he waded to the cave and he ignored the prick of rock shells on the soles of his feet. Inside, the dinghy slapped its buffered sides against the stone wall on small peaks of tide while Gull loaded it with fishing tackle, bait and wet-weather gear. He left the four-stroke engine clear of the water and set oars. It was one of those days when he needed to savage his way through the harbour – to labour through it and pull and strain and sweat the tension and frustration out of him. At these times the easy pulse of the motor made him want to scream. Before he untied the dinghy he felt behind a rock below the mooring ring and put a bottle he'd hidden there in the tackle box. It was one bottle of half-a-dozen cellared in the cave – one bottle of more than that cellared all over the property and beyond it, hidden so well from Marlin it made him laugh. He had a network of secrets, caches all over the Fishcastle, around the yard, amongst the rocks and even under the harbour in a fish trap. He lied easily about his home drinking and the belief in his lies made him proud. Marlin bred good liars – and one cunning drunk.

He pushed the dinghy out safe across the rocks and slid into it easily, with no splash and little sound, as though it was a second skin. He rowed away from the calm of the windward shore and out across the chop, grunting with the effort of every quick pull, and he did not pause until he was almost at Greys Point and out of the sight of Marlin. Only then did he anchor, set a line and unscrew the top from the bottle. The chill of the late sea wind cut across him hard. Like a smack. Like a kiss.

From the eaves of its meathook tree on the fringe of the driveway a butcherbird flew. It was startled by a child running to the harbour front. Jennifer closed the gate behind Miriam, who still moved weakly after her illness.

'They won't be there now,' Jennifer called to Beccy. 'It's nearly five. The children have to be home by five.'

'But Marlin's still here,' said the child. 'I can smell him.'

Miriam laughed. 'Beccy? Excuse me? You can smell him? What does he smell like?'

'Coffee and fish.'

From the side door Jennifer saw her father down by the carp pond with two strays. She tried to herd her friends inside without him noticing but Beccy broke loose and ran.

'See?' she shouted back to them. 'I told you.'

'Well, blow me down, if it isn't our Jennifer at last,' Marlin said. 'And she's brought the two pretty ladies with her.'

'What are they still doing here?' Jennifer pointed to the two small children. 'They should have been home ages ago.'

'All our clocks stopped,' he said to his leftover audience. 'All the clocks in the world stopped and we won't know the time until the moon comes up.'

Beccy laughed loudly, delighted to have even a scrap of him. Marlin gave her a few crumbs for the fish and she poked them through the pond's protecting wire.

'Is the other pretty lady coming to say hello to Marlin?'

'Miriam's been very sick. She can't. I'm going to make them a hot meal.' As gently and as firmly as she could, Jennifer pushed Miriam through the doorway. Miriam was too drained to resist but she did pop her head back outside to call 'Hi' and give Marlin a wave.

'You go upstairs,' Jennifer told her, and fussed with plastic bags and her tote, pushing them into the hall with her foot. 'Go up where it's warm – turn the TV on – I'll rescue Beccy. Beccy! Come on upstairs, darling!' Agitated like a sheepdog at a rustling, trying to cut what was hers from the rest. 'And get those two kids out of here, Dad. The next thing we'll be getting complaints.'

'No complaints, worrybelly. They only complain if they're sent early.'

'Just five minutes – pleeeese.' Beccy went down on her knees, her hands pressed together in prayer. Very theatrical. Very Marlin.

Jennifer thought, *It's all him, this play-acting. He makes idiots of them all.* 'Just five then. I'm going to start your meal now and, Beccy, when I call you you must come right away, okay?'

'Okay.'

'If you're going to the kitchen will you make your ol' dad a coffee?'

'I don't think I'll have time.'

'Pleeeese!' He whined on his knees with his own hands pressed together. The children shrieked with laughter and clutched their bellies. Jennifer turned quickly and marched up to the house. The others resumed their study of the carp pond. She was aware of their chatter but did not hear what they were saying. She was afraid for Beccy. She was afraid of every moment she was with Marlin – being drawn closer and closer to his web as the others had been. He was too strong. And once caught on his sugar silk he devoured their minds. He enchanted them, mesmerised them until they were loyal subjects to the point of absolute fearlessness. Whether he knew it or not, he had made a cult, and he was its high priest. Jennifer did not slam the side door. She did not want Beccy to know she was anxious.

The chatter around the carp pond on that occasion, however, was not only harmless, but informative. The high priest was also a teacher – as is the way of high priests.

'That fish there got whiskers.' A boy named Brett pointed at the pond.

'Looks like de ol' catfish got in there,' said Marlin.

'Do catfish have kittens?' Beccy asked.

'Catfish lay eggs and they lay them in a nest.'

'Like birds, Marlin?'

'More like birds than fish. More like eggs than kittens.' Marlin squatted on the edge of the pond and the disciples squatted in front of him. 'Our freshwater catfish, *Copidoglanis tandanus*,' he told them, and he made them say its name by taking the syllables to pieces, '*Cop-ido-glanis tand-anus*. They make nests for their eggs out of river grit and pebbles and such, and sometimes they're a metre across the top. We think that bird fish preeetty clever, yes?'

'Yes!' All eyes and ears and he knew they would never forget.

'Beccy!' Jen called from the window. 'You can come and get Marlin's coffee if you like and then you must come upstairs.' Beccy was at the door almost before she'd finished the sentence. The honour of the coffee mug. The honour of being chosen.

'Okay, Jen,' she said, grinning with the thrill of it.

'Now be careful, it's hot. Hold it by the handle and walk slowly.' Jennifer had filled the mug three-quarters of the way so it wouldn't splash. 'Give it to him, then straight back upstairs. The others are going home now.'

'Okay.' She carried the mug in slow procession, holding it in front of her like a holy chalice, a grail, and not a drop was spilled. Marlin accepted it with exaggerated ceremony.

'I'll get your coffee next time, Marlin.' Brett, who'd spotted the whiskered carp and was a regular after-schooly and therefore considered himself of higher rank, was peeved.

'I'll get it if I want to,' Beccy said to Marlin. 'He's in my class at school. Once he kicked dirt at me. He smells.'

'She's a Hill kid. We hate Hill kids,' said the boy.

'And why don't you like pretty ladies from the Hill, young Brett?'

'They got no money. *She* lives in a shed and Mum says they're all druggies.'

Tears she would not allow to spill had formed in Beccy's eyes. She walked over to the sea wall and leaned her elbows on the rough cement and bit her lower lip hard. Marlin took the other two aside.

'Tell me again what the catfish do?'

'They lay eggs in a nest like a bird.'

'And what's its real name?'

Silence.

'Best get home and find out then,' Marlin said. 'And young Brett – maybe you bring Marlin coffee next time. Now, *home!*' They walked, gossiping away, and when Marlin heard the gate close he said to Beccy, 'You better go up to your pretty mummy, poor little Hill chil'.' And Beccy ran to the house dry-eyed but with an expression of shattering defeat on her face. She ran up the stairs as though she were being chased and sat on the floor in a corner of Jen's room, afraid to breathe heavily in case the breath brought floods with it. Miriam lay on Jen's bed. She had a magazine opened across her face.

'Have a good time, Bec?' she asked drowsily. There was no answer and Miriam looked across the room. 'Beccy? What is it? What on earth's the matter?' She slid off the bed but she knew, by the expression on Beccy's face, that it was not the time to touch her. 'What happened down there?'

'Nothing,' said the child. She was hugging herself so hard around the knees her arms looked like muscled twigs. 'Nothing!'

Jennifer struggled up the stairs with a laden tray. She'd made a beef and vegetable stew the night before and on the tray was the pot, three bowls, spoons, milk, bread and fruit. She put it on the table under the window. 'There!' Then from her bedside cupboard she took a bottle of Merlot and glasses. 'And there! You're not on antibiotics or anything, Miriam, are you?'

'No, Jen. God that smells good.'

'It *is* good. And a glass of red won't do any harm at all.' She glanced across to Beccy. She was still sitting in the corner. 'Why the long face, darling? Didn't you have a good time down there?'

'Some,' said the child, and Jennifer studied her face more closely.

'Did something go wrong downstairs, Beccy?' She served the child a bowl of stew and bread on the floor where she sat and the steaming, rich smell of it somehow broke the spell of misery on her face.

'Brett said he hates Hill kids and Marlin didn't tell him to shutup.'

'Is that the kid who's in your class?' Miriam asked.

'He's really mean to me. I hate him.'

'Kids! You shouldn't take that much notice of him. He's a brat,' said Miriam. 'Eat up your dinner, Bec, you'll be all right.' Miriam spooned stew and dipped bread with the greatest pleasure. 'This is really great, Jen. At last I can taste something!'

'Have you got the strength to open the wine, Miriam? I just have to go down to the kitchen – I think I left the stove on.' But Jennifer flew down the stairs and into the yard, letting the wire door slam behind her. She found Marlin still sitting on the edge of the pond. He was reading a book, his legs straight out and bare feet crossed. She knew he knew why she'd come but he didn't look at her.

'Listen to me!' she hissed. 'Next time you have those children here you might try teaching them some manners.' He continued to read and slowly turned a page.

'The dewfish – *Tandanus tandanus*, yes, maybe they'll remember that one . . .'

'You can't be normal, can you. It's impossible!'

She would like to have pulled the book from his hands, but didn't. The weakness in her make-up prevented luxuries such as assertion, a wildness, a fury, a frustration of aggression, a terrible need to touch him with violence. These things were all crammed into the bottle of her brain to ferment until they destroyed her. She had sometimes thought in moments of almost unbearable frustration that she wouldn't mind if the bottle burst, as long as she was near him and had at least that moment of pure satisfaction. 'How *could* you let Beccy be hurt like that! They're my friends and when *my* friends come here I don't expect them to be hurt. And I don't expect them to have their heads filled with your madness!'

'Don't you forget, daughter, when your pretty ladies come here dey come to *my* house.' He spoke softly and evenly – even worse.

'And who do you think *pays* for *your* house?'

'Dem people who loves their ol' dad.' He laughed – worse still.

'You can't even talk in a normal voice – not for a minute, can you?! You're as mad as a hatter!'

'Thank poppies for that.'

'I'm telling you, leave my friends alone,' she said with any passion she could muster. 'You wouldn't like them, anyway,' she said. 'They're Jews!'

Marlin smiled at her. Like the snake smiling at its mouse before it eats. He turned away from her and continued to read his book. There were broken clouds now in the sun-setting sky and the wind had dropped. Jennifer felt very tired and turned to go.

'Where's Gull?' she asked.

'He's out fishing for bottles.'

Jennifer couldn't think what she could possibly say in reply and let the matter drop.

Miriam was sitting on the floor next to Beccy when Jennifer returned. An end-of-day tiredness had smudged grey around Miriam's eyes but she was pleased to see that there was little left of the stew and a wine glass had been sipped. Beccy was more cheerful and was eating grapes.

'Will you make that meat next time, Jen?' Beccy asked. 'I could eat it all over again.'

'You were a long time turning off the stove.' Miriam looked into Jennifer's eyes. She'd heard the door slam. 'Is everything okay?' She stretched and yawned and rubbed the tips of her fingers through her hair. Her white neck, arched and supple as a bird's, was exquisite, Jen thought. Pity to hide such beauty on the Hill, like fine china stored in a dirty cupboard.

'As okay as it ever will be, Miriam.'

Miriam uncrossed her legs and stretched them in front of her, massaging her bare heels into the luxury of carpet pile. Beccy leaned on the sill of the lookout window and watched the top of a maxi-yacht's mast as it rounded the point.

'Can we read "This is the House"?'

'I think we should get your mum home, darling. She needs lots of rest.'

'Please, Jenny.'

'I'm all right.' Miriam closed her eyes and leaned against the wall.

'Just a bit of it then before you go.' Jennifer took the old nursery rhyme book that had belonged to her mother's family. She sat on the bed with Beccy close beside her.

> *This is the house that Jack built . . .*
> *This is the cat,*
> *That killed the rat,*
> *That ate the malt*
> *That lay in the house that Jack built.*
> *. . . This is the maiden all forlorn . . .*

> *This is the man all tattered and torn . . .*
> *This is the priest all shaven and shorn . . .*
> *This is the cock that crowed in the morn . . .*
> *The cock that crowed in the morn!*
> *. . . That lay in the house that Jack built.*

'You didn't say it right,' Beccy said. 'You said "the cock that crowed in the morn" twice.'

'Sorry, darling. I guess it all reminds me of something else. Miriam?'

'What?' Sleepily.

'I was just thinking – and tell me if I'm out of line here – but have you thought about leaving the Hill? I mean maybe getting a job down here and renting a couple of rooms? I could help with everything, Miriam. I'd help look after Beccy. I might even be able to get you into Dolan's – just part-time – see if you like it.'

'I've thought about it.'

'It'd be great, Mum. We could live here.'

'I don't think so, Bec.' Miriam dragged herself to her feet. 'I'll think about it, Jen. When I'm not so tired I'll really think about it.'

'Whatever you decide, Miriam, I'd honestly like to help. You're like family to me – no, not family, more very, very close friends.'

'When I'm stronger and I get my head straight, Jen, I promise I'll think about it. Right now, we'd better get home. Get your things, Beccy.'

'Can we just go out in the yard for one minute?'

'Just one minute.' Miriam was too weary to argue. Jennifer rummaged through a drawer and brought out a fringed shawl. It was light wool and the colour of watermelon.

'Here,' she said, wrapping it around Miriam's shoulders. The colour suited her well. 'We can't have you getting a chill.'

'It's fabulous.' Miriam turned in front of the mirror. 'Isn't it pretty, Bec? Can I just wear it home, Jen? I'll get it back to you tomorrow.'

'No, keep it. I want you to have it. You look beautiful in it.'

'You sure? My God!'

'I'm sure. It belonged to my mother. I never wear it,' she lied. She'd worn it often when the days were cool but now it would better serve as a new layer of binding, a cohesive to help hold fast their friendship.

There was no sign of Marlin on the harbour front lawn. Jennifer strolled across the grass while Miriam and Beccy coooed sweet nothings to the death-row pigeons while Beccy had a conversation with the python, stroked a blue-tongue lizard, held a tortoise in her hand and counted the carp in the pond. She asked if she could go down the steps to the water 'for just one minute' and while Miriam, all watermelon and gold, leaned against the sea wall and gazed out on the bay, Jennifer took Beccy's hand and said, 'We're going down to the jutty for a minute.'

Miriam waved to them. 'Wait a minute, I want to come too. Why is it called a "jutty"?'

'I used to call it that when I was a baby. It's supposed to be "jetty", of course, but I named it "jutty" and it's been that ever since.'

Jennifer's smile was private, behind her hand, as she watched Beccy standing on the tip of the stone outcrop, with a breeze whipping her skirt around her legs and blowing her hair to one side. Somewhere there was a photo of herself standing there, windblown in exactly the same way. She was not sure where the photo would be – maybe Bindi Hope had it – but watching Beccy at that moment was like watching a replay of her own childlife. There was so much about Beccy that she recognised – and loved – and was afraid for . . .

Miriam had the flat of her hand above her eyes and was looking out to the harbour. 'Is that someone waving to us out there? See? In that boat.'

Jen recognised the dinghy. 'That's my brother, Gulliver. He goes fishing a lot.'

'So you tell me. It's about time I met him, I think.' She waved and Jennifer barely lifted a hand.

'Now would not be a good time.' *He'll be full as an egg by now*, she thought. 'He'll be stinking of bait, and filthy.' The dinghy had turned and was headed for home. 'Besides that, I do think you should be home now, out of the late air. It's too breezy for someone who's been as sick as you. Come on, Beccy,' she called, 'your mum's going home now.'

'Oooh, do we have to?'

'Yes. We have to.' Miriam and Jennifer turned and started back up the steps. At the top, near the pond, Miriam took Jennifer's hand and warmly held it. 'Jen, I can't thank you enough for looking after us the way you do. You really care about us, don't you?'

'I love you, Miriam – both of you.'

'And we love you.'

'Love' was a word Jennifer seldom heard away from the TV or the cinema. 'Love' was a word she dreamed of. 'I love you' were words spoken to other Jennifers, not her. After all, she didn't even love herself. But now that she had heard the words, and she was sure she had not been mistaken, she was filled with something that shone and was warm as crystals must be before they are made cold away from their homes. The warmth was reflected in her eyes and as a brush – just a feather of touch – of colour on her face. She was the only one who was aware of these things, but for that moment she was stronger than she had been for years.

At the gate, two surprises waited for them. The first was Marlin, standing quiet and holding a large preserving jar.

'So,' he said. 'The beautiful ladies are going?'

''Fraid so,' said Miriam. 'It's a long climb home.'

Marlin handed the jar to Beccy. It was half-filled with sea water and a bluebottle, its jellyfish bubble inflated on the surface and its bright, sea-blue tentacles trailing to the bottom. 'Something to learn about when you go to the library,' he said. 'You tell us what you know next time you come, little Hill chil'. We show that Brett a thing or two, hey?' Then he left them and went inside the house. Beccy was speechless with joy and gratitude. Even though sea creatures were something she feared, she was overcome with Marlin's acceptance of her. She would be his slave for life. She would do anything for him.

'What a thing to give her!' said Miriam. 'I hate blue-bottles! You know you mustn't touch the tentacles, Beccy. They sting and they're poison.'

'He's great! I'm going to call him Marlin!'

Jennifer was horrified but not really surprised. She mumbled something about it being 'his way', 'typical of him' and thinking 'everyone's as mad as he is', but Beccy carried the jar as though it were a life force and started to walk along the Sandpath, oblivious to anything else. Miriam, after kissing Jen quickly on the cheek, was forced to catch up as well as her weak legs would allow. Jennifer waved until they were out of sight.

The second surprise was something that had lain in the letterbox, missed by the afternoon collection. It was a Tibetan prayer-wheel card from Hesta. It bore a Blue Mountains postmark.

'Oh, good! She's back home,' Jennifer said to herself. And with higher spirits than she was accustomed to, and still refreshed by the strength of the word 'love', she made her way to the kitchen and another night in the man house that was the Fishcastle.

Out on the harbour, his mood softened by liquor and the tranquillity of the bay, Gull, as he reached the dinghy cave, wondered when he was going to meet the blaze of red hair above a watermelon shawl that had posed on the jutty in the spotlight of the end-of-day sun, standing there like a beacon lighting up the world.

Chapter Seven

HELL RISING AND HEAVEN FALLING

The mind and dreamings of Hesta Mainwaring left her to go wandering long, long before she was able to follow them. She and Marlin had somehow grown from plain, dry seeds in a brown, double-bricked plain household with even plainer householders. Sombre parents they were, who seemed in the mist of her memory to be the same colour as the bricks. They were clean-scrubbed people almost to the point of disappearance, toneless in their pitchless voices, dressed in shadows of grey and fogs of brown and neither lax nor strict with the fruits of their dry couplings. Hesta and Marlin envied other children who found passionate fault with their parents, or love, and wished *they* could boast of a strapping for bad and lollies for good.

But Hesta and Marlin had grown in spite of it all. They had grown strong in spite of their raising amongst plain things spectacular in their nothingness: dustless rooms where it was difficult to know where a dress began and a curtain ended – whether it was a coat lying across a chair or merely the chair itself (or possibly someone sitting in it). Even their food sulked on plates in a dry late autumn of colour: singed pumpkin, dead beans grey in the face, dull cheap-cut meats and mashed potatoes that turned ashen in sympathy with the rest. At the end of the day these children longed for breakfast and the oatmeal their father made in his black, iron pot, the only food that seemed able to defend itself from ruin.

Conversation, if there was any at all, was sparse and intoned in low mantra – words from a swamp of topics, all joined together to save air:

'Rabbit prices gone up again corned silverside slimy wiped down with vinegar milk billy-can leaking hardly enough for a cuppa bird droppings on the gas meter turned brown in the sun new priest under fifty well you know what they say Hesta's uniform hems need coming down can't you do it yourself your marks for arithmetic not good enough for a job behind a counter let alone your airy-fairy ideas better learn Pittman's shorthand always handy grey socks Marlin what do you do to the toes what does he do to the toes of his socks I ask you Father shoes don't come grey black's good enough why does he stuff his pockets with yabbies and lizards Father I ask you who do you think does the scrubbing at the tub toe nails need cutting boot soles too thin and heaven help us where will it all end the indigestion the boils and constipation . . .'

Marlin, Hesta remembered, escaped the ghosts of home as soon as he was old enough to move independently. He hunted for colour and life in bushland that greened thick and lush in a gully behind their house. He was forever calling her to see lizards or spiders under rocks, or birds' nests and eggs and telling her wild stories about it all. He showed her yabbies and tadpoles in the creek and he was sure he knew where there was a platypus hole. They counted fruit bats hanging high in black bunches and he stroked the emerald scales of tree snakes curled like ribbons around a branch. He showed Hesta how to tie newspapers around her legs to protect them from thorns and help him pick wild blackberries, and once, when they were older and sitting amongst maidenhair ferns on the creek bank, dangling their toes and staring into the water, Marlin had said, 'If I had gills I could live down there.'

And Hesta had said, 'You'll never get a girlfriend with gills.'

'I've already got one,' he'd said. 'I paid Birdie Lee sixpence behind the weather shed to show me her fanny and she said she would've done it for nothing.'

'When was that?'

'Wednesday.'

'Birdie Lee's got measles. She wasn't at school on Wednesday. You're just full of lies.'

'Well, it must've been somebody else,' he'd said, and splashed water on her. 'Birdie would've done it anyway.'

Hesta, in her own way, decorated herself away from the dull smog of her brown nest by stitching bright coloured scraps of fabric together (which she'd begged for at the haberdasher's) and draping herself in cloaks of different meanings, speaking strange tongues, pretending to be a dozen people in a week, dressing her hair with wild flowers and dancing fairy rings around the bracken in the gully.

And as a bonus there was for Hesta's eyes another dreaming world of endless richness and beauty that stretched as far as she wanted to stretch it outside the frames of her classroom windows. Forever gazing out through the fly-spot glass at craggy mountains, lakes and pine trees and small islands in coral bays with palms and sand and handsome black men. She was once rapped on the knuckles with a ruler for it. The teacher was a coarse woman with fat wrists too close to her hands and a wedding ring strangling the wrong finger and Hesta, brought suddenly back from a royal wedding in Hungary, had said: 'How dare you, madam!' She wished that Marlin had been there to see a teacher startled and speechless.

'What are you going to be when you grow up?' she'd once asked her brother as they scooped tadpoles into jars, he in dirty grey, and she draped and crowned Queen of the Creek.

'I'm going to collect every animal in the whole world and write them in a book,' he'd replied. 'And what will you be, Hesta?'

'Somebody else!' she'd said.

Hesta's homecoming to Sydney after travelling from one side of the world to the other was an arrival that brightened some of the red eyes who left the aircraft with her. After four changes of flights from Iquitos via the United States over a period of two days she was almost beyond exhaustion when her flight touched down on a wet tarmac at six in the morning. Her legs, still in their pantyhose, had become too swollen for shoes and too painful to support her, and a wheelchair had been ordered in which she sat as though it were a royal litter. Creased and stained and cramped she was wheeled away by grinning courtiers, wearing her hat on the unwound springs of her hair and carrying boots and bags in her lap. She was very pale but for two ominous red spots on her cheeks and Qantas, fearing for her health and their good name, raced her through Immigration, collected her luggage, sped through Customs and had her in a cab headed for her room at the YWCA in Kings Cross almost before she'd yawned three times.

She did not contact Proudie Bay that morning. She didn't want to speak to Marlin or Jennifer until she'd rested, and she knew that Jennifer would be getting ready for work. She would stay quiet at the 'Y', as she usually did when she returned from a tour, shower and sleep and change her clothing and take the train to the Blue Mountains the following day. Then she would write to Proudie Bay – when she was in her home and sure of who and where she was.

After the dense air of the jungle and the musty air of the aircraft the clarity and eucalypt-scented breath of the mountains – the purity, the rarity of it, almost took her own away.

She walked with care through a garden that had gone mad with growth in her absence. Everywhere were signs of recent rain. Trees and shrubs were lush with it and flowers bloomed anywhere they chose. Hesta stopped to admire a deep purple salvia – the best of all the purples in her opinion, better than the tibouchinas that grew along the coast whose colour, she'd always thought, was ordinary.

Wheeling her suitcase behind her, she pushed her way along the path that led to the door, past bracken overspilled and hen'n'chicken ferns spread wide beside her, pecking at her feet. At intervals giant cobwebs straddled the path, and their owners, too fat to move, resigned themselves to having their homes demolished by the swish of a branch. Overhead, king parrots flew in close-knit family flocks; bellbirds, wattle birds and magpies flew to higher trees and somewhere in the distance a koel cuckoo cried for a mate. Only the hoons of the bush – the currawongs – dared to swoop close to Hesta's head. At the door she looked behind her again at the tangle of growth: at conifers hiding behind vines, clinging, ancient English roses dewing in their centres, camellias, giant bunyas and kurrajongs, blue spruces and eucalypts, a forested harmony of natives and exotics in their own wild world, and she sighed and thought of Lucretia and wished she could have been there to share the sight of it.

Inside the house there was another air – stored air, and not so pure. But the dust and must was no less welcoming than the garden. She was pleased to see that nothing seemed to have been moved. Dust was the indicator of movement and dust still lay where she'd left it. To Hesta, dust was the soul of a house: she rarely disturbed it.

Her good sense of smell detected no intrusion by man or possum but she scanned the walls and ceilings for huntsman spiders, for they are the first to know when a house is empty. On a chair by a window lay the book she'd been reading till the moment she'd left the house for South America, a volume of Isabel Allende's stories, opened on a cushion at the page to be continued.

It was a comfort of a house. She warmed in it like a cat. It was a house to curl in – to stretch in and stroke. She licked the back of her hand but the skin still tasted of seat sixteen B.

And after telling her suitcase with its rickety wheels to 'sit' inside the door, she went to the kitchen and did what nesting women have done since the beginning of women – boiled water for tea and, after drinking it, calmed like a cat whose paws had been buttered. She sat at her desk with its back to a window and wrote to Jennifer.

> *... it's from trees to trees I've come, dear, but the*
> *trees here breathe; in the jungle they*
> *choke on water and strangle each other, poor things ...*

She tried to phone the village for a food delivery but the telephone was dead. Since Colin's death Hesta had, on three or four occasions, been cut off from one service or another, not because she was too poor to pay but simply because such mundane affairs rarely entered her head. The newsagent had stopped her papers months ago and had had to write off her debt when he finally used the last of his red stickers. But her power had been cut only once. Hesta had been so frightened by the dark that it was the one bill she remembered to pay.

It was towards the middle of the day that Hesta had tried to telephone the village and she was still barely awake. She had never learned the management of jet lag and it overcame her totally. She wasn't sure when she'd gone to sleep again but it must have been soon after trying to phone, and realising she'd been cut off. Jennifer's card still lay on the desk, sealed in its envelope and stamped but there it would stay for the time being because Hesta slept in her chair all that afternoon and most of the night.

It may have been the next day or the day after that when she woke, she couldn't be sure. To Hesta it was six minutes past nine on a day that would no doubt reveal itself to her as it ticked on. She was vaguely aware, at some stage, of buttering half-frozen bread and drinking tea. She knew she must have eaten because there were crumbs on her chair and the mat below it. She would sweep them later, she thought.

While she waited for her bath to fill she stripped and studied her tired image in the mirror on the back of the bathroom door.

'An old body is a terrible thing to behold. Terrible!' she said to it. 'And I'm glad, Colin, you're not here to see this one.'

She looked pale and shabby – second hand, like the things for sale in charity shops. Her breasts, her belly, the skin of her arms and legs sagged and spilled downwards as though she were being pulled to earth before her time. What was once plump and pert and firm had folded into creases, and the creases, which would never fill out, had to be powdered like a baby's. Her knees were not quite level and her dance-loving toes and hands were twisted like deadwood twigs with arthritis. Her pubic hair was as sparse as a bald man's pate and the hair on her head had dried too long in the cabins of planes. *A sight only for embalmers*, she thought, *or mortuary mice – or buzzards*. When she had the strength she would take the mirror down and kill it. She had no further use for one so long. She had no wish to be tortured by a full-length mirror. *Better if it could no longer reflect. Better if it died!*

She sank into the bathtub and filled it even more with tears.

Hesta was surprised by the heat of the morning when she walked, holding Jen's postcard, through the garden to the road. The flurry of wild things that had been disturbed by her arrival had settled back into their trees and hides and hollows, but the path spiders had not made new webs. There was a hum of heat in the bush that was like a hum of electricity. Cicadas shrilled sharp as ear-piercing stabs, crickets and small things never seen crrricked from rocks and fern roots. Immigrant mynas and sulphur-crested cockatoos cried out in an irritated way. Alarm bells, cautions and signals they were, she was sure of it. She wished, as she had wished many times before, that she could understand them. Perhaps there was a bushfire somewhere in the mountains. She pulled her hat down over her hair, down so that her eyes were shaded. She walked slow and heavy. Her land legs had still to join her.

Hesta's nearest neighbours lived at the top of the road, almost where it joined the main, and approximately two hundred metres from her house. Their names were Mr and Mrs Clarke; Hesta had never known their first names. Mr Clarke was a retired violin maker who still made violins. Mrs Clarke was a craft-fiddler. She made things for church fetes, inventing all the time with ribbons and cottons and crochet hooks. She bottled fruit and vegetables and was fond of housework. She had hand made all her pot holders. They were gentle people. Mr Clarke was in his garden when Hesta called to him. He was balancing an umbrella over a bed of seedlings to protect them from the heat.

'Aaah, my dear Mrs Mainwaring.' He spread his arms in a gesture of welcome and broadly smiled. 'Welcome home! Come in! Please, come in for a moment. We thought you might be back. We tried to ring but your phone seems to be kerplunk.' Mrs Clarke appeared suddenly by his side. She slid her arm through her husband's and smiled a greeting. They were small people, trim and small, with small, straight features and feet and hands. Hesta thought, not for the first time, that they were perfectly matched, like salt and pepper shakers shaped like birds.

'I'm on my way to the postbox.' Hesta held up the card. 'I'll call in on the way back if you like. It's terribly hot.' They nodded in unison.

'Nothing terrible happened when you were away, dear,' said Mrs Clarke. 'We peeped around your garden once or twice but there was no mischief that we could see.' She held up a little thumb. 'All okey-dokey! Your phone's out of order though,' she said. 'But you're welcome to use ours.'

'I would like to order groceries, thank you. I'll be back in a short while.'

At the postbox on the corner of Wellings Road and the main street, Hesta felt the worst of unsheltered heat. Cars, coming and going, were a wavery mirage of metal and on the road were dead lizards and a small snake, still curled like an 'S'. Near the postbox lay a possum – flat and squeezed, its toothpaste innards covered with flies. The ruts in the dirt path hurt Hesta's swollen feet and the postbox cover burned as hot as a stove top when she lifted it. For a moment the world swam around Hesta's head and she swayed a little. She sucked a dry breath of air and hoped she'd reach the Clarkes' before she fell.

'It's the worst feeling.' Mrs Clarke dabbed Hesta's forehead with a damp cloth. 'That awful feeling in your head as if you're not quite on the ground.' She poured more juice into Hesta's glass. 'It's apple, dear. Homemade.' The juice was cool and refreshing and Hesta drank two glasses of it. It occurred to her that probably one of the reasons for her faintness was lack of food. She'd barely eaten since she'd come home.

'It's passing,' she said. 'I'm so sorry to do this to you. I don't think I've ever been jet-lagged so badly.' They nodded and tutted around her, fanning, dampening, clucking. 'I will telephone for a food order if I may.'

'Perfectly all right, absolutely all right, dear lady.' Mr Clarke dashed to the telephone and guarded it until Hesta picked up the receiver. 'I will also report my own phone out of order if you don't mind.'

'Of course not. Not at all ... but, as a matter of fact we reported it ourselves – well, you see, we knew you couldn't.'

'And what did they say, Mr Clarke.'

'Well now, it seems – and mind you, we all do it from time to time heaven knows – but it seems you might have forgotten ...'

'Oh.'

Mrs Clarke, triggered by the mere suggestion of food and want and unpaid bills, had already rushed to the kitchen to fill plastic bags with homemade pickles and jams and rose-hip jelly and shortbread and other non-essentials. And she threw in a can of Baxter's Game Soup, its use-by date overdue by two months, but how could anything as grand as Baxters go off, she'd thought as she packed it.

It was one o'clock when Hesta walked slowly back and along her path. The unusually heated day had silenced the hum of morning sounds. It was as though the earth had taken a deep breath and was holding it. She was afraid that her own panting breaths would be heard for miles and she found herself tiptoeing and trying to stop the rattle of pickle jars in the bags. 'Sssshh', she whispered at the door, 'hush to the world.' And she thought of the loud, screeching, wet heat of the Amazon and compared it with this stillness and wondered at such extraordinary differences on one small planet, only hours apart. 'Hush to the world ... sssshh ...' as she turned the key in the lock and was startled by a single green cicada on the door frame who drummmed drummmed

drummmed until it too was consumed by silence.

There was still a lightness in Hesta's head but Mrs Clarke's apple juice had relieved the faintness. She put their donations on the kitchen table and hunted for something that would satisfy her. At the back of the freezer compartment was a bag of linguini, not too old; in the cupboard was a can of tomatoes and one of mushrooms, olive oil, dried oregano and evaporated milk, and she made a meal and a pot of tea. She ate at her desk by the window and then, in her chair, continued Allende's stories where she'd left them, on page thirty-nine, 'Toad's Mouth'. But that was as far as she went with it because she fell asleep again, but this time feeling better with food in her belly, and she slept until a quarter past three – at least that was what her watch showed: a quarter past three, but it was so dark inside the house, despite the lamp glow on her desk, that she wondered if her watch had stopped. The second hand indicated that it had not.

The darkness came from outside. It was a darkness heavier than night. From her windows she could see that the sky did not seem to be where it should be. It seemed to have fallen to the tops of trees and the trees, terrified, stood still and waited. She wondered for a moment if it was all a trick to her tired eyes, an illusion, like the hot mirage of cars on the main road. Hesta opened the front door and looked out.

Great clouds – mountains of them – hung heavy and low, heavy enough to crush anything under them. Along a split in the sky lay an eerie green tinge but for the most part it was black as night. Through the trees, in the distance to the south-west, she watched the black mass twisting over upon itself. But there was no wind – there was no movement of any kind. The garden seemed to have folded down on itself, and on wild things silent beneath it. There were no sounds of comfort, no birds or crickets or cicadas – just the lowering of the sky, pulled down by its black weight, to touch the earth. 'The sky is falling, the sky is falling,' she recited with a nervous giggle to ease her anxiety, make light of it, to simply make a sound. Inside, she locked the door and, acting on an instinct, locked the others, and the windows. *Is this what 'outside' was trying to tell me*, she thought. *It must have been*. She hurried from room to room as best she could on sore legs. She unplugged the television, acting on old advice about power surges. She tried the telephone again in the vague hope that some miracle had set it working but it was as dead as the world outside.

Hesta sat in her chair – it seemed to be the best thing to do at the time. It was a comfort to her. She sat hard against its back, as though the chair's wings would protect her or fly her somewhere else if they couldn't. She sat there as still as everything else, though she didn't know why. She tucked her purse in beside her and pulled her straw hat firmly down, almost over her eyes. She held a cushion tight across her chest and looked for all the world like a bird hiding in a shrub. Shortly, the table lamp on her desk went out and, then, a click and silence from the refrigerator.

A memory suddenly came to her. It was a few moments before she realised what had brought it to mind. She remembered when she and Marlin were very small they used to run to a bridge over the railway line when it was time for the freight train to roar through the tunnel. They'd lean over the guard rail, quiet and excited, and listen for the rhythmic rush of the engine as it came nearer and nearer until it whooshed into the tunnel below them, then rushed out the other side in a terror of smoke and steam and noise and fire so fearful, so breathtaking in its power, that they hated it if the driver waved and ruined their monster fantasy. She remembered the sound of the rushing train, for at that moment she was listening to exactly the same sound. It was a throbbing roar in the distance: she could not tell from which direction it was coming but with every second it became louder.

The first sign of movement outside was a sudden blizzard of leaves hurled against the windows with such force by the wind that they seemed almost to be embedded in the glass. Through a patch of clear window she saw flashes of sparks as trees crashed to the ground somewhere near the road. Now the sounds outside were no longer those of a freight train but the truly terrifying howl of a wind so strong she would not have thought it possible. She held the cushion over her face and cried: 'Don't be frightened, don't be frightened, don't be frightened . . . ', keeping as clear a head as she could. Every second or so there was the crash of a fallen tree, a smash of metal somewhere. Over the top of the cushion she saw timber planks flying past the house, twisting and spiralling until they were out of sight. A huge eucalypt branch crashed against the window where the desk sat, shattering the glass and showering her with splinters. The house rocked alarmingly on its foundations and the front door shook as though all of hell was trying to break in. The back door gave up the fight; it banged open once, hung on its hinges for a second and was blown away. The refrigerator cast off and slid towards the opening. And hard rain, forced horizontal by the wind, cut through the house from every possible opening and, with the wind, soaked and destroyed everything in its way. A crying currawong, caught in flight, was blown sideways against the jaggard shards of a window pane and died, impaled and bloody. And Hesta still clung to the chair – she couldn't have moved if she'd wanted to. Even when she heard the roof move and grate, as though it were being prised away with a tool, she did not move. She stayed tense as a stick in the chair and she sat still and terrified even when a section of the roof above her came off and spun away like a frisbee – and she sat still even when the remains of a conifer smashed through the opening and on top of her, pinning her, wet and bleeding, under it. And it was there she stayed, in and out of conscious-ness, crying little cries like a bird drowning in its feathers, for the remaining ten minutes of the worst storm the Blue Moun-tains had ever known.

When Hesta finally woke to a sort of reality, she was crying; she had no idea why. Everything around her seemed to be green or blue or white with lights. She would like to have said something, there was a lot she wanted to say, but she shivered so violently that speech was almost impossible. There was the face of a man hovering over her. She wanted to warn him, 'Be careful, be careful.'

'You're in a hospital,' said the face. 'You were caught in the storm. You'll be okay.' The face seemed to be smiling and she felt vaguely irritated by it – *Didn't it know what was happening?* She wished she could stop shivering so she could tell them. 'You're in shock, Mrs Mainwaring,' someone said. 'There's nothing wrong we can't put right.' The face said it was Doctor Heath; he wore glasses, she couldn't see his eyes. There seemed to be a tube taped to the back of her hand, and another hand – she had no idea whose – was patting her wrist. Hesta took a breath and forced words from her shivering mouth.

'Where is my hat?'

'We'll look for it, dear,' said a voice, as though the question had been perfectly natural. 'Don't you worry about it. We'll find it.' And Hesta, comforted for the moment, drifted back into half-sleep.

When she was awake and could speak again, and she had no idea when that was except she believed it was daytime, she asked the question:

'What on earth happened?'

'There was the devil of a storm, Mrs Mainwaring. The worst.' This time it was a woman. 'You were right in its path, I'm afraid. The house ... well, everything in your area was pretty badly hit.' She moved closer to the bed. 'I'm told you were found under a tree sitting up in a chair. The SES got you out. You're very lucky, considering.'

'Am I all right?'

'You'll be okay. Your left arm is very bruised, there are three broken fingers and some minor cuts and scratches,' she was told. 'You'll be a bit sore for a while but you'll be okay. We all think you were very lucky.'

'What about the Clarkes?'

'Where do they live?'

'Not far from me. On the same side, near the main road. *If the State Emergency Service rescued me*, Hesta thought, *then they will have attended to the Clarkes.* 'Ask the SES about the Clarkes, will you? They'll be wondering about me too, I imagine. I hope they're all right, the Clarkes. They'd just planted seedlings.' She wondered if she'd imagined a brief look between two staff members. Hesta glanced down to the left. Her arm had been immobilised and was swathed in something white.

'A patch job, I'm afraid. We were run off our feet with injuries,' the woman said. 'Sometime in the future, when you're stronger, we'll straighten things out properly for you. We'll have to cut your rings off.'

'You'll do nothing of the kind,' said Hesta. 'I'd rather have crooked fingers. Were many people hurt?'

'A few.'

'Badly?'

'Some broken bones – you know, that sort of thing.'

'I hope – well, at least no one was killed.'

'You need lots of rest.'

'Where is my purse?'

'Locked away safely. Do you want it right now?'

'No.'

'It was sensible to keep it with you. The contents saved us a lot of time.'

197

'Is there anything left of my house?'

'Not much, I'm afraid, dear. There'll be a great deal of work to be done. It'll take a while. Is there someone, a friend – some family member we can contact? Someone you could stay with when you leave here? They'll be a long time clearing your area and repairing damage.'

'It's all gone, isn't it? All my things? All my treasures?'

'We don't really know, dear,' the woman said. 'I'm sure they'll find a heap of things when the trees are cleared away.'

Hesta cried softly, not for the everyday, material essentials of a household, except perhaps for her chair and clothes. She cried for all the poor, helpless objects she had collected over the years and loved so much. She cried for her pictures, her books and her music. And there were letters: dozens of letters and photographs and childhood albums of Colin, and his journals, and the trophies he won for school sports – his silver napkin rings, one for each birthday, her purple scarves from a world of markets, a coffee pot from Bulgaria that she had nursed in her lap all the way home in 1981, and sari silk from Madras and dolls from France and all the rest of the history of her life that was there to remind her when her own memory failed. And she wept for the house Colin had given her with such love and the garden that had survived for half a century – and finally, she sobbed for the currawong impaled on glass shards, the sight of it most terrifying of all, like the final scene of a devastating drama. The woman was holding her right hand. 'It's good to cry,' she said.

'I want you to enquire about my neighbours, Mr and Mrs

Clarke. I want to know if they're all right. And then – and then, I expect you'd better contact my niece, Jennifer Hardwick. She lives at Proudie Bay.'

'You leave the details with Sister.' she said. 'I'll send her in shortly. We'll look after you.' And she smiled reassuringly and left the ward.

She had given 'the details' to Sister who had then passed them on to one of a huge body of volunteers who had given their services for the rescue and welfare of the storm's victims. The SES, the Salvation Army, the Red Cross, and ordinary people from everywhere – busy, helpful, proud to be part of it, happy to be pulling together, happy to have something to unite them. Just like a war, she thought. Just like a war. And her conversation with Lucretia about such matters came to mind.

A female officer from the Salvation Army came to see her.

'I hear you're leaving hospital in a couple of days. Is there anything we can help you with? Do you have any money?'

'My purse is here in the drawer.'

'Would you like to have a look?'

'You do it if you like.'

There was a fifty-dollar note and credit cards, a wet passport and a damaged, used Qantas ticket.

'I believe you're going down to Proudie Bay.'

'Yes.'

'Do you have anything to wear?'

'I don't believe I have. I hadn't thought.'

'It will be a while before you can shop for replacements. I'll bring you a few things. What size are you?'

'Fourteen.'

'And shoes?'

'Eight – size eight.' *So this is what it's like, charity. She had nothing – nothing! It had not occurred to her – never!*

The day before she was to be released a bundle of clothing, a pair of shoes and underwear, all clean and neatly folded, was delivered to her. *Second-hand*, she thought miserably. *Second-hand – but then, so am I . . .*

A social worker came to help her. 'The local taxi companies have got together and have offered their services for relocation: Mrs Mainwaring, you'll be travelling to Proudie Bay in style.'

'People are so kind, aren't they. You've all been so kind.'

'Mrs Mainwaring,' she said gently. 'You wanted to know about Mr and Mrs Clarke of Wellings Road . . .'

'They're dead, aren't they.'

'I'm really sorry. How did you know?'

'A certain silence when I asked. One learns a great deal from silence.' Hesta sat on the edge of the bed. Her legs were bare and still bruised but they were no longer swollen from the flight that brought her back from South America – a thousand years ago.

Chapter Eight

THE MIGRATION OF SISTER BIRD

The monarch of a Huon pine forest had been cut down to provide the Hardwicks with a kitchen table. It had once towered, straight and strong as a pylon for the earth, on a bank of the Huon River in Tasmania. From its peak, and if the air was clear, the tree could see the valley where apple trees grew, and beyond the valleys, clear over the crests of hills, to watch the river wind south from the mountains of Wedge and Bowen.

It could also on a still day hear the saws working in a timber mill owned by James Hunter & Sons – but it meant nothing at all. It was long years, decades, before the tree realised that a Huon pine of good age and richness of timber, to be in such a place, not far from a cleared slope to the river – not inaccessible – needed to resign itself to a certain fate. And in 1902 it was James Hunter who decided its fate when he sent Jess Paterson and his team into the forest to execute it.

The dismembered, enormous body of the tree provided (among a hundred other things, including new beams for a church) a table that was six-and-a-half feet long and three feet wide, solid, heavy and now scratched and dented from generations of use, colour patched from deep honey to spilt ink. Marlin had bought it from a second-hand dealer one year after his marriage to Lissy. He had since used it for food and pliers and screwdrivers and putty and glue and fish heads and books and hooks, not necessarily in that order. That it had once lived had slipped from his memory. He'd forgotten it had ever breathed.

Now, the table, freshly cleaned and oiled by Jennifer, was set early on a Sunday evening with a cold meal. There was salad, bread and cheese and plum jam that Bindi Hope had made, cold minted potatoes, tomatoes and basil, hard-boiled eggs, sliced ham, mustard pots, dressings and a bowl of bright red crabs.

In the centre of the table sat a pewter pot of geraniums and nasturtiums mixed with stems of rosemary and thyme. *It all looked simple and rustic*, she thought – a frame from a foreign movie – Italian, perhaps, or Spanish, in the south.

'So!' Marlin said when he came to eat. 'Who's coming to dinner, as they say? Don't tell me it's the Duchess of Wellings Road – early.' Gulliver, who was in his usual evening fog, sat down and said nothing.

'No, Father dear. You know she won't be here till Tuesday; there's been no change. But things will be different in this house when she does come. She's used to decent food on decent tables and we need to smarten up, so get used to it.'

'We'll have to sit up straight then, will we? Like pins?'

'Yes, you will.'

'She won't be in childhood number two, will she? She's not going to rush about in coloured capes and be different people? I hate crowds, Jen.'

'How could she possibly rush at all! For heaven's sake, she's been injured. She could have been killed! Are you listening to me? Your *own sister* could have been killed. I don't understand you – either of you. You just don't seem to care.' Jennifer cut bread. She watched Gulliver spread his with the concentration of an artist – slowly – as though he were painting a still life with plum jam and brush. 'She's going to need a lot of support from us all. She'll be a nervous wreck.'

'That'll make two of you, then,' said Gull.

'Well, naturally, I was upset about it. What would you expect?'

'You were all over the place like a blowfly.'

'I can't sit around and do nothing like you. There were things to be done.'

'Quite so,' said Marlin. 'But how are we to *transport* the duchess down from her mountain?' He pinched his lips, raised his head and looked along the bone of his nose through a monocle of finger and thumb. 'Are we to send a royal coach?'

'Can't,' said Gull with his mouth full of bread. 'It's in for repairs.' And he laughed and choked in a spray of crumbs.

'God, how sickening! When she comes down she's going to think the zoo's moved *inside*!' Jennifer plugged in the water jug and snatched coffee from the shelf. 'You know very well she's coming by cab.' She banged three mugs on the bench. 'You know very well she's coming on Tuesday. You know – I just wonder if it had been this house blown down – and I wish to God it had been – wouldn't that be a different story?' She threw coffee into the plunger pot and poured water. 'And what's more, if it had been this house and it was the two of you trapped, bleeding under a ton of trees, I wouldn't take two steps to help either of you.' Of course she knew what was behind Marlin's snide remarks. It was his way of expressing apprehension of a threat, jealousy. Hesta could very well be a threat to his limelight, she knew that. She was capable of eclipsing it altogether if she was in good form, but that was unlikely during this visit. She sat down heavily and scraped her chair forward.

'Ah, come on, Jen Wren,' Marlin said. 'We just havin' a bit o' fun. We'll be good as goog eggs for Sister Whoever.' He swallowed a mouthful of food like a pelican and kissed the tips of his fingers. 'Nice crabs, Jen. Did you knit them yourself?'

There had been a week's notice to clear out the spare room opposite Jennifer's. The jumble of junk that had grown in it was sorted and discarded or stored down in the laundry and under the stairs. Jennifer washed the curtains, cleaned the window, checked the sofa bed and made it up with fresh linen. A central, swinging light seemed only to reflect the shadows of the room's dark cedar panelling, and to give it light she hung three bright prints, a dried arrangement of native flowers, a red Indian cotton spread for the bed and two cushions from her own room. Bindi had lent a small chest of drawers and a cane chair. Jen had cleaned and dusted and checked it every day – sometimes twice a day – since they'd been told about Hesta and the storm.

Jennifer had been in touch with the hospital on three occasions and had spoken to Hesta twice. On the second-last day of her stay it seemed that some of her belongings had been salvaged. A washing machine that had moved only a short distance and the refrigerator that had rolled as far as the creek seemed to be in shock, she'd said, but otherwise unhurt. Hesta's voice had been flat and resigned. There were sodden books, she said, a few trinkets, ruined clothes, torn pictures and no furniture worth saving, not even her chair that had stayed upright and in one piece only long enough for her to be more easily found. There were no fittings or accessories, except for a mirror: a hideous thing, she'd said, that had been on the back of the bathroom door and had not broken even though the door had been torn away.

'The garden is a devastation,' she'd said. 'But gardens grow again, don't they. Photographs can't grow again and journals and the history of Colin can't grow again – what will I do when I can't remember Colin? Or the house, or the story of my own life?' And she had told Jennifer about the Clarkes and she'd cried for the small, neat, matching pair. And she had told her in detail, about the currawong. All wet feathers and blood and glass. That was something, she said, she couldn't possibly forget. Its beak dying open after a scream. She could never forget that.

It had been a sad conversation. A side of Hesta Jennifer

had not really known, and she was relieved when, towards the end of it, a little of the old spirit squeezed through a minute crack in Hesta's depression. 'The Salvation Army came this morning, dear. They have dressed me in sack cloth. There was nothing else to give me, just sack cloth. The ashes, of course, were too wet to use. You will have to shop for me, dear, and dress me up.'

The effects of the storm had been filmed from every possible angle by the media. Jennifer followed the stories on TV. Every tragedy recorded – possibilities of tragedy, tragedies that would have happened if only so and so hadn't been a hundred miles from the Blue Mountains at the time, and even one or two possibly tragic interviews with people who had not heard of the storm at all.

Storm witnesses were interrogated and sobbing faces magnified until they filled the screen. There was, on one channel, a shot of a child's teddy bear, presumed dead, lying in the rubble of a house in an area that was not the Blue Mountains at all and could very well have been Lebanon. But there was, to Jen's horror, on one channel, a shot of the ruins of Hesta's house and the chair in which she'd been found. And in the background of all this drama rock bands, with bass rhythms strong enough to alter heart patterns, belted out something about loss. Hesta had said: 'They're everywhere with cameras on their shoulders and something to do. Just like a war zone, but safer. They're enjoying themselves and not being hurt. Today they're not bored.'

'When Hesta moves in,' Marlin said, 'and your ginger-top

friend comes with the little Hill chil', we'll be full of wimmin, Jen – a hundred to one! Save us all!'

'It's all right, ol' Dad,' said Gull. 'I've taken the redhead off your hands. That'll be one less.'

'You can't do that,' Marlin laughed, ''cause I saw her first.'

Jennifer glared at Gull. *'You* keep away from Miriam.'

'Too late,' he said, grinning. 'I've run into her a couple of times.'

'You mean the pretty Jew lady?' asked Marlin.

'That's the one.'

'But Jews don't have red hair.'

'This one does – all over,' Gull said, still grinning at Jennifer.

She knew they were just baiting her: picking away at scabs never given time to heal, some old, some recent. It was a game they played. She refused to rise to the bait and breathed in deep and slow and bit her lip. She left the table without a word and walked outside to the harbour front and stood shaking by the wall. She thought of a conversation she'd had last week at the cafe. A woman had chatted about her family dinner table and how it was the only time they all really came together. 'The only time of the day,' she'd said. 'We're all so busy.'

'What do you talk about?' Jennifer had asked.

'Oh, you know, the usual things. School, homework, what people are reading, what films we've seen – at the moment, the Monet exhibition, have you seen it? – just chitchat.'

'Oh,' Jennifer had said, 'well, I guess that's more or less what everyone does at the dinner table.'

'Yes,' the woman had said, 'I imagine it is.'

'If you could hear us at the table – and ours is in the kitchen by the way' – Jennifer might have said, but didn't – *'you could not possibly believe what you hear ...'* She glanced back at the house. A thought wandered in and out of her mind but stayed long enough for her to wonder if one of Gulliver's 'hidden' vodka bottles would be enough to fuel a fire bomb. And the next time she met the woman at the cafe she could say, *'Oh, by the way, our dinner table conversation didn't go exactly to plan the other night so I burned it down.'* (Huon pine is excellent for the fire, though slow to burn.)

The thought of either of the men touching Miriam or Beccy horrified Jennifer. But she was sure that Miriam would have told her if she'd spoken to Gull. And Beccy too. It would have been an ordinary, natural thing to do. *'I ran into your brother today at the shops. I didn't have time to talk.'* But neither had mentioned it. Or maybe they could have met him briefly and forgotten all about it. Even better. But what could Miriam possibly find that was interesting in Gull? Nothing at all. Nothing!

Jennifer eagerly anticipated Hesta's stay with them: it was almost a breathless sort of clockwatching. The thought of it made her shoulders seem lighter. It would be wonderful to have another woman under their roof, somehow a completeness – even if she was a bit fanciful on occasions. *As if fanciful would make the slightest difference in this house!*

Tuesday was wet and chilled, as early summer Tuesdays can sometimes be. Something of a summer surprise, a trick, a game to catch people in tank tops and Ts and summer skirts, unawares. A cool, sharp south breeze cut along the Sandpath, pushing showers in front of it and ringing wind chimes on the way. A grey sky and a funeral procession of clouds gave a sombre look to Proudie Bay, and the few people prepared for it, all umbrella and boots, scuttled in and out of doorways. To the ocean end of the road and above it, the Hill was veiled in a swirl of rain and mist. Conditions were not comfortable for Jennifer and Bindi while they waited at the gate for the cab to arrive. They were cold and their feet were wet. But it all seemed appropriate somehow.

At one-fifteen a cab rounded the corner of the Sandpath and drove slowly until it gently stopped at number fourteen. On the back seat, a woman half sat and half reclined. The woman seemed old. She had a dry, papery look about her that was relieved only by the colour of bruising, and her thin grey hair was caught behind her ears with bobby pins. She wore a plain white short-sleeved blouse and a cotton skirt, decorated with large green flowers with red centres. No style at all. Absolutely none. On the blouse a spot of rust showed on the point of the collar and the buttons were odd sizes.

The driver opened the door on one side and Bindi, in excitement, opened the other. The woman sat and looked sadly at both of them. Tears of relief and surprise ran down Jennifer's cheeks.

'Hesta?' Bindi was ready to take her hand luggage but

was too shocked by what she saw and stepped back. 'You've lost so much weight,' was all she said.

Jennifer slid into the cab and sat beside her aunt and stroked her hair.

'I'm afraid I might cry too, if I speak,' Hesta said to them. 'Don't let anyone see me today. Bindi, dear, come and see me tomorrow.'

Further down the Sandpath the Perkers could be seen walking up with welcoming smiles. Bindi hurried to them and explained. She invited them back to her house for tea.

Jennifer and the driver helped Hesta out of the cab and she stood shaking and shivering on the path, supported by both of them. There wasn't much luggage: a small suitcase, her purse and a walking cane the hospital had provided. Jen was anxious to get her into the shelter of the house.

'She's had a pretty rough time of it. She'll be shaky for a good while I think,' the driver said.

'Can I make you some coffee or something?' she asked him.

'No thanks. I've got a sister lives ten minutes from here. That's why I took this job on. Good excuse to see the kids.'

'We can't thank you enough.'

'Take care, dear man,' Hesta managed through chattering teeth.

The cab turned and drove slowly back again. For a moment the cold breeze dropped, out of respect to a woman who had just seen the God of winds and would not be interested in the games of one of its children.

Jennifer took Hesta's right arm and together they

shuffled along the drive. It was then that she saw some of her injuries.

'What on earth's happened to your hand?' She touched Hesta's left hand gently. 'They haven't mended your fingers.' *Why would they leave her fingers twisted like corkscrews?* 'Why did they leave your fingers like that?'

'At the time they couldn't do anything that wasn't urgent. They were so busy with injuries . . . but they wanted to cut my rings off, Jen. I wouldn't let them do it.'

'But rings can be mended – or you could have other ones.'

'Darling, try to understand. My rings were all I had left.' She closed her eyes tight against the memory. 'At that time, at that awful time, they were the only things that gave me some sense of dignity – some sense of *me*.'

'Well, let's get you upstairs, warm and dry.' At the side door Jennifer peeped around to the harbour front, but there was no sign of Marlin or Gulliver. She was thankful for that. They walked slowly to the stairs, Jennifer still focused on the injured fingers. 'But aren't you in pain?'

'Not badly. The doctor told me if I change my mind I can have them straightened – but of course they'd have to break them again first.'

'Oh my God,' said Jennifer. 'What a thought.'

At the slow turn of the stairs footsteps could be heard below. They were quite clearly the pad of bare feet. And there was quite clearly the sound of something tapping against glass and an occasional plop and splash – throaty coughs and underbreath grunts and exclamations muted but audible. Hesta paused and sighed and coughed in reply. Two close strangers signalling their presence, like birds. Clearly, Hesta and her brother were aware of each other.

'Where is Gulliver?' she asked.

'I think he must be at the bike shop today. Sometimes he's offered work at odd times. He's bought a bike. I'll tell you all about it another time.'

'And Marlin?'

'I believe he's working downstairs,' Jennifer said, keeping strictly to the script. 'He said he'd be up to see you when you'd rested,' she lied. He had said no such thing. But she camouflaged the lie with a smile.

Jennifer took her into the room she had prepared. She had expected – pictured – Hesta throwing up her hands and crying out with pleasure at what she'd done to it. But the room could have been nothing but a shed, a Hill shack – the bed could have been a stack of hay and the chair a pile of boxes for all the notice she took of it. She simply lay down on the bed limp and exhausted, oblivious to the bright wall prints and the flowers – and almost oblivious to Jennifer. But it was only a moment of disappointment.

'I'll look after you, darling.' Jennifer stroked her again.

'You're a very good person, Jennifer. I tell everyone what a good person you are. And brave.'

'Bindi made a pot of chicken soup for you.'

'She's a very good person too. So many good people.'

'Would you like some now? Before you sleep?'

'No thank you.'

'Would you like a brandy?'

'God yes, darling. I'd love a brandy.' Hesta began to cry. But there was no tension in her crying. The tears flowed of their own accord, relaxed as the flow of a stream.

'Don't cry, Hesta, you're safe now.'

'I know that, dear. I'm just tired. Very, very tired. And I'd better not see anyone until I am cured of it. Why aren't you at work?'

'Of course I'm not working today! Or tomorrow. I'm here to take care of you.'

Jennifer poured Hesta a large brandy with a splash of water and while she drank it she sat on the edge of the bed, very close to her. There was no familiar perfume on her skin – no Blue Grass, Hesta's favourite – nothing she'd expected, nothing sweet or exotic, just the smell of skin dried by fear and the clinical smell of antiseptics, a hospital smell that clung to her, even drowning the breath of brandy: an alien trace designed in a laboratory to cling forever. Her fine hair, styled usually to give an illusion of fullness, smelled as though it too had been chemically scrubbed.

When the brandy was gone she closed her eyes and slept, smiling.

On Wednesday morning it was as though Tuesday had never existed. The wind had changed and the sun warmed the Bay. On the harbour, small boats slapped against the last of Tuesday's swell and the wake of trawlers and ferries. Hesta had slept from afternoon to morning and felt more at ease than she had felt for a long time. Jennifer had brought her tea and toast and honey at eight o'clock.

'You have made me a very fine nest indeed,' she said, looking around for the first time. There was a pale tint of colour on her cheeks. 'I particularly like the Jeffrey Smart print.'

'It wasn't by chance. I know you love his work.'

'And of course I love everything else.'

'Bindi provided the chest and the chair; she really wanted to help. She's been looking forward to seeing you again.'

'I have never known so many people in my life who have wanted to help me. Such kindness. It's the part of human nature I'd forgotten existed.' Hesta sat on the edge of the bed. Jennifer had made sure the mattress base was well padded so none of the metal of the sofa could be felt. The mattress was new. Hesta pointed to her suitcase. 'There are two small Indonesian figures in there and a sari. The colour has run of course, but we can thread something into it. There are a few other bits and pieces. It's all I've brought to the Bay. Two more boxes are being cared for by the good old Salvos – I don't mind at all now – it will be good to be without possessions, all those fussy material things we cling to – it will be good to be poor.' She eased herself to her feet. She was still dressed in the plain clothes of charity. 'While I'm in the bathroom, dear, look in the suitcase. You will find something in a small green bag that the storm gods saved for you with all their love.'

Jennifer opened the bag and took out of it a music box she had loved from childhood. It was a small, black lacquered box from China delicately worked with gold dragons. She had been given the box to play with as often as she wanted when her mother died. It was a comfort box. It played a strange Eastern tune but Jennifer could have hummed it from beginning to end in her sleep. She wound the key and opened the lid and was amazed to hear the tune again, clear as a bell.

'Well, bless the storm gods for saving its life,' was all she could think to say to Hesta when she came back to the room. 'Thank you, darling. I hope they'll let you stay with me for ages.'

'We'll see, dear ... we'll see. Now, tell me the news. Is the household behaving itself? Has your brother ravaged all the Bay's females? Did you starch the porridge as I suggested? Have you found a prince of men amongst the tables at the cafe? Has one of them snatched the tray from you and tossed it into the bay and carried you off?'

'No,' Jennifer laughed. The music box played on.

'I lost all *my* music, you know?' Hesta held her hands against her face. 'All of it drowned to silence.'

'Then we'll have to get you some more.' Jen kissed her cheek. 'We'll play grand concerts: just you and me.'

From the top of the steps that lead to the jutty and the harbour it was possible to look down on a hammock drowsing in the sun. The hammock was strung between a pole and the ancient stunt of a shrub. The hammock was old and patched and had been brought to Proudie Bay from Bali.

Little of its occupant could be seen but over one side was draped a brown tree limb of an arm, its blond and grey hairs catching light like tight metal curls from a lathe. Finger twigs hung ape-like from the hand, hooked of their own accord, and the nails, filled with paint, putty and brine, brushed the ground with their split ends. At another end was an ankle, also hanging over the hammock's side, and from the distance of observation there appeared to be a barnacled foot and bunioned toes: a sea foot needing a scrape. Where a face might have been was an open book flattened against it. The book was entitled *Crustaceans: Ancient, Modern and Mythical.* And as for the rest of the hammock, the rest was simply a hanging bag of body that almost touched the ground under it.

It was a few minutes after four o'clock and Jennifer crept down the steps and stood quiet and watched the hammock sway very slowly with the man's breath. She had left Hesta to wash and change and had decided the time had come to ask Marlin when he might consider receiving a sister he had not seen for five-and-a-half months.

She looked more closely at the arm, the hand, the ankle, the foot and *Crustaceans: Ancient, Modern and Mythical,* the gentle sway, a certain inconsistency of movement, no matter how slight, in relation to the breath, and she suspected – no, she was certain – that he wasn't asleep at all. There was a certain tension in the parcel of body, the main trunk, that Jennifer recognised. A possible trick of his trade. She wondered how long he'd lain there, pretending. She would like to have thrown a bucket of water over him. She was tempted to stand there and let him suffer for an hour.

'I expect if I let you lie there like that for another hour you'll only get cramp and be no use at all!' she shouted just above his head.

'Mmm? Mmm?' Marlin stretched and feigned a yawn and moved the book from his wide open eyes and rubbed their sides with his knuckles. 'Ol' Mr Sandman got me for sure, Jen.' He looked up at her and swung the hammock from side to side. *It was a fleapit of a performance,* she thought, where you paid nothing and got nothing – in a way it was not worthy of his talents. She ignored the whole act.

'Hesta's well rested now, Dad. She wants you to come up and see her.' Marlin looked at her quickly as though he'd been called to arms.

'*I* can come up and see *her* can I? Oh, my God! An audience, and me not dressed proper.'

'Just come upstairs and behave yourself. She's had a terrible experience. You can't imagine the things that have happened.'

'She tells a good yarn, our Hesta.'

'Dad!!'

'Aye-aye!'

The arrival of sister Hesta – whenever there was an arrival of sister Hesta in Proudie Bay, was another knife point of pain in a certain part of Marlin's mind. She was the reminder of a past he'd locked into the back, back drawers of his brain. Imprisoned there were memories he hoped would one day rot to nothing for lack of use, as fine as the dust of Lissy's body. But memories do not do that – memories are indestructible, even if the drawers are locked solid and the keys tossed into the sea. Simply the thought of Hesta had them opening their cells of their own accord to assault his consciousness with a clarity of Lissy's illness and death (and other things) that was almost unbearable. The memories even had a smell to them, Hesta's link to them had a smell to it – a sweet, rotting sick smell that became stronger every time the memories crowded, as though they had grown cancers of their own. The ghost of Lissy was a stink that woke him, foul, in black night terrors, and he would lie sweating and howling for something to cling to – something – flesh that was not dying, a body that had life and warmth for comfort. And then the memories would release a woman, all alive-o and laughing, who was not dead at all, not even dying – and it was Angie the Irish who Hesta had found him with just after Lissy's funeral. She had stood gaping like a mullet at the door of his room, dressed in black to her ankles, and had stayed in shock and had watched and listened to the Irish squealing while he pumped on top of her in a fury of anger and grief and fear – and revulsion at the slow rotting of his wife.

These were the knife points that Hesta brought to Proudie Bay, and each time the points grew sharper.

She had never forgiven him. She couldn't possibly have understood his reason. She had once whispered to him that not only could he not escape the past but while they both lived she would be the past's messenger.

He had been grateful, however, that she had not shamed him before his children.

He walked up the steps and across the grass slowly, and only quickened his step when he reached the stairs, marching up, forceful and strong, hoping the sound of his step would warn her that he was not afraid.

'Well, Marlin.' Hesta had washed and changed to sack-cloth of a different colour. For the fun of it, Jennifer had draped the water-stained pink and gold sari over her shoulder hoping it would share its colour with her aunt's face, but Hesta's skin could not absorb it. Jen had brushed the sparse, grey hair back and secured it with a band at the nape. But despite the use of lip colour and a necklace of shells, her brother was so surprised by her thin and wan appearance, the look of exhausted resignation in her eyes, her bowed shoulders and twisted hand, that all his swagger, all the bluster was blown out of him and to Jennifer's astonishment he crept up to her, gentle as a mouse, and pecked her on the cheek.

'Well, Sister. How fares the Duchess of Wellings Road?'

'Wellings Road has been blown away, Marlin.' She looked at him from the sides of her eyes.

'And all the birds with it?'

'Yes. All the trees, Marlin, and all the birds.'

'Everything deady-bones?' He asked quietly, and for a moment they might have been sitting, the two of them, small and bare-legged on the edge of their childlife creek in the middle of the bush, lost in their imaginings.

'Almost all,' she said.

'But not one,' he smiled at her. 'A small grey bird with pink and gold feathers and a broken wing survived.'

'Oh yes, Sister Bird survived.'

Jennifer was so astounded and relieved by what she had seen and heard that she fussed about tea or coffee or drinks or anything at all – as though she were waiting table at Dolan's.

'I know Hesta will have a brandy,' she said.

'Yes, dear. Not too much water.'

'I don't think we keep brandy for the ruination of women in this house, Sister Bird.' Marlin, daring to taunt them both, and then grinning sheepishly to make it better.

'Still such a moral creature, Marlin?' Hesta said evenly, then looked away as the roar of a motorcycle distracted her.

'Coffee for your ol' dad, then,' he said.

It was Miriam's idea that they all take Hesta to Shack Hill's market day. It wasn't too far to walk from the Fishcastle to the jumble of stalls, boxes and ground mats, bells, whistles and drums and grill tops of soy burgers that gathered on the first Saturday of the month on a patch of public lawn near the Cove Beach car park.

'We sell hemp clothing. You might find something you like, and Lauren makes excellent wraps, any colour you want.' Miriam had taken an immediate liking to Hesta when they'd met, and Hesta had likened Miriam to a certain portrait by Degas. 'She crochets shawls on the most enormous hooks. They're like huge cobwebs.'

'And!' Beccy, breathless in the presence of a woman who could be her grandmother if she wanted to, 'you can get one of Luce's muffins – and I'll let you hold one of Avian's crystals. She won't mind.' Beccy was convinced that she could cure Hesta's hand by stroking it with a finger as often as possible.

'We don't want to make her too tired, darling,' Jennifer had said to her, but Beccy had taken no notice.

'Do you like pumpkin?' Beccy asked Hesta.

'What was that?'

'Do you like pumpkin?'

'Yes. Sometimes.'

'Me too. Sometimes.'

'Beccy?' Jennifer, wanting to remind her whose friend she was. 'Beccy?'

'What?!'

'Would you like a sandwich and a drink?'

'No. I want to show Hesta things.'

'Say "no thank you",' said Miriam.

'*No thank you*! Come on, Hesta.'

The lights of their days, it had seemed to Jennifer, had begun to shine brighter on and around the house. There was a calm about the place. The harbour peaked and splashed gentle against the jutty and the wall, and a certain warmth wound a thread like silk around them all. Even the snake unwound its coils and stretched and pigeons on death row coooed soft and gave no hint of their impending doom. Between Hesta and the males, a somewhat starched aura of tolerance and civility existed and the aura had stayed undisturbed for longer than she could have imagined. Everything had been almost exactly as she'd hoped when Hesta made a family of them all at the Fishcastle. It was just – well, just this absurd adoration Beccy had for Hesta – and Miriam too, to some extent … But what was she thinking? She knew it would pass, of course. *It was just the novelty of the thing* – the tales of the storm, the stories of death and destruction, the media attention, recalling the sound of express trains and the story of the tunnel and the bridge when she was young with the boy Marlin. She knew of course, it would pass. Beccy would get sick of it like any other child. Miriam would be too busy to help care for frailty. But it had all added intrusions to a mind already crowded with them.

Jennifer had shopped for Hesta. She had tripped to the city for one whole liberating day, alone and courageous, with the authority to spend what was needed at David Jones, and to buy a treat for herself if she saw something she loved. She'd been like a child on a special excursion – a big day out, and she'd kept it all for herself. She had not invited Miriam to go with her. She had bought clothes for Hesta and had not included Miriam or Beccy in her choice. She had bought accessories and underwear and sandals and mules – all without the help of anyone at all. She was proud of that. She was proud of her strength to choose, even if it was only for one day, between the hours of eight and four.

In one of the bags was a linen dress for Hesta, size fourteen to sixteen, beltless, cut on the cross and elegant. It was the deep blue purple of salvia that she loved. The day of shopping had been empowering. It had cleared her head of destructive thoughts – for that one day.

Beccy and Hesta had been delighted with the purple dress. A wave of a wand over sackcloth and there she stood, *ta da!*, in purple linen. The dress was too long and a little loose here and there, but it was the sweetest thing she had worn since the storm. Of course the colour reminded her of the salvia in her ruined garden. She wondered how it was healing. She wondered if the garden missed her and thought she had abandoned it.

An hour before they were all due to leave for the market Beccy had insisted on 'making her over'. Hesta had allowed her to paint her cheeks and lips, shadow her eyelids, tie back her hair with green ribbon and drape the sari around her. With red wooden beads from the dress-up box, Beccy had added the last adornment. Hesta looked like a very old prize at a fair – or the grandmother of circus dolls. Miriam and Jennifer privately laughed while Beccy worked very seriously and Hesta, for the sake of the child, remained a serious subject. After admiring her work Beccy insisted on helping Hesta downstairs to show Marlin what a beautiful sister he had, and out in the sunlight she stood in glorious colour, the model posed and Beccy pointed. But the child had been confused by Marlin's reaction:

'Good grief, Sister Bird! Not at your age!' He covered his eyes with his hands. 'It's too bright for the naked eye. By far too bright!'

'Good, Marlin,' Hesta said. 'I'm glad you're surprised. Beccy did it all. Isn't she clever, and so good with colour. And as for *age*, Marlin – age is merely a number – I don't concern myself with numbers. Do you see trees counting their rings?' She tossed the sari end over her shoulder. 'Of course you do not, Marlin, because a tree knows it is *nothing* until it is aged. Nothing!' Jennifer, who had watched the scene from the upstairs window, smiled. *This is what he was afraid of,* she thought, *this is where she has the edge. Brilliant!* 'And because you think my appearance too bright for your naked eye, I will be proud to go to the market and dazzle everyone else, and darling Beccy shall lead the way.'

A small group of women that included the child Beccy stood at the gate of number fourteen and waited while Jennifer flew upstairs for the second time, like a mother hen, to collect sunscreen, a carry bag and an extra hat. While they waited, Gulliver wheeled his bike out onto the Sandpath. It was well timed: as though he'd been waiting in the shed for the right moment. It was not usual for him to want to be seen with the women of the house, but he smiled as if it pleased him very much. He stood the bike in front of Miriam.

'Can I sit on it, Gully?' Beccy pleaded. 'Pleeeese?'

'I'll run you round to the market if you want.'

'*Yes!* Cool! Can I, Mum? Pleeeese?'

'I wouldn't let her.' Bindi Hope said in her wisdom. 'She hasn't got a helmet.' But it was Gull she looked at side-on when she said it. And side-on she saw the flick of eye contact between Gull and Miriam. 'It's illegal,' she said. She knew what was going on.

'I don't think so. Not a good idea, Bec.'

'Mum?!'

'I'll run her around slow,' Gull said, and Beccy was already astride the pillion, thin-lipped and hard-eyed enough to kill anyone who tried to take her off. 'I'll go slow round Cliff Street. She'll be okay. I'll look after her.' All the time looking at Miriam, and Miriam, finding his eyes too much, turning her head and finding the gate post interesting. 'We'll meet you round there, okay? You have to hold on to me really tight, Bec. Put your arms around me really tight and hang on.' He kick-started the bike and took off down the road with Beccy screaming with pleasure and clutching the Brando for dear life.

Gulliver had lately given a great deal of time to Beccy and to Miriam, through Beccy. He'd offered to take them fishing, and even allowed the child to explore the dinghy cave. He turned a few tricks of his own for them. Telling fish stories of his own, jokes he'd heard in the pubs, and old tales of sea adventures to Beccy that she'd related to Miriam, full of praise for the storyteller: 'He's nearly as good as Marlin, Mum. Do you like Gull?' Jennifer had observed all this too. And she wasn't fooled for a moment.

'Where's Beccy?' she asked at the gate, and was furious when they told her. She slapped her sides with her hands. 'Why did you let him take her on the bike?!'

'I told them she should have a helmet. I told them,' Bindi said, watching Miriam, who'd folded her arms in a none-of-your-business pattern.

Hesta tried not to think of it at all. Gathering strength for the market and preparing to walk in unfamiliar sandals took all her energy.

It was a slow, unusual procession of high colour that strolled along the Sandpath. Miriam walked on one side of Hesta and Bindi Hope, the other – too close, in Jennifer's opinion. *She didn't need that much support*, she thought, *They were suffocating her.* Jennifer walked behind them; there wasn't room on the sides.

'Shouldn't you rub some of the red off your face, at least?' Bindi asked.

'Beccy would be devastated if I did.'

'She won't notice,' said Miriam. 'Once we're at the market, she won't notice. She goes wild at the market.'

'I have tissues here somewhere.' Jen rooted fussily around inside a carry bag.

'It's okay, Jen. I've already given her a packet,' said Miriam. And Hesta took Miriam's tissues, not Jennifer's, and wiped a layer of paint from her face.

Beccy and Gull were waiting on the hem of the market-place. Beccy waved a length of dowelling decorated with coloured ribbons, like a miniature maypole.

'Did you see me? Did you see me? Did you see me riding?'

'You looked very grand,' Hesta said. 'Like a lady on a horse.'

'You could have *killed* her!' Jennifer snapped at Gull, and then seeing the angry look on Beccy's face, 'the stick's pretty, Bec. Who made that?'

'Delia,' said the child. 'She makes them all the time. Come on Hesta, I'll show you where to go.' She took Hesta's arm and gently guided her away. She paid no more attention to Jennifer. Hesta paid no more attention to Jennifer, and Miriam walked with Gull. Jennifer stood alone in the crowd, holding their hats and carry bags, sunscreens and water bottles like a stick of hooks. She would not have been surprised if passing strangers had hung things on her as well.

Around the edge of the market, a savant with busy eyes and a dying face moved about in a sort of counted dance of half circles: three times clockwise and three times anti-clockwise, the same movements over and over and over. Pigeons squabbled around the feet of a boy eating chips. A plain woman with a shopping basket picked her way from stall to stall with a girl with green hair and three nose rings. The girl had a cold, and mucus clung to the rings, stale and sticky as week-old dew. Feral children ran like ground squirrels in and out of feet, eating cake and ices and waving stick streamers. There were stilt-walkers and face-painters and pan flutes and drums, and through all of this Beccy led Hesta, introducing her to stall children, reaching on tiptoe to demonstrate the excellence of wind chimes and the magic spin of a mobile. She made Hesta feel the texture of painted fabric and buy two of Luce's fruit and pumpkin muffins. And Hesta trailed around as best she could like a Delhi albino in purple and pink. She was hot and very tired. She turned and caught Jen's eye and mimed hot and tired by fanning her hand and closing her eyes, but when Jennifer moved towards her Beccy pulled her on through the crowd, out of reach.

Children must be the cruellest creatures in the world. Jennifer sat on the grass with the hats and bags. She wondered at what age was the threshold of cruelty for a child, and what influenced a child to leave it or to continue on a life path of cruelty for the sheer pleasure of it. It was a moment before she realised that the shadow above her was Hesta's.

'I think I must go back now, dear,' she said. 'I am not as strong as I thought. I'm very tired.' Hesta's skin was oiled with perspiration and there were two dark wet purple patches under her arms. Jennifer rose to her feet and gathered their belongings.

'Where are the others?'

'Gull has taken Miriam and Beccy up the Hill.'

'On the bike?!'

'Yes.'

'But that's ridiculous – and dangerous!'

'I think he's done it before, Jen.'

'Hesta!'

'Don't mind too much, Jen dear. Let's go back and have a cool drink – a nice brandy – and watch the harbour.'

'You're wrong about them! She would have told me.'

'I don't think I'm wrong, dear.'

It was a long and silent walk back to the Fishcastle. Jennifer walked, bowed down as though she carried a cross. There was no threshold to cruelty at all, she'd decided. She walked heavily on. For the rest of that day she looked forward to nothing at all. Hesta walked on and looked forward to her bottle.

Chapter Nine

THE SEVENTH WAVE

From below Shack Hill, at the bottom of the cliffs where the black night sea heaved and crashed against the rocks, there were sea creatures moaning. They curled up to a shack they knew well and parted the timber of the wall with white wet fingers and brought with them a dream of fright to Rebecca Holt.

The dream she dreamed in her small head was her own recurring night terror. It was the dream of a great, shrieking wall of ocean, so high that its top could not be seen, moving green and heavy towards her until it was almost close enough for her to touch, and she knew that if she did touch it she would die. It would close over her and she would drown. But as she had done before, she'd clawed for her life, and still in her sleep howled herself wide awake for one last gasp of air.

Even when her eyes were open and stared wildly into

the dark the demons still moaned – the demons still moaned, and she lay there listening, too frightened to move. She covered her head with her blanket and still they moaned – but the moans seemed to have moved to her mother's room and had become the sound of her mother's voice.

'Mum?!'

A silent pause – a breathlessness – a whispered '*shit!*' in a strange voice.

'Mum?!'

'Bec, go to sleep. It's after midnight.'

There was movement. A squeak of bedding, a rustle of clothing.

'Mum!' Beccy lay absolutely still in her own slick of fear, wide-eyed, staying purposefully sleepless, in case the night terror came back to her.

'Bec! Go back to sleep!' Miriam called. There was an edge to her voice.

'I'm scared. I'm having that dream.' She thought she heard her mother's feet touch the floor but it could just as easily have been a splash of water, or something plopping back into its sea, so acute were her senses.

'I have to go to her,' she heard Miriam say. 'No, don't! I'll have to go – she has these dreams.'

'Ahh, shit, Mirry!' Not a muffled voice this time. 'Get her to sleep in the van next time, for God's sake!'

'Shut up, Gull! It's not her fault.'

Gulliver Hardwick's motorcycle had become a more frequent feature outside the shack, parked against the wall between it and the van like a black horse tethered. And during the late-night visits Beccy was dimly aware of sounds through the partition that she felt, somehow, she shouldn't be listening to. They were the sounds of a life she knew she could not share with her mother and she'd angrily block her ears with her fingers. Once she had asked Crystal if the sound was Gull loving her mother but Crystal had laughed at her and said, 'Probably just fucking, Bec.'

Early in the mornings when Gull had slept at the shack Beccy would sneak outside and sit astride the bike and twist her hands around the handles the way Gulliver did. She would shake her head so that her hair looked as though it blew in the wind, and she would pull her skirt up high the way the wind blew it when she rode behind Gull and he laughed and winked at her in the rear-vision mirror. But Gull rarely gave her rides now. For a whole, sweet time she was sure that he liked her as much as he liked her mother – more even – and certainly as much as Beccy loved him. But all he did now was swear if she played with his bike and whine if she was in the shack when he had things to do, or if she disturbed him with her nightmares.

She was convinced it was the night dreams that caused the trouble, that brought out the worst in Gulliver. If she could stop the sea dream then maybe their relationship would go back to what it was. With all the courage in the world she visited the ocean and confronted her enemy.

It was on her way home from school one afternoon that she crossed the Hill path and walked through the scrub until she reached the fence at the highest point over the cliffs.

She looked down and watched the great waves tear at their base, battering and sucking the rock and spitting it out, gouging it out bit by bit. She knew they were crumbling the cliffs, dissolving them, so that one night they could pull the cliffs down into the ocean and take the Hill with them.

She leaned over the middle rail of the fence as far as her pounding heart would allow and threw down to her terrible sea a small china dog she had loved. Her sacrifice flew out of sight in the wind and she felt sorry for it, throwing it down to hell like that. She waited and listened, but above the wind she heard not the slightest sound of it having been received. Not a splash. Not even a gulp.

'If you don't come to me at night,' she shouted down to it, 'I'll give you something nice every Friday after school, okay?! Can you hear me down there, you bloody *bad water*?!'

She kept her bargains with the ocean to herself. She knew the spell of it would be broken if she told another soul. And only night would tell if the sacrifices worked. She tried not to be frightened of bedtime.

In the meantime, when Gull came to stay overnight, she had to camp in Crystal's van. It was a terrible thing to have to do. She had to sleep on a mattress on the floor with the cockroaches. Sometimes, if she was lucky, Crystal didn't come home, but if she did, she was either pot-brained or drunk or mad, or snoring loud as a roll of drums. Beccy hated her all the more no matter how she was. But even more terrible in her mind, even worse than Crystal, was her mother making her sleep there because Gull wanted it (though she was aware of Miriam checking her from time to time), and Gull's betrayal of her love for him. On the nights she had to sleep in the van, she hated him almost as much as Crystal.

'So! It's about time you got here!' Jennifer was angry, her voice sharp as pain. She'd had a hard working day; it was stifling hot and the table fan in her room seemed to circulate heat. Outside, the haze of it was dense enough to cut. Trees drooped and birds swayed on branches with their wings stretched to catch something cool. Over the rooftops a yacht's mast glided past with no wind at all in its sails, cheating under its stern.

'I said I'd be here about five.' Miriam threw a cotton bag on the floor of Jen's room in a sudden fit of irritation. 'When did you say I had to be here by a certain time?' Her head ached and her eyes stung from the hot, dry air.

'It's *five-thirty*, Miriam. She's still down there listening to his rubbish. She hasn't been upstairs at all.' Jennifer's words and her tension flew around the room like jaggards. Miriam sank to the floor, exhausted by them and everything else.

'Jen, you know I can't hurry, the way I feel now.' She stretched her feet out on the carpet. And you can't expect a kid to stay up here with you when there are other kids to play with – and if you want to know what I think, I think Marlin's stories are great fun. She's full of them when she gets home.'

'No wonder she has nightmares!'

'Oh, for God's sake, Jen, chill out!'

For the last three days Beccy had been coming home from the cafe with Jennifer. She ran down the hill from school and played on the sand near the tables, looking for periwinkles, tossing shells into the bay, fidgeting and waiting impatiently for Jen to finish work. Miriam had caught yet another virus that had left her weak and nauseous, and as with other emergencies Jennifer had jumped into the role of surrogate mother. But as soon as she arrived at the Fishcastle, Beccy just became one of *his* after-schoolies. She'd found it impossible to hide her irritation and frustration. She was powerless to alter the child's switch of loyalty.

Beccy sat on the harbour front grass, happy and straight as a joystick, oblivious to the heat and the bickering upstairs. She sat cross-legged and goggle-eyed with two stragglers, while Marlin dazzled them with an epic lie. Earlier, Marlin had delighted Beccy even more by promoting her to 'Keeper of the Coop' and 'Head Tester of Pigeon Breasts'. He had called her to him. 'Our Rebeccy here,' he'd said, 'will test the coooer's breasts and tell whether they're ready to have their heads screwed off for the oven – kneel.' She had knelt. 'I place on the head of our "Keeper of the Coop" the crown of the pigeon twig.' And he'd placed on her head a twig with two leaves that had fallen at his feet. Beccy had solemnly bowed and graciously accepted applause. Her elevation once again confirmed her status as his slave for life.

Upstairs in Jennifer's room, the spirit of Rebecca's coronation seemed to have had a calming effect on two women.

'Jen, I'm really sorry I was late – and I'm sorry I snapped

at you. The truth is, this afternoon I fell asleep again. It's all I seem to want to do now – sleep.'

'Are you still nauseous?'

'Yes.'

'You did go to a doctor, didn't you?'

'They said it was just a low virus. A hangover from the flu – something like that anyway.' Miriam stood at the lookout window and searched for a breeze. She was a greying pale. The natural light and shades of her skin disappeared into sallowness. Her eyes were dull and lacklustred and her copper hair needed a clean and polish.

'Did the doctor give you something to take for it?'

'I don't need anything. I'll be all right.'

'But you're obviously not eating properly. You've lost weight.'

'*Please* stop fussing, Jen. I'm okay!' She clamped her mouth tight and shut her eyes. 'Oh, God, there I go again. I'm sorry.' She put her arms around Jennifer and tried to hug her. 'Jen, you're as stiff as a board. You get so tense. You worry too much, but I hate it when we spat. I really love you. I don't know what I'd have done without you down here: I'd have gone mad. I'll always be grateful to you.' She held Jennifer at arm's length. 'Still friends? Are we? Yes?'

'Oh for heaven's sake. Of course we are.' Jennifer turned the fan up a notch. 'It's just that . . .'

'Just what?'

'Oh, nothing. It's just me. It's the heat. My period's due. Nothing!' But what she would really like to have said if she'd had the courage to be truthful, was: *'It's just that, I wonder if you'd love me as much if I wasn't doing anything for you ... just for myself and not lifting a finger. I'm everyone's friend as long as I'm useful – good old Jenny, the working she-ass – or Jenny, the chained monkey: throw a dollar hug to her or a ten-cent smile every now and then to keep her dancing. She'll do anything for a crumb of love and you all know it. It's bloody pathetic!'* That's what she would have said if she'd had the courage to be truthful ... *'And, what's really the matter with you, Miriam?'* she'd have added. 'It's nothing,' she said. 'Nothing's wrong. It's just me.'

At the door of Jennifer's room there was a light rap. From a new habit formed she glanced at her watch.

'Can I come in, dear?' Hesta called.

'Of course you can come in.' Jennifer was pleased in a way, to have the spell of her thoughts broken. 'Miriam's here.'

'Lovely!' she said to Miriam. 'How are you, dear?' Hesta watched Jennifer pour the first of her brandies. 'Are you feeling better?'

'Not too bad, really.'

Hesta still had a light, wispy look about her. She had gained no weight at all. Her fine hair hung in threads around her face like a frayed hem and it was damp with perspiration. A fresh bruise on her arm was the mark of a recent fall in the bathroom and a reminder of the day that Jennifer had confiscated the brandy bottle. *So much for the joy of Hesta!* She'd been shattered by the incident. *So much for nice family units: so much for someone to talk to woman to woman. She might have known it was nothing but wishful thinking! They're all cripples here, every one of them. It was like running a bloody asylum!*

'This heat is awful, dear, isn't it?' to Miriam. She'd almost finished the first drink: two-and-a-half swallows to a tot. Jen and Miriam exchanged glances. 'Am I to drink alone, dear hearts?' And when neither of the 'dear hearts' responded, Hesta sat at the table by the window and fanned herself with a magazine.

Miriam picked up her bag and kissed Hesta on the cheek. 'I've got to go. You take care now.'

'Where's little Beccy?' Hesta asked.

'She's still down the front with Marlin.'

'Then you must take her home, Miriam. The sooner the better.'

At least they were always in agreement on that issue, Jen thought. At least there was still some clear thinking above the brandy.

They left Hesta drinking and humming flat tunes to the air outside the lookout window. On the stairs Miriam swayed for a moment and held the banister.

'Are you sure you're all right?' Jennifer took her arm.

'I'm okay. I was light-headed for a minute. Is Gull here?'

'I think I heard his bike.' Jennifer's tone altered in an instant. She took her hand away from Miriam's arm.

'Do you think he'd give us a lift to the Hill? Do you think he'd mind?'

'For God's sake, why would he mind?' *Why would he mind!* she thought. *He's probably already out there waiting!*

But he'd had to be asked, and at the gate, Gull waited sullenly quiet for his passengers.

'Miriam,' Jennifer said. 'I'm going to be late tomorrow. I don't want Beccy here without me and I can't have her waiting around the beach forever. I don't think I'll be home till after six.'

'She can come to me. It's okay. I'm feeling a bit better in the afternoons now.' Miriam took the child's hand when she protested.

'Mum, I want to come here!'

'Well, you can't. You can't come here every day. It's not our home!' There was a crabbiness in her voice again and she felt queasy with heat. Sweat ran between her breasts. She was beyond any pretence to sweetness and light.

'I'll pick her up from school if you want.' Gull said suddenly. 'I'll watch her for a couple of hours – okay, Bec?'

Miriam thanked him but with not much enthusiasm. 'Is that okay with you, Jen?'

No! It's not okay, not okay, not okay, not okay! 'Oh, I expect so.'

Beccy spun circles and shouted, loving him all over again in the blink of an eye, forgiving him for a flash of a grin. Gulliver glanced at Jennifer and saw the signs.

'Hesta will be here. The kid can stay with her if you're worried.'

Jennifer said nothing more. She was not absolutely sure why. She did not thank Gull for his 'favour', only searched his eyes for a second or two for a clue – a reason for it. As Miriam and Beccy squeezed aboard the bike, all she could think of to say was: 'You be a good girl for your mum, Beccy.'

And as they rode off she tried to limit her thoughts to relief that she'd persuaded them to buy helmets. *There she goes again ... the good mother hen Jennifer ... good mother wren, pecking around them with its work hands, its drying womb, a brain limp and constant dread in the pit of its belly, coiled like a wildthing, trying to read truths behind all their eyes.*

They waved to her and she waved back. And as they turned the corner a small pink helmet caught the last of the sun.

At the bottom of the dirt track that served as Shack Hill's road, Miriam told Beccy to hurry on up and start her homework.

'You haven't been up to see me for a few days, Gull,' she said when they were alone.

'I've been busy at the bike shop.' He kicked a stone out of its hole and sent it rolling down.

'So? You work at night?'

'Well, you've had that flu again. I don't want to catch it from you.'

'Bullshit, Gull! Bullshit! You know damn well I haven't got the flu.'

'How long is it now?'

'Over four weeks.'

'That's nothing.'

'I'm pregnant, Gulliver!'

'So what if you are! How do you know it's mine?' Anger made his pretty-boy face ugly. She wondered why she'd taken so long to see what was behind the big doe eyes and the long lashes. Behind them, by the side of the track, small bushes listened and wandering Jews nodded knowing heads in a current of air. 'The way you lot live up there, it could be anybody's.'

She didn't have the strength to hit him but the fear she saw in his eyes compensated for it.

'You're scared shitless, aren't you?' she said, 'but that was a terrible thing to say.'

'Okay, I'm sorry. We'll think of something I suppose, but for God's sake don't tell anyone. You haven't told anybody, have you?' By 'anybody' she imagined he meant Jennifer and his father – particularly his father.

'No, I haven't. It'll be our little secret for the time being, but you'll damn well have to help me.' She started to walk up the hill but turned and said to him: 'When you pick Bec up tomorrow you hand her straight over to Hesta or your father, okay? And tell her to do her homework.'

'Whatever ... if he's there, and if the old girl's awake.' He turned the bike and rode off, the engine sputtering sullen and quiet and pensive as its rider.

When Miriam reached the shack after a slow, stone-rutted climb, she threw up behind it, more or less on the spot where Gull parked his bike. She vomited noisily and Beccy ran to her on the verge of tears.

'Stop it, Mum!' she screamed. 'Stop it. You sound like Crystal!'

'Make me some tea, Bec . . . . and try and find me an apple. And don't worry, I'm okay.'

'You're not. You're sick!' Beccy cried. 'You're always sick!'

'Not always, Bec. Just a little bit right now,' she said between heaves. 'Just a bit.'

'Well, who's going to look after me when you die? That's what I want to know.'

'Bec, I'm not going to die. I'm just throwing up.' Beccy was angry with fear but the tears that had threatened stayed, as usual, deep in the bottom of their well. Miriam wiped her mouth with her hand. Her heaving was mostly dry. 'Now how about that tea?'

'Okay. There was an apple in my bag but I gave it to the waves. It was an old one. I'll find another one. Do you want me to find another apple?'

'That's a good girl. Ask Luce. They make me feel better.' Her throat and voice were scratched dry from retching. 'Tomorrow we'll buy a whole bag full.'

They slept early, the mother and child. They slept the deep, drugging sleep of minds exhausted. But that night at least, Beccy did not dream of the ocean.

Rebecca Holt's pink helmet, printed in black with her name, was carried to school, hanging from her backpack, in full view, like new Olympic gold. She complained bitterly when she was told to hang it on a hook outside the classroom. Only one of the after-schoolies, consumed with envy, told her that it was a cheap helmet and the worst brand and when the bike crashed her brains would be all over the road and her arms and legs and her teeth somewhere else and there'd be crows eating the bits. But it meant nothing to her – she couldn't even be bothered picturing the scene, and for the rest of the whole, preoccupied day the last thing on Beccy's mind was her death.

Gull pulled up outside the school, engine still revving, at fifteen minutes after three, and as she climbed, pink-helmeted, up behind him and wrapped her arms around his leather jacket, she could not have been more proud had she been one of Mrs Kerslake's Blossom brides. And when Gulliver gave the engine full throttle as they rode off, she imagined every eye from the school to Shack Hill would be watching her, *must* be watching her, and she shrieked with excitement. In the wind was the smell of hot oil and fuel and leather, and if she could, she would have ridden with her arms stretched out like a bird. It was not until they'd reached the turn to the Sandpath that she realised that not once had Gull laughed or glanced at her through the rear-vision mirror.

Beccy followed Gull as he wheeled the bike across the gravel and into the shed. 'Don't touch anything,' he told her. She'd never been in the shed before, where the bike was kept – in the holy of holies. Everything else was quiet. There was no deep Marlin voice coming from the harbour front. It was so quiet she could hear the pigeons coooing. Even next-door's dog wasn't barking.

'I'm first, am I?' she asked him with her hands on her hips, still high as a kite from the ride.

'First for what?' He'd produced a bottle from somewhere and unscrewed the top.

'For *stories*, Gully!'

'No stories today, Bec. Marlin's in town today.' He drank from the bottle and licked a spill away from the corner of his mouth. He stamped on a bull ant near his boot. Beccy was plainly let down.

'What can I do then?'

'You can stay and talk to me for a bit.' He hung his jacket and helmet, opened his tool box and began to work on the front wheel. 'Do you want a drink or something?'

'Jen gives me orange juice.' She squatted down near the wheel. 'What are you doing?'

'Changing a fork bolt.'

'What's that?'

'You wouldn't understand if I told you.' He sucked at the bottle again. 'So the wheel won't fall off if you have to know.' She squatted closer, watching him work. He coughed.

'You smell like Crystal,' she said.

'What the hell's that supposed to mean?'

'I don't know,' she said abjectly. 'Just when you breathe out. It's a bottle-piss smell.' To her great relief he laughed out loud. 'Christ, Bec, the stuff you come out with! Where did you hear that?'

'Crystal, I guess,' she said. 'She calls everything piss or shit.' And when he laughed again she laughed too. *She'd made Gull laugh!* She tried to think of something else.

'How's your mum?' he asked, not looking at her. 'How was she this morning?'

'She throws up all the time.'

'But she's got somebody to look after her – a boyfriend maybe, right?' He kept working.

'You're her boyfriend, aren't you?'

'Well, not as serious as maybe somebody else would be. Tell me who else there is.'

'Don't you like us any more?' Beccy felt the afternoon begin to fold inside out: all the fun of it turning sour. 'Don't you like Mum now because she vomits?'

'Well, yes. Of course I like her, and I'm sorry she's sick ... but ...' his spanner slipped, and he swore and sucked a nicked thumb.

'You're just her boyfriend, I told you! You have to look after her. Crystal told me what you do in bed.'

'Christ, Beccy!'

'So that's how I know, okay?'

'Okay – okay. Jesus!'

'I want a drink,' she demanded angrily, furious at the way Gulliver and the day and her mum's sickness had crushed her.

'Go round to the kitchen then.'

'Where's Aunty Hesta?'

'My guess is asleep.'

'Can I go and play with the animals then?' She stood and pulled her skirt down.

'Yes – go play with the animals.'

'The snake?'

'Whatever! The snake, the lizards, whatever you want. I have to finish this.'

'I don't care anyway! Do you want me to tell Mum you don't like us any more!'

'Don't you do that, not if you want to ride on the bike again.'

'I don't care about your stupid bike either!' Glaring at him with her hands on her hips. The on again-off again love affair off again.

Beccy stamped out of the shed, leaving her backpack and helmet on the ground near the door, and went in search of a drink and something to love until Hesta woke and Jennifer came home.

It was for Beccy one-and-a-half absorbing hours later that Marlin found her playing a story game on the grass, surrounded by two tortoises, a blue-tongue lizard and the python, flopped in a curl of disinterest near its coop. She was ranting to them in the lowest voice she could manage and every now and then moved a recalcitrant tortoise back to its allotted place within the circle of her audience. She spun around when she heard Marlin's voice but was not in the least embarrassed that he had caught her at his own game.

'Well, well. Is our lil' Hill chil' Beccly, too early for the next session or too late for the last?'

'Why didn't you come today?' she asked him. He was dressed in a shirt, trousers and shoes. Almost a different person.

'Work-a-day, Bec. A fish workday at the museum. And now poor ol' Marlin's tired and wants his coffee and he wonders who will make it for the poor ol' thing.' Beccy laughed and took his huge bony hand in hers. Who? *His*

245

slave for life, of course! 'I will,' she said, grinning.

Later, while they sat together on the edge of the carp pond, she told him, 'I've checked the pigeons. There's one nearly fat enough for Marlin. I fed it some corn. It will be deee-lissh-uss!'

'What a good keeper is our Beccy. And where's the nice mountain lady?'

'She's upstairs. She's had her sleep and I brushed her hair and gave her her bottle.'

'For gosh sakes!' He threw up his arms and rolled his eyes and grinned all over his face. 'Our Jen *will* be pleased. And where is the Gully Bird?'

'In the shed, fixing his wheel.' And that was all she said. There was nothing more she wanted to say about Gulliver. 'What will I do now? What can I do till Jen gets home?

'Well now, let's have a think, lil' Hill chil'. You let old Marlin put away his papers and throw off his city clobber and he just might let you see some sea pictures.' He put his face near her ear and spoke just above a whisper. 'Like, for instance, what lives way down at the bottom of the sea where there's no light.'

'Wow!' she shivered.

'Ghosty fishes they be, my Beccly. They make their own light so they can see with their big, big eyes.' And he widened his own eyes and flapped his lips together and made sucking sounds. 'Would you like to see pictures of that!?'

'Yes,' she shouted. 'Yes.' Even though she was afraid of what she might take to bed with her and dream that night. She had not told Marlin of her nightmares and would never tell him, but at that moment she believed that she was about to be confronted with pictures of her real enemies – the demons from the deep black with staring eyes and white claws. She was fascinated and afraid at the same time at the prospect of seeing the real ones for the first time . . . and she would search the pictures for signs of a small china dog and an old apple, lying there, on the floor of the ocean, in the dark, blacker than anything.

On the kitchen table Marlin spread out sea books with pictures and sketches of things rarely seen. He gave her paper and pen to scribble notes. It was wonderful and frightening to her. There were sinuous creatures with strange eyes deep diving from sea mountains – there was a moray eel's dark rock home with nothing but teeth at the entrance, and in the deepest blackness, black and heavy as wet velvet, were sad glowing things with no shape at all, changing their forms like spirits. There were sparks of light like lost fireflies crying, curls of worms with eyes and lights in their flicking tails, white wisps of something veiled blowing in a water wind, a million fish darts moving this way and that, all tails and one brain – and other things, all aliens from the planet sea that visited earth only in her nightmares, rising from way down deep, way down where Beccy imagined the bottom of the world ended and lay on the roof of hell. She had seen no evidence of sacrifices.

'I hate the water,' she said after a long silence. 'I hate the sea. I'll never touch the sea.' And straightaway she knew she'd said the wrong thing.

'Can our Beccy swim?'

'No,' she said miserably.

'Then ol' Marlin will have to do something about that. We can't have our Coop Keeper landlubbing forever.' He gathered the books together. 'But not today.'

'Not ever!' she shouted and ran out of the room.

Beccy was upstairs, sitting on the floor in green tulle from the dress-up box and watching television when Jennifer came home. Reminders of homework had been thrown out the lookout window. She studied with great concentration the muddled families in 'The Bold and the Beautiful'. Even worse than her own.

'Beccy! What a thing to be watching. Have you done your homework?' She threw her purse on the bed.

'Yes.'

'Have you had a drink and something to eat?' She kicked off her shoes.

'Yes.' Still glued to the set.

'Have you been with Hesta?' Changing her blouse.

'She's asleep. She did wake up and I brushed her hair and she wanted her bottle.'

'Oh no! And what else?'

'Marlin showed me pictures of terrible fish. He wants me to learn to swim but I told him I don't want to.'

'Well don't take any notice of him. What about Gull?' Slipping on sandals.

'He talked a lot.'

'What about?'

'Mum.' Standing perfectly still now, and listening.

'What about your mum?'

'He wanted to know how many boyfriends she had.'

'Why would he want to know that?'

'I don't know. I told him he was Mum's boyfriend but he said he wasn't really.'

'Why would he say that?'

'I don't know.'

'Why do you think he's your mum's boyfriend anyway? I mean, they just see each other now and then ...'

'Gull sleeps at our place lots.' Beccy still watched the screen, not really absorbing the drama. She didn't see Jennifer's face. She was glad to have someone to talk it over with. She was sick of it all. 'Sometimes he gets angry with me if I have my bad dream. I have to sleep in the van with Crystal.' She held her nose and screwed up her face.

'How many times has Gull slept at your place?' There was something in Jennifer's voice that was colder and steelier than 'The Bold and the Beautiful'. Better.

'Lots. But I don't think he wants to any more because Mum throws up all the time.'

Jennifer clamped her hand over her mouth. She'd turned as red as a beet and simply stood still and stared at the floor.

'What's the matter, Jen?' Beccy asked, staring at her. 'Don't you get sick too!'

'Beccy.' Jen's voice was low and even. 'You get your things together. I just have to go downstairs for a minute. You stay here and then I'll take you back to the Hill, okay?'

'Can I watch TV?'

'Yes. Watch TV.'

Hesta was in the hallway outside Jen's room when she emerged with the dark demeanour of an avenging angel. Darker.

'What on earth is it, dear?' Hesta was jolted out of the brandied corrugation of her mind. 'You look like the Black Queen.'

'Stay with Beccy for a few minutes. I'm going down to talk to Gull.' And she knew as she flew down the stairs that her instincts had been right all along.

Gull was still in the shed fiddling with his bike when Jennifer burst in like a cyclone.

'What have you done now!?' He flinched from her real and extreme anger. 'What have you done to Miriam?!'

'I don't know what the shit you're talking about.'

'Don't you swear at me, you bastard!'

Never before, never before, he thought.

'You're nothing but a trouble-making idiot – always have been and I suppose always will be! Don't you speak to me the way you talk to those garbage fish-stinking pub mates of yours!' She moved closer to him, barely inches away. 'What-have-you-done-to-Miriam!?'

'Nothing that I know of,' he shouted. 'What the hell are you talking about?' But he was already red with guilt. She was very close to hitting him and she had no idea that it was the second time in two days that he had narrowly escaped assault.

'Yes you do. You know damn well! Is Miriam pregnant?'

'I don't know. And what if she is? What's it got to do with

me!? The kid said she's got a dozen men.' Then Jennifer did slap him. For the first time in her life she slapped him hard across the face and he was so shocked his jaw dropped.

'And on top of everything else, you're a liar – a liar and a cheat! You're just no good and I'm just glad your mother isn't here to see you now – if the cancer hadn't killed her, you would have!' Her voice was chillingly even – not what they were used to in that house. She didn't wail or cry or fly into hysterics and that frightened Gull even more.

'But even if she is gone, I don't know if it's mine. How would you ever know with someone on the Hill.' He was immediately sorry he'd said that. 'Who told you she was pregnant anyway? Beccy?'

'Beccy doesn't know – nor will she until she has to. In the meantime . . .'

'You're not going to tell Dad, are you?' He sounded like the boy child she once knew and loved and protected. But the little voice was not enough. She was not moved by it.

'That would really mess you up, Gulliver Hardwick, wouldn't it!' she hissed close to his face. 'I'll just have to think about that.' And she turned to leave.

'What's all the commotion?' Marlin asked as he passed the shed. 'My little fishlings fighting over some bait?'

'Oh, shutup!' Jennifer snapped as she pushed past him and marched back to the house.

Chapter Ten

SNAKE

The length of Hesta's stay at the Fishcastle had been dictated by the extraordinary state of her affairs. While her health and strength had improved she was not able to cope with the mental strain of dealing with wrangling insurance companies, solicitors and municipal councils – none of whom knew what the other was doing, and Hesta had no idea at all what *any* of them were doing. She had given her own lawyer, Colin's lawyer, the task of sorting it all out.

That she still owned a patch of ruined land off Wellings Road in the Blue Mountains was an irrefutable fact, but that was, so far, the beginning and the end of it. She was not, however, without funds. By the grace of Colin Mainwaring there was still a healthy bank balance and she contributed generously to the running of the household at Proudie Bay. It irritated Jennifer that the two men took for granted lobster tails on the table instead of poor man's leatherjackets or

yellow tails, and duck and corn-fed chicken in place of
strangled pigeons, perky pink potatoes instead of bagged
scrubbers.

Hesta had authorised Jennifer to handle her financial
affairs and because of a forty per cent proof alcohol tremor
she had developed in her hands, and a similar fault in the
head that sometimes caused it to tic-toc from side to side
like a pendulum, she found it easier to have Jennifer do
whatever was needed to be done beyond the gate of number
fourteen, the Sandpath. She rarely went outside now. It was
as though she had developed a fear of space.

Three boxes had arrived from the Salvation Army, Blue
Mountains' Storm Relief Division. They contained all that
remained of Hesta's possessions. In the eyes of some survi-
vors of the storm the contents of the boxes would have been
a disappointment: no VCRs, no crammed money boxes, no
microwave ovens, no hard drives or fax machines or mobile
phones or trophies won at bowls. Hesta's boxes housed
treasures of a different kind, all important to her – and even
one alive-o – that breathed.

She had waited until evening in order to share the box
openings with Jennifer. 'Everyone loves opening boxes,'
she'd said.

They sat on the floor of her room, Hesta with a large
brandy and Jennifer, not for the first time in the last week
or so, with a slightly smaller brandy. Jen's nerves had been
stretched to their limit – she had no idea they could still be
put on the rack! – and while she had no intention of becoming a Hesta or a Gulliver, she was grateful for the seductive

numbing warmth of the spirit. They picked through the boxes with care and Hesta held each piece gently in her hand and told its story, most of it true. One or two pieces, a small, hand-painted box lined with mirrors, for instance, had dried mud and a leaf still clinging to it and Hesta put them aside so that the remains of Wellings Road could be preserved.

In box one was a bag of fabric remnants she'd collected simply for the joy of their colour: *torn, dirty: need washing*. A wood puppet from Burma: *head dislodged, foot broken*. Two masks from the Sepik River, New Guinea: *intact*. A bronze dragon from Chinatown, Sydney: *crushed tail*. A small wooden rocking horse, carver's stall, Como, Italy: *tail missing*. A penis cover, New Guinea highlands: *empty*. And then more and more surprises. It was for Hesta a shower of memories – a celebration of losts and founds – a Christmas of gifts! She held the dirtiest to her face and closed her eyes and smelled the earth of her home on them. Jennifer sat and watched a trembling, delighted old child at play.

In the second box were books. Sixteen water-damaged and three miracles. One of the miracles was *Wind in the Willows*, dry and whole.

'You loved this story. I read it to you when you were tiny – you and Gulliver.'

'I still love it – that, and the Chinese music box. Even though they remind me of bad times I still like to see them again. Does that make sense?'

'Yes, Jen, that makes sense.'

She rummaged through the third box that held mostly

ruined clothing. The slacks she'd worn to South America, still striped with mud of a different kind. A purple Moroccan caftan that had lost its colour to a white shirt. Two smelly winter sweaters clinging to each other for comfort. Thick socks, pantyhose, gloves, scarves and underwear were either thrown in a rubbish bag or put aside for the laundry.

'Lately, I've been trying to remember Mother's face, Hesta. I do when I'm feeling low – but it's a sort of mist,' Jennifer said. 'Hazy pieces I can't put together. It's awful.'

'That's normal, dear heart. Don't worry about it. It will all come to you when you most need it. Naturally, memories of Lissy will be part of those you've tried to erase.' Hesta held up two pillowcases, wrinkled her nose and threw them out. 'I think memories grow clearer as time passes; that is until you're so old you can't remember anything at all. But she was a pretty thing, your mother, small and pretty, lovely eyes. Clever in the garden and the house. Those are the memories you'll find and keep. Lissy Gibson, meek and mild. Just right for Marlin of course. No competition.'

'Why do you suppose she couldn't see the truth in him?'

'She might not have wanted to, darling. He was very appealing – and very good looking. And *very* persuasive. Your mother was mad about him. He can still be a charmer when he wants to.'

'And doesn't he know it!'

'He charmed her parents in the blink of an eye. But thank the gods they didn't live long enough to watch their daughter dying. If they had to drive off the Hawks Nest Bridge it was better they did it when they did.'

'They didn't *drive* off it. They were *nudged* off by a truck. It was ridiculous. The press made it look like the end of *Thelma and Louise*. I don't believe any of those old reports.'

'I wonder if this would shrink if we washed it?' Hesta held up an alpaca poncho.

'Probably. Tell me, how long after they married did Mum start to be unhappy?' Jennifer idly took the poncho and put it aside for dry-cleaning. 'Bindi used to make remarks. I know *she's* never liked Dad. I've often wondered just how long it took him to ruin everything. I know he saw other women.'

'So they say, dear.'

'I hope Mum was a happy child.'

'I think so. Probably happier than Marlin and me. I'll always remember one story she told me. When she was very small her father sometimes took her to Cove Beach at dawn to see what the tide had washed up. One morning, on the high tide, there were two wooden crates full of onions and tomatoes that had been dumped at sea. They brought them home and made an enormous pot of vegetable soup, just the two of them. The best soup she'd ever tasted, she said. It was one of her fondest memories.'

'I'm glad she was happy then. I'm glad she had something to keep her going,' Jennifer said. 'And I'm glad, really, she didn't have to go through year after year of dramas in this place.'

'Stop worrying about Miriam, Jen. If she's pregnant she's pregnant. You can't do anything about it.'

'But they lied! They're all liars!'

'Just trying to protect you, dear. Not wanting you to worry so much. I'm sure that's why.'

'No. You know that's not true. They just lied. There's no one in this entire world I can trust!'

'Jen, please . . . just try to think of the baby. Think of the fun you'll have with a little one to play with.'

'No I won't. Not if it's Gulliver's.'

'And when do we tell the old grandfather?' Hesta laughed at the prospect, and even Jennifer's mood was lifted for a second by the vision of her father in that unthinkable role.

'Not until we have to. And anyway, Miriam still hasn't admitted to it.'

'Well, dear, it won't be long before she'll have to.'

In silence, Hesta took the last item from the third box: a single bed sheet. It was yellowed and stained as though its owner had wet the bed every night for a year. She picked it up with finger and thumb and tossed it into the rubbish. But under the sheet lay a small grey-brown frog, barely alive and pulsing with fright but not cracked or broken or filthy or with bits missing. *A real survivor. Another miracle.* Jennifer put it into a water glass and Hesta, in a state of excitement, hurried to the top of the stairs and called for Marlin.

'Please find somewhere for it to live.' She gave it to him. 'It was at the bottom of a box. It's from the mountains. It's come through everything, brave little thing. It must have been at my house. I can't think how it's survived.'

'I'll put it in the carp pond,' he said, licking his chops and grinning.

'But they'll eat it.'

'Probably,' he said.

'Marlin!'

'Aaah.' He studied it closely. '*Crinia signifera.*'

'Nonsense!' said Hesta. 'Its name is Wellings. And make a pond just for him. He deserves it.'

'Aye aye, Sister Bird.'

A bundle of mail, re-addressed from the Mountains, followed in the wake of the boxes. It was a normal bundle of mail on the whole – overdue subscription notices, periodicals, Art Union lotteries, a letter from the YWCA, a card from the woman who lived not far from the mailbox at the top of Wellings Road – but there was one envelope that was decorated with German stamps. Hesta threw the others onto her bed and tore it open with hands that shook, not with brandy alone. The letter was written in carefully word-processed script.

My dear friend, Hesta.

It is winter in Koblenz and I think of you. In the cold I remember our hot days with the animals in Phillipe's camp. I am living with my mother in the hotel. I will live here for Christmas then I think I will visit my friend in the Blue Mountains. Will I stay with you, Hesta? There is too much cold here and I will like to see the sun and your beach and your mountains. It will be good to talk again. I will not wear my swimsuit all the time. I will wear a skirt for you. I laugh sometimes when I think of you. Do you remember the spider? Do you remember the bad Beppi? Do you remember the little

*rat animal? No maybe not the capybara. I think that will
make you sad. I come to Sydney in January, airline Luft-
hansa. Can you tell me where I must go? Please write soon.*

Always your friend,

Lucretia.

Heaven help me! Hesta thought, *it's only just after two; hours
before Jennifer comes home to hear this news – Marlin's in the
city – goodness knows where Gull is – and her letter is already
over two weeks old! Lucretia will wonder why she's not heard by
now. She'll think I've forgotten her.*

Hesta was in a fever of excitement and helplessness. She
began to write to Lucretia on a postcard but the words were
uneven and spidery, like a right-hander trying to write with
the left. She discarded it and instead held Lucretia's letter
tight to her chest in case she should lose it.

Jennifer had not reached the top of the stairs before the
news was shouted down to her in a town crier's bellow.

'I have a letter! I have a letter from Germany – from
Lucretia! She's coming to Sydney!'

'Lucretia?'

'The woman I was with in the Amazon. I wrote to you
about her.'

'Oh.'

'She'll be here in January. Isn't it wonderful?'

'Yes . . . I think so. It'll be nice for you.' As usual Jennifer
was tired and preoccupied. She just wanted to kick off her
shoes and relax. She couldn't be less concerned with
German tourists. It did not occur to her that she would in

any way be concerned with tourists from Germany. 'I need to soak my feet.'

'Jennifer, please pay attention.' Hesta still had the envelope crushed against the poor sacs of her breasts. 'The letter was addressed to Wellings Road. They've had it for ages. How am I going to tell her where I am?'

'When is she coming?'

'The beginning of January, Jennifer!'

'There's plenty of time before January. Just write to her.'

'Will you do it, dear, please?' Hesta gave the letter to Jennifer. It was written on the hotel's letterhead. 'You see, she might think I've forgotten about her. I need to get in touch with her quickly, dear. Perhaps we could phone her.'

'Well, there is a fax number. Why don't you write a message and I'll try to fax her from Dolan's tomorrow, is that all right?'

'Thank you, dear. Thank you.'

And it did not occur to Jennifer that this news of a German tourist would mean the addition of another woman to the menagerie. She was too tired to think of it at all. She took off her watch, stripped to her panties and went to the bathroom for a shower.

'So! We are to have an old *sour kraut* in Proudie Bay!' Marlin was working with glue and a book spine on the kitchen table. 'And where are we to put this one, Jen Wren? Which corner of our crowded refugee camp are we to put the *kraut*?'

'I don't know yet. She'll probably have to bunk upstairs

somewhere,' Jen said. 'But don't you spoil this for Hesta. She's excited, and the woman's not coming here to live, for heaven's sake.'

'And who will provide for another mouth to feed? Who will pay for *die Frau*?'

'Oh, don't be ridiculous. She'll have money of her own, and if she hasn't, Hesta and I will pay to feed her – the way we pay to feed you!'

'Don't snap your beak, Jen.' He suddenly smiled sweet as a ferret. 'Maybe it will be good. She can make us dumplings and stuff cabbages and bake big cakes with cherries and cream and fatten us up – do you think she'll do that for us, *die grosse Frau*?'

'Not if she has to listen to your rubbish,' she said. 'And I don't think she's a *Frau*, I think she's a *Fräulein*. Where's Gulliver?'

'Out fishing for mullet and mermaids. I don't see him much lately. I think our Gull's got something on his mind.'

'What mind?' she said.

Jennifer cleared the table of the remains of the evening meal. She worked easily, not having to think about it. *What a good serving wife I'd be*, she thought. The man who read poetry at the cafe had been back three times. The last time, he'd brought his son. His son's name was James and James was sixteen. The man had spoken to her on each occasion and had said, 'I want you to meet James. He has a talent for music.' She still fantasised about the man in her room in the secret times of her nights. He told her his name was Alwyn

Pepper. She had not seen a Mrs Pepper and had been afraid to ask.

While she worked in the kitchen she tried to imagine what it would be like to work in the kitchen of another man, that man for instance – but then, what on earth would be the sense in leaving one kitchen for another? A bench is a bench and has to be wiped; a table to be scrubbed only differed in shape and size; a floor is a floor to be polished, only different in the width of its boards – but wood is wood. Of course, in another man's kitchen there might be a dishwasher and there could be a microwave oven, *but in the long run*, she thought, when the milk and honey had turned sour, the rose-buds dried and the silk dress wrapped in tissue and buried in a coffin on a top shelf, *it would still be a life of servitude*; made no different by the size of the roof over her head, the quality of the sheets to be laundered or whether it was Wedgewood or fish tanks to be dusted. A housewife was a house's wife and to the husband, the housewife was a mistress. And no matter how much she was attracted to Mr Pepper, she would rather have him in her dreams. To Jennifer, the sweet old term of passion, 'To be swept off one's feet', reminded her of nothing more than a kiss with a broom, disguised with flowers. And as for sex: a few moments of heartbeats under the sweating blanket of a man, lying in a wet dream, wanting to shower and be rid of it all. *No. What I'd really like now*, she thought, as she put the last bowl in the cupboard, *is a unit to myself, paper plates, music, passing lovers and night dreamings. Paradise!*

Jennifer faxed Lucretia. She'd given Hesta's change of address and telephone number and explained briefly the reason for the change. 'I seem to remember that your post-card said you didn't like her very much at all.'

'It was true, in the beginning.' Hesta said. 'But we became very close. Do you know she once killed an enor-mous spider that was on my bed? She stamped on it with her bare foot! She's absolutely fearless. I know you'll like her. We were very close at the end.'

'She'll have to sleep up here, somewhere. Probably with you for a while,' Jennifer said. 'Until we work things out.'

'Of course – I know. It was to have been Wellings Road; isn't it sad, dear?'

'Don't worry, darling. We'll make her comfortable.'

'I think we need to go shopping, dear heart.'

'Again?'

'She must see me at my very best.'

'You mean you want to go too?'

'I do. I've decided that I must go out. Lucretia would be very cross if she knew what I had become. And maybe Miriam will join us. We can have a nice day in town and think of nothing but shopping. It will take our minds off things for a while.'

It was a weekend, and the summer mood of Proudie Bay changed from sweet to sour. It was as though the seamless blue of its sky and the eye of the sun were bored with the sights of basting bodies and sandcastles – irritated by good-natured pre-Christmas children, minding their manners just in case; diners lounging, sun-drugged at Dolans' tables, boats bobbing like bath toys and cruisers cruising, balloons flying to the moon, ice-creams avalanching off their cones, babies on swings, park lovers, wisps of Shack Hill cook smoke, and flocks of gulls eating dropped chips and small boys' bait on the end of the pier.

Dark clouds rolled in from everywhere. Wind gusts turned boats back-to-front and flattened windsurfers, mothers searched for warm tops, chased umbrella missiles and packed their bags for the ferry. And when the rain cut down, cold and sharp, those who lived at the Bay ran home and slammed their doors in its face.

And it was the sour mood of Proudie Bay that brought about, so it was thought, the events that followed:

1: Dolan's Cafe having at last to buy extra windbreaks and covers for luncheon parties.

2: The despair of ice-cream sellers, sunscreen sellers and boat hirers for the loss of their earnings.

3: After-schoolies on holidays, underfoot at the Fishcastle at all hours with the blessing of their mothers.

4: Shack Hill mud slides, rivulets and cascades and ruined pot plants.

5: Marlin padding around the house with children, like a trapped shark with minnows, watching from a window, his pigeons cowering breast to breast in the dry end of their coop.

6: And in another part of the house, an unexpected encounter with a snake.

And it was on a wet Monday that the women chose to

bus to the Imperial Arcade in Sydney. Jennifer had agreed to work extra time to compensate for the day, but wet Monday's bookings at the cafe were so sparse, it was a cafe day not worth bothering about. At nine-thirty, Hesta had already been dressed for an hour. She'd clearly steeled herself for her encounter with the outside world. She had dressed in her purple linen and sandals and carried a purse and umbrella. Miriam, still suffering from her lie, had been persuaded to join them. She admitted to nothing but a virus that had improved well enough, she said, for a day in town. Jennifer avoided the subject altogether. *The truth would be revealed soon enough*, she thought. The truth behind a lie reveals itself sooner or later.

It was Jennifer who held Beccy's hand.

'But I don't want to go,' the child said for the umpteenth time. She'd narrowed her eyes and pressed her lips together hard in a grimace of defiance. 'Marlin said he'd show me a book about whales. Go and ask him; he'll tell you.'

'We'll have fun in town, Bec. And a nice lunch.'

'That's not fun!'

'Maybe she could stay,' Miriam said. 'We won't be that long away.' Children's' voices drifted up from the kitchen. 'And she won't be alone by the sound of it.'

'I wonder where Gull is,' Jennifer said.

'I think he's out, dear,' said Hesta. 'I heard the bike at least an hour ago.'

'What do you think, Hesta?' Jennifer asked.

'I think she'll be perfectly all right, dear.'

'I'll talk to Dad, then.' She turned to Beccy. 'Now listen,

if you get sick of things downstairs you come up to my room – don't go wandering off. You can watch TV or read or whatever you like. You can even lock the door if you want . . .'

'Oh, for God's sake, Jen!' Miriam and Hesta exchanged quick glances. 'What would she want to lock the door for? Don't make such a fuss about it. She'll be all right. She's a sensible kid.'

'Promise me you will be,' Jennifer said to the child.

'I *promise!*' Beccy spat on her hand, crossed herself and ran out the door. 'I'll tell Marlin,' she called back to them. 'You don't have to.'

Marlin padded down the drive to the gate with them, bare-headed and wrapped in a sarong in spite of the rain. He held Beccy's hand.

'Don't forget to bring us back some s'prises,' he said.

'Yes!' sang a jubilant Beccy.

'And don't forget some hair nets for the flutterbys, and jelly snakes for a necklace, and . . .'

'Oh for goodness sake, stop it, Dad!' Jennifer said while the others laughed. 'Let's get to the bus stop before we're soaked.'

And the three left the gate, sheltering close under umbrellas, their heads down, almost under their wings like birds. Three off to market, to market; two rainbows and a brown wren hopping down the Sandpath to perch in the bus shelter. They did not look back at Marlin and Beccy, wet and laughing – she, holding the man's bony hand tight as though it belonged to her.

Marlin showed Beccy and two other children the book of whales. He'd given them notepaper and pencils. 'Now, write down whale – the order Cetacea. Got that?' He showed them photographs of blue whales longer than a dozen dinghies end to end, baleens scooping oceans in their jaws and making tidal waves with tails. And he told how killer whales ate the tongues of dolphins and swallowed baby seals whole ... ssssllllpp ... And notepaper fluttered out of sight while they watched, bug-eyed with their hands pressed against their faces. He showed them southern rights being chased for their best whalebone, and a blue that was measured one-hundred-and-thirty feet long with a twenty-seven foot long baby. He showed old pictures of caught whales being stripped of their flesh with flensing knives and told how it was an Eskimo who traded the first whalebone – 'No, he didn't know his name', and how he'd once eaten whale meat in a Japanese village with the captain of a whaler and an old woman who had no teeth and chewed the meat with her gums and tongue like a parrot, and Marlin had them squealing with delight when he crumpled his face, drew his lips over his teeth and slapped them together to demonstrate.

Beccy sat and listened and watched the man with terrified fascination, her hands clenched in her lap and every muscle tensed. She didn't need to take notes because everything, everything Marlin told her, she knew, would live in her brain till she died.

And then there was another book – not whales. 'This here is a toadfish. It puts out a sound, a hum like a powerline, so loud ships can hear it.' And he turned page after page over fire worms alight on black sea nights, angry squids changing their colour, sea spiders and jellyfish with see-through bodies and shapeless things in the deepest dark where the sun of the world couldn't reach. She was learning about everything that frightened her. She could put names to them. If she wanted to, she could tell them she knew where they lived – how high they were or how low. She had come to know them.

Her last sacrifice to the ocean had been a small posy of bush weeds weighed down with a stone. She wondered which one of Marlin's sea things had eaten it.

'And speakin' of whale meat and such,' said Marlin suddenly. 'It's chow time for this old man of the sea.' He closed the books like a preacher at the end of a sermon.

'I'll make you some food, Marlin,' Beccy said quickly. 'I'll make you some coffee and I can make a sandwich if you want.'

'Well, well. Our Beccly's going to be the ol' man's cook is she?'

'I can cook anything,' she said with her hands on her hips.

'I bet you can't cook McDonald's!' one of the others said.

'You'll have to go home now,' she told them, standing firm, narrow-eyed and defending her territory.

'We don't have to!'

'Yes you do!'

'Why?!'

'Because I said so!'

And Marlin laughed down on them from the loft of his height, happy to be so possessed by them, delighted to have them fight over him like little slaves begging for favours.

Lunch was no more than rye bread cut ragged, whole tomatoes, a lump of cheddar and instant coffee strong enough to paint with, but Marlin accepted her offerings and savoured them as if they'd come from the table of Bacchus himself.

Lunch in the city was no less a novelty than it was at the Fishcastle. The shopping trip to outfit Hesta had been so successful that Jennifer and Miriam were forced to trail some steps behind her as she sailed in and out of boutiques, fanning herself with credit cards. She had bought fine beige slacks, caramel silk shirts, a linen jacket and a pant-suit, shoes, belts and bags, Hermes scarves and gifts for everyone else. She'd left a trail of shop assistants behind her like crumbs in a forest. The tonic of such a day had given her the height and strength and spirit she'd thought she'd lost forever, and by lunchtime, she'd emerged an empress of moths from the trembling, wrinkled chrysalis in which she'd been trapped since the mountain storm.

In a coffee shop she had sat, straight as a stick, opposite a mirrored wall, and made no pretence to the study of her new image. She ate heartily, managing with her bent hand as though it was as straight as the other, and conducted a lively conversation.

'And all this for your German woman,' Jennifer said to Miriam. 'She must be pretty impressive, Hesta.'

'Yes she is, dear.' Hesta tried to spear a crisp potato wedge but it flew off her plate and landed in the lap of the man at the next table. The new Hesta strode majestically to him and picked the wedge from his fly. 'I think this, young man,' she said, 'is mine!'

'Isn't she something?' Miriam shrieked with laughter. 'I hope I'm like her at that age.'

'God help us all if you are.' But Jennifer, despite her embarrassment laughed too.

'I haven't had so much fun since I came home from South America. You see?' said Hesta. 'I said it would cheer us up.'

'And speaking of "home",' Jennifer fidgeted with bags, 'I think it's time we got back to the Bay.'

'It's only ten to three,' said Miriam. 'Bec will be all right, you know.' She'd relaxed in the warmth and dry of the arcade and her lunch still lay contented in her belly. There'd been not a hint of nausea.

'But you must be feeling tired, Miriam.' There was a slight edge to Jennifer's voice.

'No, I'm fine.'

'Then your virus must be disappearing.'

'Yes,' Miriam said without looking at her.

Hesta, coming in on the tail of it, asked, 'Are we off, then?'

'No,' said Miriam.

'Yes,' said Jen.

'Well, I don't mind if we go,' said Hesta. 'I want to see Beccy in her new dress, and her other "s'prises".'

Outside, in the real world, it was still raining. A line of

wet and drooped people stood like penguins at a taxi rank with patience and little hope. Jennifer led the way to the bus stop where a line already shuffled into the shelter of damp seats and steaming skin and dripping brollies.

But the spirits of three shoppers were not dashed for one metre of their journey back to Proudie Bay at the end of the line.

To Beccy's astonishment the two children had gone home soon after she'd told them to. She ran around the kitchen and tidied and straightened and tut-tutted and grumbled in the way of Jennifer after a meal. She left on the floor, still damp from rainy feet, patterns of her own amongst the larger ones.

'Well, look at Miss Boss-in-Boots! Or is it poor ol' Cinders we got working here?' Marlin passed through the room carrying a pile of books and a spectacle case. 'Old Marlin has to go to his cell and do some fish work so Beccly will have to twiddle her thumbs until the mother comes home.'

'Where's Gull, then?'

'You got me there, girl,' in his deepest voice.

'The bike's in the shed.'

'Well, there we are. The bike's in the shed, the Gull's done a bunk and all's right with the world.' And then, in what might have been his own voice, or as close to it as he could get, 'You'd better go up to Jen Wren's dryland room, Bec, and look at her land books. I reckon they'll be back soon enough. I have a mess of work to do.' And he padded off down the hall, past the fish tanks and into the room at the end whose door latch clicked the loudest in the Fishcastle.

Beccy didn't mind at all being left to herself. She went to the pantry cupboard and took two biscuits from a tin, feeling the wonderful warmth of familiarity in the house she thought of as her own. The rain had eased but only insofar as it was no longer a torrent. She left the kitchen in the direction of the stairs but then suddenly turned and ran outside to Gull's shed. The bike stood propped and shining against one side of it, and with the greatest care, and as quietly as possible, she positioned his tool box and climbed from it to the bike's saddle. One biscuit was part swallowed while the spare sat in her pocket.

'Brrrmmm ... brrrmmm ... brrrmmm,' she growled, leaning forward and stretching for the handles and blowing crumbs everywhere. She mimicked the twist of Gull's hands on the gears and the way he lowered his head when the wind whipped against him. She tucked her knees in the way he did when he rode and looked as if he were driving a stallion clear off the face of the earth. There was nothing in the world like this ... nothing!

'What the shit do you think you're doing?' Gulliver leaned, dripping wet against the door. She had no idea how long he'd been there but it couldn't have been long because she would have known by the smell of him, all wet clothes and bottle piss. He leapt across and snatched her from the bike. 'When did I say you could muck around on the bike, you little shit! It's not a fucking toy!' He was red with anger but his voice was hardly more than a hiss. He snatched a rag from a shelf and wiped rainwater from the leather and smudges from the handles. Beccy stood against a wall and glared at him, perfectly still and quiet – quiet and dry-eyed even though her heart pounded like a trapped bird's. 'Get out of here! Don't you ever come in here by yourself again! Get out of here before I land you one across the bum!'

Beccy walked stiffly out of the shed, then ran through the rain to the house. She ran up the stairs to Jennifer's room and sat crouched and dripping in a corner. And she stayed there still until her heart allowed her to breathe more easily.

Jennifer had once read Beccy a story about an emperor's palace in Japan. It was an ancient and exquisite palace that sat on a special floor. The emperor called it the 'Nightingale Floor'. It was made of huge timber boards but they'd been pinned and tined together with metal rods in such a way that the floor 'sang' whenever it was walked upon. It was the emperor's warning system, for no matter where in the palace he happened to be, he would always be aware of approaching feet by the tune they played, no matter how softly they trod.

On that day, Beccy could have told Jennifer that the stairway to her room, in its way, was similar.

The sounds Beccy heard coming from the stairs were no more than the creaks of boards, and the sounds were spaced. She knew it wasn't her mother or Jennifer's quick, hard steps or Hesta's slow ones or Marlin's heavy pads. They were whisper sounds – creeping, hesitating, creeping up again. She crouched in her damp corner and pretended she was the emperor, ready for anything.

Since running from the shed she'd occupied herself with

TV, picture books of the ballet and the dressing-up trunk from which she'd taken her favourite green tulle skirt. She'd borrowed Hesta's lipstick and blusher and eye pencil from the bathroom and had given herself a new face. And it was this small, painted creature who might have escaped from a fairground that Gulliver saw when he propped himself unsteadily against the doorway.

'Sorry I yelled at you, Bec.' He breathed fumes through the room strong enough to light fires. 'But you made me mad down there.'

'Sorry,' she said in a voice she couldn't hear.

'You know it was wrong, playing around with the bike.' He swayed away from the door for a moment.

'I suppose so.' She still didn't move, ignoring the wisdom given to all women from the beginning of women. She just pulled her knees up under her chin and wrapped her arms tight around them.

'What're ya doing all dolled-up like that?' He suddenly grinned up one side of his face, switching his voice from venom to honey with a flick of his tongue. 'You look like a mad fairy.' He took three unsteady steps into the room.

'You'd better get out of here!' she said, ready at battle stations. 'Jen wouldn't want you in here.'

'Well, she's not here is she.' He was still grinning but only with his teeth.

'I'll tell her. She'll be home in a minute.' She hadn't moved from the corner. She didn't think it would be a good thing to do, to move from the corner. *Stay still. Stay still. In her mind.*

'They'll be away for hours. What are you dressed up as, Bec? What're you supposed to be?' He shocked her by sitting on the edge of Jennifer's bed. 'It's hard to stay mad at you, Bec.'

'I'm not going to tell you anything! I'm going down to get Marlin.' Her heart, which had had such a short time to recover from the shed, began to bleat in her chest like a lamb in fright.

'Well you can't get Marlin cause Marlin's gone round to the beach.'

'He wouldn't go in the rain.'

'He's looking for bluebottles washed up.' He laughed at the great-eyed look of her, staring out from pencil marks and red shadows. 'Jesus, you look funny, Bec.'

'You get out of here, Gull.'

'You get out of here, Gull ...' He aped her small voice. His mouth was wet-lipped and loose. 'Come over here and tell me how the green fairy's mum is.' He patted his lap. 'Come on, Bec. Is she still throwing up?'

'No,' she said, not moving an inch. 'So you can go and see her if you want to because she doesn't vomit any more.'

'Can't take the risk, Bec,' he said, rubbing his buttocks against the bed edge. 'Can't have the snake here spewed on.'

'What snake?'

'My pet snake. You come over here, Bec, and I'll show you. This one's a friend of your mum's too. Come on, you like snakes. This one won't bite you.'

She wasn't sure what he was talking about but she was tense with caution. She didn't want him coming over to her;

there was something far more menacing about that. *Maybe it would be better to go to him – maybe then he won't get angry.* And she gingerly moved to the bed.

When she was next to him he unzipped his fly and eased his penis out. 'Beccy, this here is old snake. The best sort in the world. Snake, meet Beccy Holt, the green fairy of the Hill.'

He had taken hold of her arm and Beccy folded, silent inside herself. His breath was pure bottle piss and he grinned and the corner of his mouth leaked, like the thing in his hand seemed to grin at her with the corner of its mouth leaking. The snake was veined and red and its shape changed and grew. Beccy would not have known how pale she'd become, tucked inside herself the way she was, or how her eyes were shut tight and her mouth tight as a slit.

'Ah, come on, Hillbilly girl. Don't tell me you've never seen one of these before. Not where you live – not with your bed right next to that mum of yours.' He massaged his cock with one hand and held Beccy's arm with the other. 'Come on, Bec,' he said breathing hard. 'Come on. Feel me up, Beccy. Bone it up for me, Bec.'

She was vaguely aware of wanting to be sick. She wanted to be as sick as her mother had been and now she knew the reason for her vomiting. She wished she could be sick all over him – vomit so much he'd drown in it. She turned her small, angry head away from it and tried to pull her arm free but he suddenly pulled her face down so that the terrible, leaking thing was against her cheek. And in silence she heaved dry retches like her mother.

'Come on, Bec,' he said, low, under his breath. 'Give him a nice wet kiss.'

She tried to pull away but suddenly it was in her mouth anyway, and in a rage of anger and revulsion she bit down as hard as she could until he screamed like a stuck pig and hit her again and again across the side of her head, but the more he squealed and hit out, the harder she bit until her mouth was so full of blood she had to let go. She wasn't sure where the screams were coming from. She had felt no pain.

When he lurched from the room, crying and hopping and swerving and bumping into door and walls, holding his crotch and staining a path to Jennifer's bathroom, Beccy walked stiffly and icily back to her corner and squatted there. Her eyes were two dark furious points and in order to draw her lips together in their hard, angry line, she emptied her mouth of blood by opening it wide and letting it run and drip onto the green tulle of her skirt. She curled herself tight into the corner of the room – tight enough to become part of the wall, and therefore invisible. She saw nothing but the blackness of her mind. She was hardly aware of Gull's own retching from the bathroom and his cries of 'Oh God! Oh Christ! Oh Jesus! Fuck! Fuck! Fuck! ...' as he tried to stop the blood flowing from his torn and dying cock.

Beccy stayed curled tighter in her cocoon of wet, green tulle; tighter into her corner and rocked from side to side stiff as a metronome, but silent, and let the new tempests of sound rage outside of her being. The sounds were a very long way away. She couldn't have known it was Jennifer who ran to the bathroom, following the spoor of blood – Jennifer running backwards and forwards, her hair flying, skirt flying, feet slipping in blood on the carpet and shrieking: 'What is it?! What is it!? What is it?! What's happened?! What's the matter?!' – over and over again, racing between the groaning mess in the bathroom and the chillingly quiet Beccy, looking up at her, covered in blood and make-up, squatting tight as though she'd been sewn into green tulle, like a small, vio-lated sprite ... a ruined spirit, the right side of her face already swelling a terrible red.

Jennifer, almost collapsing with thoughts of what might have happened, terrified of what she suspected, tried to think clearly, but for those frightening moments she regretted every breath she took: every frantic beat of her heart, and she hated that she could see anything at all. She wished she were blind. And deaf. She wanted more than anything at that moment to be dead.

Earlier, when the three had returned from their shopping trip, Jennifer had gone straight up to the house and had left Hesta and Miriam at the front gate chatting about their day to Marlin who had just strolled back from Cove Beach. And as though she were watching herself from somewhere else, somewhere above her, she had run back down to them and told Miriam that Beccy would like to see her right away. She saw herself tell Hesta not to go upstairs for a while, and she watched herself tell Marlin in a voice that fought for breath and one she hardly recognised.

'You think kids think you're a god, don't you! You think you're their saviour, but you don't really care what happens to them – you don't care if they live or die! When they're not sitting around your feet lapping up your garbage, you don't care what happens to them! There are some kids who hate you, Dad ... I hated you! There! I've hated you so many times! You should see your precious Beccy now – go up and see her now! Go and see what's happened to her while you mucked around on the beach not caring less! And then, you'd better get that ... that ... son of yours to a hospital. And *I* couldn't care less what happens to *him*!'

And it seemed to her that beyond the mist of it all she was shaking and crying and screaming and fainting at the same time, but all of it on the inside. On the outside she was something like stone.

Marlin, for once in his life, could think of nothing to say; and no strange way of saying it.

Hesta held a shaking hand to her mouth, her eyes wide with anxiety, and Miriam, suddenly terrified, ran as fast as she could into the house and up the stairs. Jennifer, absolutely exhausted, leaned against the gate post and looked to the sky for relief, and finding none turned to Marlin.

'I don't think I can stand you another minute! I think you're mad!'

'Hate's a cancer, Jen,' he said quietly, in the voice he was born with. 'Don't hate me. Don't hate me as much as this – one way or another it could kill me or you. I know hate can kill.'

'And do you think I'd care!' Jen cried, loud enough for the whole street to hear. She stood stiff as a ramrod, her arms tight against her side.

Hesta had stood silent and trembling through the whole thing. All she could think to say was, 'What a terrible place to bring Lucretia to.'

Chapter Eleven

STILL LIFE, PROUDIE BAY

There came a time in Jennifer's life when the outlines of the world looked as the world always had, but their colours had drained away and the lines were a blur.

There was not, in her world now, even the sharpness of black and white; it had become, from her window, a slur of slow grey with undefined lines, a smudge of view from the window as though it rained forever on glass. Ships ploughed as slow as sea slugs through a still of ocean, birds flew in a pause of motion, rain might have been no more than a tap's drip or a torrent – she could not have said. The wind that blew against her face as she stared out could have been tepid or ice sharp from the Antarctic, and all of Proudie Bay, as far as she could see, had merged and become nothing at all – a blurred landscape not worth hanging. The stillest of life.

Jennifer sat day after day, gazing out at the grey through

the mist of her eyes. But despite the dullness to the sight of her world, the sounds of it had increased to a painful pitch in her hearing, no matter how slight. The single call of a finch would cause her to stiffen and flinch and the squeak of her chair if she moved was almost too loud for her to bear. There was at once a greyness and a clarity.

Hesta crept in to Jen's room from time to time, desperate for her to be whole again. There was once a rainbow over the rooftops near the Cove.

'Do you see it, dear?'

'No, there's nothing there,' Jennifer had said flatly.

And once there was a new moon.

'You must have seen the new moon last night. Did you bow to it nine times, dear heart? Did you turn your money and make a wish?'

'No.' But on that occasion there'd been a faint quiver to Jennifer's lips and Hesta had put her arm around her thin shoulders and hugged her tight. It was possible, Hesta thought, that she was approaching the peak of her grief.

'Rebecca is all right, heart.' With her finger, Hesta moved lank hairs from Jennifer's face. 'And you must be well soon for them.'

'How can Beccy ever be all right? How can Miriam *ever* be all right again?' She shrugged away from her aunt's touch. She had no wish to be touched at all.

'I wish you'd let me call a doctor, Jen.'

'No! I'm not going over it all again – for anyone!'

'Miriam's been down to see you many times.'

'I can't face her. I can't talk to her. I don't want to talk to anyone!' Still watching grey things from the window.

'She's worried about you, heart.' Hesta spoke softly, for this was the longest contact she'd had with Jennifer for days. 'And I think she needs you. I think she's nervous about her pregnancy.'

'That's Gulliver Hardwick's baby she's having; let him worry about it.' Jennifer turned her head and Hesta was shocked by her ravaged expression, the dry, dull skin of her face framed with oily strands of hair, the pencil thinness of her. She looked at Hesta with her dead eyes and began to shake. 'Isn't it all the most disgusting thing you've ever heard of? He might just as well have killed them both but instead of that he added another one!' She took a long shuddering breath. 'I wonder what the bastard has in mind for the baby!' And then suddenly she was shaking in a spasm of grief and the gates of the dam began to open.

Hesta held her very close. She wanted so much to be her strength but broke and wept with her, her emotions, like Jennifer's, absolutely out of control. They clung and cried a river of tears together until they were all but exhausted by it.

'Rebecca is very strong, Jen.' Hesta cradled her niece in a comfort of arms. The softest of shields. 'Children have the strength to climb out of the most awful pits.'

'I wish I could believe that.'

'You must. She already misses you.' Hesta stroked Jen's face then moved away and poured two brandies. She said, for no reason at all, 'Lucretia and I drank whisky in the jungle. It was all they had.' The sandwiches she had brought earlier still lay on their plate untouched. She put them next to Jennifer's drink, hoping to tempt her. 'Now, we'll just sit together for a while. There's no need to say a word. We'll just sit and hold hands.'

'Who scrubbed out the bathroom?' Jennifer suddenly asked. It was an even, carefully chosen question as though it had been number one on a list of questions she'd been saving for the strength to ask – Question one: Who scrubbed the bathroom?

'What, dear?'

'Who scrubbed out the bathroom – after it happened?'

'Your father.'

'Ha! That would have been something to see. Did he have to kneel to do it?' There was a glimpse of strength in her voice.

'It is possible.'

'Good!' And anger that had festered behind the dam of tears began to rise. It threatened to break through at any moment. 'Good!!'

The season of summer moved on, sluggish and humid through its warm waterveil. Cloudbanks hung sculptured and heavy over the Bay.

Humidifiers and electric fans were set to work in closets and bathrooms, and clothing was aired and cleaned of its mouldy beards. Outside, the bay tides ribboned thick and heavy against all but the working boats. Fish swam slow through kelp. St P's twelve bells rang out through the air like fog horns and everything in the Fishcastle moved in a hot lazy way. The python slept, the tortoises coupled for want of company, the lizard's blue tongue hung and pigeons picked at itchy quills. But the laughter of children came from other houses.

Christmas had come and passed by number fourteen the Sandpath without even opening its gate. Christmas had risen and spirited over the roof like one of Scrooge's ghosts; there was not so much as a holly or an ivy, or wreath or ribbon of tinsel, and the herald angels had been forced to sing else-where. Christmas cards left by the postman for Jennifer, who refused them, were read by Hesta, who kept them in a box until the world might turn light again. Among the cards was one Beccy had made herself, a card from Miriam, full of love and forgiveness, a note from Dolan's to say they missed her and one from Alwyn Pepper and son, hoping she would soon be well.

Marlin had reacted to the disturbing incidents of the past weeks like a wounded animal. He was agonised to the point of growling. A rage of wounds. Bereft of the company of children who'd been kept at home by the sniff of trouble, the loss of a son, the hate of a daughter, a loss of pride and his liking for himself. He paced in his square of study like a fish trapped in a tank too small for it. He ached with shock.

He'd been told about Miriam's baby after the horrifying news of what his son had done to the child, and his fury had been so great that he had all but demolished the inside of Gulliver's room, and particularly every bottle found. He had then gone to the shed, still white with rage and, groaning with every blow of a hammer, had inflicted as much damage on the bike as he could, and everything on the shelves, not knowing that part of it was where the ghost of his wife lay. And when he found the shed's cache of alcohol – three bottles of it – he smashed them over what remained of the bike until splinters of glass left stripes of blood on his palms. He had thought of destroying the dinghy cave too, but that was part of the sea, and sacred – even though it had been dirtied by one of his own. He'd stood bleeding and panting outside the shed when Hesta found him.

'What a lot of blood is spilt, Marlin.' She spoke slowly to disguise the tremor in her voice. 'Let there be no more of it, please.'

'What is to become of this affair, Hesta?'

'Miriam wants it swept away, Marlin – for Jennifer's sake, for Beccy's sake and for her own, and the baby's.' Marlin looked at her with eyes full of sadness and fury. 'I think it is right that no more innocents are hurt.'

'And what about the runt of *my* litter?' he demanded. 'What do we do about our bad seed?'

'That is for you to decide,' said Hesta.

'I could kill him! Hesta, at this moment I could kill my son.'

'But that would only punish you,' she replied.

Gulliver's pain had been as intense as his father's but there was a difference. Gull's pain was localised. It was *centred*. His pain bled on the outside. He could put a finger on it. His pain was a recognisable being, a lava burn that sucked all thoughts from his mind – no matter how fleeting – all thoughts but self-pity. Twinges of remorse or shame, or a fear of consequence were blown away with the fire that burned at the centre of his being, on his patched and damaged cock.

He had spent a painful and humiliating two-and-a-half days in hospital. The attending doctor had lectured him, while dressing the wounds through a silent scream, of the dangers of playing sex games that get out of hand. 'In your case, literally!' he'd said and grinned. Very droll. But Gull had said nothing. He knew he must not say anything.

And he'd been given a lecture on safe sex by a kindly, middle-aged male nurse, which made him want to scream again.

'Even with oral it should have a dress on, love.' He waved a finger at him. 'You'll think twice before this happens again – well, never mind, love. I hope *he's* as healthy as you are, is he? It's important to know that. He's not one of our poor darlings, is he?'

'He's healthy enough,' Gull muttered.

'Good news then,' the nurse said, gently crowing and fluffing pillows with a feather-duster hand and caring like a father hen.

At that time, Gull had no way of knowing what was happening at the Fishcastle. The last contact he'd had with his family was when Marlin dropped him off, unceremoniously from a taxi, with an overnight bag and two hundred dollars at the door of Casualty, where he'd spent a painful forty-five minutes sitting on towels and moaning quietly to himself. He had no way of knowing what the consequences of his actions were to be, but for the time being, to be nursed by a gay as if he were gay himself, was convenient. The treatment was caring – painful but caring. During one moment of it he'd spared a thought for Stevie Thomas and wondered if he just might be more merciful in the future as a gesture of thanks to his tribe. There were, however, no thoughts to spare for Rebecca Holt, or her mother or Jennifer. After its focus on the pain of the *centre* of his *being*, his mind was exhausted, and emptied itself of all other considerations – except, perhaps, what might happen when he next met his father.

Gulliver had taken a taxi home to the Fishcastle, for there was nowhere else for him to go, no other place he could safely go to earth until he was whole again. He'd crept slyly, nervously and unchallenged into his wreck of a room and lay down on the first space he came to, like an animal after a night of rutting on the tiles. He had been told of some discomfort during urination and 'erectile difficulties', both of which were 'fucking understatements' in his opinion. He had been given two courses of antibiotics, but more than anything in the world he needed a drink. He needed a drink badly but he'd seen the state of his room and smelled the smell of wasted bottles and the smell of Marlin that still hung in the air, strong enough to touch, and he knew there would be none to have.

It was Hesta who tapped on his door. 'No one else knows you're here,' she said. 'I rang the hospital. I've been watching for you. Your father is out ... and Jennifer is not very well. Jennifer is most unwell,' she said quietly. 'I think you must hide yourself away. It will be best if you hide yourself from them all.' She carried a plate of toast and a mug of coffee but her hands trembled so much that most of it was lost. 'There is damage, Gulliver. There is a great deal of damage and I don't know how it will be mended.'

'What's going to happen then? What's he decided to do?' He propped wearily on his elbow. 'What about Dad? What did he say? What did he do?' Hesta looked around his ruined room and shrugged by way of an answer. There was no mention of Miriam – no mention of the child.

'You haven't asked how Beccy is, or Miriam.'

'Ahh, you don't have to worry about kids like Beccy, or Miriam for that matter,' he said, like a man whose heart and brain were forever in his pants. 'Things like that happen on the bloody Hill all the time.'

Hesta glanced at him briefly with distaste. 'You're very fortunate, Gulliver, that Miriam wants to put it all behind her. She doesn't want the child hurt any more, or your sister. And she doesn't want the worry of it. It's enough for her to know she's carrying your child.'

'Yeah, well, so she says.'

'Don't you be arrogant with me!' Hesta was suddenly very angry. 'I'm the only human you will have to talk to in this house until you leave it. It's terrible to think that there must be thousands of people like you who are excused their crimes simply because of the shame and agony their disclosure would bring to their family. It is not right, Gulliver! But I don't know yet what Marlin will do. I have never, never seen him so furious.'

'It just happened,' Gull said. 'I don't know how. It just happened. I might have had a couple of drinks.'

'You were drunk! And as soon as you're well enough I believe you must leave this house.'

Gull glared at her. 'Who the hell are you to say I have to leave here? Not that I'd want to stay, but it's not your bloody house. But I'll tell you something: if I could throw my leg over it and sit on the saddle, I'd get on the bike and go right now!'

'I don't think so, Gulliver,' she said quietly. 'I think you may have to find some other form of transport.'

'What're you talking about?' He saw her glance around his room and at what was left of his possessions. 'Oh no! Oh, Jesus, no! The fucking bastard! The mad bastard!'

'You are a foul-mouthed young man, aren't you.' She would like to have treated him with more ferocity but she was as worn out by it all as the rest of them. 'I'm glad your mother can't see what you've become.'

'Ahh, piss off, you mad bitch!'

He turned painfully so that his back was to her. He was desperate for a drink. He wanted to urinate but couldn't bear the thought of it. The only thing between his legs was burning and an itch. His possessions lay in ruins and he wondered what punishment could be worse. He was very close to tears.

'Later, I'll leave food outside your door,' Hesta said. 'In the meantime, I'll bring you a brandy, though heaven knows you don't deserve it.'

But the craving for alcohol was a pain she understood,

she felt it. His craving became hers and, though he'd said not a word, she'd felt it; one sot communicating to another. She could only imagine the rest of his pain and heaven knows she wanted him to suffer – but *she* didn't want to suffer *his* withdrawal. As she left him she didn't hear a murmured 'Thank Christ'.

Sea dreams more terrible than before had returned to Beccy despite her sacrifices. The latest offerings to calm the demons had been a purple bead necklace from the doorknob of Crystal's cupboard, and a yellow scarf from her mother's drawer. They had blown miles out to sea in the wind and she could not see where they'd fallen.

Sometimes, from the nightmare of water, there hung the heads of fishes with huge eyes that curled down as the water curled, their tails caught in the solid green bank of it and their mouths wide and full of razor teeth and nails. And behind them in the waterwall was a fire of red light and she felt the heat of it even though it too, was drowning.

When the dreams came and she woke in a fever of terror, Miriam could only hold her and rock her quietly, crooning, 'There, there Bec. It's all right, it's all right', while she lay panting, hot and damp in her arms like a wounded bird. And again when the child was fully awake: 'Everything will be all right soon, Beccy.' But not really knowing how. Miriam prayed for the wisdom to set it all right again, and one afternoon, after the dream before, wisdom came from an unexpected source.

From all the wise of the world and Proudie Bay, it was

Crystal who had been chosen by the gods to be Beccy's saviour.

'Did you take my purple beads?' Crystal demanded. 'The ones I left on the cupboard?' Beccy sat on the step of the van, tired and red-eyed.

'Yes,' she said, not caring.

'Well?'

'I threw them over the cliff,' her voice flat as paper.

'What the shit did you do that for?'

'You never wore them.'

'Well, I want to wear them now!' Crystal rummaged through her cupboard like a brush turkey, scattering junk everywhere. 'Jesus Christ, Beccy!'

'I threw them into the waves so they wouldn't come in my dreams,' Beccy said in a misery. 'I thought they'd work because they're pretty.'

'I know they're bloody pretty!' Crystal shouted. 'That's why I want them!'

'They didn't work anyway – nothing works now.' Beccy drew her knees together, dug her elbows into them, buried her face in her hands and shut tight her dry, sad eyes.

'Hey, Bec.' Crystal stopped clawing through the cupboard and faced the child.

'What?'

'Are you getting those bad dreams back just because some shit put his dick in your mouth?'

Beccy looked up sharply and stared at her. She couldn't believe what she'd just heard – the words – the real words for it, as though it were nothing. She swallowed hard and made a face. Lately she'd hated the feel of her own tongue in her mouth and was given to letting her mouth fall open so that for a brief time she would not feel it at all.

'Your mum's told me all about it,' Crystal said while she searched through a bag ... as though all she was talking about was a bee bite or a grazed knee. 'It's a bummer, okay, but it's only meat, isn't it, when you think about it – just some old skin and stuff, right?'

'Mmm?'

'Just think, it could just as easily have been his finger – or his big toe even, hey.' Crystal giggled. 'You know what I mean here, Bec. I mean they're all just bits aren't they – I mean, bits are bits, right?'

'Sort of,' Beccy whispered.

'It's a bummer that you feel bad,' the bottle-piss philosopher continued. 'But it is just a *feeling*. You're really all right – you just feel bad, hey.' She grinned at Beccy, raised her brows and lightly held her bottom lip with her teeth. 'Your mum tells me you bit him real hard, did you?'

'I bit him so hard he screamed and screamed and screamed.' Beccy's words rushed out like bad air from a balloon. 'There was blood and stuff all over the place!'

'Good on you, Bec.' Crystal licked a finger and drew an imaginary cross in the air. 'One up for the kids. You'd be a saint for every kid who's had something like that, if they knew about you. Saint Beccy! Patron Saint of the Bummers!' She went back to the cupboard and tossed a string of cheap pearls over her shoulder. 'Here, you want these? I'm sick of them.'

'Yes please! Thanks, Crystal.'

'Well, okay. But don't go throwing those over the cliff. It's a waste of time,' Crystal said. 'When you get over the dickhead down the Bay, you'll probably stop having those dreams anyway. I don't know for sure but you probably will. Do you know where your mum's tie-dye skirt is?'

'Yes, do you want it now, Crystal?'

'Soon.'

'I'll get it for you, okay?' And she dashed off to her mother's drawers, glad and eager as a lap-dog.

'You don't look so tired today, Bec.' Miriam dumped shopping bags onto their table and oranges spilled out. Beccy was arranging a bunch of scrub cuttings in a jam jar. 'Did you get through school all right?' Miriam was thin and weary smudges of shadows darkened her eyes. The baby hardly showed. She walked around slowly like something gold and white moving on air.

'School was okay,' Beccy said. 'Crystal borrowed your tie-dye for tonight.'

'Oh? She could've asked me.'

'I said she could, Mum.'

'Why?'

'She said you told her about what Gull did – you know . . .' It was only the third time the incident had been mentioned since that day.

'You don't mind that I told her?'

'No, it's okay.'

'I had to talk to somebody. Jen won't see me. It's been

hard.' She sat Beccy down and held her hand. 'Crystal's good to talk to. Everything you tell her goes into her ears but I don't think she listens, so she's good to tell stuff to – not for advice – just someone to tell.'

'She talked about it a lot to me.'

'You mean what happened to you.'

'Yes.'

'What did she say, Bec?' Miriam had serious misgivings about remarks Crystal might have made.

'She said it was a bummer.' Beccy took an apple out of a bag and polished it against her dress. 'And she said I could be a saint for what I did but mostly she said it was a bummer – and she said anyway it was only meat.' The child smiled up at her in an embarrassed way but Miriam hugged her daughter to her, tears of relief wetting her eyes, and she combed her hand through Beccy's untidy hair. 'Can we maybe see Jen tomorrow? I miss her. I'll make her another card if you want.'

'You do that, Bec. She's feeling very bad right now, but I'll try again on your way home from school.'

'And I want to see Marlin too.'

'I know, Bec.'

'But not that Gull! Is he going to gaol?'

'I don't know, but if he doesn't go to gaol there are other ways to punish men like him.'

'What other ways?' and Beccy saw Crystal propped against the door, grinning, and already dressed in Miriam's skirt and a grubby top of her own.

'Oh, well, let's see,' Crystal said. 'Hang him up, no lights at night, make him eat lizards and put a ferret down his pants.'

'Crystal! For God's sake! I don't want her having any new dreams. What she's got now is enough.'

'Well, it'd be no good putting him in gaol anyway. They'd only kill him in gaol. They do that to rock spiders.'

'What's a rock spider?' asked Beccy.

'A rock spider is *some guy* who does *some thing* to *some kid.*'

'Who told you that?'

'*HQ* magazine,' she said. 'Mirry, have you got a top I can wear? This one's only got two buttons.'

'I'll get it!' Beccy jumped, renewed, out of the cloud that had been covering her. 'What colour do you want, Crystal?'

'White, I guess,' she said.

'You must decide what's to be done with Gulliver.' Hesta and Marlin had seen Gull creep out of the laundry door and into the shed where he'd stayed in grim silence for an eternity. He had caught his father's glance, as cold and hard as dry ice, and had looked quickly away.

In Marlin's mind, the punishment of his son, worse than anything a court could have inflicted upon him, had begun. His recovery was slow. An infection had fed on his wound and more medication had been needed. He was unsteady and weak. The most precious of his possessions had been spoiled, and the others damaged. He existed in a realm of pain, humiliation and silence. His room was his cell and he had to rely on Hesta for food, and for him, a belly scrape to the lowest depths when he was forced to beg her for a ration of liquor. There was an aura of blackness around his locked door that hung heavy as dust – blacker than any prison could make. The whole house existed in a whirlpool of emotions and sadness and it remained so until two of the blackest clouds lifted on the same day.

Miriam came to visit. Instead of searching for Hesta to enquire about Jennifer in whispers, she marched straight up to her room and went into it without so much as a tap at the door. And Jennifer, accustomed to the tips of toes and hushed voices, was jolted out of her chair as though she'd been struck, and stood facing Miriam like a startled bird. Miriam put a parcel on the table and said, 'I made some biscuits. Oatmeal and fruit. I brought you some valerian; it'll calm you down. It's a herbal. I'll make the tea if you don't feel like doing it – or do you want coffee? Bec's coming straight here from school so we'd better save some for her.' Jennifer had not blinked since the door had opened. Her mouth hung open. 'Well?! What's it to be, tea or coffee?'

'Tea?' It was hardly a sound at all. Jennifer put her hands to her ears to muffle the sudden noise. 'Beccy mustn't come up here.'

'Well, she is!' She went to Jen and held her hands and gentled her voice. 'Listen to me. Beccy is all right. Every day she asks can she see you. She doesn't blame you for what Gulliver did.' Jennifer flinched from his name. 'And neither do I! It was a bad thing, Jen, but we've got to get over it.'

'Look what he's done to you,' she said in a voice dry of tears.

'I never loved him, you know.' Miriam looked directly into Jen's eyes, trying to drive her message home. 'You know what he's like. He's good looking; I was pretty lonely for a guy, and, well, it just happened. Jen, look at me! It was just sex and it was an accident.'

'But there's a baby.'

'So? It's not what I planned, let me tell you, but I don't want to get rid of it or anything. We can look after the baby together – you and Bec and me.'

'But what about – him?'

'We can do something about him later. Right now I'm worried about you and Bec . . . and me, I guess.'

Jennifer had not moved from the patch of grey sun on the grey carpet near her grey window. She pushed a lank string of hair off her face with a slow-motion hand. 'You're very thin, Miriam.'

Miriam laughed out loud. 'Well, look who's talking. If you turned sideways you'd disappear. You've been sitting up here too long. How long has it been?'

'I don't think I know,' Jennifer said.

From an upstairs window Miriam could see Hesta, sitting on the harbour wall reading. She wore her victim clothing, Salvation Army cotton, flat sandals, no make-up that she could see, and a devastation hairstyle: all windblown wisps and frazzles and useless pins. *What a lot of work they all had to do to climb to the tops of their lives again*, she thought, *all of them!* She went to the kitchen, hoping she would not see Marlin or Gulliver but not really caring one way or the other. She turned on the jug, took down three mugs and called Hesta from the side door.

'Tea in five minutes in Jen's room, Hesta. Okay?'

'Sorry, dear. Did you say Jen's room?' She waved to Miriam with a letter in her hand.

'Yes.'

'Oh, my goodness, Miriam – oh, my goodness! I didn't know you were here. This *is* good news. You've seen her – you've talked? You're a wonder. I'll come now and help.' She tried to tidy herself, smoothing her skirt, brushing her shoulders, smoothing her hair, only to have it all brushed back the wrong way by a stiff breeze.

Hesta was so surprised and pleased to see Jennifer preparing to eat and drink with her friend that she was unable to remark upon it. She simply went to her niece and kissed her on the cheek. She clutched a letter close to her but decided that it was not the right time to tell them her own news. She ate a biscuit and praised the cook. She drank tea and chatted about the harbour and a ferry she'd just seen with a choir of male singers on board. 'It was lovely. They sang all over the water.' she said. 'I imagine they're Welsh.' Suddenly, small talk in a small room in which a storm was passing. Her letter from Lucretia Haldane could wait until the clouds had moved further away.

Jennifer had put two biscuits and her own mug, wiped clean, aside for Beccy, and when she heard the child's feet running up the stairs she sat tensely on the edge of her chair and waited for a small, dark-eyed woman child at the door, with her hands on her hips. But when Beccy came she ran to Jennifer, threw her arms around her and buried her head in her lap.

'Will you like me again now?' the child said in her specially deep voice, hoping to make Jen laugh.

'Oh, Bec, I've missed you so much.' Jennifer wearily hugged her and stroked her back.

'I don't care about that *Gully* any more, Jen.'

'Oh, God! Beccy! I'm so sorry.'

'Bec!' Miriam held up a warning hand. 'Remember what I said.'

'Don't worry about it, Miriam,' Hesta said. 'He's been sent to his room, darling. He has to stay there for a very long time and not bother anyone again.'

'Is it dark in there?'

'I suppose so, dear.'

'Well, Crystal says he should eat lizards and have a ferret down his pants!' Becky giggled behind her hand as children do when they speak of things that really belong to adults. And despite the pall of emotion that still hung over them, weary smiles, little more than a dry parting of the lips but smiles nevertheless, lightened the faces of Miriam and Jennifer. Hesta's smile, on the other hand, was juicy as a cut melon. And it had little to do with Rebecca's remark.

It was two more days before Hesta told Jennifer and Miriam that she'd had a letter from Lucretia and that she was to be with them in three weeks.

'In three weeks she will be here. Then we'll all see some surprises.'

'I can't possibly cope,' Jen said in a state of panic. 'Three weeks is too soon. It's too soon. You'll have to do everything yourselves.'

'We'll do everything, heart. You're not to worry for a minute. Miriam will help. And Marlin.'

'Ha!'

'It will be good to have Lucretia in this gloomy house. She will shake us all awake. Lucretia will cheer us up – and she will know what to do. She will tell us what we must do. She is very strong.'

'If she had any idea at all of what she was coming to,' Jennifer said, 'she wouldn't move an inch away from Germany.'

'You don't know her, dear. She wouldn't miss it for the world.'

Chapter Twelve

THE GERMAN WOMAN

Hesta disposed of her days with a brainstorm of activity. She knew she'd been without responsibilities and the need to think for herself for too long. Her brain was too slow to react, and her nervousness too quick. Her world was not quite upside down – the sea was not the sky, the flame tree in the yard still stood, rooted right way up – but everything around her seemed slightly askew, and everything had a shudder to it.

Gulliver had only just begun to creep to the water's edge to watch and wait near the dinghy cave for bottles and six packs rowed to him on the quiet by smuggling fisher mates – and he had only just begun to sneak to the shed, low to the ground as a lizard, to tap and wrench and screw what was left of the bike. Marlin had taken to his study to lick his wounds and dream of after-schoolies – to bury his nose in books already read, edit lectures already given and suffer Hesta's 'Hail Mary' cooking from a head full of recipes where everything was left out. And there was poor Jennifer, her poor dear heart, who'd at last ventured outside on her weak gangles of legs, but only when she could be alone; and inside, capable of nothing more than switching on the water jug.

In order to prepare for Lucretia's visit Hesta had had to somehow put herself in the role of a woman with much more strength than she possessed, and play the part as an actor would play it. She became a Mrs Danvers with key bunches and hard mouth for Gulliver, a sister bird to Marlin, obliging to a point, as warm as milk but with not too much sweetness, a mother comforter for Jennifer, Miriam and Beccy and a mother of the earth to creatures tanked and caged and cooped – but the part she played for herself was a frantic and confused Little Red Hen who chirped from time to time:

'Who will help me clean the house?'

'Who will help me coop the snake?'

'Who will help to pluck the pigeons?'

'Who will help me cook the meals?'

'Who will help me hang the sheets?'

'Who will meet Lucretia at the airport?!'

'Who will meet Lucretia at the airport?!'

It had been decided that Hesta would share Jennifer's room when Lucretia came. Under the circumstances, it seemed best. Again, it was Bindi Hope who lent an old-style single bed that took up little room.

In six days, in six days, in six days she'll be here. Hesta recited lists to her nervous mind. She worried that no one would be well enough or civil enough when the day came. She was afraid that she might not cope alone and that her friend would leave in disgust at finding so much sadness and confusion.

'I cannot believe,' Marlin said with a tongue dipped in ice, 'I cannot believe that your *kraut* is still coming to this house at this time!'

'We've had no time to change the arrangements, Marlin. There was nowhere else for her to go.'

'You're going to have to keep her busy, Hesta. And away from me and away from here!'

'Of course she'll be taking trips and seeing the sights, Marlin. She won't be here all the time,' Hesta said. 'And Marlin, please try to remember that if Wellings Road had not been destroyed, neither of us would be here. We wouldn't be bothering you at all.'

'There's no comfort in telling me that now.'

'I am more than aware of difficulties,' she drew herself up to what little height she could muster, and covered her face with the face of a sterner woman. 'But she is a visitor. She is to be *our* guest, and we will! We will be civil! And we must try to present a reasonably normal household.'

'And how is the *kraut* to come from the airport, Sister Bird?'

'You must collect her, of course,' she said, ignoring the look in his eyes. 'You will collect her in a taxi.'

'I damn well will not!'

'Then, Marlin, I expect I must try and go myself. But I will tell everyone it is because you refused.' She was flustered despite the help of her new roles. Her fingers feathered through her hair, searching for the pin she'd forgotten to put there.

'And tell me,' Marlin said, 'who's to explain the runt in his cell to her – and Ophelia up there . . .' he nodded to the ceiling, '. . . wafting around like a half-gone willi. Who's to talk to the *kraut*? Who's to cook? Heaven help us all if it's our Sister Bird.'

'Well then, Marlin, perhaps you could do it yourself. I'm sure you could if you put your mind to it.'

'I'm breakfast,' he said, and he padded away to his study and latched the door.

'It won't be long now, heart.' Hesta soothed Jennifer with low tones and music. 'And I do want Lucretia to see how lovely you are.' She stroked Jen's shoulders and pushed her gently to face the mirror on the dresser. 'She'll be here on Wednesday, dear. Are you looking forward to it as much as I am?' She watched the faded reflection of her niece. 'Would you like me to brush your hair? Would you like to wash it, dear, and then I'll brush it for you? Would you like that?' Jennifer looked at her reflection too but appeared to see nothing at all. 'Would you like Miriam to buy you something pretty, dear?' She stood behind Jen and spoke to the mirror. 'Something nice, to cheer you up? Dolan's asked after you again, dear. They all send their love. They can't wait to have you back with them.'

'Heaven knows when that will be.' Jennifer's voice was a flat line, hardly registering.

'It may be sooner than you think.' Hesta gave her arms a gentle shake. 'Lucretia will set us right. I guarantee it.'

'How is she to come here, to the house?'

'I've booked a taxi.' Hesta stood back a pace and fluttered nervous fingers. 'I'm sure I can manage it.'

'What about Dad?'

'He refused.'

'Oh, what a terrible family.'

'Never mind. You mustn't worry about a thing, but later, Jen, I would like you to come downstairs and help me plan a shopping list and tell me what I must cook.'

'Is there anything else to be done to her room?'

'I don't think so, dear. You must come in and see what I've done to it.'

'Yes,' said Jennifer. 'I expect I'd better.'

It was Saturday.

On Sunday a tentative snail's pace of activity took place in the Fishcastle. Marlin emerged from his study and patrolled the harbour front, checking python, fish and fowl, battening down and securing before 'the invasion of the Hun'. Then, as a last thought, he tucked a tortoise into the top of his sarong and ran the mower over neglected grass. Gulliver had been sighted, sneaking down to the cave, and slow Jennifer, tired after every step, wandered through the kitchen with an apron tied around her thin waist and tried to make some sense of Hesta's shopping plans. Hesta, on the other hand, seemed to move about with the speed of nervous light, settling dust from one place to another, chasing blowflies, draining the dish drainer, checking the refrigerator, wiping what was already wiped, drying dry cups, and checking the upstairs bathroom again and again and again for even invisible traces of carnage.

That was Sunday.

On Monday, Hesta shopped with Miriam's help, from a muddled list corrected by Jennifer, and from it a reasonable menu for a week was planned. The strain of the day had Hesta sitting on the edge of her bed at nine o'clock on that moonless night, knitting nervous fingers together and silently pleading for the strength to continue, for all their sakes.

Jennifer, however, went to her bed genuinely physically tired for the first time for weeks, and slept deeply.

That was Monday.

On Tuesday morning, and against all their plans, laid well or not, Lucretia arrived at the Fishcastle.

She arrived at eight forty-five, alone and unannounced, bellowing and laughing with the cab driver loud enough to have every curtain on the Sandpath pushed aside. She threw a heap of packs and bags onto the path. She arrived with all the gentleness of a brass band to a salon of chamber music. She looked, to a shocked Jennifer and Hesta watching from their window, to the yapping Carters' dog from a crack in its fence and to Marlin who'd just padded home from Cove Beach with a bundle of kelp, like a wild woman, bright-eyed and bushy-tailed, who'd travelled no further than the next suburb.

The woman saw Marlin's hand on the gate of number fourteen.

'You live in this house, *ja?*' she demanded, but smiling, while the cab drove, grinning past a gauntlet of lifted curtains, back to the airport. 'You know my good friend, Hesta?' Marlin, for some reason, lowered the kelp to below the waist of his sarong, as if there was a need to protect his soft underbelly.

'I am Hesta's brother,' he said with a chill. 'You will of course be the German woman.'

Marlin's first impression of Lucretia was the same as Hesta's had been; distaste for the blustering creature who looked so brazenly into his eyes. She stood firmly on the path, treading new ground of another country, moving her feet as though she owned every stone of it. A bold woman. *An insolent woman*, Marlin thought. *An arrogant, typical* kraut!

Lucretia threw Marlin one of her packs and he had to drop the kelp to catch it. It seemed to his man eyes that she wore no underwear at all – certainly not under her top. And when she bent over, her tracksuit pants clung, creased and sweaty to every split, every crevice of the bottom of her. Marlin held the pack where the kelp had been, for despite his first impression of her he felt movement around the area of his long-deprived balls.

'I come one day early,' Lucretia said. 'You don't mind?' She swung bags over each shoulder and carried another. 'Hesta I think will be surprised.'

'I think we can be sure of that.' Marlin unlatched the gate

and stood aside for her but before she walked through she bent and picked up his kelp bunch. She put it to her nose and sniffed it as though it were roses.

'This is very good for the earth, *ja*? Or maybe you are constipated?'

Marlin looked to the sky. Whatever it was that had moved behind his sarong had ducked for cover. The Fish-castle, he thought, had become a monument for madness. He followed her as she marched up the drive, crunching gravel, as though she'd lived there all her life.

Upstairs, Hesta was much, much more than surprised. She ran about, she dithered, she fidgeted, wispy-haired, cotton-shifted, barefoot and unbathed. Her hands and fingers flew around like twigs in a wind.

'You must go downstairs, dear.'

'I can't!'

'You must, Jen. You must try. Make her some coffee. It will give me time, dear . . .'

'I can't, Hesta.'

'Please, please, Jen. Do this for me. Heaven knows how Marlin is treating her. Brush your hair and go, darling. Say we've all been sick . . . say we've had the flu or something. Please, darling! How could she have come a day early!' She gave her niece's hair a few strokes with the brush. 'Go on! Go on, dear!' And as she hurried to the bathroom she was relieved to see Jennifer, deeply sighing, go slowly down to the kitchen.

Marlin had already turned the jug on. His belly was crunched under his ribs as if he'd taken a deep breath and couldn't let go. Jennifer sighed again at the sight of the man's vanity.

'Aaah, so, here is our own Jenny Wren – our Jennifer.' He had begun to perform already in some small way for Lucretia; to make his mark; peeing around his territory in the only way he knew. He padded around the kitchen with mugs and milk and sugar bowl. 'And where is our Sister Bird, Hesta?' Jennifer glanced at him and closed her eyes briefly, but it was almost a relief to hear his rubbish again.

'We've all had the flu as a matter of fact.' Jennifer shot her father a look. 'Hesta will be down shortly. She's thrilled you've come early.' She went to Lucretia and kissed her cheek. 'Welcome to the Bay, Lucretia. I'm Hesta's niece.'

'I have heard about you. You are the beautiful one. Hesta tells me all about her niece . . . You are all sick?' Lucretia sat at the table and eased off her joggers. 'Is Hesta still sick from the bad storm?'

'It's taken her a while to get over it. But she's feeling better now. We're all feeling better.' Jennifer spoke as brightly as she could. She took spoons from the drawer and saucers from the cupboard. She glanced at the instant coffee jar Marlin had put on the table. 'We won't use that, Dad.' She admonished him with a frown and a shake of her finger. *Another act for the stranger*, she thought, and felt ridiculous for performing it, but these were the games families played. She took a sealed bag of ground coffee from the freezer and a plunger pot. 'You must be tired, Lucretia. Would you like your coffee strong?'

'Black and strong – like a negro.' Lucretia laughed and

pushed her hands through her wiry black hair. And it was difficult not to look at the dark wirewool of her armpits. She sat there, relaxed and instantly at home, her legs stretched and crossed at the ankles, grinning from Marlin to Jennifer, smelling of all the smells of a full life on the earth: traces of spice and sweat, wet forests, riverbeds and smoke – smells that were not unpleasant. And Jennifer looked at her wistfully, knowing there was probably nothing on the face of the earth that could cause Lucretia a moment's anxiety, that the German woman was absolutely in control of her life.

'I'll make you toast if you like. Are you hungry?' Jen asked.

'Toast is *gut*.'

'An' somethin' for your dear ol' dad, Jen?' Marlin wheedled, performing for all he was worth. 'A wee toasty for the man?'

Jennifer didn't answer him but put out extra slices of bread. She hoped Lucretia wasn't too sickened by his rubbish. She hoped Hesta had told her what he was like.

'You have a strange language.' Lucretia laughed straight into his eyes. 'You talk in a tongue – is this player's talk, brother Marlin? I like it. I do not understand, but I like it!'

Marlin folded his arms and laughed with her. These were new and strange sounds in a house that had been so troubled, so black and Jennifer, plunging coffee and buttering toast and fussing slowly around them, felt while they laughed that life at the Fishcastle *could* return to normal madness as Hesta had promised – anything was possible. She'd felt a flash of irritation with her father's idiotic hamming, but the irritation was at least a feeling and it was better than no feeling at all. She even managed to smile.

Hesta joined them. She too was smiling and she held her arms out to Lucretia. Her hair was wet from the shower and she'd tried, too heavily, to disguise a paleness with blusher and lipstick but her eyes were alight at the sight of her friend. She wore the purple linen, creased now from over-use, and mules.

'We're so very glad you've come, Lucretia.' Somehow she'd adopted a clear, confident voice on the way down the stairs. 'And so very glad you have given us an extra day with you.' Lucretia jumped up and wound her powerful arms around her friend.

'But you look wonderful! *Schön!*' She kissed Hesta soundly on both cheeks and almost sent her flying. 'It is good to see you again!'

The sparks of human warmth that generated in the room radiated and touched them all. Marlin was able to express himself with an explosion of laughter that was not noticed in any particular way. Jennifer was flushed with exhaustion but pleased that so far they were surviving the morning without calamity – she wished briefly she had a camera to record the strangeness of it all.

Lucretia's boisterous affection threatened to overcome Hesta who teetered to a chair. And outside the window, it was as if the Fishcastle had suddenly been jollied into move-ment. Pigeons coooed against each other's feathers, the python uncoiled and stretched, lizards licked blue tongues, sea birds screamed for scraps and Gulliver managed to lurch

312

up from the dinghy cave unseen, bottle-pissed to his feet soles, to curl and sleep unchallenged in his cell.

The sounds of the harbour played in the background in a soft way, not wanting to intrude, but Lucretia ran to the window when a tugboat trumpeted out of tune. She smiled and yawned all at once. There seemed to be row upon row of white, sharp teeth in her mouth.

'I can swim with the fishes here?' She winked at Hesta.

'Yes, Lucretia, you can swim. But here you must beware of sharks. Sharks may not be afraid to bite you, German or not.' Lucretia smiled and yawned again. 'But come along, dear,' Hesta said. She picked one of the packs from the floor. 'It's time for a shower and a rest, I think. Come upstairs and I'll show you where you are to sleep while you're here.'

'*Ja*, yes, that will be good.' And she left with Hesta, yawning, and leaving behind her a wake of her naked smells that had Marlin shifting on his chair. Jennifer, for an extra-ordinary moment, thought she saw him blush.

'You can clear up,' she said to him, still sitting there, struck unusually dumb. 'I'm going to rest too.' She knew there was amusement in the situation but she was unable to laugh at it. Without a word, Marlin began to work at the sink. A sight unseen beyond the hour of breakfast.

'So, that is what Sister Bird found in the Amazon. An Amazon Borgia!' Jennifer was already leaving the room but clearly Marlin needed to recover authority lost. To mark his territory with stronger piss. 'Was that a fat ring of venom I saw on her finger, Jen? We must keep her well fed, daughter – a side of cow a day and a net full of fishies or she'll stalk when

313

the moon's up, Jen, and eat us all; teeth, nails, gizzards and innards and spit nothing out!' He put a hand to his mock-horrored face. 'Snakes alive, Jen, did she bring her own leash, I wonder?' His ridiculous theatrical words, something she hadn't heard for a long time, sounded so abnormally normal that Jennifer laughed for the first time in ages. And he seemed pleased to see a change begin in her. 'That's all right for you to laugh. It's not the Jennifus the big ol' Amazon *kraut* is after eatin'.'

Jennifer glanced around the grey kitchen with her dulled eyes and suddenly saw a spot of colour. The light from the window shone for a second on a willow-patterned bowl. It was only a small patch of blue and faded at that but it was better than no colour at all.

'What do we do about – your son?' she asked him. 'How are we to introduce him? Someone we don't even talk to.'

'We won't have to, Jen Wren.' Marlin winked. 'I'll leave a trail of mincemeat leading to his door. She'll do him in an Amazon second!'

Lucretia Haldane slept, except for brief feeds and waterings, until almost noon on Wednesday. She slept heavily and unmoving, on her back, with her mouth open and gently snoring – a strange noise, like a cricket. Hesta hovered near the door, looking in every so often in case something was needed. She envied the totally relaxed body of the woman. There was no foetal curl. No comforting pillow hug. No belly protection by lying face down. There was, in the posture of her sleep, almost an arrogance of fearlessness. There were certain features of her friend Hesta wished she could steal.

When Lucretia was fully awake, Hesta slowly helped her to unpack. Bending with difficulty. Handling with difficulty.

'My friend Hesta is not so *formidable* I think; not so tall as I remember.'

'The mountain storm blew me down, Lucretia.'

'And your hand is hurt.'

'Yes, dear. It seems it was broken.'

Hesta began to tell her stories of the storm, and Lucretia stopped what she was doing and listened. She expressed shock; she sucked in her breath; she hit her chest with her fist; she said 'yi yi yi yi . . .', for Hesta's story of the storm was jaw-clenching in its drama (as though such a thing needed elaboration, for goodness sake). But like all good tales, the tale of the mountain storm had become old enough to grow in height, in width, in ferocity. The tale of the mountain storm had grown a mould of lies so convincing that the teller was unaware of them. But that is the way of such tales. It is how truths become legends. A bone broken became several, two trees crashing became four, glass shards speared birds mid-flight, blood spilled was blood *poured*, a crack was a ruin and Wellings Road an extinction – the day the world ended. But Lucretia, the good listener, exhibited amazement and sorrow at every turn.

'You should write this storm for a movie,' she said. 'Then you will be rich enough to put your mountain back.' She sorted through clothing and found a blouse and skirt. She stripped naked without a thought and began to change.

'Don't you think you ought to wear panties, dear?' Hesta

watched a body wearing nothing more than its skin and obviously more comfortable in it than the cloth it was being wrapped in.

Lucretia turned and shook the backside of her skirt. 'You see? Who will know I do not wear such things?' Marlin will, Hesta thought. 'Only once in the month I wear panties.'

'That's very practical, dear.' Hesta felt a vague irritation but pushed it aside. 'This evening you will meet Miriam Holt and little Beccy. They live in a community not far from here. They're our friends. I know you'll like them.' She helped Lucretia put clothing into drawers. 'When you're ready we'll walk down to the harbour front, there's so much for you to see. The weather has not been good to us lately but I see a change. I know you'll find a whole bay of things to enjoy.' This was small talk, she thought, and how good it was to speak like this – how soft on the ear, the patter sounds of normal houses. She hoped the winds of change would bring more of it or nothing at all. 'We'll all eat together – that is, except Gulliver.'

'Who is this Gulliver?'

'He's my nephew, Jennifer's brother. I'm sure I told you about him. Mostly he's called Gull. But he won't be here tonight, he – he has been –'

'The flu?'

'He's still not well. You'll see him another time.'

'Is he also strong and fine like his father?'

'I'm afraid so, dear.'

She sat cross-legged on the end of the jutty, the German woman, moist and salt-sprayed, and she stretched her arms and rolled her neck and shoulders like a seal. She seemed absolutely at home. Entirely part of the landscape and the sea. *She had come to the right place*, Hesta thought, watching her. Proudie Bay was where she should be. And she wondered if the Blue Mountains might have been alien to her, uncomfortable, away from water.

Sitting at the kitchen table that evening with Miriam and Beccy, Marlin, Jennifer and Hesta, Lucretia showed no signs at all of jet lag. She had endless energy. She told them about the American she'd met in Singapore on the way to Proudie Bay, sparing them few details. She told them travel stories about every corner of the earth, above and below the equator and beyond – even the Galapagos Islands and a remote valley of Kauai. And then there were a hundred optional extras: white-water rafting, ballooning, climbing, diving, chewing betel nut, learning the tango. Travelling so far and doing so much from a kitchen table exhausted them all until they could hide their yawns no longer. She was still eating, drinking and talking when Miriam and Beccy slipped away, when Jennifer pulled herself upstairs, then Hesta, until she was left with a tired but mesmerised Marlin. The woman radiated enough energy, he thought, to power a city. She left the table at one-fifteen.

Jennifer and Hesta's agonising over how best to cover the existence of Gulliver, how to introduce him as though there was nothing wrong, was solved by Lucretia. She simply followed her nose one morning during a swim with the fishes and introduced herself to him in the dinghy cave, where he'd gawped and spluttered and scuttled into a corner of stone like a roach caught in light.

'Your son drinks too early I think,' she said to Marlin, who had strolled down to the harbour with a bucket in his paw. 'He hides in the dark. He is not a happy man.' Marlin glanced in the direction of the cave with distaste but held his tongue.

'There's been a bit of trouble,' was all he said, and in a rare moment, sensed the virtue of silence.

'That is too much sadness for a *bit* of trouble.'

'The son has been a *bad* boy.'

'*Ja*? Making too many babies I think?' She winked at him but he didn't laugh.

Marlin disliked having adult strangers around the Fishcastle for more time than was absolutely necessary but he had made an exception for Lucretia Haldane. It was, however, a discomfort; an embarrassment to hear a stranger speak so intimately and lightly about matters that tore at the heart of the Fishcastle and everyone in it. Lucretia watched his face and knew she had angered him.

'I'm sorry,' she said, 'my tongue is too strong for my brain.'

'You must learn to curb it, woman!' He grinned at her. It was difficult for him to maintain a rage with this woman who was so unafraid.

Jennifer, watching from an upstairs window, saw that her father had spruced himself early. He wore white drill trousers rolled mid-calf below his brown torso with his belly held in so tight she wondered if he could breathe at all. *More theatre*, she thought. Act one and more to come. It was endless. What a whore he is, she whispered. And Lucretia's pale olive skin had already added to it the shade of lightly burned sugar and probably smelled as sweet. It would not have been necessary to tell Marlin that the woman in the black swimsuit, sea- and sun-basted, was good enough to lick. *What a show they were in for*, she thought.

Hesta joined Jennifer at the window. She'd heard their laughter.

'She has a strange effect on men,' Hesta whispered. 'When I first met her I thought she was hideous, but then, I'm not a man.'

'She's pure sex,' Jennifer said. 'They can smell it a mile off.'

'Yes, dear, I expect you're right, but she terrified Gulliver. She told me she found him in the dinghy cave and frightened him into a corner.'

'Ha! I'd like to have seen that.' Jennifer could still hardly bear to hear his name. 'Maybe the smell of sex was a bit much for him.'

They watched the two of them wade amongst the rocks, scraping, plucking, picking – he, filling the bucket with weed and kelp and water, and she, behind him, pointing to this and that, talking, sitting on rock shelves under the water tops, apparently not in the least troubled by the blades of spent oyster shells that littered the area.

And they secretly continued to watch them, as Marlin had once watched Lucretia from a window as she drew the element of water to her as intimately as if she were Proudie

Bay born – and netted a male as easily as she'd charmed the python, whispered to his lizards, stroked the throats of birds and petted the carp.

And it was Marlin, from a hide, who'd watched her one evening as she lay under the flame tree, hands behind her head, ankles crossed, watching the moon rise. And he'd stayed until she moved.

'How long is your wife dead?' A miniature school of grey fishlings cruised and darted around her toes, inquisitive. Marlin had his back to her and she watched the line of his spine as he bent over his sea garden.

'Too long.'

'It is lucky to have your daughter still to help you.'

'The daughter washes the dishes and boils the spuds,' he said. 'There's more to it than that.'

'She should have a man of her own, that good girl. It is not good to live with a father. I would not live with a father.'

'And I would not live with a daughter if there was a choice,' he said with a sharpness, then made an effort to change his mood. 'So! Our Lucretia is the *bairn* of a Scot.' But he looked at her briefly, uncomfortable with her blunt and guileless manner. 'Is it the Scot or the German you are most like?'

'Not one of them!' she laughed. 'There is only me.'

'I can believe that.' He waded deeper with his arm under the water, grinning hugely. She leaned forward to see what he'd found. 'Is it a man fish with pearls, Marlin?'

'Better!' he said, grinning down. He pushed his arm between two rocks. 'Better than that!' And with a howl of triumph he brought his arm out, covered to the elbow with clinging and sucking octopus, its tentacles wound tight against his skin and its head pulsing dark with anger. 'This is what I've caught for the bairn of the Scot!' And he waded to her and swung the arm and the creature close to her. Lucretia shrieked with amazement and kicked water over him. Marlin was delighted she was not afraid. 'Help me get it into the bucket, woman!' he roared. 'Don't jest stand there a'laughin'!'

Together they unsuckered and untwined the octopus while it clung to one then the other until, weak with laughter, they had it snaking and inking in the salt-watered bucket.

'Feast fit for a king and a *Fräulein*,' Marlin shouted, waving his fishing arm, red with sucker spots. 'But we'll have to chop up this occo ourselves. Our Jennifer's frightened by wee sea pets.'

'We'll eat it near a fire by the sea, *ja*?' Lucretia easily fell into his ways. 'We will eat him under the moon, okay?'

'Is okay for the wild Scot's bairn, is okay for de ol' Marlin.' They climbed the steps together and he put the bucket on the grass and his hands on her shoulders. 'Maybe you better stay on here at the Bay and help ol' Marlin farm the sea.' He was grinning all over his face. 'Now, you stand guard and slap his wrists if he tries to go home, and I'll fetch the chopper!'

'You must not let my brother frighten you, or carry you off with his strange ways, Lucretia,' Hesta said. She had come outside to see what the commotion was about. 'You must take him with a grain of salt. His head is full of fins and scales and feathers – and women – in no particular order. No particular one.' She looked at the seething bucket of water and remembered Lissy's horror if there was an octopus to be cooked, slapping and sucking one tentacle after another over the side of the can, its live eyes black with hate. And she remembered the child, Jennifer, once watching her mother's fear and vomiting at the sight of it, and Marlin scolding the small child for it.

'Not to worry, Sister Bird,' Marlin said, winking at her. 'The Scot's bairn would eat it live if she could. At least I'll put the poor manny asleep first.'

Sheltering on a patch of harbour front grass, in the shade of the flame tree and not far from where Lucretia watched the moon, sits a grey stone lion. It sits compactly, straight-backed and still, with unblinking eyes and a hard stone frown. The lion is forever on the lookout for magpie beaks or bird droppings and sticky children, and it has sat in that fashion for so long that parts of its grey coat have greened with mould and moss. On the side of its neck, just below the right ear, is a dense white patch of web where spiders nest, and on the tip of the left ear is the scar of a wound that was inflicted in 1983 in silent combat with Jay Lennox and a bag of marbles he'd been given for his fourth birthday. This lion, for the most part ignored for being lifeless, had become a special place for Rebecca Holt to sit and contemplate the knots and fathomless cares of her world. It had become almost as holy as baby Alice's grave in the garden of St P's.

On an early, humid February afternoon there was a

silence that humidity brings – a lazy air. The harbour was full of tide that spilled all over the Bay, even over the end of the jutty. Seagulls too lazy to fly draped themselves like pennants on the spars of yachts or preened on bobbing buoys. There were two soft bells ringing, just loud enough to keep the Bay awake. One was from a charter ferry and the other from St P's, silvering down in a Japanese way for one of Mrs Kerslake's weddings.

From the sea wall across the bay it was possible to see the sidewalk tables of Dolan's – and possible, if the current of air was right, to smell the last of the crabs drowning in pots and fish with eyes staring at nothing, blindfolded with batter and fried. And it might have been possible to catch a glimpse of Jennifer, back at work in her serious, pernickety way.

In the yard of the Fishcastle, the grass, in need of a cut, buzzed with thick, humid life and lay still in peace and quiet before the after-schoolies, happy to be back with their storyteller, came gravel-crunching up the drive again to get the best seats in the house. Upstairs, Hesta snoozed on her bed. Lucretia had gone to Cove Beach for a swim and the ghost of Gulliver tinkered and drank and made impossible plans in his marked, shadowed territory. Marlin, wearing only skin and his sarong, padded from the harbour front to the house and back again, anxious for the silence to be broken.

And Beccy, not anxious at all to be disturbed, sat as quiet as breath by the stone lion. She'd watched Marlin out of the corner of her eye but it was not until he'd paced for the third time to the sea wall that he saw her.

'Ho ha!' he shouted, pretending to be surprised. 'Has our brown top Hill chil' run away from the schoolyard?' He padded towards her, crushing grass and slaughtering ants. 'Has the Beccy come to tell dis ol' lion her secrets?'

Beccy shrugged, unhappy. She sat close to the lion and put her arm over its back. She did not answer him.

'Well, I'm hearin' nothing at all, at all – has the Bec gone mute?' He leaned over and whispered in her ear, 'Did she sell her tongue at the markets?'

The child pressed her lips together and kept as straight a face as she could. She turned her back to him. Marlin sauntered over to the snake's hutch, lifted the creature and draped it over and around his shoulders. He began to writhe about.

'Oh! Oooooh! Dis ol' snake man he get me! Save me! Save me!' He flopped its coils around him in mad movements, and he staggered and cried out. 'Help me! Heellp meee!' His hand clutched his throat while the python, limp and half asleep from sun and boredom made no effort to play his own part in the drama. Beccy put her skirt over her head so he wouldn't see her laughing but there were tears streaming down her cheeks and eventually she had to come out, choking for air.

'Well now,' Marlin said. 'The Bec's laughing tool is working, any rate.' And he threw the snake a short way into the air and caught it.

When she could catch her breath the child said, 'I stayed home today. My mum got sick last night.'

'Vomit sick, Bec?'

'Yes, all over the bed.'

'Poor copper-top. And poor brown-top.' Marlin felt deeply sorry for the child.

'Can I wait for Jen?'

'As long as you want,' he said.

'Where's Cretia?' From the beginning she'd had trouble with Lucretia's name.

'She's round the Cove fishing for a merman, that's for herself of course, the merman – and a mermaid for me, Bec. Anything you want her to catch for you?' Marlin had become as fond of the child as any human he had known. At that moment he longed to hold her hand or just stroke her hair, but he didn't dare touch her. Not now.

'I'm really hungry,' she said.

'What about some bread and honey and a drink?'

'Yes please, Marlin.'

'Milk?'

'Yes please.'

'At once, madam!' He bowed in an old-fashioned way. 'I will go and scrape the bees and milk the pigeons ... at once!' he said. 'Immediately, madam!'

She still sat and hugged the lion but *it was good*, he thought, *to see her laugh*.

'How sick is she?' Beccy followed Jennifer up to her room, preferring quiet for a while to the squealing on the grass. 'Is she in bed?'

'I don't know. She was feeling better after lunch. She said she'd come down and pick me up.' The child's hair had the

messed look of restlessness and there was shadow under her
eyes.

'Have you been dreaming again, Bec?'

'A bit.'

'And you look as though you've been crying. Have you?'

'Marlin made me laugh too much,' and she began to
giggle again. 'He pretended old snake man was killing him –
I nearly peed my pants.'

'Oh, him and his rubbish! No wonder you have dreams.
But its better than crying your eyes out at something sad I
suppose.' She called to Hesta to help her with teas and bread.
Beccy heard Lucretia's voice outside.

'I'm okay now,' she said. 'I'll go and show Cretia what to
do.'

An hour later, while Hesta and Jennifer sat at the table
with their coffee, Miriam came. Outside, the open-air theatre
was still playing the first act. Beccy and Lucretia sat in the
back stalls so the child could explain the more obscure
snatches of plot to her.

At almost four months, Miriam's pregnancy barely
showed. The bloom and serenity that made other women
beautiful at that time was not there. The translucent quality
of her skin had vanished and there was a paste of dullness,
bordering on grey – a matte coating through which nothing
shone. Her eyes, even when she smiled, were vague looking,
almost expressionless. She sat heavily and drank weak
black tea.

'What did the midwife say, dear?' Hesta asked.

'Iron deficiency. The same as last time.' Miriam's hand

shook a little. 'She's given me a supplement and some herbals. I don't know what else I can do.'

'Go and see a proper doctor for a start.' Jennifer went to the window to check Beccy but really to hide her irritation. 'Midwives might be all right to deliver babies but what do they know about medicine?'

'Heaps, Jen. They're okay. They deal with these things all the time. I just had a bit of trouble last night.'

'What trouble?'

'Well, throwing up is nothing new, but I had a bit of spotting. I'm sure it's just the strain of everything.'

Jennifer looked with concern at Hesta. Neither knew of such things from experience, but simply by virtue of their womanhood they assumed an air of knowledge.

'Was there much blood?'

'No.'

'Did you have any problems with Beccy, dear?' Hesta warmed Miriam's hand with her own.

'No. There were no problems with Bec.' Miriam picked at the crumbs of a biscuit. 'I'm seeing the midwife again tomorrow, but I promise I'll go to the clinic if I get worse.'

They were silent for a moment but it was difficult to think with the noise outside. They occupied their hands uselessly with whatever cup or spoon or crumb was closest to them.

'The thing is – I think you're brave to want to continue with the pregnancy at all, under the circumstances.' Hesta said it suddenly, almost to herself, an escaping thought, but the look on Jennifer's face made her wish she'd not allowed it to be heard.

'That's our own flesh and *blood* you're talking about!' But she added quickly, 'I mean what a thing to say, Hesta. As if she's not feeling bad enough!'

Miriam told Hesta not to be sorry for what she'd said – she'd thought about it a hundred times.

'It just slipped out, dear.'

'Sometimes I've been so sick,' Miriam held her arms tight across her chest. 'And so sick about all that's happened – worried for Beccy, worried about the baby, and thinking about the father. My parents don't even know I'm expecting. I mean I know Gull's your brother, Jen, but what sort of father is that! Well, I've thought about abortion; don't think I haven't.'

'But you won't, will you? You wouldn't. I long for it now. I mean, I've lost so much, you know. You said it would be *our* baby. That's what you said and you'll hardly have to lift a finger. Miriam, look at me! You won't think about this any more, will you? We've lost the father. I've more or less lost my brother, Miriam. Please go to a proper doctor. Go to the clinic. I'll pay for everything.' Miriam and Hesta exchanged astonished glances. Both were frowning. Jennifer's new fears spilled all over the kitchen table like hot wax, burning ruts into the pine.

'Dear heart,' Hesta said gently, 'it is *Miriam*'s baby. You can't cling to it just to make Gulliver clean again. Do you understand, dear? Miriam's baby will not be someone pure in your life, to cleanse its father's sins.' *Tragic. It was a tragedy*, Hesta thought, but it was clear to her what was in Jennifer's mind. There was so much locked away in her niece's head. So much clamouring for freedom. 'And what will happen when you have babies of your own, dear? You can't look after all the babies in the world.' But her niece had her hands knotted tight in her lap and sat miserably, staring at the table.

'And when do you think that's ever going to happen!' she said. 'What chance is there for that?'

The light from the kitchen window played around in dust shafts. As the trees outside the window filtered it, the dapple of light spotted coffee mugs, spoon handles, strange patterns on their hands. There was less tension in the silence of the kitchen now. Cheers and hoots from the after-schoolies' circle denied that indulgence. The three women sat at the table, reflecting on the state of things as women do in the kitchens of houses, where quiet is allowed and truths are hung out to air. And the thought came to Hesta, after Jennifer's outburst, that kitchens are surely where all the records of female lives are stored – in their walls, in the cracks of their floors, in the blotting-paper surfaces of rags, cloths and towels hung on hooks. Revelations of old wisdom, records of births, deaths, marriages and couplings out of order, recipes and cures, must hang in the air of kitchens and glue like oil to their surfaces and settle safe on shelves where cracked pots sit and old jugs are never lifted. And she thought briefly about the smell of kitchens. Does grief have a smell? Does laughing leave an aftertaste? Was there something sugary in the smell of gossip that was addictive? Was the rancid stink of a used dishcloth the accumulation of the tears of the women who'd used them?

She had always believed that nothing was inanimate. She believed that everything was alive in some way with the touch and breath of its user. But this was a hard house, the Fishcastle – a hard house with a poreless skin that hardly ever smelled of woman. It was a hard-skinned man house that showed little signs of their souls.

From the rim of a flowerpot, a blowfly grew. Jennifer watched it in the light of the window-sill with no interest while it climbed to the top, quiet and lazy in the silence of the room. It washed its legs and tested the air for something more rotten than biscuit to nest on, then stood perfectly still and pointed like a hound at a spot behind the three women. *'Found it,'* the fly would have said if it could have spoken.

Gulliver leaned against the hall doorway. He seemed at least part-sober. Miriam swung around and stared at him with an expression of surprise and anger. Hesta seemed less disturbed. Jennifer could not believe her eyes. In the room came the uneasiest of moments in which there was not even the movement of breath. The fly regarded the man and flew away. If the fly could have spoken she would have said, *'Rotten, yes. But rotten should be dead for maggots.'*

'I've come to say goodbye.' He was sullen and looked at no one but Miriam. 'I'm moving out of this shithole.'

'What am I supposed to say?' Miriam asked. Hesta and Jennifer might not have been in the room at all and Jennifer hated him for passing her by like that. She sat there hating him all over again, but wanted to ask him: *'Where?'* A sudden panic – a loss. *'But where? Where are you going?'* But she held her tongue.

'I don't give a fuck whether you say anything or not,' he said to the only woman in the room he could be bothered with.

'Good riddance then!' Miriam turned so he wouldn't see sickness and tears in her eyes. 'I hope you fall off the bloody end of the earth and go to bloody hell.'

'Don't talk about going to hell.' He had the cheek to smile. 'I'd finish up back here.'

'Fuck you!' Miriam swore in a voice that was strange. Intense and furious.

'Miriam! Be quiet!' Hesta had never heard Miriam speak like this. She looked coldly at Gull. 'As a matter of courtesy you could tell us where you're going.'

'Far enough.'

'But where?!' Jennifer wanted to scream. *'What will you do for money? How will you manage?'* Even after all he'd done, she had these thoughts. She looked hard at him, squinting her eyes in order to search his face more closely for some sign of goodness that must be there somewhere – hiding. *'How long will you be gone?' Good God! Why can't I say good riddance like Miriam – why can't I say 'fuck you'. He isn't worth more.*

But then Miriam was crying and being comforted by Hesta.

'I'm going to be working at the shop. I'll send a bit of cash if that's what you want.'

'I don't give a shit what you do.'

Gull raised himself on the balls of his feet and peered down her body.

'What're you looking at?' Miriam was flushed with anger. She pushed Hesta aside. 'You want to see if I'm still knocked up?' She stared at him, tight-lipped. 'I haven't decided what to do with this kid you say *might not be yours*. I haven't decided one way or the other.'

'Well, it's your business, I guess.'

'Yes, that's right, you shithead!'

I don't know this Miriam, Jennifer thought. *This is a Hill voice yowling – this is a Hill voice screaming at my brother!* She sat silent still, gagged by her grief, her anger, humiliation and weakness. *Why am I caring anything for this man. He's ruined our lives! It makes me sick! I make me sick!* 'And I don't care where you go, either,' she said to him, too late. 'I don't care what happens to you now, not for a minute.'

And Hesta thought, *If all those words and tears didn't crack the walls of this kitchen*, this man house, and soak, sobbing forever into the corners of it, *she didn't know what would*.

From the open-air theatre outside there suddenly came a loud cheer and Beccy burst into the kitchen dragging Lucretia by the hand.

'Marlin's going to chop two pigeons and he wants the meat cleaver.' The child was wide-eyed and breathless. 'I told him to do it. I told him which ones were ripe.'

'That's all we need,' Jennifer said, shaken from the heat of one situation to the chill of another. 'It's disgusting to do that in front of children.'

The blowfly that had left the kitchen for richer fields returned, as though it knew there would soon be a nest to lay in.

'I tell him better it be chicken,' Lucretia said. 'The little birds have no meat.'

'Yes they do!' cried the Keeper of the Pigeons, and then suddenly seeing him she said in her special, low voice, 'Hello, Gull!!' She barely spared him a glance and, having so briefly acknowledged him, dismissed him in a second, in the flash of a closed eyelash, and turned to the others: 'Mum, Cretia says when you chop off a chook's head it can still run around. But not pigeons, they can't run.' She looked into her mother's face. 'What's the matter? Are you crying?'

'No, Bec,' Miriam lied. But her daughter swung around and faced Gulliver, her chin up and her small hands in fists.

'You keep away from my mum! You keep away or I'll chop *your* head off and watch while you look for it!'

'She has the courage of a German, this one,' Lucretia said with admiration. 'She will be strong with men I think. She even frightened the cave man,' she laughed, and pointed to Gull.

'Aaah, get stuffed, the lot of you!' He turned to go. He left Jennifer, hands clenched in her lap and staring into the table as though she would find some message of comfort deep in its timber.

Lucretia held the cleaver away from Beccy. 'I think I should carry this, my young warrior.'

'But I'll give it to Marlin, okay?'

'*Ja*, okay, okay.' She grinned and winked at Miriam and pointed to the little fury. 'This one I like to see when she is a woman! When the men come to wave their cocks.'

'Lucretia!' Hesta said sharply.

'I am sorry. I say the wrong word, *ja?*'

'Yes dear, you did,' Hesta said. 'Later, Lucretia – later this evening there is something I have to tell you.'

'Okay, my friend,' and the woman gently led Beccy away.

'Bec,' Miriam called. 'Don't be too long. We have to go soon.'

And the child, sensing some gravity, simply said, 'Okay, Mum.'

Outside on the grass, outside of the room where their emotions had been flayed and their souls laid bare and where cleavers were stored, a great cheer rose from an innocence of children as the first of the pigeons lost its head. It sounded like a day at the guillotine. She wondered idly if one of the little darlings was sitting there knitting something.

'But Dad, he's gone! He just left. He didn't tell us where. I have no idea where he's gone. Not that I care.' Jennifer drew breath at last.

'Ol' Marlin knows where his runt's gone.' He looked down at her with a smear of smile that hardly moved his mouth. 'Did the runt make you think he was a man of property? Did he make you think he was oiling around the world like a slicker?' He glanced down at Jennifer's tight hands. 'I can tell you where he's gone to ground. The runt has a room over the bike shop where he curls up with his grease and his nuts.'

'You knew all the time?'

'I know the movements of my herd,' he said.

Jennifer clicked her tongue and closed her eyes. 'Well, you'll never know my movements, not from one day to the next. Not now.'

'Oh, yours? Dear little Jen Wren, I know yours best of all. I put salt on your tail a long, long time ago.' He smiled and his words held no particular menace but she shivered just the same.

In the thin light of an early morning, down by the carp pond, Lucretia watched Marlin scrape the porridge pot and watched as the last of the gulls snatched drying gobs from the sea wall. They had not spoken. Lucretia had seen in his eyes the need for silence and had held her tongue, but when he looked at her at last she spoke softly.

'How does one ocean know when it meets another?'

He said nothing. He leaned against the wall and stared out over the water.

'Do the colours change? Is there a sign that says, *Welcome to the Atlantic*?' She pointed to a freighter rusting its way towards the ocean. 'How will that captain know these things?'

'He won't leave the Pacific. There's no need for him to know.' He only briefly glanced at the vessel. 'That rust bucket's going to Newcastle. It would sink if it crossed a line.' He scraped the empty pot.

'It is sad for a man to have such a son, *ja*?' Sea birds screamed pink-eyed above their heads and the golden fish plopped nervously in their chicken-wired pond. The morning sky was already veiled by a fine, steam haze that promised another humid day. 'Hesta told me. It was hard for her to say the words I think but I know where his cock has been.'

Marlin was suddenly angered by her intrusion into a very private domain, opening closets and tossing skeletons all over the place. Airing and outing as though the affairs of *his* Fishcastle belonged to anyone who wanted to pick at them. And worse, he had, he thought, locked the sins of the runt away in the cells of his mind, with all the other sicknesses, to rot away unnoticed. It was as though she'd lifted the top of his skull and had gone rooting around in his brain looking for dirt. He banged the pot with the ladle and threw it, black bottom, down onto the grass.

'It was only so I do not say the wrong words to the little one.' She slid around in front of him and looked into his eyes. 'We do not do this to hurt you, Marlin. And what Hesta tells me is not the worst thing one human can do to another. It was a bad thing for the child but it is not the worst thing I know. Your Proudie Bay will never have to live through such things.'

'Mmm,' he said. He held a hose in the pot. 'Turn on the tap, *Fräulein* – hard,' he said to her. And the rush of water that cleaned the pot also cleared the air. He seemed, in a way, relieved.

'Tonight Marlin, I will come to your bed, *ja*?' There was something totally open in her expression. There was absolutely no guile at all. 'We will get angry together, *ja*? We will make a mountain of anger until pooof! – the mountain explodes and there will be no more of it and we will lie quiet. I think that will be good, yes?'

He didn't answer her. There was nothing to be said, for

from their first day such a night had been inevitable.

'So? You will work today?'

'Yes, ol' Marlin has snots in lecture halls most Wednesdays. No playdays on Wednesdays. The bairn of the Scot will have to play with someone else.'

Behind them, but out of earshot, Jennifer and Hesta hung washing on the line strung between a palm tree and the house and, while they did it, Jennifer, who knew her father's body language so well, wondered when Lucretia's panties would be hung on the line at dawn – that is, if she wore them.

'Today I will walk!' Lucretia hooked her arm through Hesta's and steered her towards the harbour. 'I will walk up there.' She pointed to the hill of St P's.

'It's going to be very hot, dear.'

'Hot like the Amazon?'

'Heavens, I hope not, Lucretia.'

'Then it will be nothing.' She put her arm around Hesta's shoulders. 'Will you walk with me?'

'I'd like to try, dear, but it's a long time since I've walked so far.'

Lucretia hugged her. 'If you stop I will carry you.'

'No need, Lucretia. We do have buses.'

Jennifer had been sceptical about the outing. She'd fussed around Hesta in a spin of meddling. 'You can't possibly walk so far – you've hardly been out at all – it's all uphill of course, you realise that, don't you? You'd better wear my joggers; you can fill them out with socks – and don't forget your hat – and wear a blouse and skirt – and don't forget sunblock and money for a taxi if you feel faint – doesn't Lucretia know you've been sick?' Sounding to Hesta like her own drone of a mother a hundred years ago just before she escaped to the schoolyard or into the bush with brother Marlin. But she tolerated the fuss for Jennifer's sake. She allowed herself to be dressed and lectured. It was good for her niece to do these things.

Even before half-past nine the Sandpath was already hot enough for Proudies with bare feet on their way to Cove Beach to have to hop from shadow to shadow, the cooler stripes of poles and fences and trees. A humid haze had fallen over Shack Hill and softened the look of it and in the distance the spire of St P's could barely be seen. Just a suggestion of it. Like a water painting.

As the two women walked past Dolan's Cafe they caught a glimpse of Jennifer sorting cutlery, but she did not see them. They walked across the park on grass high as their ankles, a sea of new green too quick for the council mowers. Lucretia slipped off her sandals and curled her toes amongst the blades.

'It is good, this park. Do you come sometimes with the little girl? Do you have picnics here on the grass?'

'Of course, dear,' Hesta lied. She had never done so. She hated to sit where dogs had been.

For Lucretia, the effort of the walk to the church showed itself as no more than a gloss of oil on her arms and perspiration that dampened her face. For Hesta it had been a rock face, an Everest; as daunting as climbing a giant bunya in

Wellings Road, and St P's seemed to distance itself from her, whenever she had the strength to look, as if it were on wheels and being pulled away with every step she took. Her own skin was a bright rose, her ears rosier still and her breath came in tiny gasps, bubbling like gills drowning in air. She was unable to speak and at the turn of the road, where the steepest stretch began, Lucretia moved behind her and pushed until they were through the gate and on St P's garden path.

St P's stood unchanged, a small stone flower-bedded fortress with its back to the wind and the furious ocean. Shrubs still sheltered against its body, and shrub birds, too small to fly, nestled safe against the sea winds and warmed their eggs. Lucretia was enchanted.

'We will go inside, Hesta. It will be cool and we'll rest for a while.'

'Aaahhh yes, dear . . . aaahhh.' Every word an effort.

'Poor Hesta. We will have to make you strong again.' Lucretia helped her spent rag-doll friend through the doorway and steered her to the back where the pews were even cooler.

Inside St P's, the light was no greater than a dusk and there was a dry shadow of air that flowed easily into them. The smell of old stone and timber was as comforting as the air. They sat quiet, side by side, with only the soft sound of soft breathing joining them like clouds touching. Lucretia closed her eyes and seemed to Hesta to be at prayer.

'I had no idea you were godly, dear,' Hesta said when at last Lucretia's eyes were open.

'Not godly,' she said. 'It is a feeling sometimes, only a feeling.' She stretched her arms behind her. 'I like this place. There are churches I have seen, big and cold like bat caves with no end to them, where everything echoes – I feel nothing in such places. But here it is small; I feel I am in the circle of a *Kirche* like the old times of churches. I do not lose myself in this place. In Scotland there are such *Kirchen* as this one, small and made of warm stones – no, not godly. I don't know what I am. My mother a Jew, my father a heathen ...' She turned to Hesta but her friend had fallen asleep with her chin on her chest.

At the front of the church a light was switched on and there was a man at the altar. He carried cloth and a can. With one hand he took a bunch of white lilies from a brass vase and tossed them onto the floor. The lilies were made of a substance not known to the earth. He poured liquid from the can on the cloth and put the can on the floor. He began to rub the brass, stepped back to a better light and knocked the can over. So was the ritual at the altar of St P's on that Wednesday morning. 'Bugger!' said the man. And he was so frightened by the laugh of a woman that he kicked it again.

'I've made a bit of a mess on the carpet I'm afraid.' He did not apologise for his word. Lucretia had already marched down the aisle to him. 'I don't know what Mrs Kerslake will say about this. You don't know how to get Brasso out of carpet I suppose?'

'What is this Brasso?'

The dark puddle on the blue carpet had formed itself into a badly drawn flower.

'It's for cleaning brass and ruining everything else,' Robert Brae said. 'Not really the sort of thing for a bride in white to be near. And the smell doesn't improve with age.' Lucretia kneeled, put her finger on it, sniffed it and laughed again.

'Maybe you call this the blood of Christ and people will come to your little church from the whole world and leave money.'

'I'm afraid this blood has too distinctive a smell. Any housewife would know the truth in a minute. But it's an entertaining idea nevertheless.'

Still on her knees she offered her hand: 'I am Lucretia Haldane.' He shook it warmly.

'Robert Brae,' he said. 'You must be a visitor to Proudie Bay I think.'

'I am living at the Fishcastle with my friend. Hesta is Marlin Hardwick's sister.'

'Aah yes,' Robert said. 'Actually, the Hardwicks are not amongst my flock – or anyone else's I imagine,' he smiled. 'But I remember Hesta of course. I'd like her to know that we all said a special prayer for those who suffered in that terrible storm.'

'I will tell her. She is here, but asleep. We will tell her when she wakes up.'

Later, outside in the harsh, salted real world, Robert offered a quick tour of the grounds and the old graveyard. They read the stone of Sarah and little Alice with a sadness that Robert had become accustomed to.

'Once read never forgotten,' he said. 'It brings people

back time and time again. There is one little girl who lives on Shack Hill. She comes often to the grave and makes flower chains for it. I find it very touching. She tries to be little Alice's friend. I secretly took a photo of her once. I keep it on my desk.'

'What is her name?' Hesta asked, expecting no other answer.

'Beccy – just Beccy.'

Outside the window of the Fishcastle, in the blue satin sky of late dusk, a moon was raising light for when the night was dark.

'Do you know what the native people in New Guinea call the moon?' Hesta asked. 'They call it "lantern bilong Jesus Christ". Isn't that poetic? Everyone, isn't that poetic? Marlin?'

'It is beautiful,' said Lucretia.

'By the way, dear. What was that you said to me in the church? You said something but I must have been dozing.'

'You were asleep, my friend, but you asked if I was godly and I told you I don't know what I am because the mother is a Jew and the Scot is a heathen.'

'I see, dear. But it doesn't matter. We mustn't worry,' said Hesta.

Much, much later, when the moon over the bay was high and deep and honeyed, an oboe was stroked to life by Bach. There were two naked bodies on a bed, one lying, one kneeling. There were tongues that twined and licked like serpents and hands that cupped and explored. Breasts brushed a mouth and a mouth sucked mother parts. A finger drew

S-bends along a spine until it was lost in the shadows of wet creases. Eyes were wide open and full of tears or closed to hide a private vision. There were acts of sex that were full of love or base and loveless and urgent. They were all at once an offering, a giving, an act of grace, a dominance, a submission – a sweetness of seduction with the smell of animal about it. And even while Jennifer dreamed this dream in her wetting sleep she seemed to be aware that on her father's bed a similar play had begun, with low lights and soft music, but real – with live flesh.

Jennifer's dream was one and more than one. But it was not enough to wake her.

Chapter Thirteen

BIRTHDAY

It was still night in Proudie Bay.

All over the Bay, women held pillows close and dreamed of different lives and pleasures denied the sleepless. Men grated dry breaths and damp-dreamed away the worries of their day while babies in their snugs of quilts moved their mouths in pink-bud dreams of nipples, and dogs wheezed and whimpered in their quick sleeps through visions unknown to man. It was night.

And Proudie Bay, free to do what it liked for a few hours, buzzed and splashed and washed its shores with a gentle of tide. Seagulls roosted on places that were their day secrets and cried soft night cries. Fish plopped cheekily close to fishing boats at the moorings, bobbing bluish in a light from the bottom of the moon. And underneath the surface of the water, where the black of night was deepest, kelp forests and weed gardens moved and swayed in their own way, disturbed only by the creatures that sheltered there.

In Proudie Bay it is clearly understood that night is the province of water and will be freely shared only when a rising sun allows it.

On Thursday morning the porridge was late. Everything was late. The gulls flew like paper in a gale and screamed for the pot. Breakfast had to be eaten in relays. Jennifer had already dressed for work and was pegging washing on the line when Hesta came downstairs. Hesta looked drawn and pale, probably, Jennifer thought, as a result of the climb to St P's in the heat. Her clothes too were pale. It was difficult to tell where skin ended and cloth began.

'Good morning.' Jennifer took a peg out of her mouth. 'There's no porridge this morning. You'll have to make yourself some toast. The water in the jug is still hot. It's going to be a nice day, I think.' As always, morning had made everything clean. The world smelled as fresh as the sheets and towels. Hesta handed her a top that belonged to Lucretia. 'It's all so quiet, isn't it?' Jennifer said.

'You know, heart,' said Hesta, 'I think your father and Lucretia might have spent the night together. Her bed was not slept in.'

'I know they did,' Jennifer said, remembering her dream, seeing it all with her eyes closed tight, feeling with every breath of her sleep. She pegged one of his shirts to the line. 'I know they did, even though there're no pants on the line. Maybe she doesn't know what to do after a night with Marlin.'

'That's all nonsense, dear, you know, that silly rumour about the pennant flying. You know how loose tongues love to build on that sort of thing. It might have happened once ... a very long time ago.'

'You mean the Irish woman?'

Hesta glanced quickly at Jennifer, surprised. 'It's possible, dear,' she said. 'Does it bother you very much that Marlin might have spent the night with Lucretia?'

'Why on earth should it bother me? It's nothing new. I can't think why they've waited this long.' But Jennifer was at least sure of one thing – the German would not have toppled head-over-heels into his net. She would have dictated the terms.

The bay had begun to give up the peace of its night to the disturbance of another human day. Fishing boats, which the good eating fish had played with all night, chugged out in search of them. The first of the ferries whistled for its city workers and a tide slapped against the jutty with a purpose. The Fishcastle's menagerie stirred and the Carters' dog yapped the pigeons wide awake, but there was a clear sky and a dry breeze and the clean, wet washing flapped in celebration of it.

'Summer's here, de grass is riz, I wonder where de boidies is?' Marlin came, padding on his bare soles from the side of the house with nothing on him but a sarong and a grin. The gulls heard his voice and swooped above him. He ducked and feigned terror. 'For gawd's sake. Who let du Maurier in here with her flocks?!'

Jennifer ignored him.

'Breakfast cooked in a minute, Jen. Your ol' dad slept in.'

'Don't cook oatmeal on my account. I've already eaten,' she said, concentrating on other things.

'Well, the Jen Wren's not the only beak to feed.' He glanced at Hesta. 'Good lord, Hesta. You look like a nun!'

'Thank you, Marlin,' she said.

'Where's Lucretia?' Jennifer asked with bitter on her tongue.

'The *Fräulein* is having herself a swim in the Cove. There'll be porridge for her, for sure.'

'Well, I expect she's earned it.' Jennifer balanced the laundry basket on her hip and marched off. She felt no animosity towards Lucretia but she was angry that he once again had treated her like a child who had no idea what was going on in her own house. She slammed the door behind her.

'You should talk to her more,' Hesta said. 'Let her feel part of your life instead of forever treating her like a kitchen maid.'

'She's jealous, Sister Bird.'

'Marlin!'

'Well, what's to tell? What's to talk about?' He reddened slightly when he saw the look on his sister's face. 'It's none of her business!'

'Yes it is, Marlin. You know how sensitive she is. When you have your affairs in this house it is her business. You owe her a word, Marlin – she works so hard and you shut her out without a thought. You owe her a word, and more, Marlin, much, much more.'

'Great balls of fire!' he boomed. 'What is this?! Interrogation in my own house? Are there spies at peepholes? Are there cameras hidden in the chandeliers?'

'You know we don't spy, Marlin,' Hesta said. 'No one has to spy. You flaunt too much for the need to spy.'

Marlin blew a hiss of a sigh.

'I come round here all sunshiny this morning, Sister Bird, and all you lot do is throw a bucket of rain over me! Shame! Shame! Be damned, the lot of you!'

'Nevertheless Marlin, you do make Jen very unhappy,' said Hesta. 'I wish I knew why.'

'The Jennifus is a martyr to misery – like a Jewish housewife – she wallows in it. One day, Sister Bird, she will die, smiling of it, tied to a cross of broomsticks with dishcloths!'

'What an absolutely terrible thing to say, Marlin! Terrible!'

'By the way,' Marlin said, as though he'd just been discussing some light reading. 'It's the *Fräulein's* birthday on Saturday. I think maybe we should have cream cakes and lolly water. What thinks you, Sister Bird?'

'What an extraordinary man you are.'

That afternoon Miriam and Beccy wandered around the beach below the cafe. They waited for Jennifer and walked along with her, chatting about their day and listening to Beccy's animated story of how Bret Anstell in grade four was sent home for putting his hand up Belinda Grey's skirt and making her cry, and how his mother was told to come and get him, and Bret crying too and Mr Ford making them all stay back after school while he told them that boys weren't allowed to do that any more, and anyone else caught doing that would be thrown over the cliff!

Jennifer and Miriam listened with serious expressions – the best they could manage – both of them trying to suppress smiles, but when Jen glanced at Miriam she thought she had not seen her looking so well for a long time.

'Oh, come on, Bec. Mr Ford did not say he'd throw anyone over the cliffs,' Miriam said. 'That just sounds like something Marlin would say.'

'Well . . . yes, he did.'

'Beccy?'

'Well, that's what he meant!' She put her hands on her hips and planted her legs defiantly apart. 'And he could if he wanted to. He's the boss of the school.' Beccy, still with her hands on her hips, marched ahead of them with her nose in the air.

'You look better today, Miriam.' They were approaching the Sandpath. The sun, even at that hour, beat down on their heads like a furnace and Jennifer envied the loose, flowing clothing favoured by Miriam and the women of Shack Hill. 'There's a bit of colour back in your face.'

'I am tired though,' Miriam said. 'I won't come to the house. I'm dying for a sleep.'

'But I can stay with Jen, can't I?'

'No, Bec. There're things to do.'

'But you'll sleep better without me, Mum. I can do everything later – pleeese!'

Jennifer smiled at Miriam and nodded.

'Oh, all right, Beccy. But you can't go to the Fishcastle every day of your life. You've got your own home – you know, up there – h.o.m.e.!'

'Your mum's right, darling,' Jennifer said quickly. 'Today you come for a while but tomorrow you go straight home, all right?'

'Okay.'

'And then on Saturday,' said Jennifer, seizing the opportunity. 'I hope you can both come to Lucretia's birthday dinner. Can you, Miriam? We can start early so you won't get tired.'

'Okay, we'd like that. Thanks. What time?'

'I haven't really thought. Hesta phoned me at the cafe. Apparently Marlin told her this morning that it was Lucretia's birthday on Saturday. She thought a dinner would be nice. Come around six, I suppose. Do you think that's too early?'

'It sounds fine, Jen, thanks. I'll look forward to it. It's a nice idea.'

'It will certainly make a change. I don't get much of a chance to cook something decent.'

Beccy squirmed and twirled and hugged Jennifer. 'Can I come and help you cook it?'

'All right, if you want to. But ask your mum.'

'Whatever,' said Miriam, and as she turned to go. 'Have you heard from you-know-who?'

'No, Miriam.'

'Not that I care,' she said, walking away. 'To hell with him!'

Yes, to hell with him! Jennifer whispered in her mind despite the pain it brought to her heart. She held Beccy's hand and walked up the Sandpath and the feel of the child's hand reminded her of something shocking. *Yes, to hell with him!* Beccy tugged Jennifer's skirt to make her walk faster. *But his bike's still here . . . as long as his bike's here he'll have to come back . . .* Beccy pulled her up the drive of the Fishcastle. *Of course I wouldn't have anything to do with him. I wouldn't even look at him – not for a minute.*

After Jennifer had changed and washed and wet-combed her hair for the cool of it she heard the high pitch of voices down on the harbour front grass and vowed to herself – as she had vowed many times before – that if *he* thought she was going to run to the kitchen to make all their little teas and *his* coffee and all those stupid little fairy breads and run around them all like a bloody maid *he* could think again, she went downstairs to the kitchen to do just that.

'Ah! The beautiful Jennifer has come home.' Lucretia stood by the table and smiled broadly. 'I will make you a coffee – sit down for a while. I have almond biscuits.'

'Oh?'

'Hesta is sleeping. You like almond biscuits, *ja*?'

'I suppose so.' There was a certain churlishness in Jennifer's voice. It was a mystery to her until she realised it was because her kitchen had been invaded. 'But there's no need for you to do anything at all, Lucretia, thank you. You see, at this time of the day there are things *I* must do – it will be easier for me to do them. I know where everything is.' *My kitchen*, she thought. *Why in God's name am I thinking this!*

I must be off my head! 'But you see, there are special things to do for the children first . . .'

'I will do it all for you.' If Lucretia had heard anything at all offensive in Jennifer's voice she did not show it. 'You should rest at this time, poor Jennifer. In this place you work too hard. You tell me and I will do it.' From the air, it seemed to Jen, Lucretia produced two mugs of excellent coffee. 'First you drink, then you tell me.'

Jennifer was confused. She felt as though her train of after-work thinking, regular as clockwork, had been shunted onto a strange branch line – her routine journey interrupted and sent too far away for her to quickly come back to it.

'You are always too tense, I think. Too tired. Everyone makes you work too hard.' Lucretia raised her mug and toasted Jennifer. 'Sometimes, do you have a holiday?'

Jennifer sat stiffly on her chair. She looked around at her undone chores with a sense of panic. Lucretia had put the coffee pot on the wrong bench and she'd left the sugar bowl uncovered for the ants. Bread that ought to have been on a board on the table was drying by the sink, there were plates unwashed and a tea towel out of place. With an effort she sipped her coffee.

'I used to stay with Hesta sometimes, when she lived in the Blue Mountains. That's about all really. Is the fridge door shut properly? You've got to push it hard.'

Lucretia seemed not to have heard her.

'One day we will all go to these mountains. This I would like to see.' Lucretia bent down to her coffee and sniffed the rich, aromatic steam. 'Hesta told me stories of her mountains when we were in South America. They made us feel cool when the jungle was hot around us and the bugs were flying. She told me about the trees that make the mountains blue I think. And she told me much about her Jennifer. She is very loving to you, I know.' Lucretia paused and drank. 'This week,' she said without looking up, 'I took your father to his bed. We had sex. He is an unhappy man I think. He is confused.' Then she glanced at Jennifer and winked. 'But the cock is still good!'

Jennifer nearly dropped her coffee. She lowered it as gently as she could to the table. Outside, the drone of Marlin's voice and the buzz of children made the passage of time in the kitchen almost surreal.

'Why are you telling me this?'

'Because you are his daughter. This is your home. It is only right I tell you. I would want to know these things in my own house.'

'Thank you,' she said quietly.

'You do not mind?'

'No, Lucretia, I don't mind. But it's not the first time, you know. It's not the first time he's had a woman in his room since – since my mother died.'

'Of course it is not the first time. He is a man. A man is a man! He will do it again, many times. You must not mind.'

'I wouldn't like him to break your heart too.' Jennifer's voice was childlike and Lucretia looked at her with pity.

'Men are too stupid to break hearts! A man could not break my heart; I am the one who breaks theirs!' she

353

laughed. 'You are like my mother I think – a mat at the door for men to wipe their stupid feet. I tell her she must pull the mat away when they stand on it and make sure the floor is waxed and *hard!*'

Despite it all, Jennifer laughed. 'I wish I had half your strength, Lucretia – just half of it.'

'You will learn.'

From outside came the chant for after-schoolies' teas and a booming order for coffee from Marlin. Jennifer eased herself to her feet and stood at the side door.

'I'll do it when I'm good and ready!' she called to him. It was a trembling attempt at half a strength but Lucretia cried 'Bravo!' loud enough for the whole Bay to hear. Jennifer caught a disapproving glance from Beccy, but the open-air theatre, finding no answer to it, absorbed itself in another play.

From the window they watched Marlin stride to the garden tap, cup his hands under it and drink.

'You after-schoolies want a drink today, the Jen Wren says we have to lap it up like dogs.' And he left the tap dribbling for a line of children. Jennifer rushed guiltily to the fridge for cordial.

'Let them enjoy the water,' Lucretia said. She had lazily poured herself another coffee and sat with it as though there was nothing at all happening outside. 'It is good for children and men to drink water. Leave them and sit with me, busy Jen.'

Jennifer hesitated for a moment but she did put down the bottle. While she was at the bench, however, she covered the sugar bowl and moved the coffee pot to its usual place.

At least she did that. At least she maintained that much control.

On Friday afternoon Hesta waited for Jennifer at the gate and helped her carry shopping bags into the house. She had insisted on paying for the cost of the meal but had left the planning of it entirely to Jennifer: 'I will be the bottle washer and the waitress, dear heart. You'll tell me what to do.' In one of the bags was a poaching pan Jennifer had borrowed from the cafe. 'I don't know how you managed to carry it all, dear.'

'I managed.' Jennifer sorted and plated and packed with the ease of a chef. There was almost a glow to her. 'You forget I carry food all day long. You could put the poacher in the cupboard to begin with.'

'Have you decided upon a menu, dear?'

Jennifer fished around inside her tote and brought out a slip of paper. 'I want to keep it simple. I think it's nicer in the summer. What do you think of this? Scallop, prawn, mango and avocado salad with lime, honey and herb dressing to start . . .'

'*Exquisite!*' Hesta said.

'Poached chicken with white wine, garlic and tarragon sauce . . .'

'Oh, my stars!'

'. . . with English spinach and new potatoes – and maybe a few spears of asparagus, and a small mixed salad if anyone wants it!'

'Jennifer, my mouth is watering.'

'So is mine as a matter of fact. Then, fresh figs with mascarpone and almond wafers.'

'*Delicious!*'

'And I bought a good selection of cheeses and fresh ground coffee.'

'Darling heart, it's a pity you can't do this more often. You have a gift.'

Jennifer blushed with the pleasure of praise. 'For wine we have Blanc de Blanc and a light Merlot in case she wants red and a Heggies for dessert. It's all cost a fortune, I'm afraid.'

'That doesn't matter at all. Lucretia will be so delighted. I'm quite excited. And it's such a romantic menu.'

'You think? Well, let's hope they don't have it off again on the table.'

'Jennifer!' This was a Jennifer she hadn't heard from for a long time. She was delighted. 'You see? I told you Lucretia would make a difference to us all.'

'Did you ask Bindi to come?'

'Yes, dear, but she won't. You know how she feels – she won't sit with your father.'

'I understand. I wouldn't either if I could help it.' It was a remark made more from habit than feeling. She made notes and covered plates with plastic as she talked. 'We'll cover the table with white sheets. They'll have to be ironed, and I bought candles. I thought candlelight would be nice.'

'And what else, dear?'

'Tonight we can start the sauce and make the salad

dressing – and we can prepare the bouillon for poaching and the cheese platter.'

'You only have to show me what to do.'

'Then tomorrow I'll come home early. The rest will be easy. Miriam and Beccy are coming at about six, though Beccy will probably come earlier. She wants to help.'

'I'll tell Marlin to keep Lucretia away from the house. It will be a wonderful birthday for her.'

'Hesta?'

'What is it dear?'

'Did you ask Lucretia to tell me she went to bed with Dad?'

'No, indeed I did not.' She blinked with surprise. 'We haven't talked about it at all.'

'Then I'm glad. She told me because she thought I had a right to know. I'm glad she wasn't put up to it.' Jennifer laughed, remembering their conversation. 'She made it all sound so normal – even boring. Nothing fazes her, does it?'

'Not that I know of, heart. Lucretia is very unusual, I think.'

At ten minutes past four on Saturday afternoon Beccy burst through the side door and into the kitchen like a cyclone. She carried a parcel that was an awkward shape and badly wrapped. An inch of wood poked from one torn corner. She was breathless and her hair had blown to a tangle.

'Can I wear something out of the dressing-up box?'

'If you want to.' Jennifer smoothed odd creases from the sheets that covered the table.

'I made something really nice for Cretia.' The child put her parcel on the table. 'And I made the card too.'

'Oh my God! I forgot to buy her a present!' Jennifer cried. 'How could I have forgotten to buy her a present!'

'Good heavens, Jen, you're cooking her a present much more beautiful than anything we could think of.' Hesta buffed knives and forks with a cloth.

'Did you get her a present, Hesta?' Beccy asked.

'Yes I did, Beccy. Just something small.' She took a small box from the dresser. In it was a silver chain and hanging from it a Star of David and a Celtic cross. 'It's just a thought but she will know its meaning.'

Beccy had opened the biscuit tin in the pantry and had two in each hand.

'You're making crumbs, Bec.'

'Sorry.'

'Look, why don't you go to the yard and cut something pretty to put in a vase for the table. That would help.' She took a pair of scissors from a drawer. 'You be careful with these.'

'Okay. Where's Marlin?'

'We told him to take Lucretia for a long walk, dear,' Hesta said. 'And they're not allowed to come back until half-past six.'

Beccy ran to the door, then stopped and said to Jennifer: 'Oh, I forgot. Mum says if she's a bit late don't worry and start without her.'

'Why on earth should she be late?' *There's always something to go wrong*, Jennifer thought. She knew there'd be something!

'She just had a headache. She's taken some pills and she's lying down for a while. She's okay. What sort of flowers?'

'Anything, darling. You choose.'

The poaching kettle was on the stove, its stock ready for the chicken. Everything else was set out in order. The prawns were pink and sweet and the scallops like creamed satin. They looked so nice Jennifer wished she enjoyed seafood. Mangoes had been cubed and hass avocados were ready to slice. Vegetables stood by clean and crisp for finishing and the figs, creams, sauces and dressings and the cheese platter sat ready to be served, in the fridge. On the table was a bowl of nasturtiums that Beccy had arranged, a silver bowl of wafers and the tray set for coffee.

'I wish I could paint a picture of this,' Hesta said. 'I could never, never be so organised or creative. What a treasure you'd be for someone, heart,' she said in her old-fashioned way.

'Thank you, darling. Maybe I'd like to be a treasure for someone – very nice, very good looking and very very wealthy.'

'The trouble is,' Hesta laughed, 'most of the rich good-looking ones are gay.'

'How on earth would you know?'

'I've known a few in my time, heart. I even fell in love with one of them once.'

At six thirty-five Miriam had not come but neither had the guest of honour or Marlin. Jennifer was already agitating between bench, table and stove and looking anxiously at the clock. She checked the dark green candles in their holders and rearranged the gifts at Lucretia's place. She tested the CD player she'd brought down from her room and the disc of gentle Bach and Mozart. *It should be*, she thought, *a very nice night if nothing goes wrong*.

The first to fly into the kitchen was an explosion of pink and white tulle. Beccy had helped herself liberally to the dress-up box. She was flounced and frilled, and ribbons trailed like parrot tails. She had painted her face and stuck glitter and stars to it. She danced around Jennifer like a dervish in a party world of her own.

'Do you like me?!' she squealed, planting herself in front of Jennifer with her arms stretched out and her head back.

'You look beautiful, Bec.' But there was something about the look of her that made her shiver. The memory of green tulle and blood in the corner of her room. 'You look just like a dancer, darling. But you'll have to stop tearing about. You'll knock something over.' *A painted face with its mouth full of blood.* It was difficult for Jennifer to look at her without shaking. The green tulle had been burned and the ashes scattered on the sea. Terrible, terrible days. Perhaps the whole dress-up box should have been burned as well. 'Are you sure your mum's all right? She should be here by now.'

'She's okay. She'll be here soon.'

By contrast, Hesta looked almost funereal in elegant beige pants and a cream shirt buttoned to the throat. But there was a sparkle in her eyes and she had not been too aggressive with her make-up.

'You look very nice, darling,' Jen said. It was clear to her that some of the sparkle in her aunt's eyes owed a tot or two to the brandy bottle.

'What can I do, dear?' Hesta walked carefully to the table and supported herself on the back of a chair. 'Where would you like me to sit?'

'Take the chair to the left of Marlin's usual place . . . and Hesta, just sit down, there's not much to be done now. I just wish they'd all hurry up.'

Hesta sat and stared at the table. 'It looks too beautiful to be real, dear.' She spaced her words and Jennifer poured her a glass of water.

'Here – you just sip that for a while.'

Marlin and Lucretia arrived, dressed and behaving as though they were visiting strangers. Manners, polite chatter, *nice* smiles, nods all round. Lucretia wore a soft green fabric, *probably rayon*, Jennifer thought, and her father was all white cotton and drill, except for the Roman sandals on his feet. Jennifer hardly recognised either of them.

'Aaah, the table groans already. But where are the hounds and the jugglers?' Marlin smiled from his teeth and his scrubbed close-shaved baby-bum face. 'And do I smell the work of a master chef? Or is it our Jenny Blue-bird who cooks such superior chow for lucky us?' Marlin crowed. He shone in the room. His entrance was perfect – his patter, his timing, perfect. He shone and outshone as he knew he would. Dramatically he escorted Lucretia to the place marked with gifts and held the chair until she was seated. It seemed to all of them that she had genuine tears in her eyes.

'Happy birthday, Lucretia,' they said.

'I do not in my whole life have such a birthday as this.' Jennifer felt the warmth of her smile to the bottom of her soul. 'Thank you, *danke*, my good friends. This – this is all very beautiful!'

'Open your presents,' shrieked Beccy, bringing them all back to earth. 'Open mine! I made it all myself.'

Lucretia regarded the child with a slight frown. 'And who is this lady?' she asked. 'I think I do not know this fine person in such fine clothes?'

Beccy giggled. 'It's *me*, Cretia!' She ran around the table and stared into Lucretia's eyes.

'It is Beccy?! How can I believe my eyes. But where is your mother? Shouldn't we wait for your mother?'

'No, she's late. Do it now, Cretia.'

Jennifer took the child's hand. 'You sit here. Next to me.'

'Why is Miriam so late?' Hesta whispered.

'I have no idea! But I'll have to start the dinner or it'll be ruined.' The chickens were well and truly poaching. She took things from the fridge. 'At least Miriam could have phoned.'

'Well, maybe Miriam will not mind if I open the little fury's gift or she will explode, I think.' Lucretia stripped away endless sticky tape and brown paper and Jennifer, with another glance at the clock, took a bottle of wine from the fridge.

'We'll at least have a drink.' She opened the Blanc de Blanc with the ease of cafe experience and poured. She realised then that her own tensions must be spreading through the room like a disease. She gave the first glass to Lucretia.

'Ahh, a glass for all except the pure white and virtuous Marlin,' Lucretia laughed. 'He will only have holy water I think. Why does Marlin not drink wine?'

'Wine be the tears of women, so they say,' he said. 'But tonight I don't mind sharing a woman's tears on her birthday.'

Jennifer was almost sorry he'd agreed to join in. She wouldn't have minded if he'd been left out like a shag on a rock. Hesta accepted hers with urgent gratitude and she poured a little for Beccy who behaved as if all the birthdays and Christmases in the world had suddenly landed in the Fishcastle's kitchen. Lucretia held up Beccy's wooden coat-hanger with its coloured paper butterflies hanging from it on string.

'*Danke!* Beccy. Thank you, thank you. I will hang it near my bed.' She blew the child a kiss.

'It's a mobile,' Beccy said, flushed with praise and pride.

'I know it,' she laughed. 'I will find a good wind for it.' She unwrapped Hesta's small gift and held the star and the cross in her hand for them to see. 'I will wear this always, my dear friend.'

'If you do,' boomed Marlin, producing a purple box with a flourish, 'your neck will be as crowded as a queen's what with one thing and another.'

Lucretia opened the box with great care, as though the contents might be alive. Marlin's gift was a slice of stone, irregular in shape and slightly larger than a fifty-cent piece. In the centre of the stone was the fossilised impression of an ancient fish. It was attached to a leather thong for the neck. She drew breath in genuine surprise. She studied it and felt its surface before holding it up for the others to see.

'I have never seen anything like this!' She kissed Marlin on the cheek. 'It is a magic thing, this stone. It is a great treasure!'

Of course it is, Jennifer thought as she topped up Hesta's proffered glass. *He must have searched forever to find a present better than anyone else's!*

But then Lucretia was holding her glass up to Jennifer. 'And I toast the best gift of all – well, almost the best,' she said quickly, seeing Beccy's scowl, 'This wonderful dinner. *Danke schön,* my dear Jen. Thank you. I toast the chef!'

'But you haven't tried the food yet,' Jennifer said, laughing for the first time.

'Well, why don't we, dear,' Hesta said, 'or very soon we'll all be on our ears!'

The chicken was eaten with pleasure and praise between the hour of eight o'clock and fourteen minutes after it. Potatoes had been used as a mop for the sauce, and the spinach, with its nutmeg and a dop of cream, and asparagus spears were consumed at respectable intervals.

'I thought we'd used all our praise after the first course, heart,' Hesta said. 'But here we are singing it again, dear. What a marvellous cook you are.' Lucretia kept raising her glass to Jennifer and even Marlin was speechless for a while, licking his chops and dabbing at his mouth, loose with creams and juices. Only Beccy was unimpressed and concentrated on bread and cheese and wafers.

It should have been, Jennifer thought, *a remarkable night amongst so many others that were unremarkable*, but it had become just another of her feasts of tension and agitation. She had eaten a salad and picked at the chicken but there was little room for food in the churn of her belly. Beccy, who leaned sleepily against Jennifer's arm, tugged at her sleeve as though she'd read the signal.

'Do you think Mum's all right?'

'I'm sure she is, darling. She's fallen asleep probably. We'll give her a few more minutes.' But she knew the child was tense too.

Hesta had become tipsy quiet. Marlin and Lucretia talked together but Jennifer only caught the edge of their words. There was something about her university.

'I imagine it's very cold in Bonn now.' She made a flat attempt to contribute.

'Cold as bergs,' Marlin said. He drank wine then water then wine then water. Jennifer imagined the ritual was to keep his purity intact. 'All the good Bonny girls will be standing around hot coals with their chestnuts. Am I right or am I right?'

Lucretia laughed. *He always made Lucretia laugh.* Jennifer rocked Beccy in her arms. 'She's almost asleep,' she said.

Lucretia nodded and licked her fingers. 'I think this chef has a French lover, *ja*? – and they cook such food as this and make love. Guide Michelin would give it three stars, I think.'

'Our Jen with a Frog?' Marlin roared with laughter.

'We're eating off her sheets, *Fräulein*, and I don't see no Froggy stains ... pure as driven snow, our Jen Wren's sheets!'

'You don't think I'd tell you if I had a lover, do you? Not for a minute!' Jennifer snapped.

'Be more kind to your daughter, Marlin,' Lucretia slapped the back of his hand and he pretended to hang his head in shame. 'Of course a father does not know the daughter's lovers – it is none of his business!' She winked at Jennifer.

'Talk about chestnuts.' Hesta was as sleepy as the child – both of them lullabyed by the opposite ends of age, and wine. 'I think Lucretia told me about the old chestnut trees in Bonn,' she said drowsily.

'Yes, that is true ...'

'Ssssshh!' Jennifer put a finger to her lips. 'I heard a noise in the hall.'

'It's Mum.' Beccy jumped from Jennifer's lap and ran out the kitchen door, but it wasn't Miriam, it was a young blond man trailing in hemp clothing and carrying a lantern.

'Good Christ!' Marlin exclaimed.

'No, my man. Kris Carpenter. The door was open. I did knock.'

'Kris says my mum's *really* sick!' Beccy was on the verge of tears.

'What's happened? What's the matter?' Jennifer waited for the worst, expected anything.

'Crystal says Miriam's losing the baby. She says Bec better go home.' There was little urgency in the man's voice.

He stood rooted to the only spot of still air in the room. Around him flew a panic of women and child. Jennifer had begun to cry. Hesta dissolved into a sorrowful silence in her chair.

'Oh my God! My God! My God! I knew it. I knew there was something wrong ... Beccy, I'll go, you'd better stay here with Hesta.'

'I'm coming too!' she screamed.

'I'll have to run all the way!'

'I'm coming too! I want my mum!'

'Well get your shoes on quickly – hurry!'

'I come with you, Jen.' Lucretia ran up the stairs with the child to find her shoes.

'Where is she?' Jennifer shouted at Kris, furious with his laid-back attitude, wondering how long it had taken him to wander down from the Hill. 'Is there a doctor with her?'

'I don't know. She's in the shack.'

'Couldn't you phone us! God! Fancy her in that filthy place. Why didn't you phone?!' Jennifer told Hesta to make coffee and to drink it until she was awake and to stay awake in case she was needed. She pushed past Kris Carpenter and grabbed the lantern out of his hand. 'You make me sick – the lot of you!'

'Crystal told me to get Beccy. That's all she said.'

Jennifer ran outside and down the drive. Lucretia and Beccy struggled to catch up. When at last the hurricane of noise and movement had left the house, Marlin said with unusual gentleness, 'Come along, Sister Bird. We'd better be the bottle washers while the cook's away.'

At the foot of the Hill, where the streetlights ended, they were grateful for the tilly lamp and the light of the moon. For one irrelevant moment something that Hesta had once told Jennifer flashed through her mind – *Contemplate the moon; think upon it and you won't be frightened* – and it had calmed bad moments in her childlife, but now there was no time to contemplate the moon and her heart beat so hard against her she could hardly breathe.

'I know the quick way up.' Beccy, still in her flounces of torn tulle and stars, scrambled off the track and climbed and scratched her way through the scrub. She broke a twig from a shrub to move cobwebs out of their way. Jennifer was in such a state that when they arrived at the shack she had not realised that she was scratched and bleeding from head to toe.

Inside the shack, on the floor of the bedroom, lay Miriam. Someone had put a pillow under her head. Crystal sat on the bed, shaking and smoking a joint. Another woman squatted beside Miriam. On the floor between her legs, in a mess of blood and urine and faeces lay a tiny form of flesh, a jelly mould of shape, unmoving and no bigger than a tub of butter. Miriam's eyes were closed and she gently moaned. Jennifer tried to speak but retched into her hands. Beccy stood in the doorway and stared, fists stiffly at her sides and, in one of them, the twig she had picked on the way. Her dark eyes were huge with fright. For seconds that seemed like hours, they did not move or speak, then Lucretia shook Jennifer's shoulders.

'This is not the time to be sick. You can be sick when you are away from here!'

Jennifer coughed and held a hand tight across her mouth. It was Beccy's small voice that brought her to her senses.

'It's okay, Mum – Mum? – it's okay. Jen's here.'

'Who did this!?' Jennifer screamed at the Hill women. 'Did you do this? Did you make this happen?'

'Nobody did anything.' The woman squatting by Miriam's head spoke calmly, not looking up. 'I'm Miriam's midwife. She's just lost the baby. She's all right. She's in shock. She'll be all right.' The woman looked at Jennifer for the first time. 'You're her friend from the Bay, right?'

'Yes.'

'Then take over from me. Sit with her and stroke her head while I clean her up.' She looked at the child. 'It's okay, Beccy. Your mum's okay.'

'She should be in a hospital!' Jennifer couldn't bring herself to look below Miriam's waist. She turned away from the terrible sight and stroked Miriam's shivering head. 'She needs blankets, for heaven's sake! She's shaking all over.'

Lucretia tried to take Beccy's hand but the child pulled angrily away.

'Come outside with me for a while, little one.'

'No!'

'Go to the van, Bec,' said Crystal.

'No! You go to the van!'

'Don't fuss over her,' said the midwife. 'Let her stay if she wants. Crystal, you come and help me. Don't worry,' she said to Jennifer, 'If I think she needs to go to hospital, I'll take her.'

'Can't you cover – cover – that?' Jennifer indicated the lost being by nodding but not looking. She whispered comfort to Miriam and kissed a cheek, damp with her own tears.

Lucretia had left with the other women and Beccy squatted near the tiny form on the floor. Jennifer was deliberately unaware of it. She could still not look at it. The child moved closer to the foetus and poked it again and again with the twig, hoping the shock would make it move and breathe, maybe something like a newborn's slap, and she squatted there, grey-faced, until Jennifer, glancing at her out of the corner of her eye, screamed for her to stop. But Beccy was reminded of the day Paul's puppies were born on the Hill and the two he had thrown over the cliff into the sea . . . 'Dead', he'd said, but she'd never been sure. She stayed by the foetus. She would guard it forever.

An hour later, Miriam, cleaned and bound and padded, lay warm in her bed. She managed to sip herbal tea and had held Jen's hand.

'Thanks for coming,' she whispered. 'It just happened, Jen. I'm all right. I'm sorry. I've been nothing but trouble, Jen. Look after Bec for me, hey?' She squeezed Jennifer's weak-as-a-kitten hand, sighed and slept.

In the second room of the shack Lucretia had somehow produced drinks and snacks for the group.

'But where is the child?' She spoke quietly so Miriam would not be disturbed.

'She wanted to go to the van. She said she'd go to sleep. The kid's had enough for one day, I reckon.' Crystal licked herself a smoke.

'What is it you do with the foetus?' Lucretia asked with almost clinical detachment.

'Oh, God!' Jennifer moaned.

'She was part of our community. She'll be treated gently.'

She? She? Jennifer was shocked to hear it. 'You mean that – that little thing on the floor was a *she*?!' She wished she could stop her hands shaking. She watched Crystal sucking smoke down to the soles of her feet and the lazy look in her eyes and just for a moment she wished she could do it too. Or a drink, or pills – anything. 'I'm going to check Beccy,' she said.

'No worries,' said Crystal. 'I'll check her.' Padding out on a wave of pot – for all sorts of reasons not wanting strangers in her van. She knew Beccy would have dragged the old mattress down on top of the cockroaches and smoke stubs and would be out like a light. Moments later she padded back again.

'She's not there,' she said to whoever might be interested. She pinched the smoke to her mouth and drew on it. 'I can't see her anywhere.' Then she whispered something into the midwife's ear.

'Well, look for her!' the woman hissed back. 'Move it, Crystal!'

'What did she say to you?' Jennifer said. 'What's the matter now?!'

'She's taken the foetus with her.'

'*What?!*'

'Sssssshhh! Don't wake Miriam. We'll have to look for her.'

'But where? Where would she go?' Jennifer was already at the door. 'Hurry up!'

'Maybe she went back to your house, Jennifer,' Lucretia said. 'The child will be very frightened by this.'

'Yes. Yes, of course. I'll go back there now. You stay here, Lucretia – yes, that's what she's done. Dad will help. Isn't there a phone here?'

'Only the public down near the car park.'

'Oh God, what a place!' Jennifer ran out into the night and gave thanks to the moon. She stumbled and tripped her way to the beginning of the car track, all the time calling for Beccy in a voice she hoped would not reach Miriam. Behind her, the sound of the ocean thrashing against the cliffs made her sick with anger.

But Beccy was not at the Fishcastle.

Marlin and Hesta had stayed by the phone to wait for news. Jennifer flew in like an injured bird. Even Marlin was shocked by her appearance.

'The Bec didn't come back here,' he said, 'but I'll go a'huntin' for her, Jen Wren. I'll track the critter down.'

She leapt at him and pounded him with her fists. She kicked his leg so violently that he pushed her away and held her at arm's length.

'Don't – you – realise – what's – happened?!' she screamed and sobbed at the same time. 'Can't you – for once in your life – be normal! – be normal!' she screamed, and frightened Hesta. 'Be *normal!!*'

'Only trying to cheer us up,' he said and sank into a

chair. Folded into it. She thought it might have been tears she saw in his eyes but it could have been something else.

'I'm going to ring Robert Brae up at St P's.' Hesta's fingers flustered about with lives of their own. 'It's just a thought, mind you, but I'll ask him to watch for her.'

'You can't ring him at this hour,' Jen cried. 'It's the middle of the night – oh, God, what am I saying. Of course we must ring everyone – and the police! – everyone!'

Hesta did telephone Robert Brae, and it had not been necessary to wake him up. He'd answered after the third bell.

'Yes, she's here, Hesta.' He sounded as though he'd been crying too. 'She's worried about her fancy clothes being torn and dirty. I found her trying to bury a box next to Alice's grave, Hesta. She was trying to dig a hole with her hands and a stone ...' His voice cracked and wavered. 'She thought Alice would like a friend to sleep with and she said "keep each other safe".'

'I don't think I understand what you mean.'

Jennifer ran to her and grabbed the phone. With difficulty Robert Brae repeated the story.

'I'll comfort her until you come,' he said. 'We'll be in the vestry.'

Marlin ordered a taxi. He asked Hesta to stay in case Lucretia called, and he and Jennifer drove to St P's.

He had not entered a church since childhood, and as he did so he wept.

Chapter Fourteen

SEA PICTURES – THE LAST SACRIFICE

One day Gulliver Hardwick crept back to the Fishcastle to visit skeletons.

It was a Wednesday. He had checked with the museum and knew his father was in the city. He had spied on the cafe from the pier and knew that Jennifer was at work and at the house he imagined there would probably only be Hesta and the German to confront, that is, if one was awake and the other wasn't swimming. But on that day Hesta had taken Lucretia and Miriam in a train to the Blue Mountains to visit the remains of Wellings Road.

The first of the skeletons were the bones of his bike, rotting in their ruined shed with its door still hanging on a hinge and the mother side still desecrated. The other was his dinghy, bucking impatient against its line in the cave. And when Gulliver toe-sneaked across the yard towards the harbour steps, sniffing the air for life or danger, the only human he saw was Beccy Holt, sitting by the stone lion; sitting with her arms wrapped tight around her knees and whispering seriously into his grey stone ear. Her back was to him but her senses told her there was someone there and she turned and tensed and narrowed her eyes.

'Hi, Bec,' he said. 'How's it going?' as though nothing had happened between that day and this.

It was one-thirty. He did not ask why she wasn't at school. He did not say anything at all for a while. She just stared at him, thin-lipped and scowling. She was not afraid.

Miriam had recovered remarkably well from her ordeal and, for Jennifer, after the tragedy of it all there was joy in seeing true colour and freshness return to Miriam's face – a beauty so long gone. After two weeks of care by the women of the Hill and the women of the Fishcastle, she'd been ready to face life with new strength.

'*Little She*', the tiny human who had been lost and named by Beccy at St P's in a proper fashion had, after all, been buried next to baby Alice's grave, with Robert Brae's blessing. The Reverend Brae had also provided a small metal plaque set in sandstone with the simple epitaph:

Here lies Little She.
A friend for Alice.

Beccy seemed satisfied with that. Future generations of graveyard visitors, Robert decided, would simply have to guess the year and make up the rest. Beccy continued to visit the graves, sweeping away dirt or rubbish and weaving weedflower chains, one for each. No one questioned her about the terrible night she had run away with the box; she had simply been told, first by Robert and then by the others, that what she had done was not the usual practice in such cases but had been an act of love.

'She is strong and clever, that one,' Lucretia had said. 'She will help herself first. She will not need us to interfere.' And the women agreed to the wisdom of this. Lucretia, they had come to know, had a sense that was common and uncluttered and the strength to reduce the insurmountable to a mound.

The excursion to the Blue Mountains was a revelation to Lucretia but for Hesta, it was a mix of sadness and joy. She had been so long away from her trees – too long.

Marlin had offered to drop Beccy off at school on his way to the city and the group had left Central Station at eight twenty-one. Lucretia and Miriam sat by windows and, when the train had left the outer suburbs and began to climb, Lucretia pressed her nose to the snotty glass like a child.

'So much forest! So much land is here,' she said. 'It never ends.'

'Not forest, *bush*, dear,' said Hesta, delighted to be guide for the day. 'Here we call it the bush.' The train clung to its rails and rocked its way through a whole album of views.

'At the top of the mountains, will there be snow?'

'I hope not, dear. But it might be cool – autumn is not far away. It will be cool and fresh, I hope.'

'Or hot as blazes.' Miriam stretched her legs up on the opposite seat. 'You never know up this way.'

'How is it you know the Mountains?' Hesta asked.

'When I was little we used to come down to Medlow Bath for holidays. The family. Not every year – just sometimes.'

'Heavens, I've never thought of you being anywhere but on the Hill.'

'And I guess it looks as though that's where I'll be staying.'

'We'd all miss you terribly if you didn't, Miriam.'

Hesta the guide drew their attention to points of interest with finger points and hand waves. 'The main station in the Blue Mountains is at Katoomba, but we can go on to Mount Victoria if we like. It's a quaint town. We can have morning tea there. There are old book shops and an old hotel. Poor Wellings Road is way behind it all. I shall hire us a taxi.'

With affection Hesta watched great stands of eucalypts speed past the window, postage-stamp farms with tethered goats and train-chasing dogs, horse yards, curls of country roads and apple orchards and, in the distance, glimpses of rock shafts plunging into valleys and veils of falling water. She was proud of it all. She hadn't realised how much she'd longed for the sight of open country and trees. She glanced at Lucretia and was pleased to see she was so impressed by it, proud of the expression of interest and delight on the face that stared out the window.

At Mount Victoria they had an old-fashioned tea with scones and jam. The jam was homemade, Hesta told them, and only in a supermarket jar for convenience, and the cream freshly milked from a cow out the back and whipped while the water boiled, and she assured them that the tea bags had been hand-sewn by local craftswomen. She could think of nothing to say about the scones, which were hard as rocks.

Miriam smiled and nudged Lucretia, 'Hesta, you're a true Hardwick,' she said.

'But it's a pity, isn't it, that everything is such a sham,' said Hesta.

There were signs here and there, just small reminders of the storm. In a shop window were photographs of its devastation at fifteen dollars each (unframed) but a picture of Hesta's area was not amongst them. At a quarter to eleven Hesta hired a taxi to take them to Wellings Road.

'They had a whopper of a storm round there a few months ago,' the driver said.

'I know,' Hesta said, 'I was in the middle of it.'

'Yeah? Well, I reckon it was more like a twister, or a hurricane. Was your house damaged?'

'It was blown away,' she said.

'Yeah? That'd be a bit of a bloody nuisance, hey.' They smiled and he grinned at them from the rear-vision mirror. Hesta asked him to stop at a point by the road where she knew the grandeur of the mountains could be seen, especially the distant, dramatic contrast of greens and blue against the stark faces of rock. Lucretia drew a sharp breath of surprise.

'I have no idea of this,' she said. 'It is so – so *grand*! As though men have never been in there; as big as a country!

I have no idea. I have never learned about such beauty in Australia. It is just as you tell me in the jungle but even then I cannot imagine this!'

In Lucretia's eyes the mountains steamed thick and rich all the way to the end of the earth, and there was a silence of sound only the wind makes through mountains and leaves. A slick of oil colour in the air around them and the scent of it in the clean sky was almost painful to breathe. There were rock faces of painted ochre and rock faces wet and black, dropping into gullies and out of sight, and crowns of eucalypts a mountain high and falls of water spilling into pools never seen. It was a hard landscape, strong and powerful to her senses. This wonder of the earth was the province of wild things and birds and ancient spirits. It was a landscape that held her at bay, allowing her a glimpse and no more. She was in awe of its beauty.

'I have missed it,' Hesta whispered.

And then, as they drove on, all were quiet with their thoughts and, despite the hum of the motor, they were aware of the endless silence of the land.

At the top of Wellings Road, Hesta asked the driver to wait for them. She noticed that a new mailbox had been set at the corner of the road and she remarked upon new timbers added to old in broken fences and spaces where sheds had been. She led them down the old fire trail, more deeply rutted now after the relays of heavy vehicles and machinery that had driven over it after the storm. The day was cooler and there was a newness to the feel of it. Hesta remembered the heat of the last day she had walked the trail, heavy as a press on her shoulders, and the strange air that had been so hard to breathe. They passed the place where the Clarkes' house once stood. Anything that had remained of it had been demolished for reasons of safety. There was nothing left except a short winding of path and two beds of rose bushes. Stands of trees stood, still splintered but with new growth straining through.

'They were both killed, you know,' Hesta said.

'Yes, Hesta, I remember your story of the storm. It must be very sad for you here.' Lucretia put her arm around her friend's shoulders.

They walked on and then weaved and ducked their way through the tangle and wilderness that had once been Hesta's garden. Shrubs struggled through a blanket of potato vines. Dying conifers clung still to their uncertain roots. Wild salvia forced its spikes through wandering Jew and black-berries – and bunya trees, still in shock on the storm sides, held giant seed balls ready to drop and start again. But through all the chaos of vegetation, under the shroud of vines and bracken and weeds, the outlines of a garden that had once been one of the most beautiful in the district could still be seen. At the end of the walkway, in a clearing, was a pile of debris that had once been Hesta's house.

'Such a pity ... such a pity,' she said, but she did not cry. She climbed and limped over the rubbish, gingerly searching under timber and broken tiles. 'We must be very careful of snakes at this time of the year.'

'I do not mind snakes,' said Lucretia.

'Our red-bellied black snakes are not as domesticated as

Marlin's python, dear.' But Lucretia had already pushed timber and metal aside and had found the broken head of a doll. 'That poor little thing was French,' Hesta said, taking it in her hand. 'I bought it in Paris. It had a black dress and a bonnet.'

Miriam stood back from the ruins. She tore weed vines from good plants and slapped at mosquitoes on her legs. Hesta was about to speak to her when she saw something familiar poking from under a pile of split floorboards. It was a very old, painted tin platter, oval in shape, very much the worse for wear and storm. It was painted with scenes from nursery rhymes and Hesta held the bent thing to her chest and whooped with pleasure. 'Lost and found!' she cried, 'lost and found!' She held it up for the others to see. 'Not worth a cent of course – the searchers must have thrown it back.' But the true, flushed delight on the woman's face in the midst of such devastation made the visit to the mountains more worthwhile than they could have imagined.

'Do you think you'll build again?' Miriam asked.

'I don't know. The insurance companies take a lifetime to sort things out. I might not have a lifetime to wait for them.'

'Well, you'll always have a home at the Bay. I think Jen would like you to stay forever.' Miriam uncovered a daisy bush and picked two buds from it. 'We'll take these back as souvenirs.' And she looked at Hesta. 'I know Beccy and I would hate you to move back up here.'

'Thank you, Miriam, but I do feel more at home here

than at the Bay. I had no idea how much I'd missed it. And
I look forward to being independent again. I don't think
Marlin would want me to stay in his house longer than I
need.' And holding the tin platter tight against her, she
turned her back to the ruins of her house and walked away.
Not once did she look back. 'Time to go,' she said. 'We
mustn't be late. Miriam needs to get home to Beccy.' She
marched as briskly as she could back up the trail to the taxi.
She felt lighter than she'd felt for a long time. There'd been
ghosts laid to rest and she'd had no idea what a relief it
would be.

'Mount Victoria?' asked the driver.

'No. Take us to Medlow Bath. Miriam used to holiday
there, you know,' Hesta ordered. 'Then we'll catch the train
at Katoomba.'

'This is costing a fortune,' Miriam whispered.

'It's worth a fortune, my dear heart.'

'So then, where *is* everybody?' Gulliver asked Beccy on that
Wednesday. She closed her eyes and turned away. 'It's not
some big secret, is it?'

'They've gone to the Blue Mountains, if you want to
know.'

'Your mum, too?'

'Yes.'

'What they go up there for?'

'How would I know? I wouldn't tell you anyway!'

'Don't give me cheek, you little bugger. You been playing
with the bike?'

'No. I hate it.' He bent to toss a lizard aside and she saw tattoos on his arm. Something new.

'What's your mum like then? She still throwing up?'

'No.'

'Well? No what?'

'Just no. She doesn't get sick now. The baby's dead.'

He stared at her with his jaw hanging. 'What the shit are you talking about?'

'It's true!' she screamed at him. 'And it's all your fault!'

'You're making this up.'

'I'm not. And I buried the baby up at Alice's grave. You can ask Mum.'

'Jesus! When's she coming back?'

She didn't dare tell him she'd wagged school for the afternoon.

'I don't know, and anyway she's not coming here and she doesn't want to see you.'

'I couldn't give a shit. I want to know what's going on.'

For Gulliver life was still a hard bitch. He needed to sell the bike but his memory of it was better than the wreck he'd just seen, bones and spokes with the sea air rotting them. There'd been a lock put on the door of his room, and now this! He didn't want the baby, he wanted the baby – it was his, it wasn't his – and now she'd got rid of it, without even telling him; not that he cared, but he cared enough to feel less a man because of it. And all he had now was one greasy room over a grease shop where he'd have to work forever to pay what he owed on a bike he couldn't bloody ride. His misery and his anger had dried him up – he swore there'd better be something to wet him in the dinghy cave! He was in a state of dry, itching agitation.

'So, what the hell else has been going on here?' he asked the child.

'We had a party. You missed Cretia's birthday and Hesta gave me wine to drink.'

'When was that?'

'A long time ago.'

'So? And did they save any for me, Bec? Any birthday wine left?'

'I don't know.'

'Where did Jen put it?'

'I don't know. In the fridge I suppose. But there won't be any left for you!'

He left her and slammed through the side door and into the kitchen and when he came back he was holding a bottle and grinning like a cut throat.

'Not even opened,' he said, holding it up. 'You're not all bad after all, Bec.' He marched across the yard and down the stone steps to the jutty, the harbour and the dinghy cave. 'See you,' he called back to her.

Beccy stayed by the side of the lion and hugged it for comfort. She was not bothered about taking the afternoon off from school. Mr Ford patted her head a lot lately and said, *there, there*, so why would he mind. But she had not expected danger to be so close to her sanctuary. She had never expected to see Gulliver so close to the lion. She had never thought it a possibility.

When he had gone from her sight she went into the

kitchen herself and poured a glass of water and buttered a slice of bread. She took her snacks back to the lion and sat close to it. She knew Gull would be bottle-pissing in the dinghy cave. The tide was coming in. She heard it splashing and sucking underneath the jutty. She walked down to the carp pond near the sea wall and fed the fish crumbs. From the dinghy cave she heard Gull grunting and muttering to himself and she thought she heard glass breaking. They were angry sounds, she thought, but they were muffled by the tide and she was not afraid. She stayed by the sea wall and listened and waited.

When she saw the stern of the dinghy poke out of the cave mouth she stood on her toes and peered over the wall. She saw Gull pushing it out into the harbour, cursing and slipping over the rocks. When he'd pushed it into the clear she saw that his fishing tackle was at his feet and two bottles were jammed into the side. And as he turned the boat he looked up and saw her.

'Too wet in there, Bec,' he called in a voice already oily with drink. 'I'm going to sea where it's dry.' He grunted and leered at her and rowed further into the harbour. Beccy walked down to the jutty and sat and watched him.

He rowed in the direction of Greys Point and she watched him ship the oars and drink and drink again and throw a line over the side. She narrowed her eyes in order to see more clearly. She watched him drink and drink bottle piss worse than Crystal, and try to tug the line away from something in the water, a snag. She thought it strange that no one else on the harbour seemed to be watching Gulliver Hardwick. She looked around her but she was the only one. Maybe he was invisible to them. If her mum was here, she thought, she'd be watching him. She'd be able to see him.

His line came suddenly loose and he fell back into the boat; she even heard the thump. It looked funny and she laughed. She looked around the bay again but she was the only one laughing. And then she watched while he leaned over the side and coughed and vomited – she knew it was vomiting, it couldn't be anything else. She knew what it looked like. And she was glad he was sick, as sick as her mum had been. *'Good!'* she said, sitting there, with the wind blowing her hair to one side. *'Good!'* Then the dinghy rocked and bucked in the wake of a speedboat and she saw Gull fall into the harbour. There was no splash. There was no sound. He just fell in. She strained to listen. She thought she might hear him scream or choke on water, but there was no sound. He slid into the harbour like a seal, a perfect diver; no splash at all, and only once did his head come up and mouth something wet before it went down again. Then there was nothing – nothing at all. Gull had slipped into the water just for her. He must have planned it that way. When she was sure the play was over, she clapped. 'Yes! Excellent!'

And I'm not going to tell anyone! She sat still on the jutty and hugged her skinny arms around her chest. *Nobody – except maybe Alice and Little She!*

Beccy searched for some sign of him under the water. What a gift this would be for her night-dream waves, better than anything she'd given the sea. She wanted to see how well it would be received. She could not see him with her eyes open so she closed them and watched him in her mind.

She could see him clearly then, floating down through the kelp, twisting to the bottom the way leaves fall in air. She could see him staring into the eyes of the big-eyed fishes and brushing against sharks' fangs and grabbing at seaweed and being suckered by octopus and then lying on the slimed, dark bottom of the sea – and she could clearly see his wide, frightened eyes, but only with her own shut tight.

She drew her knees up under her chin, wrapped her arms around them and concentrated as hard as she could on her visions. She saw an eel, bigger than anything she'd seen, snap his leg and make him bleed and bite his face and she remembered the taste of his blood. And she saw a shark take his arms and all the fishes feeding until only his head was left lying on a rock, with the eyes open and knowing everything and seeing everything that was happening ... everything! And she did not move an inch from the jutty until the sea picture in her mind went black and there was nothing left to see.

When she opened her eyes the dinghy rocked aimlessly on the top of the swell. She went back to the lion and told it the story. And she was still there when Jennifer found her.

'What on earth are you doing here, Beccy? You're supposed to be at home, waiting for your mother.' Jen fussed around her and brushed crumbs off her uniform. 'Look at you, you're a mess. Are you all right? How long have you been here?'

'I came at lunchtime,' Beccy said flatly. She sat firm near the lion.

'Lunchtime? What did you do that for?'

'There's head nits at school. We had to go home,' she lied.

'Beccy?'

'It's true.'

'Beccy, you mustn't do these things.' Jennifer searched the child's face. 'There's something wrong, I can tell. Did something bad happen here?'

'No.'

'At school?'

'No.'

'Tell me, Beccy.' Jennifer squatted to be level with her eyes.

'Gull came back.' The child looked guiltily away and Jennifer felt a wave of anxiety. A familiar feeling of dread. A tortoise ambled past, touching their feet, but neither noticed it.

'He – he didn't touch you, did he?'

'No.'

'When did he come?'

'A long time ago. He took all Cretia's wine out of the fridge.'

'Where is he now?' *I just want to see him, that's all.*

'He went out in the boat.'

'Oh?' Jennifer stood and searched the harbour. She shaded her eyes. *I knew he'd be back for the bike – or money – or something.* 'I can't see the dinghy, Beccy, are you sure?'

'I watched him. He got bottle-pissed and he took out the boat and then he vomited and he fell into the water ...' Jennifer shook her. 'I don't care, it's true ... and now he's down on the bottom and the sea's eaten everything!'

Jennifer didn't think there was anything left in her life that could terrify her as much as this. She was afraid that the child had finally lost her mind – afraid of what might really have happened this afternoon while she'd been clearing tables and the others had been swanning around the Blue Mountains. There *had* to be a limit to fright. She simply couldn't take any more. She was weak and exhausted from it. 'You mustn't tell me Marlin stories, Beccy. You must never make things up like this ... never!'

'But it's true.' Beccy had cancelled any resolve to secrecy. She couldn't hold all this in a bottle. 'It's really true, Jen. I watched it all. An eel ate his face ... it's true!'

Jennifer ran to the sea wall and searched the harbour again, and then, in the area of Greys Point, she saw a flurry of craft and the police boat with an empty dinghy tied astern of it. She tried to scream but there was nothing left. No breath, no will, no heart. She sank to the grass and wept. She was unaware of tears – perhaps they were from other eyes – perhaps they were her mother's tears that fell onto the grass. Tonight, she would ask her mother if she'd cried that afternoon.

Marlin had been notified during a lecture on the preservation of the blue whaler shark. *Carcharhinus mackiei*. He had been called aside and given a note. He did not take fright. He did not weep. He resumed his place at the podium and said in measured words: 'I have just been informed of my son's death. He has gone to sea and has died on its bed.' And without another word he left the hall.

Inside the Fishcastle were pockets of mourning of different shapes and lengths of time. For Jennifer it was a period of grief that was physically painful – the sadness of it all was bottomless. She wept for her brother and she grieved for the child he had planted so carelessly into the world, but at the end of a black day she comforted herself with the thought that at least she now knew where he was; she no longer had to worry about him hurting himself or others. But when she continued to cry Lucretia suggested that it might be because she thought it wouldn't be right to stop. 'It is not necessary, dear Jen. We will not think less of you if you dry your eyes and get on with your life.'

Marlin's pocket of mourning was brief and private. He mourned for what his son might have been, during the night hours of emptying Gulliver's room of every possession – every trace of him. He kept nothing, and when he glanced around the empty shell his eyes were dry. Miriam too was dry-eyed and more concerned for Beccy and Jennifer than the death of a drunk who had made them all suffer so much. And Hesta, in her feathery, finger-knitting way, grieved only for poor Lissy's sake and the terrible, terrible waste of it all.

Beccy's feelings were her own and unfathomable. She remained fiercely self-contained, furiously strong. There seemed to be not a shred of sadness in her eyes ... or innocence. They were not to know that since she had allowed the sea to take Gulliver she had not had her night terrors and the green wall of ocean had stayed behind the cliffs. It had been, she thought, the best sacrifice of all. And now, when she went to bed, if there was a storm or the waves were breaking like furies, all she had to do was close her eyes and watch the sea pictures of Gull falling through the water to the bottom of the world and she was comforted in her way. She talked about these things only by the graveyard at St P's.

'She will be the strongest woman in the world, that little one,' Lucretia remarked as she sat with Marlin on the sea wall. 'A hard life is making her strong. Nothing must interfere with that.'

'As strong as the *Fräulein*?'

'I think so.' She put her hand over his. 'But you must help your daughter, Marlin. *Her* troubles make her weak; you should help her to be like Beccy. She should have a lover. She should not be living in this house.' She stretched her head back and shook her hair in the sun. In the sky a streak of cloud chased seagulls to the park. There was a peace about the Fishcastle as though a thorn had been removed from its side. Lucretia had browned to the colour of milk coffee during the summer and her skin had absorbed the smells of the Bay.

'Stay!' he said suddenly. 'Stay here with me.'

'I am already late for my work, Marlin. I go back to Germany I think.'

'Marry me then!' he said. 'I will give you Proudie Bay.' She laughed and kissed his ear.

'I am not good with only one man, Marlin, but for you? I will think about it.'

'I love you,' he said, and despite having never once said those words to his wife, or indeed to any member of his family, it had not been too difficult.

During an afternoon, among so many that had passed, a ring of after-schoolies sat cross-legged at the feet of their master, their storyteller, their guru.

'Once upon a time,' boomed Marlin.

'Once upon a time,' they chanted.

'There were three sons of a father. The North Son. The South Son. And the middle son, as handsome as you like . . .'

'You!' they screamed. '*You!*'

'The North Son grew snakes for belts and pigeons for the pot . . .' And the children began to recite their mantra and they squealed in anticipation of what came next.

In the kitchen, Miriam helped Jennifer with afternoon tea. Together they buttered bread and poured drinks and heated the water for Marlin's coffee. Hesta dozed in her room.

'I miss Lucretia already,' Miriam said.

'She told me Dad asked her to marry him.'

'Great! Do you think she will?'

'I think she'd be mad.'

'But it'd be good for you too, wouldn't it?'

'Maybe . . .'

'You're getting too set in your ways, Jen. You could do with a change.' She set bread and drinks on a tray with a blue cat on it.

'That's not the right one,' Jennifer said.

'What?'

'That tray with the cat on it. It's not the right one.'

'What does it matter!'

'I've always used the green tray, that's all.'

'Good grief!' Miriam transferred everything to the green tray. 'I can't believe I'm doing this. You know, Lucretia said she hoped you'd move out of this place and get a life. Why don't you? You don't do anything – you just work! Maybe you and Hesta could get a place together.'

'And what do you think would happen here if everybody left?' She put a bowl that Miriam had moved back on its correct shelf.

'Life would go on, Jen. The world would keep turning, for God's sake!'

'Well, anyway, I've thought about it, don't think I haven't. I've thought about leaving a hundred times.' *But I can't, I can't. I don't have the courage. My whole life is here and I'm frightened to leave it, I hate it and I love it and I can't leave. Where do I get the strength to do that, Lucretia? Why is everyone getting strong except me? Why didn't you tell me that before you left?* 'Hundreds of times I've thought about it.'

She poured Marlin's coffee and stirred it. Across Proudie Bay moored boats turned their backs to the wind and sea birds perched, gossiping on their sides. A fishing boat unloaded at the pier and the last of the tourist ferries whistled for the pub crowd. Jennifer stared vacantly at it all from the window. She avoided the area around Greys Point.

Marlin cried out for his coffee and, from the top of the

stairs, in a sleep-smudged voice, Hesta called for her bottle an hour early.

How can there be an end to this, Jennifer thought, and when she hooked a stray hair from her face she realised she'd left jam on it. She didn't wash it off. It didn't seem to matter.

Miriam watched with sadness as Jennifer took the tray and pushed the door open with her foot.

Outside, Marlin looked up at her with heavy eyes and watched her put the tray on its patch of grass. The usual patch of grass. For a moment he closed his eyes. *How can there be an end to this*, Fräulein? *She's got us trapped, the Jennifuss. She's got us all trapped. Come back and help me . . .* Just for that moment with his eyes closed.

Beccy looked at Jennifer and scowled and shook her finger. 'About time!' she said in her low, play-act voice. She gave Marlin his coffee.

Jennifer went back to the kitchen and said to Miriam: 'I hope he doesn't think I'm going to wait on him for the rest of his life!' But she was pleased the Fishcastle was settling back to its ordered ways.

Beyond the sea wall, Proudie Bay licked its lips over weed gardens and sea graves where the corpses of mistakes were buried. That night it would stroke the jutty with its tide . . . *there, there . . .*

THE PENGUIN CENTURY OF AUSTRALIAN STORIES

Edited by Carmel Bird

This landmark collection brings together the best Australian short stories written in the twentieth century.

From early bush life, through the Depression and the Second World War, to the fast lane of urban contemporary existence, Australian short-story writers have explored and reflected our national identity and experience. *The Penguin Century of Australian Stories* represents, in one volume, our finest writers in all their modes: the lively comic fiction of Henry Lawson and Steele Rudd, the distinctive imaginations of Christina Stead and Patrick White, the experimental style of Peter Carey, and the highly lyrical prose of Brenda Walker and James Bradley.

The themes in these stories, selected by Carmel Bird, mirror the concerns of our past and our present, creating a map of the short story in Australia. Celebrating one hundred of Australia's most gifted writers, *The Penguin Century of Australian Stories* will enlighten and entertain for many years to come.

AN ACCOMMODATING SPOUSE

Elizabeth Jolley

'It really did seem that he had married them both. Two angels, she said, two accommodating angels, very plain angels.'

When the Professor marries Hazel, Lady Carpenter warns that his new wife is so like her twin, Chloe, he will have trouble telling them apart. So inseparable are the twins that the Professor lives with both women under one roof.

Into their generous and harmonious household return their daughters – triplets – fresh from their round-the-world travelling, and ready for whatever excitement they can grab next in their lives.

Family life in the otherwise quiet house swells to a chaotic dazzling crescendo as the Professor struggles to keep in step with the seven women in his life, and a strange request from Dr Florence.

'*An Accommodating Spouse* is vintage Jolley, always cutting between pain and laughter, dislocation and consolation, chaos and order . . . lit by Jolley's special sense of absurdity and the meaning that flows from it.'

– *The Age*

'There is a fine musical line running through *An Accommodating Spouse* which takes you gently by the ear and leads you through it . . . a fantastic book in all senses of that word.'

– *The Sydney Morning Herald*

80275498